LAURA ZIEPE

Made in Essex

AVON

A division of HarperCollins*Publishers*
77–85 Fulham Palace Road,
London W6 8JB

www.harpercollins.co.uk

This paperback edition 2014
1

A catalogue record for this book is
available from the British Library

ISBN-13: 978-0-00-748648-9

Set in Sabon LT Std by Palimpsest Book Production Limited,
Falkirk, Stilingshire

Printed and bound in Great Britain by
Clays Ltd, St Ives plc

MIX
Paper from
responsible sources
FSC C007454

FSC™ is a non-profit international organisation established to promote
the responsible management of the world's forests. Products carrying the
FSC label are independently certified to assure consumers that they come
from forests that are managed to meet the social, economic and
ecological needs of present and future generations,
and other controlled sources.

Find out more about HarperCollins and the environment at
www.harpercollins.co.uk/green

Firstly I'd like to thank my agent Hannah Ferguson for believing in the Essex Girls books from the very start; I hope to continue working with you in future. I'd like to thank Caroline Hogg for her help and also my lovely new editor, Lydia Newhouse. I'd like to thank all the Avon team that have worked on both *Essex Girls* and *Made in Essex*. Becke Parker – thank you for helping to make the Essex Girls book launch a huge success! It's a night I'll never forget.

Thank you to everyone that read *Essex Girls* and contacted me to let me know they enjoyed it via Twitter/ Facebook. You'll never know how much your kind words mean and I've really appreciated the feedback! Keep it coming . . .

To my husband, Terry, for putting up with me when I've had deadlines and have been rather preoccupied; I'll always be thankful for your endless cups of tea. You just need to learn how to cook now! Haha.

I'd like to thank all my friends and family for coming to see me at book signings and for spreading the word about my books! I'm truly grateful to you all.

My lovely friends Danielle, Claire and Carolyn; thanks for helping me out whenever I've asked and giving me suggestions. Shirley Harrison, you're one of the funniest people I know and you've helped with lots of lines in the book; I'm sure you'll have fun spotting them (again!). Last but not least, Becky Cooley; thanks for always being yourself, you gave me so many ideas for the characters and you may be from Kent, but you're a true Essex girl at heart ☺

CHAPTER 1

'Open your eyes after three. Ready?'

Jade squeezed her eyes shut and nodded, excitedly. 'One, two . . . three.'

Her hand flew to her mouth and she gasped loudly as Kelly coolly strolled into the room, wearing the very first bikini in their new collection. It was amazing seeing something that they'd actually designed themselves as a finished product, and it looked far better than she'd ever imagined.

'How hot is this bikini, babe?' Kelly beamed from ear to ear. 'Just picture how good it would look with a dark tan and blue vajazzle as well.'

'Oh my God! You look unreal,' Jade said admiringly, eyes bulging. It was a bright petrol blue colour and had a glittery effect which sparkled in the light; it would look even better in the sunshine. The girls had decided to replace the simple tie strings on the bottoms with a row of three gold chains and then inserted some pretty gold dangling charms in between the two cups on the top. It was simply done and looked incredible on Kelly's killer figure. 'It looks easily as good as the expensive ones you buy from America, Kel. It's beauts!'

'I know! I love it!' Kelly said as she glanced at her reflection in the mirror. 'What are we calling this one?'

Jade thought for a moment. 'I like the name "Essex Showgirl",' she decided. 'What other colours can we get for this design?'

'Caitlin said she also has gold and hot pink, hun.'

Jade jotted it down in her notebook happily. Those colours would also look great. She had a feeling that the 'Essex Showgirl' bikini was going to be very popular indeed.

She was thrilled to be starting her own swimwear business, Vajazzle My Bikini, with her best friend, and couldn't wait until everything was up and running. They'd been on holiday to Marbella the year before and when Jade had realised she was the only one with ordinary, plain swimwear on her first day she'd almost been in tears. After finding a boutique that stocked similar glitzy and glamorous bikinis to everyone else's, she'd been horrified at the expensive prices and had decided they should make their own instead. It had been fun visiting the Spanish market for jewels and beads to customise their swimwear, and when they were constantly stopped by girls wanting to know where they'd purchased their costumes from, Jade had realised they were on to something. Kelly was still working as a freelance beautician and Jade had been temping in mundane office jobs to save money for their website. They'd finally saved enough now, and while their friend Lisa's cousin, Tony, was designing and creating their website at a reduced price, they were making the swimwear and planning their collections. They'd found a lovely lady online that ran a swimwear company in America, who sold them bikinis in bulk at discount prices so they could customise them. So far, everything was working out perfectly.

Jade inspected the bikini and looked closely at how well Kelly had made it; she was impressed. Kelly was fantastic at sewing, whereas she was better at sketching the designs on paper, so they could share the workload. They were going to split the administration and had decided that Jade was going to take all the calls and deal with customer queries.

Kelly looked round the room blankly. 'When can we arrange the office properly?' she enquired.

Luckily Jade had an office in her home that was big enough for the two of them. It belonged to Jade's dad, but he never used it for more than one day a month. She paused. 'What do you mean? All we need is another chair. We'll just go out and buy one.'

Kelly arched a perfectly neat eyebrow. 'Mmm . . . I was thinking we could change it a bit as well, you know, make it our own?'

'By doing what?' Jade asked in bewilderment, looking around at the perfectly practical and tidy oak wood office.

'I've brought some bits with me in my car, hun. I hope you don't mind, but I'm not really feeling it in here. I read online the other day that you need to feel comfortable where you're working to be able to work your best. The work place is an important environment, babe. You go and get yourself a snack or something and come back in about thirty minutes. Just let me have a little move around with the furniture,' Kelly told her wisely.

Jade gave a little nod and surrendered. 'Okay, whatever you think. Just don't touch any of my dad's work in the bottom drawer, or he'll kill me.'

'Cross my heart,' Kelly smiled, getting changed back into her clothes and making her way downstairs to her car.

Thirty minutes later, Jade heard Kelly calling her so she made her way upstairs, wondering what on earth was wrong with the office in the first place. As she entered the room she was greeted by fluffy pink pens in sparkly pen holders, pink and white flowers in a silver mirrored vase, decorated photo frames with their holiday snaps, hot pink feathered

3

cushions, and a white furry rug in place of the plain brown one.

'Ta-dah!' Kelly sang as she twirled round on the spot, pleased with her work. 'What do you think?'

'I think it looks like Barbie and Sindy have decorated the room!' Jade snorted with laughter. 'What is my dad going to think?'

Kelly giggled. 'Oh come on, old Jimbo will love it,' she said with an amused smile.

'I can't imagine my dad appreciating you calling him Jimbo,' Jade joked.

Kelly swivelled round on the spot, looking at her work. 'Do you not like it?' She pouted.

'I'm sure I'll get used to it,' Jade replied, knowing Kelly could never work in an office without a bit of sparkle. If it inspired them to create the best swimwear then the sparkle would stay. It did make the office a bit more girly and personal too, she thought, and was unable to contain her grin when she spotted a photo of her and her boyfriend, Sam in one of the frames.

'That's such a gorgeous photo of you two,' Kelly said, when she saw Jade looking at the photo. 'I just a hundred per cent *had* to put that one up.'

'Thanks,' Jade said, flattered, as she picked up the frame. The photo had been taken at Kelly's boyfriend's birthday last year in Nu Bar. They both still had a slight tan from Marbella, where they'd met, and it made their teeth look amazingly white. They looked so happy, and luckily they still were.

'You two make such a sweet couple,' Kelly grinned. 'I'm so glad that Sam's become good friends with Billy too. I love going out just us four.'

Jade nodded. She had to agree it was great that they all got on together so well. If only Lisa had a boyfriend too though, she thought, remembering her other single best

4

friend. Not that Lisa minded being single one bit. Ever since she'd split up with Jake, her long-term boyfriend, the year before, she'd been having the time of her life. It was difficult for her and Kelly to even get a minute of her time because she was always going out. She had been in a relationship since she was sixteen though, Jade reminded herself – Lisa was simply making up for lost time. She was constantly on dates with different guys and it was impossible to keep up! Jade didn't blame her though, and she was happy if Lisa was; that was the most important thing. She had really thought that Lisa would have married Jake a year ago and they'd even been engaged, but after Lisa cheated on him with Billy's friend, Jonny, in Marbella, Lisa had realised she hadn't really been as happy as she'd always believed. Thank goodness Lisa finished it, Jade thought, otherwise she would have been divorced in her early twenties!

Kelly interrupted her thoughts. 'So what are the categories going to be on the website?'

Jade opened her red notebook. 'We decided on the places where all the best pool parties are, didn't we? So we have the "Essex" section, which is going to be our most over the top, blinged-up swimwear, the "No Carbs before Marbs" section, the "What Happens in Vegas" section, the "Romantic Getaway" section, which will be a bit more toned down for when you go away with your boyfriend or husband, and the "Ibiza Zoo Project" section, which will be all animal print.'

'Love it,' Kelly beamed, running her fingers through her thick blonde hair, 'it's going to be so much fun naming all the bikinis. I just love this job already!'

Jade felt the same. 'Me too. We need to meet with Tony tomorrow at six o'clock to go over the web designs, so make sure you're free. I'll meet you straight from work.'

Kelly nodded and there was a long pause. 'I *so* need a diary.'

'You need one of these,' Jade said waving her red note-book in front of her, 'diary and notebook in one.'

Kelly poked her tongue out cheekily, 'Alright, Miss Organised!' She took a package out of her bag ebulliently. 'I forgot to show you some of the sequins and beads that got delivered to my house this morning. They're gorge.'

'Wow, they're great,' Jade agreed, as she watched Kelly pull out various colours of sparkling sequins and pretty beads from the package. She couldn't believe how good they looked when they were so cheap to buy. It filled her even more with excitement, and ideas for new bikini designs were flying around in her head.

'I know,' Kelly sighed, 'although I'm going to have to call the company up we bought them from and complain about something.'

'What?'

'Well, look here at the receipt,' Kelly pulled out a piece of paper received in the package, 'it says flat shipping rate, £3.99.'

Jade squinted as she read it. 'So?' she asked, bemused.

Kelly looked at her with a surprised expression, as though Jade had missed something. 'I don't live in a flat, so why should I have to pay that? The package was delivered to my house!'

Jade laughed. She was going to have to get used to hearing these silly comments all the time working alongside Kelly every day. 'Kelly, flat shipping rate doesn't mean they've charged you because they think you live in a flat. That just means standard shipping rate, you dope!'

'Oh,' Kelly said sheepishly, packing the sequins away again, 'well they shouldn't call it that then, it's confusing. Anyway, I must dash as I have a client coming at seven for a spray.'

'Why? What's the time?' Jade asked in a panicky voice.

'Quarter to seven,' Kelly replied, glancing at her watch.

'Oh shit!' Jade said slapping her hand on her forehead, 'Sam is going to kill me! I was meant to meet him at six-thirty for dinner!'

Kelly pulled a face. 'Oh dear. You did the same thing last week, didn't you? Just call him, babe, don't worry.'

Kelly kissed her goodbye and left.

Jade sighed, biting her bottom lip. The problem was she couldn't just call him and let him know that once again, his girlfriend had simply been too busy working and forgotten she was meeting him. What could she say? She looked at her appearance in the mirror and quickly added some MAC lip gloss and kohl eyeliner. She quickly brushed her long highlighted hair and tied it back in a ponytail. Jade threw on the first pair of skinny jeans she found, texted Sam she was on her way and ran out of the front door.

'Come on,' Jade said to herself moments later as she was sitting in traffic, feeling stressed. Why were all the cars in front of her going so bloody slow tonight? She could hear her phone ringing in her bag and the fact that she knew it would be Sam, wondering where she was, made her even more anxious. She needed to make something up. She had been extremely preoccupied with the website recently and forgetting about Sam was becoming a regular occurrence, much to his frustration.

Ten minutes later she was almost running through the doors of The Bluebell restaurant in Chigwell. She saw Sam's unimpressed expression as soon as she walked in. As Jade made her way over to the table she asked herself, yet again, how she'd managed to get with someone so drop-dead gorgeous. He was looking smart in a tight white shirt and light pink tie, which emphasised his natural olive-coloured skin and penetrating green eyes. His fair hair was brushed over to the side and Jade felt the urge to run her fingers through it.

'Hi, babe,' she said, and kissed him hard on the lips,

hoping to ease his annoyance at her being over forty minutes late.

'Where have you been? Why are you so late?' Sam asked petulantly.

'I'm so sorry,' Jade said as she sat down, 'it's just we had some issues with the new website and I had to sort them out with Tony.'

Sam nodded and the look on his face told her he'd heard it all before. 'You could have called earlier to tell me, you know, so I didn't come here and have to sit alone for over half an hour. You did the same thing last week too.' He looked offended as he sipped his glass of water.

'I'm sorry,' Jade said, gazing into his eyes to show she truly meant it, 'please don't be annoyed with me. Let's have a nice evening, yeah?' She grabbed his hand and held it across the table.

Jade noticed his expression soften and felt relieved.

'So, how's it all going anyway with the website?' he asked a few moments later, genuinely interested. She knew he found it attractive that she was taking a risk and running her own company with Kelly. He was proud of her.

'It's all coming together now,' Jade grinned. 'Kelly put on the first bikini in our collection today and it looked amazing. We know exactly what we want on the website, which is nearly done, and then we just need to make the rest of the swimwear, have a photo shoot so it all looks professional and then the website can go live. I can show you some of the categories we're putting the various bikinis in,' she said, getting her notebook out of her bag and passing it across the table to Sam.

'That's great,' Sam said browsing through the pages. He laughed, 'You take this red notebook everywhere.'

'It's in case I think of new ideas,' Jade told him, smiling warmly. 'I write everything down.'

He looked at her lovingly. 'You look nice tonight by the way.'

'You're joking? I've got hardly any make-up on and got ready in about two minutes! I'm as pale as a ghost!'

'I like you looking natural, you know that,' he said.

Jade smiled. Sam always said the right thing and made her feel good about herself. Thank goodness he was nothing like her awful ex-boyfriend, Tom, who not only used to constantly make jokes about her being from Essex, but also cheated on her. She was so happy with Sam; he meant everything to her.

'Anyway, there are some good films on at the moment at the cinema. Fancy it tomorrow night?'

'Yeah, that'll be great,' Jade said, her eyes bright. Then she remembered, and her face fell. 'Oh no, I can't tomorrow night, sorry. We have a meeting with Tony about the website design. I don't know how long it's going to go on for.'

She could tell Sam was trying to hide his disappointment. He lowered his voice and fiddled with his phone. 'No worries.'

'What about Saturday night though? We may be meeting Tony again in the afternoon but I can meet you in the evening?' Jade suggested cheerily.

Sam nodded. 'If I didn't know better, I'd be worried about you and Tony.'

Jade's jaw nearly hit the table.

'Only joking,' Sam added when he saw her shocked expression, 'Saturday night sounds good to me.'

Jade hoped he was only joking. She couldn't handle him starting to get jealous, especially about Tony. She thought of Tony and his dark hair and hazel eyes. She supposed he *was* quite good looking, in a rough round the edges kind of way, but she didn't look at him like that. Tony was far too old for her too, Jade thought, she guessed he was in his mid-thirties. He was just Lisa's cousin: their web developer. She didn't want anyone else and wouldn't dream of ever even looking at another man when she was with Sam. Why would she, when he was pretty much perfect?

'Sam, I'm sorry I've been so busy lately. I promise you, it's just work, nothing else.'

'I know,' he reassured her, 'it's fine.'

CHAPTER 2

'That's definitely the one,' Lisa said with tears in her eyes, as she was handed the tiny ball of fluff.

'So you're going to take her then?' the woman asked, getting a little emotional herself.

'How could I resist buying her with this gorgeous little face? She's adorable,' Lisa answered, stroking the puppy behind the ears, much to the dog's delight.

'You'll love her,' the woman said, with a twinkling smile. 'They're such good company; all they want is to be fed, watered and loved. My three sit on my lap all day.'

Lisa was so happy she'd found her perfect Chihuahua. She was long haired and chocolate coloured and literally the smallest dog she'd ever held. There were two to choose from; a boy and a girl. The girl was smaller and had seemed to take a shine to her, so there was no doubt she was choosing the right one. She had also bought lots of pink things for when the dog arrived, so she didn't really have much choice anyway.

She had been ecstatic when her parents had finally agreed to let her get one. Since she'd split up with her fiancé, Jake, eight months ago, she hadn't been herself. The guilt of cheating on Jake on holiday had been too much to bear and eventually she had admitted it to him. Ever since the day she had confessed to him, she hadn't heard a word. One of his friends had texted her, asking to meet so he could give her some clothes she'd left at Jake's and get some of his bits from her, but apart from that, there was nothing. Lisa had tried to send him messages at the beginning, but he'd just ignored her. Who could blame him? She was surprised she hadn't seen him around and could never go out without searching the bar or club for his familiar face. She knew her parents just wanted to see her happy again, and if a dog was the very thing to do that, then so be it.

Lisa had decided to get Jade and Kelly to look after the dog in the daytime when she was at work. Seeing as their business, Vajazzle My Bikini, was home-based, it wouldn't be any trouble for them to dog-sit. They would be so excited about her new puppy, she just knew it. Kelly's mum had a Chihuahua, Lord McButterpants, and they all adored him; now Jade and Kelly had their very own gorgeous puppy as their mascot. Lisa thought they were so lucky working together and their business was such a good idea. She couldn't wait until they started making the swimwear so she could get some for her next holiday.

'What are you going to call her?' the lady questioned.

'I think I'm going to call her Cupcake,' Lisa said, her heart melting as she stared into the dog's little coal-coloured eyes.

'I can tell she's going to be spoilt rotten,' the woman said with an easy smile.

'Most definitely.'

Lisa could tell that the lady found it difficult letting the puppy go. She could see why though. Who wouldn't get attached to this cute little thing? She placed her in the new pink dog bag she'd purchased, on the soft white blanket, and put the dog on the floor on the passenger side of her

12

car. Cupcake sniffed around inquisitively, and Lisa felt guilty as the dog began to shake and cry when she pulled away.

'There, there,' Lisa soothed in soft tones, 'now stop that crying. You're going to be just fine, I promise. I love you lots already.'

She couldn't stop looking at her new pet the whole journey back. She even got beeped by another car because the traffic lights turned green and she hadn't noticed, being too engrossed with Cupcake. Just looking at her and stroking her silky fur made her smile. She was the most beautiful dog in the world and she couldn't wait for Jade and Kelly to meet her. They'd be so happy that they'd get to look after her every day! How lucky they were, Lisa thought.

Her parents had agreed to dog-sit tonight because Lisa had a date. Now she'd found her perfect pet though, she actually felt like cancelling and spending the night with Cupcake. It's too late to drop out now, she told herself, she'd agreed to this date and she'd have to go. If only she could remember exactly what he looked like? She'd met Alex in London after work one night, but had been quite tipsy when they'd exchanged numbers. Hopefully he's as nice as I remember, she thought. Lisa had lost count of the amount of times she'd given her number to men and agreed to meet them – only to be greeted by someone she didn't find one bit attractive. She was learning that alcohol, dark bars and clubs were definitely not a good mixture when it came to dating. It was so much fun though, and getting to meet new people all the time was exciting. She had no one else to worry about apart from herself. It was a weird feeling at first, but one she was really enjoying. She couldn't believe she had really thought at one point in her life that Jake was the one. She'd have missed out on so much!

She was so happy since her friend, Nicola, had joined the television company she worked for. She, too, was single and lived in Essex and they had hit it off straight away, often having to work together on projects and new TV shows. They were always out after work meeting new men and Nicola had just asked her earlier that day to move into her new flat. After picturing how much fun they would have together, Lisa had known she couldn't say no and she was planning on telling Nicola her answer on Monday morning.

She dialled Jade on her car phone. She wanted to show off Cupcake as soon as possible. Getting the dog had been a slight spur of the moment thing after her parents had finally agreed, and she'd seen the advert online only yesterday. The girls had no idea about it.

'Hi Lisa,' Jade answered in her friendly voice.

'Hi babe. Where are you at the moment? At home?'

'Yeah. Me and Kelly are just doing a bit of work before our meeting in an hour. Why?'

'Just wanted to check you were in. I have a surprise for you both.'

'Really?' Jade replied excitedly and Lisa could tell she was smiling.

'Yep. Will see you in five.'

Not long after, Lisa was standing on Jade's front doorstep with Cupcake safely in the bag, which was half zipped up so the girls couldn't see straight away.

'Hi, come in,' Jade said as she answered the door, not noticing the bag.

Lisa followed her upstairs to the office where Kelly was sitting.

'You alright, hun?' Kelly smiled fondly when she walked in.

Lisa looked around the office and couldn't believe the transformation. 'Wow. Love what you've done in here, girls.'

'It was Kelly,' Jade nodded in her direction.

'I'd never have guessed,' Lisa smiled warmly.

'Come on then, what's the surprise?' Kelly beamed.

No sooner had she asked, Cupcake started to cry, unfamiliar with her new surroundings.

'Oh my God. What's that in your bag?' Kelly asked eagerly, standing up.

'Girls,' Lisa pulled the puppy out of her bag, 'meet Cupcake.'

'Oh she's gorgeous!' Jade said in shock, her voice high pitched as she moved nearer to stroke the dog.

'*Oh. My. God*. Shut up! I'm in love! Where did you get her? Please say she's yours? She is beauts!' Kelly practically grabbed her out of Lisa's hands.

'My mum and dad finally agreed to let me get a dog!' Lisa said happily, 'which is quite strange actually, because I've just decided to move in with Nicola.'

'What? Where to? It better not be anywhere far away?' Jade asked quickly, slightly worried.

'It's not. Nicola has bought a flat in Chigwell and it has a spare room I'm going to rent.'

'Hello, gorgeous little girl,' Kelly was saying in a squeaky baby voice as she stroked the dog lovingly.

'She's so cute!' Jade said, tickling her behind her ears, 'let me have a hold.'

'So when are you moving?' Kelly said, passing the dog reluctantly to Jade.

'Well I think Nicola is moving in straight away. So I suppose I can go as soon as I want. I haven't even told my parents yet, but I'm sure they'll be fine about it. She only asked me today and I've decided to definitely do it.'

'What's the flat like?' Jade enquired, her eyes remaining firmly on the puppy.

'I don't even know yet. I think it's meant to be quite big though. Nic's bought it and I'll be paying her rent each month.'

'That's great,' Kelly said before she turned back to look

at the dog, 'you can have a moving-in party. Jade, let me hold Cupcake again please.'

'You two won't need to fight over her, don't worry,' Lisa grinned wryly. 'I thought you two could dog-sit during the day when I'm at work, seeing as you'll both be working from home. What do you think?'

Jade and Kelly looked at each other.

'I think yes!' Kelly almost screamed. 'You don't understand how much I'm going to spoil her. There is this amazing dog's boutique down Queens Road in Buckhurst Hill. We can get her some gorgeous little Juicy Couture outfits and diamanté collars.' She looked at the dog and put on her baby voice again, 'You're going to make all the other dogs jell, aren't you, Cupcake? In fact, I'm going to call her Princess Cupcake. She's far too important to just have one name.'

'Will she be okay here all day do you think?' Jade asked, slightly concerned. 'Won't she get bored?'

Lisa waved her hand casually. 'She'll be fine. All they do is sleep and sit on your lap the lady said. Apparently they're really easy to house train too, so she'll be clean in no time. Oh, I'm so glad you'll have her. I didn't know what to do otherwise!'

Kelly hugged the dog to her chest. 'Babe, we're going to love having her all day, aren't we Jade? I'll dog-sit anytime! Can't believe how amazing she is!'

'Thanks. I can't stay long,' Lisa explained, 'I have a date tonight.'

'With the same bloke you went out with the other night? James?' Jade asked.

Lisa looked up at the ceiling thoughtfully and then finally answered 'James? Oh no, not him. I've gone off him since he turned up to the date bright orange.'

'What?' Jade cried.

'He'd clearly had a spray tan,' Lisa shook her head remembering it, 'and not a very good one either.'

'Lisa, there's nothing wrong with a man having a healthy-looking glow with the help of fake tan,' Kelly chipped in. 'Do you have his number? I'll text him to come to me next time.'

'Trust me. He was the colour of a tangerine and he was wearing a white shirt that made it look even worse!' Lisa exclaimed, closing her eyes as if trying to block out the memory.

They laughed.

Lisa continued. 'I'm going on a date with this guy called Alex, and for once he's not from Essex. He lives in Hertfordshire and I met him in London.'

'What's he like?' Jade enquired.

Lisa exhaled. 'That's the problem. I'm not too sure. He's got dark hair and blue eyes . . . or were they brown?'

'Well, good luck with him,' Kelly said kindly. 'What are you doing tomorrow?'

'Nothing,' Lisa replied, 'why?'

Kelly's eyes gleamed with excitement. 'We've a hundred per cent got to go shopping for Princess Cupcake.'

'We've got a meeting with Tony tomorrow, remember?' Jade reminded Kelly.

Kelly scrunched up her nose. 'Oh yeah. What time?'

Jade looked through her red notebook. 'Five o'clock. I suppose we have plenty of time then to go shopping and for lunch. Deffo count me in.'

'Ah thanks girls! This is going to be so much fun,' Lisa smiled. 'Right, I'd better go then.'

'Good luck with Alex,' Jade said.

'Thanks.' Lisa opened the dog bag and turned to Kelly. 'Okay Kelly, hand Cupcake back now.'

Kelly didn't move or even acknowledge she'd heard.

Lisa repeated herself, her voice louder. 'Kelly, hand me back the dog please.'

There was still no response.

Lisa took a deep breath. 'Kelly! You can see her tomorrow. Give her back!'

Kelly handed her back with a sulky pout. 'Okay, okay, fine.' Then she looked thoughtful for a minute. 'It's lucky you got a girl actually. I remember Lord McButterpants used to hump everything in sight until we had him circumcised, especially my cream Ugg boots.'

Jade and Lisa burst into laughter.

'Kelly, do you mean castrated? It's only people that get circumcised, silly! Not animals!'

Kelly grinned, before laughing with them. 'Oh come on, you know what I mean.'

*

The following day, the girls were walking down Queens Road, with Cupcake securely in the pink bag over Kelly's shoulder.

'Make sure you don't trip over and drop her in those shoes,' Lisa said, concerned by Kelly's four-inch black Jimmy Choo heels, which she was wearing with shiny black skinny jeans and a black peplum top with a diamanté collar.

'Stop worrying. I would never fall over,' Kelly said confidently, jutting her chin skywards. 'I've been wearing heels since I was about seven.'

'I doubt it,' Jade frowned.

Kelly turned to her sharply, appalled that it was being questioned. 'Yes I have, actually. I had black patent Kickers remember? They were big thick heels. We were in Mrs Horne's class, so we were seven.'

'Oh my God, so you were,' Jade remembered, shaking her head in disbelief.

'I might get a blow dry while we're down here too,' Kelly announced, as they passed a blow dry bar.

'Going somewhere tonight?' Lisa asked.

'Me and Bill are going to go for a nice meal somewhere. I always like to look nice for him. I've had a spray tan as well,' Kelly explained as she looked down at her bronzed arms.

Jade glanced at Kelly, who looked tanned, as she always did. Jade didn't even know Kelly's natural colour at all anymore; she never went out without a bit of fake tan and though Jade hated to admit it, neither did she nowadays. At Jade's uni, in Bath, it had been a different story. Jade wasn't even sure if she had owned any fake tan for the three years she was there.

'What about you, Jade?' Lisa asked.

'Just going to the cinema with Sam. How did your date with Alex go, by the way?'

'Mmm . . . he was okay,' Lisa said thoughtfully. 'I haven't fallen head over heels for him or anything. He's nice, but I really wasn't keen on his shoes.'

Jade and Kelly laughed heartily.

'You can't not like someone because of their shoes!' Jade exclaimed. Lisa was so fussy, she thought, but as she glanced at her, with her beautiful shiny long dark hair, slender legs and striking coffee-coloured eyes, Jade realised she could afford to be.

'Well I didn't really like his shirt either. It was far too baggy and didn't do him any justice,' Lisa told them before stopping. 'Right girls, here it is up here on the right. Puppy Kit Pet Couture.'

'Oh my God. Is that an actual four-poster bed for a dog in the window?' Jade asked, completely astounded by what she was seeing. How had she never spotted this shop before? It was madness! As they walked in, Jade was mesmerised. There were dog coats, jackets, t-shirts, dresses, skirts, fancy dress costumes. There was even dog perfume! They were surrounded by everything you could ever need for your pet and more.

'Hi girls,' the lady that worked there greeted them, 'awww
. . . let me have a look at her,' she said as she approached
them and spotted Cupcake poking her tiny head out of the
bag.

As the lady chatted to Kelly and Lisa, Jade walked around
the shop, amazed at some of the things she was seeing. She
picked up a gorgeous Swarovski collar and bracelet set,
thinking Cupcake would look adorable in it, and then reeled
in shock at the £150 price tag. This one is better, she thought,
picking up a little white one with pink crystals, which was
only £17.95. As Jade browsed through the adorable little
dresses, picking up some as she went, she froze. She could
hear a girl talking loudly behind her to the lady at the till.
How did she know that voice?

'Jade?' the husky voice said, sending shivers down her
spine.

She turned around, to be confronted with her worst
nightmare. It was Adele. Memories of Marbella last year
came flooding back to her. Not only had Adele, who was
Sam's ex-girlfriend, tried to keep them apart by telling lies
about Jade and snogging Sam right in front of her face,
but she had also stolen their bag of sequins and jewels
from the market and put them on her own bikini! She'd
denied it of course, but Jade and Kelly knew the truth.
She was just a complete bitch and Jade had hoped she'd
never see her again. She had spotted her once since
Marbella down Loughton High Street, but she had hid in
a shop until she had gone. There was nowhere to escape
in here.

'Oh, hi Adele,' she said, about to turn back round to the
shelves of clothing. The last thing she wanted was to actually have a conversation with her.

To Jade's surprise, Adele practically jumped on her, kissing
her cheek. 'Oh my God, I haven't seen you for ages! How
are you, hun? Who are you with? Oh my God, shut up!

It's Kelly. Kelly!' she shouted, flapping up and down and interrupting Kelly's conversation with Lisa and the shop assistant.

Kelly's face dropped and she waved unenthusiastically, looking like she'd seen a ghost.

'Come over here, babe!' Adele signalled, a huge grin plastered on her face.

Kelly said something to Lisa, who looked over, and they made their way to where Jade and Adele were standing.

Adele grabbed Kelly as soon as she was within reach, hugging her tightly. Jade had to stifle a laugh as she watched Kelly's terrified face.

'Hi Adele,' she said, trying to pull back from her forceful embrace.

'How are you, babe? Can't believe how long it's been! I've been hoping to bump into you two for ages.'

'I'm good thanks,' Kelly replied, taking another step back. 'This is Lisa by the way; I don't think you met her in Marbella?'

'No,' Adele shook her head, 'I do recognise you from Marbs though. I saw you with Jade and Kelly a few times. Hi, hun.'

'Hi,' Lisa nodded, looking bored. She knew all about Adele and how much of a cow she was.

'Oh my God! Your dog is amazing!' Adele roughly put her hand through the opening of the bag to stroke Cupcake, who cowered and hid further into the safety of the blanket. 'What a lovely Chihuahua.'

'Thanks,' Lisa replied, looking at her watch.

'I'm buying a miniature Yorkshire Terrier, so just getting some little bits for him now. He's completely adorable. Costing my dad a fortune because he's like, from the best breeders ever. Think his dad was a winner at Crufts and everything. Over one and a half grand he is. Oh well, it's worth it, isn't it babe?' she said to Lisa, as though they

F/2251357

understood each other because they both had dogs. 'What's she called?'

'Cupcake,' Lisa replied.

'Princess Cupcake,' Kelly corrected her hastily.

'Cute,' Adele smiled. 'I'm calling mine Buddy. He'll keep me company in my new amazing flat my dad bought me. You girls have to come over soon. It's stunning. Huge. We'll go out for the night and have drinks before at mine. Where are you girls living now? Not at home with your parents still, surely?' Adele smirked.

'Me and Kelly are, yes,' Jade answered indignantly. 'At least this way we can save money as luckily our parents don't charge us too much rent.'

Adele looked as though she'd tasted something bitter. 'Your parents make you pay rent?'

Jade and Kelly nodded.

'Oh right,' Adele remarked, raising her eyebrows in disbelief. 'My dad has taken care of everything for me, luckily. He's bought me all new furniture too. What about you?' she asked, her eyes flicking to Lisa.

'I'm moving in with a friend,' Lisa replied, 'and will be paying my own rent and buying my own furniture. I could never just sponge off my parents without contributing, even if it was an option. No offence,' Lisa grinned caustically.

'None taken,' Adele retorted, with one of her fake smiles that Jade knew so well.

'Anyway Adele, nice seeing you. We really better hurry up though, we've loads to buy,' Kelly said, as she turned and picked up a tiny white frilly dress.

'Okay girls, have fun shopping. I'll add you on Facebook and we can go out soon, yeah?'

'Yeah, though I don't go on my Facebook much,' Jade lied.

'No problem. Give me your phone, babe,' Adele demanded, holding out her hand.

'Why?' Jade said, trying to think of a good reason why she wouldn't have it on her without it looking too obvious.

'I'll put my number in,' Adele told her firmly.

Seeing no way out, Jade passed her the phone and Adele put her number in and called it so she had Jade's number on her own. *How annoying?* Jade thought, hoping she wouldn't keep texting and calling. Why couldn't she just get the picture? They didn't, and would never like Adele; she was bad news.

'Cheers, hun,' Adele turned to leave, 'oh, and Kelly?'

'Yes?' Kelly replied, warily.

'I really wouldn't go for that white dress for Cupcake. It'll do nothing for her figure,' Adele remarked and then waved dismissively and left.

*

Later on that day Jade and Kelly were on their way to the meeting with Tony.

'I still can't believe that Adele suggested our gorgeous little Cupcake was podgy,' Kelly huffed moodily, shaking her head; her thick, blonde, freshly blow-dried luscious waves bouncing. It was all they had spoken about since it had happened. They'd said goodbye to Lisa, who was also furious with Adele's remark, and then Jade and Kelly had had their hair done. It was so nice to simply sit there while someone made your hair look amazing. Jade's long blonde hair extensions were quite hard to handle, and she'd got into the habit of having them blow dried whenever she could. It was worth the money in her opinion.

'I know,' Jade said for the umpteenth time, 'it's ridiculous. As if a puppy could be fat. She's just jell.'

'Who does she think she is? Coming over to us like we're best mates. She even took your number! The cheek of it. I can't bear her! And I *never* hate anyone. But picking on little Cupcake, well,' Kelly shook her head violently, 'that's just taking things to another level.'

'Let's not waste any more time talking about her,' Jade said, slightly bored with going over the same thing. 'We need to get our business heads on now.'

'Yes, you're right,' Kelly said, much to Jade's contentment. 'But I just can't believe she called her fat!'

Jade sighed. Why oh why did they have to bump into Adele today?

Ten minutes later they were in Tony's office in his home in Abridge.

'Hi girls,' he greeted them with a warm smile.

'You alright, babe?' Kelly said.

Jade smiled and took one of the seats beside the computer.

'How's it all going then?' Tony enquired, his hazel eyes sparkling. He ran his hand through his jet black hair, which Jade noticed had a few grey strands. 'Got the bikinis made yet?'

'I've made a few,' Kelly explained. 'But don't worry, Tone, I'll get them done in no time. You should see me on the sewing machine! I'm a whizz kid,' she giggled.

Jade nodded in agreement. 'She's really good. I'll be helping out too,' she told him.

'Great. It would be good to get some images of the bikinis sooner rather than later,' Tony advised. 'We want to get the website up and running as soon as possible and obviously we'll need the images so people can see what you have to offer. So I suppose you'll need to get a photo shoot done.'

Jade jotted it down in her red notebook and when Tony spotted her doing so he suggested some photographers they could contact that weren't too expensive.

'Thanks, that's a great help,' Jade smiled graciously as she took their phone numbers.

She was so pleased that they were using Tony. Not only

was he great at designing websites, but a really nice, helpful person too. He genuinely wanted the girls to make a success of their business and thought their idea was fantastic. She was still shocked at Sam's remark about worrying about the two of them though. Yes, Tony was fairly attractive with his dark hair and strong jaw line, but even if Jade had been single, he was far too old for her and had a four-year-old daughter from a previous relationship. Sam had absolutely nothing to worry about.

'Will you be modelling the bikinis yourself?' Tony asked Jade with a half-smile.

Jade felt herself blush. 'As if! No, we'll be getting other people to model for us.'

Tony nodded as he rubbed the stubble on his jaw. 'I'm sure you'd look just as good in them,' he said, catching Jade's eye and making her turn away uncomfortably. Tony changed the subject. 'Okay, so I've already started Vajazzle My Bikini's Facebook and Twitter page. You just need images to put on now, as well as getting people to like your page on Facebook and followers on Twitter of course.'

'Thanks, hun,' Kelly beamed as she plaited her hair.

'In the meantime,' Jade suggested, 'let's just use the photos of us in our bikinis in Marbs, which we designed.'

'Good idea,' Tony said. 'I'll go make us tea while you two add some images and start suggesting friends to like your page.'

The girls added a few photos where they both agreed they looked nice and then started requesting friends to like their page.

'Oh look,' Kelly said excitedly a few minutes later, 'we already have three likes on Facebook!'

Jade's heart melted when she saw one of them was Sam; he was so sweet and supportive. How lucky she was to have him.

'Three likes already, well done,' Tony smiled. 'Okay, now I'll show you the three designs I have for the homepage,' Tony said, handing them a mug of tea each.

The designs appeared on the screen on the computer. Kelly's face lit up when she saw the last one. It had a black background with big pink glittery letters saying 'Vajazzle My Bikini'. It had stars which moved across the screen and looked magical. Sample images of bikinis flashed on repeat and not only did it look extremely user friendly, but impressive too.

'A hundred per cent the last one!' Kelly said, 'I just love it! Every swimwear website will be so jell of us!'

'Yes, I agree,' Jade said cheerfully. 'The last one is perfect.'

'Thought you were going to say that,' Tony said with an amused smile.

An hour and a half later Tony told them he was going away for two weeks.

'It's vital I show you the back end of the website tonight and teach you how to use it so you can get started,' he said.

Jade looked at her Michael Kors watch. It was six forty-five already. 'How long will it take?' she asked, dreading the answer.

'To show you the whole thing so you understand?' Tony thought for a few seconds. 'Maybe two hours? Two and a half tops?'

Kelly and Jade looked at each other, thinking the same thing: they both had plans.

'Only one of you needs to stay,' he added quickly when he saw their concerned expressions.

'Babe, I'll stay,' Kelly offered kindly, 'I'll learn the computer stuff easy-peasy, honestly.'

Kelly started pressing the computer screen, while Jade and Tony sat there, baffled.

'Kelly, what are you doing? It's not a touch screen!'

Kelly started to giggle, 'I thought I was using my iPhone for a minute! Need to get my brain into gear.'

Jade stifled a giggle. It was sweet that Kelly had offered, but she could hardly even use her own laptop and always needed help with the simplest things, like how to turn it on! She even remembered the time Kelly had complained her laptop was stuck and wouldn't open, not realising she had it the wrong way round when she was trying to lift the screen up. She doubted she'd ever have any clue about technical stuff. She knew Kelly hated computers and offices, one of the reasons she'd become a beautician.

Jade took a deep breath. 'Kelly, it's lovely of you to offer, but I'll stay and learn it.'

'After seeing you do that, Kelly, I'd have to agree.' Tony laughed. 'I promise I'll be as quick as possible, Jade.'

Kelly nodded, knowing that was definitely the most sensible thing to do. 'If you're sure, Jade? I'll stay too if you like?'

'It's fine; it only needs one of us. Honestly, you go.'

'I'm sorry I can't make it another day,' Tony said, looking guilty, 'it's just I really think you should get it up and running ASAP.'

'That's okay,' Jade said lightly, secretly worrying about letting Sam down again. 'I'm going to drop Kelly off and then quickly drive to Sam's and tell him I can't make tonight. Would it be okay if I came back in about forty minutes?' she asked Tony.

'Perfect,' Tony said, rubbing his hands together and getting out of his seat.

After dropping Kelly off home to get ready to go out with Billy, Jade pulled into Sam's drive. For the first time since they'd been a couple she actually felt a little nervous about his response.

'Hi,' he grinned, opening the front door and kissing her.

'Bad news,' Jade said as she walked into his bedroom and sat on his bed.

27

Sam's smile vanished. 'You can't come?' he guessed, looking disappointed and making her feel terrible.

'I'm so sorry,' Jade said, 'I'll be done in a few hours and can meet you after if you like? I could co—'

Sam interrupted her. 'I've already bought the tickets for the cinema and booked a meal. Is there no way you can get out of it?' he asked, unable to control his irritable tone.

Jade shook her head, bit her lip and looked at the floor. 'Tony is going on holiday for two weeks so it has to be done tonight.'

Sam nodded, looking even more unimpressed now she'd mentioned his name. 'Right.'

'I can meet you after?' Jade asked hopefully.

'Don't worry about it,' Sam said curtly, looking away. 'My mates are going to Sugar Hut tonight and I blew them off because I wanted to see you, but I'll tell them my plans have changed. There's no point in you rushing around for me when you have work to do.'

Jade nodded, knowing he was angry. 'Tomorrow?'

Sam raised his shoulders. 'I have a football match late afternoon and then I said I'd help my cousin move out.'

'I can help you?' she offered, desperate to make it up to him somehow.

There was a long pause. 'No, it's going to be lifting loads of heavy things. Thanks anyway though.'

Jade felt awkward. He was being slightly cold towards her and it hurt. She felt like he wanted her to leave. Sam was never like this normally; he was always so affectionate and loving. 'Are we okay?' she asked, her voice slightly shaky.

He nodded and cleared his throat. 'Fine.'

'Okay, well I'd better be getting back to Tony,' Jade told him, standing up and swinging her bag over her shoulder.

'Of course,' he said blankly, opening his bedroom door with an unreadable expression.

Jade sighed sadly. 'Speak to you soon then. Have a nice night.'

As Jade left Sam's flat, she felt unsettled. Was her business ruining her relationship?

CHAPTER 3

Adele was bored as she waited for her nails to dry. She grabbed her laptop from the dressing table and switched it on. As she waited for it to come alive, she thought about what had happened that day. She couldn't believe she'd bumped into Kelly and Jade at last. She hadn't seen them since Marbella and had been dying to go out with them on a night out. She'd been gutted when she realised she didn't get their numbers after the holiday, even if things didn't end on the best note. They always looked like they had fun when they went out and she knew they lived close to her, so it would be perfect to use them for that reason. She'd wanted to send them both a friend request on Facebook, but had worried that they wouldn't accept it because of what had happened in Marbella. Surely they were over her stealing their junk from the market to sew on their swimwear? Adele couldn't handle the thought of them rejecting her friend request, she was far too proud for that, so in the end she had stopped herself. Kelly, Jade and Lisa had all looked like such good friends today; Adele wanted to be included in their plans and go out for girly nights, lunches and shopping trips. They were nauseatingly pretty though; could she really handle being around them all the time and having to fight for attention? She cursed herself for thinking that way. Of course she could – she was easily as attractive as them, if not more so. She'd heard that Jade was going out with Sam now. She absolutely hated the thought of them together and could kick herself that her plan to split them up in Marbella hadn't worked. Oh well, Jade was welcome to her sloppy seconds, Adele thought nastily. She'd already been there, done that and got the t-shirt.

She was going to Sugar Hut tonight with an old friend from school called Donna. They'd become really close recently and Adele loved going out with her because Donna was a bit on the heavy side, which meant she ended up stealing all the limelight. Donna did everything she said too and Adele loved it that she always got to pick where they went out. Adele liked being in control; she had to be, in fact. They were friends at school, but had lost contact when Donna went to college and then off to university.

Adele had contacted Donna after her mum had bumped into Donna's mum and told her Donna worked for Mulberry in the head office. Why couldn't Adele land an amazing job like that? She didn't even want to think about the discounts she must get, which Donna was very tight-lipped about. Some people just had it so lucky. So what if Donna had a degree in fashion and marketing? She didn't exactly look the part, being a size sixteen (though secretly Adele thought she looked more like a size eighteen and that maybe she was lying). Adele would be much better suited to a fun job like that, and it angered her that sometimes life was just so unfair. She was hoping Donna could get her in the company somehow, but so far she'd been nothing but useless, saying some crap about how she couldn't and she'd have to go through the normal hiring process. Whatever! Everyone knew that if you knew someone in a company they could always manage to get you in somehow and put in a good word. Adele hadn't really worked since Marbella, she realised as she stretched her legs out on the bed. She'd done the odd couple of shifts in her mum's boutique in Ongar, but apart from that, nothing. She was getting slightly bored, she had to admit. Money was never an issue, her dad made sure of that, but she did feel the need to do *something* with her life, other than going shopping, getting her hair done and just sitting around and looking pretty. She wondered if she should try modelling or acting or something interesting like that and told herself she'd look into it on Monday.

Maybe she should text Jade and ask her to come out tonight? See if Kelly and that other Lisa girl wanted to come too? It was sometimes a bit boring being with just Donna and Adele imagined it would be much more fun with a group of them. She took her phone from her dressing gown pocket.

Hey babe. How are you? Fancy coming out tonight? I've got a table with champers? On me of course Xx

The reply came back almost instantly.

Busy, sorry x

Is that it? Adele thought, infuriated. No, 'I'm fine thanks', 'how are you?' or 'thanks for the offer'. There was no need to be so short; it was just plain rude! Who did Jade think she was, treating her like unwanted rubbish?

Adele logged into her Facebook account miserably for a browse. Donna would be round soon and she'd have to start on her hair. She noticed that one of her friends had 'liked' a company called Vajazzle My Bikini. Intrigued, she clicked on it and when the image of Jade and Kelly appeared on her screen, Adele couldn't believe her eyes. So they had decided to make their customised swimwear into a business had they? She looked at the company information and read that they were making special and unique swimwear, perfect for pool parties. She assumed it had just been a little hobby when they were away, but they were actually taking it further! She felt a wave of anger and jealousy wash over her. Why hadn't she done that? Adele would love to have her own business and make swimwear! She'd wasted so much time doing nothing, when she could have been creating her own business and getting there before those two airheads. At the bottom of their company information something caught her eye. It said 'website coming soon'. So they didn't have a website yet then? Maybe she could do the same thing and get there first? Adele's heart beat faster as ideas raced around in her mind. She needed to speak to her dad who owned a very successful property development business; he'd be able to help her and put her in touch with the right people. Picking up her phone, she called him.

'Hello,' came her dad's gruff voice down the phone.

'Hi, Dad. Really quickly. If I wanted my own website as I have a really good business idea, how quickly could you get it done do you think?'

He paused. 'I'd have to speak to Martin, he takes care of that side of things for our business. He's usually pretty quick. He did our website in just over a week, but it's fairly simple and I suppose it depends on what you want? Why, what's your idea?'

'I'll come over tomorrow and tell you. We can talk then,' Adele said happily, smiling from ear to ear.

'Okay, darling. Look forward to seeing you then,' he said fondly.

'Okay, bye, Dad.'

This was perfect, Adele thought ecstatically! Her dad

would get Martin to build Adele her very own website and then she'd make all the bikinis. It wasn't exactly hard was it? Sew on a couple of beads and diamantés here and there, big deal. Adele had seen lots of Jade and Kelly's creations in Marbella and they didn't look *that* difficult to copy. She could undercut their prices too so people would use her website instead. She couldn't wait to see the look on their faces the next time she bumped into them. They always treated her like she was a bad smell or something. She'd soon show them, and they'd be sorry for ever underestimating her.

*

Sam felt irritated. All he wanted was to spend some quality time with his girlfriend, but lately it was proving impossible. He loved that she was starting her own business with Kelly; it was ambitious and he'd always found independent women irresistible. His idea of hell was a money-grabbing gold digger, and there plenty of those in Essex, that was for sure. Sam had been surprised by how quickly he'd fallen for Jade. After Marbella, they had literally never left each other's sides and the more he got to know her, the more he fell in love. She was down to earth, loyal and thoughtful as well as being beautiful. He thanked God every day that Adele hadn't managed to keep them apart with her vicious lies about Jade being easy. He'd never really understand why she lied and kissed him that night in Marbella so Jade would see; Adele didn't have feelings for him, so what was her problem with him being with Jade? Adele really was a bigger bitch than he'd ever realised. A serious psycho that one, and he'd had a very lucky escape.

He wondered when he'd become so attached to Jade. Love was funny like that. One minute he'd been acting cool and casual, and the next, he couldn't imagine his life without her. He hadn't told her he loved her yet, but he knew he did. He'd never said it to anyone before and if he was honest, it was because it terrified him. He would be putting his heart on the line and it was a huge step. Say she didn't reciprocate? He had these worries in his head, though he knew deep down that she was just as keen on him. They were so happy together and he knew that he loved her the first time she made him really laugh. He couldn't even remember what she'd made him laugh about now, but it wasn't just a giggle; it was a deep, throaty, stomach-aching laugh that made tears run down his cheeks. He loved that Jade had a sense of humour and didn't take herself too seriously. But now she was busy all the time, letting him down constantly. Excuse after excuse – and it was hurting him more than he cared to admit. Surely there was still room for him in her life? Was there really no way she could fit him into her busy schedule? When was he going to come first? He understood she was preoccupied, but did she realise how she made him feel when she simply forgot they were meeting and arrived forty minutes late? Was he that easy to forget? Sam hated that their otherwise perfect relationship was being jeopardised by her new job. He did want to support her, but it was hard when it was at their relationship's expense. He was as understanding as the next guy, but tonight he felt nothing but angry, let down and disappointed.

Sam switched off the TV, unable to concentrate on anything apart from Jade. Maybe he was a bit harsh with her earlier? Jade knew he was being offish and had felt like she had to leave. Perhaps he should be more understanding at times? It was a busy time for her at the moment and it wasn't always going to be like this, he told himself. He picked up his phone to call her. Maybe he would meet her a bit later after all.

'Hello?' came the unfamiliar male voice down the line. Sam frowned and checked the screen on his phone to make sure he'd dialled the right number. 'Err . . . hello, is Jade there? Who's that?'

'Sorry, it's Tony. Jade's left her phone here and has just popped out to pick up a takeaway for us. Shall I get her to call you back?'

'No, leave it,' Sam said starting to feel angry again.

'Okay, bye.'

Sam hung up, fuming. So she was out buying a takeaway for the two of them was she? How cosy. The last thing he wanted was to call his girlfriend and hear another man's voice at the end of the line. He imagined them together, laughing and joking as they ate their meal. He knew he was being insecure, but he couldn't help it. His friend Steve, who was single, had suggested Sugar Hut earlier that day and at the time, he had actually felt quite relieved that he was spending the night with his girlfriend he loved. Sam had been thankful that he didn't still have to go out on the pull and wake up the next day with a hangover, but perhaps he shouldn't get too comfortable, he told himself, as he pulled on his True Religion jeans. Maybe Jade was too busy for a relationship? Maybe she'd end up marrying Tony, the bloke she was spending her Saturday night with, he thought jealously. He cursed himself; Jade would never cheat and he needed to grow up, thinking thoughts like that. What was with him? He usually wasn't the jealous kind. He needed to stop getting so angry.

Reluctantly, he pulled on his All Saints t-shirt and thought about his night ahead. He always got attention from girls when he went out and used to love it, but now it just irritated him. He wasn't interested in anyone else, not when he had Jade. He'd never wanted to move in with another girl or settle down and get married, but with Jade, all these things seemed exciting rather than scary. She'd completely changed him – and to think she'd been there the whole time in Marbella. He'd wasted so much time looking for someone that had been right under his nose the whole time. As he slipped his shoes on, he hoped their relationship would be back on track soon.

*

Adele looked down at her legs in annoyance. Her spray tan hadn't come out half as dark as she wanted and she was even looking at Donna enviously for once.

'God, I look so bloody pale!' she spat, applying more bronzer to her cheeks to compete with Donna's golden glow.

'You should go to Kelly who you went to college with,' Donna suggested, aware that Adele had taken the same beauty course as Kelly, but given up halfway through. 'She does the best spray tans ever, babe. She sprayed me twice over so it comes out darker and uses Sienna tan, which is like the best there is. She knows just how I like it.'

'I've heard Kelly is terrible,' Adele lied, bitterly irritated by the fact that Donna was friends with Kelly. 'How do you know her anyway? I didn't realise you were friends. She is so thick it's embarrassing and was crap at college. I'm surprised she even made it to the end of the course.'

Donna shook her head. 'No way! Kelly is great at her job, trust me. She does my make-up too sometimes and I love it. Don't you like her? She's such a nice girl and beauts as well. A friend recommended her to me a while back and we've been mates ever since.'

'Of course I like her,' Adele snapped, in case it got back to Kelly and she blew her chance of being friends for good. 'I just didn't think she was that great at beauty, but whatever.'

'Your dress looks gorgeous,' Donna admired, staring at Adele's gold one-shoulder Forever Unique body-con.

'Cheers, hun,' Adele said, loving the way the dress hugged her in all the right places and made her look a dress size smaller. She glanced at Donna's plain black dress that looked far too small for her and dug in her arms, making them bulge out at the sides. Thank God she didn't have her figure, she told herself happily. 'Luckily, I can wear body-cons,' she remarked, feeling glad she'd scored a point back from the fact her spray tan wasn't as dark.

Donna looked down at herself. 'I wish I could lose weight,' she sulked wistfully.

Adele had no sympathy and shook her head dismissively. 'It's really not that hard, Donna. Just stop eating so much chocolate and crisps. I'm not being funny, but it's a fact. If you eat more calories than you burn off, you gain weight. Go for a jog on your lunch break or something.'

Donna was affronted. 'What lunch break? I never have time for one!'

'How *is* the job going by the way?' Adele asked, glad the subject had been brought up. 'Is there any chance you can get me a discount on the bags yet? I've got my eye on this amazing cream clutch.'

'I'm sorry, but they're really strict on it. That reminds me though; I do have some good news for you. I asked HR again about you getting a job and they need sales assistants in Selfridges if you want me to take your CV in?'

Adele looked as though Donna had said she could get her a job cleaning toilets. '*What*? A sales assistant? Donna, *please*. I wouldn't be seen dead as a shop worker! Even if it was for Mulberry. No way. Besides, I actually don't need a job there anymore. I'm starting my own business instead.'

'That's great!' Donna enthused. 'What business? Tell me everything.'

Worried it could get back to Kelly, Adele shrugged, 'Just wait and see.' She added Chanel lip gloss to her plump pink lips. She'd had collagen injections two weeks ago and loved how big they looked. She flicked her long dark hair over her shoulder, satisfied with her appearance. 'Right Donna, call a taxi now and we'll go.'

Forty minutes later, they arrived at Sugar Hut.

'Oh my God, shut up!' Donna sighed. 'Look at the size of the queue! It goes back further than we can even see!'

Adele tutted loudly. 'Donna, don't be so ridiculous. Like *I* would ever need to queue. I wouldn't queue in that if you paid me. I'm friends with the bouncers.' She laughed at the sheer thought of joining the end of the line.

'Oh, wicked,' Donna said, brightening up instantly.

Adele marched with her head held high to the front of the line and kissed Dave, the bouncer who she knew on the cheek, giving him a saccharine smile. She'd sucked up to him the previous year so much that he thought she fancied him and asked to take her out on a date. She'd gone reluctantly, demanding he take her somewhere expensive, and they ended up going to Nobu in London, where Adele made sure she ordered the most expensive sushi and champagne so she could boast to everyone how much the meal cost. She also knew it would mean a free queue jump whenever she went to Sugar Hut. He'd been really into her, which hadn't surprised her in the slightest, and she pretended she'd got back with an ex-boyfriend to get him off her case. Luckily, Dave had understood her predicament and on a few occasions when she'd been in the club she'd given him a cheeky snog goodbye when she left, just so he didn't lose interest in her. So simple really. Men were so thick and gullible sometimes that they couldn't really see what was going on. Did Dave seriously look at his vile bald head and ever-expanding waistline and think that someone like *her* would genuinely be interested? It was laughable.

'One moment, gorgeous,' Dave winked.

Adele smiled back seductively. 'Thank you, babes. You're looking well,' she said in a soft, honeyed tone.

She looked at the queue, which seemed to have grown even longer. Donna was right; it was exceptionally busy tonight. As she glanced at the sea of faces looking at her

39

and Donna, some slightly angry that they were getting let in before them, she caught a pair of green eyes that she knew far too well. It was Sam. She looked behind him, noticing he was with his friends rather than Jade. Hopefully he'll cheat on her tonight, Adele thought wickedly. There was plenty of temptation in Sugar Hut and she imagined Sam would have lots of admirers. He looked very handsome tonight, wearing a white top which showed off his tanned skin and toned physique. She waved and gestured for him to come to the front with her and Donna. He acknowledged her, but mouthed 'No, it's okay, thanks.'

Adele was not impressed. So he'd rather queue like a civilian than jump to the front and go in with her? How pathetic. He was obviously still bothered about the stupid lies she'd told him about Jade in Marbella. It was a joke for God's sake. He really needed to get a life and get over it. God, Sam and Jade were as bad as each other. Talk about holding a grudge!

'Who's that?' Donna enquired, raising an eyebrow.

'My ex, Sam,' Adele replied blankly.

'Oh my God, he's so fit!'

'Really bad in bed,' Adele fibbed. 'I had to dump him because of it. He literally didn't have a clue, bless him.'

Donna laughed. 'I wouldn't mind teaching him.'

Adele grimaced at the thought. 'He was a lost cause, trust me, I tried.'

'What a shame, with a gorgeous face like that,' Donna said disappointedly, shaking her head.

'Mmm . . .' Adele said, still fuming that he'd brushed off her queue jump invitation so quickly.

As they walked through without paying, Adele could tell Donna was overjoyed to be out with her receiving special treatment. They walked through the entrance to the bar on the left, and Adele decided to wait until Sam came through so she could speak to him. They ordered a bottle of white wine.

'Shall we go to the table now?' Donna asked excitedly, her eyes bulging.

'No, silly,' Adele huffed and rolled her eyes at Donna's complete stupidity. 'The table is upstairs in the club. It will be dead now. No one goes up there until later so we'll stay here first.'

Donna listened to her attentively, like a child in a classroom in awe of their teacher's every word.

Not long after, Sam made his way through and Adele couldn't help but approach him immediately. She didn't know why, but she couldn't handle the thought that he didn't like her. She'd been his girlfriend once upon a time, but now he looked at her like dirt on his shoes and it didn't feel good.

'Hi Sam,' she said, kissing his cheek. She could tell he wasn't pleased to see her standing there.

'Alright?' he said vacantly, about to walk away.

'How have you been?' she asked quickly, before he disappeared. 'I haven't seen you since Marbs. Weird, because I bumped into Jade today as well. Are things going well with you two? How come she's not here?'

Sam glared at her. 'Adele, with all due respect, that really has nothing to do with you. Don't pretend to care about me, or even Jade for that matter. Please, I'm just really not in the mood tonight. Enjoy your evening,' he brushed her off.

As Sam walked away, Adele felt her face go hot with fury. Did he have to be so rude to her? Did she really deserve to be spoken to like that? It made her even happier to be copying his darling Jade's bikini business. She couldn't wait to wipe the smiles off their faces when they realised her plan. Money was no object to her so she could make her business ten times bigger and better than Jade's and so she would! They both deserved each other as far as she was concerned. A pair of complete idiots! They wouldn't last either; she'd lay money on it.

41

An hour and a half later, Adele and Donna were seated on their table. She ordered a bottle of champagne and felt extremely smug and superior to the girls on the table next to them drinking pikey Smirnoff Ices. Did people still drink those awful sugar-laden drinks? How chavvy, she decided, turning her nose up at their cheap dresses, which looked like they'd been purchased from Romford market.

Adele sighed, feeling pretty bored. She liked Donna, but sometimes she could be quite dull. Donna was so lucky to be out with someone like her, why couldn't Donna be more fun? The night wasn't going well. Sam had been rude to her twice, the only bloke she fancied who was standing at the bar had now disappeared and she was stuck with Donna. Where were all the fit men?

A short while later when Adele was in the ladies toilet in a cubicle, she heard a big argument between two girls outside.

'You've been giving me dirty looks all night, you tramp. Have you got a problem or something?' she heard one girl snap, aggressively.

There was a timid response from the girl she was addressing. 'I haven't even seen you before. I certainly haven't been giving you dirty looks.' She sounded terrified.

'Don't lie. I saw you with my own eyes. Who the hell do you think you are?' the angry girl countered.

Eager to get a better look and excited by the drama, Adele left the cubicle as soon as possible. She couldn't have been more shocked as she was faced with Chloe, Sam's younger sister, almost in tears because of the girl confronting her. Adele saw the relief in her eyes when Chloe recognised Adele. A look that begged for help. The poor thing was petrified. Adele couldn't believe the change in her! The last time she'd seen Chloe she'd been around fourteen with a cute blonde bob, freckles peppered on her nose, a fixed brace, looking every bit the young teenager she was. Now she looked like a woman! Much older than eighteen, which she guessed she was now. She had beautiful long wavy blonde hair, a stunning golden complexion, the most captivating green eyes like Sam's and the best figure she'd seen in a long time. Her slim legs seemed to never end and her natural bust was full and curvy. If Adele didn't know what a lovely girl she was, she too, like the girl before her would have hated Chloe. Adele knew as well as she knew her own name that Chloe hadn't so much as glanced at the furious-looking girl in front of her. It was clear that this girl didn't like her and never would. But it wasn't Chloe's fault and it wasn't because she'd done anything wrong. The girl was simply jealous.

'Are you okay, Chloe?' Adele butted in; making sure the dark-haired girl heard her loud voice.

Chloe's chin wobbled and she looked as though she was going to burst into tears. Adele had always been fond of Chloe. Of course, when she'd been going out with Sam, Chloe had only been a young girl, but often she'd sit in Chloe's room giving her advice on boys in school, curling her hair and doing her make-up. Chloe had always looked up to her and adored her and Adele had felt like she was the little sister she never had.

'Sorry, is there a problem here?' Adele asked the bully, sternly marching towards her.

The girl eyed her up and down, weighing her up and looking uncertain whether to carry on with her fabricated story. Her confidence was clearly evaporating by the second since Adele had showed up, and even her friend beside her edged away, as though to state she wasn't part of it.

'She's been giving me dirty looks and I was just asking her about it,' the girl retorted, attempting to keep up the bravado. The change in her once-authoritative voice wasn't lost on either of them.

'I didn't give you any dirty looks, I swear. Why would I?' Chloe said, looking frustrated. She turned to Adele with a tormented expression. 'She won't leave me alone.'

'Oh, I think she will,' Adele asserted, her head held high as she stared at the girl domineeringly. 'I think you're done here. And before you go, if I see or hear you ever speaking to Chloe like that again, you'll have me to deal with and there will be trouble. Understand?'

The girl merely nodded, backing away. 'Whatever.'

'Where do you think you're going?' Adele scowled, her voice abrasive.

'Back to the club,' the girl mumbled, trying to get away quickly.

'Not before you say sorry to Chloe,' Adele demanded, folding her arms across her chest and looking down at the bully.

'Really, it's fine, Adele,' Chloe said shakily, her large green eyes glistening.

'No, it's not fine.' Adele's eyes flicked back to the bully. 'Say you're sorry *now*.'

There was now a crowd in the toilets and girls were pretending to do their make-up so they could watch and listen. The dark-haired girl looked embarrassed and very regretful for ever starting anything now.

'Sorry,' she said shamefacedly. She visibly shrunk and turned to walk away after her friends, who had already deserted her.

'Good, now piss off,' Adele added in her direction for good measure.

Chloe sighed in relief. 'Oh my God, Adele! Thanks so much. I thought she was going to beat me up!'

Adele shrugged, 'No problem. You need to stand up for yourself against bitches like her.'

'I was scared,' Chloe said, embarrassed.

'Never mind, it's over now, you can relax. How are you? I haven't seen you for ages.'

'I'm good. How are you?'

'I'm fine,' Adele said washing her hands. 'I can't believe how much you've grown up. You look lovely.'

Chloe blushed, clearly uncomfortable with compliments. She was still as shy as she ever was and completely unaware of the extent of her beauty.

'Thanks. You look gorgeous too. I love your long hair.'

Adele smiled. 'Extensions. I get them done in London where Victoria Beckham used to go. It's one of the best places,' she boasted. She remembered how she'd had her awful, natural thin hair when she'd been with Sam back then. How completely clueless she'd been! 'Where are your friends?' Adele asked, looking round.

'In the club on the dance floor,' Chloe explained.

'You can come and sit with us, babes. I'm here with my friend Donna who works for Mulberry.'

Chloe looked amazed. 'Oh really? She works for Mulberry? I'd love one of those bags but could never afford it.'

'She gives me a discount on them,' Adele fibbed to impress her, 'has to keep it quiet though so obviously don't mention it.'

'Are you sure you wouldn't mind if we sat with you? That would be incredible.'

'Course not,' Adele said, staring at her flawless make-up. *I wonder what mascara she uses.*

'Thanks so much, Adele!' Chloe was thrilled. 'I'll get the others.'

'We've got a table with champers. It's only Dom Perignon though. We've just ordered another bottle.'

'Oh my God! I love champagne. Thank you so much!' Chloe's voice was now an excited squeak.

Adele grinned. 'Come on then, hun, I'll show you where we're sitting.'

They left the toilets and Adele was delighted that they bumped straight into Sam. The timing couldn't have been more perfect.

*

Sam watched in horror as he saw his little sister approaching him with Adele. What the hell were they doing together? he wondered suspiciously. That's the last person on earth he'd want Chloe to be hanging around with. Adele smiled in his direction, then whispered something to Chloe, pointed to a table and walked away. Hopefully that would be the end of their chat, he prayed, remembering how close the two of them had become when he was dating Adele. Of course, back then he didn't realise what a vindictive and manipulative cow Adele was.

After downing shots all night, Sam realised they were finally taking the desired effect. The only problem was, try as he might, he couldn't get Jade out of his head. If he'd checked his phone once, he'd checked it a million bloody times and she still hadn't contacted him. He was feeling more angry and hurt at how she kept blowing him out with every drink.

'Hi,' he said to Chloe as she made her way over to him. He hated how much older she looked recently. She'd started to wear a bit more make-up too and he wasn't a fan. He'd have to keep an eye on her. There was certainly no denying how beautiful she was. He'd even caught his own mates checking her out on several occasions, which made him feel nothing but sick. It was as though his sweet, innocent sister had developed into a woman overnight.

'Hi,' she said, looking pleased to see him.

Sam's eyes flicked to Adele then back to Chloe. 'What were you doing with Adele?'

Chloe squinted. 'I ran into her, why?'

'Keep well away from her. She's nothing but trouble.'

Tears formed in Chloe's eyes.

'What's wrong?' Sam asked, baffled.

Chloe hesitated. 'It's just this girl and her friends started on me in the toilets. I hadn't done anything, but she pushed me really hard and said I'd been giving her dirty looks. She was much bigger and older than me and I was really frightened. Adele saved me. She was in the toilets and overheard. I don't know what would have happened if it wasn't for her.'

Sam nodded, furious that anyone would dare start a fight with his inoffensive sister, who wouldn't harm a fly. Thank goodness Adele had been there to rescue her. 'You could have come to me. I would have sorted it. Where are these girls that started on you? Can you see them now?' Sam asked. He would give them a piece of his mind if he could.

'I couldn't come to you. I didn't even know you were here,' Chloe said, looking round. 'No, I can't see them, but it's fine now. They won't bother me again. Adele has made sure of it.'

Sam nodded, his earlier thoughts of Adele being nothing but bad news slowly disintegrating. She'd helped Chloe when she desperately needed it, despite him being completely rude to her when he first walked in. She could easily have left her. She hadn't seen Chloe in years and owed her nothing. Was she really as bad as he thought? So she'd made up a few lies about Jade in the past. Perhaps, she hadn't liked the thought of him with someone else. Sam was her ex-boyfriend, it was only natural. Maybe he shouldn't treat her so dismissively in future. Maybe she'd changed and grown up a bit? She'd saved his sister from being beaten up tonight and he'd always be thankful for that.

'I'm going to find my friends,' Chloe explained. 'Adele has invited us to sit on her table.'

Sam felt relieved. Chloe would be safe with Adele and he wouldn't have to keep checking she was okay all night. His sister being old enough to go clubbing was nothing but a worry. Especially when she looked like Chloe did.

'Okay, if you need me, come find me,' he said.

Sam couldn't enjoy the rest of his evening, no matter

how hard he tried. He hadn't eaten dinner seeing as he'd planned to go with Jade and the drinks were going straight to his head. He looked over to see Chloe and her friends who were now sitting on Adele's table. How kind of Adele to include his eighteen-year-old sister and her friends. He was sure they must be cramping her style, but it didn't show. As Chloe and Adele laughed about something together, Sam turned to Steve.

'Mate, I think I'm going to make a move. I'm smashed and don't really feel in the mood.'

'You absolute boring lightweight,' Steve joked, slapping his back. 'Only joking. See you tomorrow at the footy match. You want to sober up or you're going to play shit. A few of us are going to Nu Bar after tomorrow's game if you fancy it?'

'Yeah, should be able to. Call me tomorrow,' Sam replied and then left when the brunette girl Steve had been chatting up all night started talking to him again.

He staggered over to Adele's table and she noticed his arrival instantly and smiled as though she was expecting him. See, she was being quite nice, maybe she was different now? He leant over to her.

'Can I have a quick word, please?'

Adele jumped up. 'Of course, babes.'

He walked off to a quiet spot by the bar, where they'd be able to hear each other better.

He felt his head spinning and propped himself on the bar for support. 'Look, I spoke to Chloe a while ago and she told me how you stuck up for her in the toilets. I just wanted to say sorry for being such an idiot to you at the beginning of the night.'

Adele nodded, gently touching his toned arms. 'It's fine, honestly. I would always stick up for Chloe. We go way back.'

'I really mean it,' Sam slurred, 'thanks so much. Chloe's

so young and naïve and I appreciate that you were there for her when she needed someone. I was so rude to you earlier, but there's more to it.'

'What's up Sam? You can tell me,' Adele probed, fluttering her eyelashes, her look a face of concern.

'Me and Jade are having some slight issues,' he blurted, not even considering who he was talking to. It felt good to confide in someone. It was a release to just say it out loud.

'What kind of issues?' Adele asked surprised.

'She has this new business. It sounds ridiculous, because of course I want her to do well. I'd help her in any way I possibly could. There is nothing I wouldn't do for that girl, but lately she just has no time for me at all. Like tonight for instance. We were meant to be going out and she just blew me off last minute.'

'She's just busy, babe,' Adele replied. 'What's the business? Tell me everything about it. It sounds interesting.'

Sam waved his hand dismissively. 'Oh, it's some swimwear thing. I won't go into it. I just feel a bit down, you know? Am I being pathetic?'

Adele thought for a minute. 'No babe, you're not being pathetic. The more I think about it, I agree with you. It shouldn't matter how busy Jade is, you should always come first. I know you always came first with me, when we were dating. And I think you have a serious right to be pissed off with her.'

Sam nodded in agreement. 'She's always late to meet me recently and never answers her calls or texts me back for hours. All I want to do is just be with her and spend time with her. She's the first girl I've ever loved . . .' He stopped what he was saying, not knowing how Adele would take this news.

She laughed at his worried expression. 'Sam, please! You don't have to worry about me, hun. We were practically kids when we went out! If it makes you feel any better, I didn't love you either.' She smiled, but it didn't reach her eyes, which gave her away. He'd clearly hurt her feelings.

'I won't bore you any longer anyway,' Sam muttered, feeling slightly awkward. 'I've said too much. I'm drunk and need to make a move.'

'Well you can't leave Chloe; you'll have to drop her at your mum's. Your flat is in Chigwell, isn't it?'

He nodded.

'Perfect, then I'll come in the taxi too.'

*

Jade had been tossing and turning in bed for the past hour. She had so much on her mind and was finding it almost impossible to sleep, despite feeling exhausted.

She'd learned how to do the admin section of their website with ease and had picked the whole thing up quickly, but even still, hadn't got home until gone ten o'clock. Tony kept remembering problems they might encounter and had to teach her how to fix them, seeing as he wouldn't be in the country to help. They could still contact him, but he was going to Australia and there would obviously be a huge time difference. He'd suggested they open a bottle of wine at one point and even though Jade had felt like saying yes, she wanted to make sure she had a clear head so she didn't forget anything. Something told her that Sam wouldn't be too impressed either if he knew she was drinking with Tony and it hadn't felt right. She was glad she had stayed now so she knew exactly what to do; it meant they could get started as soon as possible. She'd agreed a photo shoot for the following week, so they would need to have a sample of every bikini in their collection made by then. They also needed a model and Jade had the perfect idea. Sam's younger sister, Chloe, would be ideal. She was slim, tall, busty and absolutely stunning. The bikinis would look amazing on her and she was certain she'd love to do it too. She was a lovely girl and really friendly and it was easy to tell she was related to Sam. Perhaps Lisa would model too, she thought, and then they'd have a blonde and brunette. The photographer looked brilliant and she was so thankful for Tony and his contacts as he'd agreed to give them a discount if they used him regularly.

She wondered how Sam's night had been. He'd seemed so angry when she went to his flat that she hadn't wanted to contact him and pester him. She was probably the last person he had wanted to hear from. It was the first blip in their relationship and it was horrible. She didn't want things to go wrong and decided she would have to start putting him first and considering him more. She couldn't keep forgetting their plans and turning up late to meet him, it wasn't on. She didn't want a successful business but no Sam, did she? The thought made her stomach flip over with fright. She'd organise something special for him this week to apologise for her behaviour. He had to forgive her. She had just wanted to do well in her career; it wasn't a personal attack on him.

As she closed her eyes she realised that she'd have to go over to see Sam tomorrow anyway, even though he told her he was busy. He wouldn't have his football match until the afternoon, so she'd go round first thing in the morning. She'd stupidly left her red notebook round his house when she'd gone there to inform him she couldn't go out and had had to write all her notes on some paper Tony had given her. She'd add the notes to her notebook tomorrow when she got it back, she told herself. After all, it contained everything about their business in it.

*

Adele strolled into Sam's flat, impressed not only with its tidiness but also its modern décor. From the stunning

51

French limestone floor to the spacious, luxurious kitchen with black marble surfaces it was every bit the perfect home. She secretly even preferred it to her own flat. It wasn't as large, but for some reason it had a welcoming, homely atmosphere.

'Nice place,' she said, looking round.

'Thanks,' Sam murmured. He looked confused in his drunken state as he narrowed his eyes. 'I still don't understand why you got out at mine though? Why didn't you get the taxi to drop you to yours?'

Adele tried to think of a good lie. 'The taxi man said we only said it would be two stops on the way back and seeing as we dropped Chloe back and then you, he wouldn't drop me and told me to get out.'

Sam had fallen asleep in the taxi and Adele had found a perfect opportunity to get back at Jade for snubbing her. She knew he didn't have a clue what was going on and even better, he would never remember.

'Well, just call a taxi,' he mumbled, as he lay down on his cream leather sofa and started to fall asleep.

'Sam,' Adele giggled, 'you can't go to sleep there, silly. Here, let me help take you to bed.'

He moaned as she tried to pull him up by his arms.

'Leave me,' he croaked.

'Come on,' Adele said, yanking him harder until he eventually gave up and followed her. She took him into his room and helped him on the bed, knowing Jade would kill him if she could see what was happening. The thought made her smile. Sam was, yet again, about to fall into another one of her traps. As he started to snore softly, Adele looked around his room. He had a photo of him and Jade in a silver antique frame on his window sill. They were both smiling and Jade looked beautiful, Adele acknowledged enviously. They were the most annoyingly perfect couple. She couldn't believe that Sam had confessed Jade was the *only* girl he'd ever loved? What did Jade have that she didn't? When was Adele going to meet someone perfectly suited to her? She hardly ever met anyone she liked. She wanted someone good looking who had money. None of this 'I'll take you out to Prezzos for a meal' crap either. She wanted to be wined and dined in the poshest West End restaurants, taken away for the weekend abroad on a luxury yacht and driven around in a Ferrari. It was what someone like her deserved and she wasn't settling for anything else. She had to admit that Sam was doing well for himself. She'd heard through the grapevine that he worked as a stockbroker in London and was earning good money, as well as getting hefty bonuses. He must be doing well, judging by his flat, Adele thought, as she nosed around. Jade was a lucky girl.

She spotted the red diary on the end of his bed thinking she'd hit the jackpot. This couldn't be true. Sam had a diary? This was turning out to be the best night ever! As she picked it up, expecting to read his deepest darkest confessions, her mouth dropped open as she read the title 'Vajazzle My Bikini' in girly handwriting. As she turned the pages, her heart beat faster and she beamed in ecstasy. This was a million times better than finding Sam's diary! This was Jade and Kelly's notebook with every single detail about their new business! She found details of where they bought their bikinis from, all their designs, a photographer they were going to use, advertising ideas, fashion shows they'd planned to attend and every other thing they'd done so far. She wouldn't have to do hardly any work now! She could just copy everything they'd done and use all their contacts. This was fantastic! Adele couldn't wait to tell her dad the next day and start getting her website built. She could buy all the same accessories to decorate the bikinis with now she knew the website they purchased them from, and just slightly change the designs. She could do better than them anyway, she thought, as she flicked through Jade's sketches. Luckily she'd used a fairly big bag tonight, she decided, as she slipped the notebook in her beige Hermès leather tote. Not that Sam was going to wake up and catch her, she realised, trying not to laugh as she slipped the notebook in one of the compartments. She was elated. This was a dream come true coming here tonight.

She walked over to Sam and looked down at his peaceful-looking face. He was fast asleep. She slowly began to unbutton his shirt, praying she wouldn't wake him. Luckily, he didn't even move. He was far too drunk to ever remember anything even if he did wake up, Adele told herself, banishing her nerves. She was safe. Before she knew it, his shirt was off and she was unbuckling his belt and pulling his jeans down. She moved the bed covers from underneath him and put them on top. As she peered under the covers at his tanned, toned, athletic body she wondered whether she should remove his boxers or not. She decided she should. Well, she had to make it look real if she was going to pretend they slept together.

CHAPTER 4

Lisa spotted Nicola instantly. Her long platinum blonde hair was easily recognisable, even from a distance. She was wearing leather trousers with a baggy snakeskin blouse and gigantic black sunglasses, despite it being cloudy. It was always weird seeing Nicola wear normal clothes; working for a television company they didn't have to wear suits, but had to dress fairly smart still. It also never ceased to amaze Lisa how professional Nicola was at work; she changed her voice so much that her Essex accent was almost undetectable, and she was completely serious and hard working. It was as though as soon as she left the office she could relax and be her true self. Lisa was meeting her in Chigwell to view their new flat and was really excited to see her room, which Nicola had told her she'd love. Nicola had been overjoyed when she'd told her she wanted to move in and they'd spent most of their day at work looking at the Zara Home website, deciding on what bedding they were going to buy and getting ideas about how Nicola should decorate. Then they'd discovered Kylie Minogue bedding and had fallen in love. Lisa had already bought two Kylie bedding sets; one stunning gold with diamanté cushions to match and a gorgeous white set with lace trim and a beautiful throw. It had cost a fortune, but it would look great, Lisa consoled herself.

'Morning, honey!' Nicola grinned as she reached her.

'Hi,' Lisa smiled, 'nice shades.'

'Thanks. I know it's not sunny but they're my new Tom Fords and I wanted to wear them. Ahhh, you brought Cupcake! Her little pink top is so cute!' she flapped. 'Oh, it has diamonds on it, how amazing?'

Lisa let Nicola stroke her dog, who she was carrying in her arms. She had to wait until she'd had all her jabs at the vet's before she could let her down and walk her.

'She's got a whole wardrobe of outfits,' Lisa laughed. 'You really don't mind me moving the dog in?'

'Babe, are you kidding? She's so cute. How could I not want her in our flat?'

'I suppose so,' Lisa said, following Nicola through the gates to the building. There was a big sign saying 'Manor Hall' on the side of the wall. Not only did the building look lovely from the outside, but even the stairway, walls and carpet looked fresh and clean. So far, so good, Lisa thought happily.

They walked to the first floor and Nicola stopped outside number ten.

'Here we are,' she sang, 'home sweet home.'

The front door swung open and Lisa stood there, amazed. It was beautiful!

'Wow. I love it!'

'It's got underfloor heating and state-of-the-art surround sound and everything!' Nicola said enthusiastically. 'How lucky are we to be living in this place? I can't believe this is my flat!'

'Show me my room!' Lisa said, putting Cupcake down, who sprinted up and down the floor, relishing her freedom.

Lisa was delighted when she was taken through to a gorgeous room, which even had its own en-suite bathroom.

'Do you like it, babe?'

'I absolutely love it!' Lisa said as she took everything in. 'We are going to have so much fun being single here!'

'I know,' Nicola agreed. Her eyes darkened. 'Do you like being single? I mean, you're happy aren't you?'

Lisa sat down on the bed, wondering why she was asking her. She thought for a moment. 'Yes, I love it at the minute. It's nice not having to worry about anyone else.'

Nicola sat down next to her and became a bit serious all of a sudden. 'I have to tell you something.'

Lisa felt anxious and fiddled with her bracelet. 'What's up?'

'What did you say the name of your ex-boyfriend was?'

'Jake. Jake Sutcliffe, why?'

Nicola nodded as though she was expecting to hear that. 'I thought that was him. I got my nails done today before I came here and my nail technician, Katy, she was going on about her new boyfriend and how he proposed to her last weekend.'

Lisa had a feeling where this was going. 'Yeah, go on.'

'Well, when I asked about him, she said he was a carpenter and he was from round here. So I asked his name,' she looked up at Lisa's face, unsure whether to continue, 'and she told me it was Jake Sutcliffe.'

Lisa froze. She could hear her heart beating so loud it sounded like someone was banging drums ferociously. Her head felt hot, like it was going to burst.

'Are you okay, honey?' Nicola asked, worried. 'Oh, babe, please don't get upset. I didn't want to tell you, but thought it was better coming from me than someone else!'

Lisa couldn't speak. She never thought she'd feel this way. She knew Jake hadn't been the right man for her and she knew her cheating on him was a cry for help, but now he was gone for good. She could never get him back, even if she wanted. He had moved on; he was marrying someone else. How could he have moved on with someone else so quickly? How could he be engaged again?

'Lisa?'

Lisa shook herself and looked up at Nicola. 'Sorry. I was in a world of my own. I'm okay. Thanks for telling me. It just feels so weird! I can't believe Jake is marrying someone else. He didn't waste any time did he? We've only been split up for eight months and he is already engaged again!'

Nicola shrugged, her brow wrinkling. 'Maybe it's just a rebound?'

'No, Jake would never propose on a rebound. He is far too sensible for that. He just loves being in relationships and he's obviously met someone else he truly loves already. I'm happy for him, really I am. But, I just feel so shocked. I always assumed it would take him ages to get over our relationship, like it's taking me. Yes, I'm happy and I like being single, but I'm still not one hundred per cent over him. I've been with him since I was sixteen! I still have days when I feel a bit lonely and question whether I did the right thing!'

Nicola cocked her head to one side thoughtfully. 'That's understandable. You know you did the right thing, don't you?'

'Yes,' Lisa said, 'I know I wouldn't have been happy to stay with him forever and that wouldn't be fair on me or him. I always knew he'd meet someone else and I thought I'd feel fine about it, but I'm so shocked. The thought of him being with someone else just seems so strange. This time last year, he was with me and we were happy. Well, I thought I was, anyway. He's moved on so quickly and is settled again. Then there's me going on loads of dates and just being the fussiest person in the world.'

'We're too young to meet Mr Right,' Nicola said.

Lisa thought for a moment. 'You're right. Let's just have fun meeting Mr Wrongs!'

58

'That's the spirit,' Nicola said getting up, 'now come with me to the kitchen.'

Lisa followed as Nicola pulled out a bottle of Moët from the fridge and got two glasses out of one of the cupboards. She squealed as she pulled the cork out and it made a loud popping sound.

'Scares me every time it does that, honey!' she explained, her hand on her chest. She filled their glasses. 'A toast. To being single, having fun and to *not* being engaged at twenty-two!'

'I'll cheers to that,' Lisa smiled. 'Also, to having the most fun ever in our new flat. Cheers!'

'Cheers,' Nicola grinned, taking a sip of the bubbly liquid.

They both jumped when they heard dogs barking.

Lisa put her glass on the glass table. 'Oh my God, Cupcake!'

'Oh shit,' Nicola muttered under her breath, worrying when they saw the flat door ajar.

Luckily the dog sounded close by, and Lisa sighed in relief when they opened the flat door and found Cupcake barking at a miniature Yorkshire Terrier dog sitting at the door of the flat opposite.

'Cupcake, that's enough!' Lisa said loudly, trying to capture the dog's attention, which didn't work. The other dog started to bark back even louder and Cupcake made a growling sound.

'Cupcake, honey,' Nicola chipped in. 'Be nice.'

'Yes Cupcake, stop that. Come inside, that's enough,' Lisa said sternly, wagging her finger at the dog.

They heard a girl shouting in the flat opposite and when she appeared Lisa stood there with her mouth wide open, agog.

'Oh hi, it's Lisa, isn't it? What are you doing here? Is that your flat? Buddy, stop that yapping!' she yelled at her dog, brazenly.

'Adele? You live *here*?' Lisa asked, her voice almost a whisper, hoping she was just visiting a friend. This couldn't be happening!

'Babe, these flats are like the nicest round here for miles. Of course I live here!' Adele cackled, reminding Lisa of a witch.

'Oh . . .' Lisa said feebly, her earlier excitement bursting like a bubble.

'So is this your flat or your friend's?' Adele asked, eyeing them one at a time quizzically.

'It's mine,' Nicola informed her politely, 'and Lisa is going to be renting a room as from tomorrow.'

'Oh amazing!' Adele smiled, 'we can do dinner and have girly nights in. How great is it we live opposite?'

Lisa nodded unenthusiastically, 'Yeah, really great.'

'Excuse the state of me, girls, I've only just got back from last night, if you know what I mean,' Adele grinned, pulling her dressing gown round her tighter.

'What's his name?' Nicola asked with a wry smile.

Adele held her hands up with a mock-offended look. 'Now come on. Do I look like the kind of girl that would kiss and tell? Sorry, I didn't catch your name?'

'It's Nicola.'

'I'm Adele.' She picked up Buddy who was still barking at Cupcake and shut him in her flat. 'Give them time and they'll be best friends,' she gave a short, gravelly laugh, which sounded like she smoked too many cigarettes. 'Do you mind if I take a look at your flat?'

Lisa looked at Nicola, willing her to say no. She wanted to get away from Adele and pretend this wasn't happening. How could she live in the flat opposite? Out of the whole of Essex, what were the chances of them both being in the same building? It wasn't fair! This was supposed to be their dream flat. A chance to finally taste freedom. This wasn't freedom – what with Adele living dead opposite, showing up at their door every night, like Lisa bet she would. Girly nights in? This was a complete nightmare!

'Of course you can,' Nicola said, scooping up Cupcake and walking inside.

Lisa followed reluctantly.

'Oh, it's *so* tiny compared to my one!' Adele exclaimed, looking delighted as she nosed around in every room. She noticed Nicola's frown as she made her way out of the bathroom. 'Of course, it's more homely or whatever this way though.'

She clearly doesn't want to get on the wrong side of Nicola, Lisa thought resentfully.

'How big is your one then?' Nicola enquired.

'It's got a much bigger lounge and the rooms are double the size,' Adele boasted smugly. 'Your one is really cute and small, though I could never live somewhere as little as this myself.'

'Well I like it,' Lisa retorted.

'Oh great, champagne!' Adele squeaked, walking to the kitchen and looking through the cupboards for a glass.

Nicola looked at Lisa questioningly and Lisa gave her a furious expression to show how annoyed she was with Adele for just inviting herself in for a drink. What a nerve she had! Helping herself to their champagne! Who did she think she was?

'We can't stay for long,' Lisa lied, frustrated that Adele had ruined her morning. First she found out Jake was engaged, now this.

'Oh I'll just have a quick glass to celebrate us being neighbours. Oh, it's Moët,' Adele said disparagingly, trying to disguise her grimace as she tasted it. 'I haven't had this since I was a teenager.'

'What's wrong with Moët?' Nicola asked, puzzled.

'Nothing, hun. It's nice. I think I've just been spoilt with expensive champers in my time and it's hard to go back to the cheap stuff. I'm a Cristal girl myself. Ignore me,' Adele said, flapping her hand.

'We will,' Lisa said under her breath, making Nicola snort with laughter. 'Anyway Adele, I hope you don't mind, but we really must be going soon.'

Adele looked disappointed. 'Oh right. Where are you going?'

Lisa was caught off guard. Where could she be going? 'Oh . . . erm . . . we're . . .'

'She needs to go to the clinic,' Nicola helped out quickly.

Lisa shot Nicola a baffled look, who then made a face as if to say the clinic was the first thing that came into her head.

'The clinic? Are we talking . . .?' Adele nodded, eyes widening as she gave them both a knowing look.

'That's right,' Nicola said, continuing the lie, 'the STD clinic.'

'But it's Sunday,' Adele frowned. 'What clinic is open Sunday and what's actually wrong?'

Lisa faked a strained expression. 'I'd really rather not say.'

'Oh, well okay then,' Adele said, looking rather uncomfortable as she downed her champagne. 'Though if you want my advice the best clinic to go to is the one in Romford and ask for Dr Stevens, he's the best. Hot too. He's helped me *loads* in the past.' Adele looked flustered as she realised what she'd just said. 'Not loads exactly . . . just the one time. Anyway, must go, I think I can hear Buddy barking for me!'

She turned and left, leaving Nicola and Lisa standing there in fits of laughter.

*

Sam woke up and groaned. His head was throbbing in pain and he was gasping for a drink. What on earth had happened

62

to him last night? How did he get home? He shivered, and wondered why he was completely naked. He had been so drunk and he could feel that he was going to be paying for it today. He got his phone from his bedside table and saw he had two messages. The first was from Jade. He squinted as he read the message, trying to focus on the words.

Morning. Hope you don't mind, but I'm coming over this morning as I left my red notebook at yours and also think we need to talk. Xx

The message was sent about an hour ago, so he needed to sort himself quickly. He didn't want Jade seeing him in this state. He was bemused when he saw his previous message was from Adele, and then memories of him speaking to her and apologising came flooding back to him.

Hi Sam. I left early this morning before you woke. I hope you don't mind. Had the most amazing night with you ;) You're still as good as I remember! Adele xx

Sam felt as though someone had punched him. Still as good as she remembered? What was she talking about? What the hell happened? Surely he hadn't . . . he couldn't even bear thinking about it. This was a disaster! He felt his face burning and a sick feeling wash over him. He deleted the message, jumped up and grabbed his dressing gown, running to the toilet and just making it on time before he spewed up vast amounts of liquid. What a mess, he thought, as he hugged the toilet seat, feeling like death. Why on earth had he thought it was a good idea to drink so much? He was such an idiot! What had Adele meant? he questioned, as he got up and walked to the kitchen to get a sachet of Alka-Seltzer. He put the white tablet in a glass of water, waited for it to dissolve and then downed it as though his life depended on it. Please make me feel better, he prayed as he wiped his mouth, and inhaled deeply as another wave of nausea washed over him.

He froze when the loud shrill of the doorbell went off. Surely Jade wasn't here already? He hadn't even had a shower or brushed his teeth! He didn't want her seeing him hungover; he knew she hated it when he went out and got wasted and now he could see why.

He opened the door, attempting a smile as he saw Jade's pretty face staring back at him. Her long dark blonde hair was loose and wavy and even though she was wearing casual jeans and a mint green jumper she still looked as glamorous and sexy as ever.

'Morning,' she said, kissing him.

He grimaced as he turned; knowing he'd just been puking up and she'd kissed him.

'Hi,' he exhaled, concentrating on acting completely normal. He didn't want her to guess anything was wrong.

'Rough night?' Jade asked, going into his room.

'No, not too bad,' he lied. 'I'm just going to jump in the shower and brush my teeth. Won't be long.'

'Okay, I'll watch the telly for a bit.'

Sam put his head under the hot sprays of water and rubbed his face. What had he done last night? Adele's message kept flashing through his mind. He had to act normal. Whatever had happened, Jade couldn't know about it. Surely he'd been too drunk to do *anything* though? He would never cheat on Jade, would he? If only he could piece together last night's events. He honestly didn't believe he had slept with Adele, but the sad and frustrating thing was, he couldn't be certain. He was so annoyed with himself for being so stupid! He had been completely drunk, which was why he'd blacked out and could only remember being in the club. The last thing he remembered was speaking to

Adele. Why did things go so wrong whenever she was around? He needed to talk to her and get her to tell him the truth. The trouble was, he was terrified what she was going to say. He wrapped a towel round his waist, brushed his teeth and put some deodorant on and then made his way to his room. Stay calm, he told himself; you're not ill, you're fine. And you did not do anything untoward with Adele last night.

'There's nothing on,' Jade sighed as she saw him, throwing the remote control on the bed. She sat down and patted the duvet. 'Come sit.'

Sam sat down, feeling nervous and paranoid. Alcohol always made him feel that way the day after, and he wondered, not for the first time in his life, why he even bothered drinking. It always seemed like such a good idea at the time.

'Listen,' Jade started easily, 'I really want to apologise for being so busy recently. I've let you down time and time again, but I promise it's got nothing to do with my feelings towards you. I just really want my business to do well, but you're more important to me and will always come first. I've been in another world recently and I'm out of it now. I'm so sorry for always being late and letting you down, I really am. But it stops now.'

Sam put his head in his hands and gave a gusty sigh. 'Jade, it's me that should be sorry. I was acting like such a spoilt brat not getting my own way, and I know it's not your fault you've not had much time recently. I was just hurt and disappointed, which turned into anger. I know it's pathetic. I want your business to do as well as you do, trust me. I suppose I just don't like sharing you. In a selfish way, I like to have all of your time, but I understand that that's not always going to be the case.'

Jade gave a natural smile, looking relieved they were having this conversation. 'So we've made up then?'

He nodded.

'Good,' she said, 'that means I didn't buy the tickets for nothing.'

'What tickets?' he asked, baffled.

'Plane tickets to Italy. I've booked a long weekend in a hotel for the two of us in September. We'll have so much fun and Kelly may be booking for her and Billy to go too. It'll still be hot and we can sunbathe all day and go for romantic dinners at night,' she beamed.

'Babe, are you kidding? That's amazing!' He pulled her to him, kissing her passionately. 'That's so nice of you.'

'You're worth it,' she replied, kissing him back.

'I love you,' Sam said without thinking. It was the first time he'd ever told her. The words just came right out and he felt embarrassed, not knowing where to look.

'Awww,' Jade looked into his eyes, 'it's a good job I love you too then.'

Sam smiled warmly, even though his head was throbbing in pain. He was so glad he'd finally said it and even happier she loved him too. Jade pushed him playfully on the bed and slid the towel off from round his waist. 'You know the best thing about arguments?' she asked him, with a suggestive glint in her eye.

'What's that?' He smirked.

'Making up,' she said, her voice soft and sexy.

Sam pulled the duvet back and got under, watching her as she removed her clothes and joined him. He kissed her hungrily, his heart beating faster by the second. As he felt under the covers to touch her warm body, his fingers brushed past something unexpected. As Jade kissed his chest, he sneakily peered underneath the covers and felt faint with fear when he saw an unfamiliar bright pink thong. Where on earth had that come from? The words from Adele's text message flashed through his mind: *You're still as good as I remember.* It must be Adele's thong! He frantically kicked it to the very end of the bed where Jade wouldn't see it, then did his very best to try to relax. Unluckily though, there was only one thing on his mind the whole time.

*

An hour later and Jade was still lying in bed with Sam, cuddling up to his warm body and not wanting to leave the bed. The TV was on in the background and Sam was playing a game on his iPhone. She stretched lazily and smiled. He'd finally said he loved her! She felt like she'd been waiting forever to hear those words. There had been so many times she was sure he was going to say it, but nothing. Now he had, Jade felt she could finally tell him her true feelings also; she was head over heels in love with him too.

'I better get going,' she groaned, getting out of bed and getting her clothes on, 'you need to leave for football soon.'

Sam looked at the clock on his wall and sighed, 'Yeah, you're right. I would rather just stay with you today if I'm honest. But, I can't let the team down and then I've got to help my cousin, Joe.'

'Are you sure you don't want me to help?' Jade offered sweetly.

'No it's fine. Thanks though, it's nice of you. When will I see you next?'

'Look at you,' Jade smirked teasingly, 'just can't get enough of me.'

'You're not wrong there,' he said, pulling her over to him as she pulled her jeans on, and making her giggle as he kissed her.

'Why don't we go for dinner one night this week?' she suggested as she wrapped her arms around him.

He nodded as he kissed her neck. 'Sounds good.'

'Oh before I go, I need my red notebook. Good job I remembered. Whereabouts did you put it?'

Sam was mystified. 'Where did you leave it? If I'm honest, I haven't even seen it. You sure you left it here?' he asked, glancing round his room.

'Yeah, a hundred per cent,' Jade replied as she walked around and searched.

'What about in the lounge? Or kitchen?' Sam suggested. He hadn't seen it in his room.

Jade pushed her hair back from her face. 'I didn't even go in there though. I only came in your room.'

'I swear to God I haven't seen it. You must have left it somewhere else.'

Jade scratched her head, perplexed. 'Maybe Kelly picked it up then? Or maybe it's in my car or something? I was certain I'd left it here though. I remember bringing it in.'

Sam shrugged. 'It'll turn up. I'll search a bit more here if you want and call you if I find it.'

'Thanks,' she answered, frustrated with herself for losing something so important. How could she have lost it? It had every bit of information they needed in there. 'I'll have another look round and then go in a bit.'

Fifteen minutes later, Jade kissed Sam goodbye, leaving his flat without her notebook. She was losing her mind. She was certain she'd left it at Sam's. She got in her car and searched everywhere, but to no avail. Where on earth had she put it? How had it disappeared into thin air? Her phone rang and she was glad when she saw Kelly's name flashing on her screen.

'Hello,' she answered.

'Hi, babe,' Kelly greeted her brightly. 'How did it go last night?'

'Yes, really well. The website is pretty simple to work and I think I'll be able to upload the products quite easily. I was just about to call you actually. Did you take my red notebook by accident?'

Kelly paused as she thought. 'No. Why, have you lost it?'

'Yeah. I was sure I left it at Sam's when I dropped you back and then went to see him, but it's not there, I just checked. I must have left it at Tony's then. I don't think it's there though. It's so strange.'

'It must be at Tony's, hun,' Kelly replied to reassure her. 'Don't worry, we'll find it. It's bound to turn up somewhere. I was just calling you because I've been up since seven this morning making some sample bikinis for the photo shoot.'

Jade felt excited. 'Oh well done. Do they look good?'

'Totes amaze. Seriously, whoever wears them is going to look so reem it's not even funny.'

Jade laughed gaily. 'Well, I look forward to seeing them. Aren't you tired getting up so early at the weekend?'

'No babe, I would work twenty-two hours a day, every day doing this. I love it!'

Jade was confused. 'Why twenty-two hours?'

'You know, a full day, hun,' Kelly answered as though it was obvious.

'A full day is twenty-four hours though,' Jade said, smirking.

Kelly gave a little giggle. 'Is it? Oh my God, how funny? I thought it was twenty-two. Are you sure?'

Jade burst into laughter. 'I'm pretty certain, Kelly.'

Kelly laughed even more at herself. 'So, shall we meet Lisa for lunch today and ask her to do our bikini modelling?'

'Yes, good idea. If there are two of us we'll be able to convince her. Then I'll go to yours after and help you do more bikinis.'

'Cool. Call me in a bit and I'll ring her.'

*

Two hours later the girls were sitting in Pizza Express in Loughton.

'What did you get up to last night?' Kelly asked Lisa as she studied the menu, running her long French-manicured finger down the page.

'Oh, I had another date actually. A guy called Mark who Nicola set me up with because her brother plays rugby with him and thought we'd hit it off.'

'And?'

'Mmm . . . he was okay,' Lisa said nonchalantly. 'His shoulders were a bit too broad for my liking. I have so much to tell you two by the way.'

'Oh good, I love a gossip,' Kelly said eagerly as the waiter came over and took their orders.

'The first thing is that I heard some news about Jake today. Big news,' Lisa told them as she handed her menu back to the waiter.

'Jake your ex?' Jade asked, wondering why Lisa was talking about him all of a sudden.

Lisa nodded. 'I met up with Nicola today to see the flat, which is amazing by the way and where the second part of my news comes in, but I'll discuss that afterwards. Anyway, so I met her and she told me that her nail technician . . .'

'What? Where and who does she go to? She could use me!' Kelly interrupted morosely with a pout.

'Okay, calm down,' Jade giggled, 'I'm sure Lisa will tell her all about how fantastic you are and she'll use you in future. Go on, Lisa. What about Jake?'

'He's engaged. Just like that. He's all loved up with this nail person Nicola knows and already he's replaced me with someone else. That quickly! I can just see him now; he's probably bought a flat, she's moved in and they probably sit there doing each other's nails every night.'

Jade sat there, incredulous. Jake was engaged to someone else so soon? She'd imagined him wallowing in self-pity for months, not getting hitched!

'Well I think that maybe it's a good thing,' Kelly finally spoke. 'I mean, at least you won't have to feel guilty now he's happy with someone else?'

'I suppose so,' Lisa replied stoically. 'It's just a really weird feeling, but I'm glad he's happy. I would be a complete cow not to be pleased for him.'

'And you'll be happy with someone else one day too,' Jade added, trying to cheer up her friend.

Kelly grinned. 'Yeah babe, you go on more dates than bloody Russell Brand, I wouldn't worry!'

Lisa snorted with laughter. 'The next bit of news is probably even worse than that. Just guess who lives dead opposite our flat?'

'Oh please say Jodie Marsh or Chantelle Houghton or someone? I could do with some celebrity clients. People love it if you've got a few celebs under your belt, my beauty business would be even more booming and we can give them a free bikini each,' Kelly said hopefully.

Lisa shook her head. 'No and no. It's not anyone famous.'

Kelly and Jade thought for a minute.

'No idea. Tell us!' they whined.

'Adele.'

'*Oh. My. God.* Are you joking?' Kelly replied, aghast. 'I just *love* her songs! Why did you lie and say she's not famous? You're hilare.' She closed her eyes, concentrating as she began to sing, 'Someone like you'.

Lisa burst into laughter. 'Not the singer Adele, Kelly,' her eyes widened, 'you know, Adele. The girl you despise from Marbs?'

Kelly's jaw dropped as reality dawned on her. 'Oh no, not her! Are you being serious?'

'I wish I was. I couldn't believe it when I saw her. She said she'd only just got back to her flat after a night out.'

'How classy,' Jade commented sarcastically as their pizzas arrived. 'Walk of shame. Did she look like a complete tart?'

'She was actually in a dressing gown, so she must have already had a shower. Urgh, she's just vile,' Lisa said, remembering how she'd barged in the flat and helped herself to their champagne after complaining about it.

'Oh I'm gutted, I really thought it was the singer Adele. I was going to ask to duet with her,' Kelly said, shaking her head in disbelief.

Lisa and Jade giggled.

'Adele's never going to leave you alone now, hun,' Kelly said ruefully.

Lisa raised her eyebrows as she cut her pizza into slices. 'I know! I've met her twice and I can't bear her.'

'Just never answer the door unless you know who's coming over,' Jade suggested as she chewed a mouthful of cheese and pepperoni.

'Or put a sign on your door saying that you're not home?' Kelly offered, looking up from her meal.

'That's a good idea. We'll have no visits from Adele, but burglars instead,' Lisa laughed.

'Oh yeah, maybe not then!' Kelly said pulling a face.

'So how was your night with lover boy, Billy, anyway?' Jade asked Kelly.

'Really nice. Me and Billy are meant to be, I can feel it,' she beamed. 'He's the perfect Ken to my Barbie. His business is doing really well too. He's like, the sweetest man on earth. He saw me looking at Christian Louboutin shoes on eBay, as I was going to buy this pair that had only been worn a few times for a hundred pounds, complete barg. Obviously I'm trying to save money for the business, so eBay is where I'm getting all my designers at the minute, but he said he'd treat me and buy me a pair from Harrods at the weekend.'

'That's so cute,' Jade gushed, secretly finding it hilarious that Kelly acted like she was trying to cut back on shopping. She seemed to buy a new designer bag every week!

She was glad Billy's business was successful though. They had spoken to him lots about his corporate hospitality company since they had started their own business and he often helped them out and gave them advice. It was starting to go really well for him and she could tell Kelly was proud when she spoke about it. It was adorable really. His business partner and friend, Gary Jacobs, hadn't exactly been pleased when Billy had left the business which they'd been running for two years to work in Marbella for the summer. But he'd been able to cope by hiring temporary staff once he knew Billy had made his mind up about going. It was something he had needed to do and now he'd met Kelly it had definitely been the right thing, Jade acknowledged.

'How's Billy's mum by the way?'

Kelly nodded her head. 'Yeah, she's doing well. I think things are looking up, which is good.'

Jade sighed with relief. Billy's mum had breast cancer and had gone through chemotherapy and radiotherapy. Kelly was often worried about Billy, who was terrified his mum might die. Kelly was the only person he ever spoke to about it.

'Would you like dessert?' the disconsolate-looking waiter asked.

'Yes please, babe,' Kelly said excitedly, 'I'll have that frozen yoghurt thing with the chocolate straw?'

'*Sotto zero leggera*?' he asked effortlessly.

'Yeah that's it,' Kelly nodded, pretending she knew the name. 'The leggera.'

He glanced at Lisa.

She perused the menu, eyes like saucers. 'Oh, I'll have the chocolate glory please.'

'I'll go for the frozen yoghurt thingy too,' Jade decided.

Ten minutes later their desserts had arrived.

'This is to *die* for,' Lisa exhaled, through a bite of chocolate fudge cake and ice cream.

'Mmm, so is this,' Kelly agreed. 'Really refreshing.'

'Okay, we need to ask you something,' Jade looked at Kelly to let her know this was the moment. 'We're doing a photo shoot this week as we need images of the bikinis for our website. We need people to model them and we were wondering if you would?'

Lisa opened her mouth to reveal chocolate-stained teeth, making them guffaw with laughter. 'Why have you let me eat this dessert then like a fat cow if you want me to model? I should have had the healthy yoghurt crap like you two!'

Kelly chortled, 'Lisa, you don't need to worry about your weight! Your figure is amazing, babe, one of the reasons we've asked you in the first place. Everything you put on looks incredible.'

'Thanks,' Lisa said with a half-smile. 'If it helps you, then of course I'll do it. I'd better cut down for the next few days.'

'Great!' Jade exclaimed happily. 'It'll be one night this week, maybe Tuesday, so I'll let you know when.'

As Lisa made Kelly promise she'd do her hair and make-up for the shoot, Jade's mind drifted as she thought about all the things they had to do that week. It was going to be busy as always, but she would definitely allocate more time to Sam. They had to make more bikinis, get the photo shoot done and then add them all to the website. There was Essex Fashion Week to prepare for too, which she believed was the week after next. If only she had her red notebook she would know for sure.

'Anyway girls I need to go,' Lisa said standing up. 'Jade, I'll see you tomorrow, about seven in the morning?'

Jade's face creased into a puzzled frown. 'What? Why?'

'You're dog-sitting Cupcake, remember?'

Oh yes, Jade thought groggily, not liking the thought of getting up early, *I remember*.

*

Adele cursed herself as she stubbed her finger with the needle. How could anyone be bothered to sew for a living? Seriously, it was tiring, boring and not exactly easy like she'd first thought. You needed patience, she mused, as she added yet another sequin to the plain black bikini she was practising on. Patience was something she definitely didn't have. She wondered whether she should pay someone to do it all for her and then decided against it, wanting a bigger profit for herself with each one she sold.

Adele exhaled loudly as she finished the last one. It was a similar copy to the one in Jade's notebook, but something didn't look quite right. She'd bought the sequins from Hobbycraft, seeing as the other ones from the website Jade and Kelly used wouldn't arrive until tomorrow. That must be it, she told herself; when she had the right sequins the bikini would look great. It would look better on too, she decided, taking her clothes off to try it.

'Shit!' she cursed, when several of the sequins flew off immediately. Now she'd have to do them again, she thought, furious with herself for not being more careful. She'd have to send a letter out with every bikini purchased that the garments were very delicate and needed to be handled carefully. Then if the customers stupidly ruined them, it was their own fault. She wouldn't allow anyone to send them back unless they were swapping sizes.

She'd already ordered a hundred bikinis from Caitlin in America, the lady who was written in the notebook. Her prices were so cheap when you bought in bulk that the girls would have made a killing. Too bad they would now have competition, Adele thought nastily. Everyone would be on *her* website because she'd make sure her bikinis were cheaper and looked better. She'd noticed in the notebook that the girls were hoping to use Chloe and Lisa as their models, as Jade had written their names with question marks. It was hilarious that they were using amateur models.

How embarrassing? Yes, Lisa *was* attractive, Adele admitted reluctantly, but a model? Absolutely not. And as for Chloe, she was about as confident as a flea. They wouldn't have a clue what to do or how to pose! She, on the other hand, had already been in touch with Skye, a professional model who had even appeared in the Ann Summers catalogues. Skye was charging three hundred and fifty pounds for the day, but everyone knew that you got what you paid for, Adele thought arrogantly. She would be worth every penny. Her images would be stunning; Skye would make a black bag look like something from the covers of *Vogue*. Now all she needed was to get enough bikinis ready so there were plenty to shoot. She'd decided against using the photographer Kelly and Jade were using. She'd looked at his website and yes he was good, but nothing compared to the photographer she'd found online, who had shot Madonna. Who wouldn't choose the photographer that had shot her? She was an icon. A *huge* megastar. Adele's photographer's prices were a lot higher, but her work was flawless. It doesn't even matter how much it costs, Adele reminded herself, you had to put money into a company to ever get some back and luckily her dad had plenty of it.

She couldn't wait for Nicola and Lisa to move in opposite. She could just see them now, heading out to dinner when they got back from work, or going round there to watch films and for a chat. Then they could all go out at weekends together. Maybe they'd even join her in Funky Mojoe at the weekend? It would definitely beat going with just Donna who she had had to persuade to come anyway, seeing as she'd made plans for some boring aunt's fiftieth birthday party. Adele had told Donna outright she couldn't think of anything more pathetic than hanging out with some dried-up nobodies on a Saturday night and at this rate she would be single forever. Donna had seemed a bit put out by this comment, so Adele had changed tactic and softened a bit, telling her it was because she had a male friend that was interested in her and wanted to meet her. It was a complete lie but she knew that would change her tune. She would just conjure up some fictitious story on the night about him being ill or something like that. Donna had only ever had one serious relationship before, in senior school. The moment she started piling on the pounds he'd dumped her and she'd been a wreck and lost her confidence after that. She seriously needed to do something about herself if she ever really thought someone was going to like her again, Adele thought wickedly.

Adele looked through her drawers and found another bikini she could practise on. She couldn't think of anything worse than sewing a whole load of sequins and beads on yet another one, but she would do it. She would do anything to beat Kelly and Jade.

CHAPTER 5

'No, Cupcake!' Jade shrieked in horror as she watched the little dog running off with a bikini top. 'Come back here!'

'She won't come back if you shout,' Kelly told her, raising her eyebrows, whizzing a bikini up and down on the sewing machine.

'And she won't come back if I whisper either, so what do you suggest I do?' Jade couldn't hide her exasperation. They'd had the dog for half a day and already she was driving Jade mad. Kelly could see no harm in her, which was making matters worse.

'Don't take it out on me,' Kelly sulked, pouting.

'I'm not. Sorry, I'm just stressed,' Jade said as she marched off down the hall to find the dog. 'No, Cupcake! No!' she shouted as she saw the dog squatting down and urinating on the floor. 'You're meant to go on the puppy pad, you silly girl.'

The dog gave her an imperious look and sprinted off, making Jade even more incandescent. She cowered when Jade caught up with her.

'Ah-ha!' Jade felt a sense of achievement, 'nowhere to run now, is there? I've got you, oh yes. Now, don't even think of running off again.' She swept her up and took her back to the office, closing the door firmly behind them.

'Cupcake, you're such a naughty little dog, aren't you?' Kelly said in her baby voice as the dog ran over to her and jumped, wanting to be picked up.

'She's weed again on the floor, so I'm going to clear it up,' Jade said frustrated. They really needed to be getting on with things and Cupcake was taking up all their time. She never realised that dogs needed so much attention. They would have to close the door at all times now or she would just keep running out. The puppy pads were a complete nightmare as she either missed or just ignored them completely. And who knew that puppies went to the toilet so many times in one day! It was absurd!

'Babe, just relax,' Kelly told her when she walked back through the door. 'I've got an idea. We'll send Cupcake for a massage for a few hours so she can de-stress. It will give us some rest and then we'll just give Lisa the bill. She feels a bit tense,' Kelly observed, stroking the dog and feeling her back.

'Are you being serious? Feels tense? A dog massage? Do they even do them? I don't know about *her* being tense, but I sure as hell am.'

'Yeah they definitely do them, Lord McButterpants always has them done,' Kelly told Jade as she looked up the website on her iPhone. 'Here you go. We'll get her the gold package yeah? She gets a bath with shampoo and conditioner, mini massage, a deep cleanse facial, nail buffing, clipping and filing, haircut, goodie bag and toy.'

'Wow. All for just one little dog,' Jade was shocked.

'Oh, but she's so worth it though, aren't you Cupcake?' Kelly cooed.

Jade wasn't so sure. She was cute to look at, but the way she was feeling right now, that was as far as it went. Kelly's mum's Chihuahua, Lord McButterpants, seemed much better behaved than Princess Cupcake. Lord McButterpants was honestly no trouble at all. 'Right, you take her then and I'll be getting on with these bikinis. Is that one done?'

'Yes, look how well it's come together,' Kelly said as she held up the purple fringed top and bottoms.

'Amazing,' Jade said, in awe of Kelly's work. 'I can't wait for the photo shoot now. Chloe should be here soon, she's coming over to borrow one of my dresses for her friend's party, so I can ask her to model the bikinis.'

'Oh I love Chloe. I'll go now and drop the dog off so I don't miss her. I want to see her try this fringe one on.'

Fifteen minutes later Chloe arrived, looking as immaculate as ever without even trying. Her long blonde hair was wavy in a side parting, with a cute little plait pinned back on the right side. She was wearing light blue jeans with a tight baby pink jumper.

'Hi,' she said cheerfully with a huge smile.

'Hi Chloe. Come in. Do you want a drink?' Jade asked her as she closed the front door.

'Yes please.'

'Tea?'

'Perfect.'

'Come in the kitchen,' Jade told her, 'I'll put the kettle on.'

They chatted for a few minutes while the kettle was boiling, until Jade brought it up.

'I'm sure Sam has told you already that Kelly and I have started our own bikini business?'

'Yes, it's such a good idea,' Chloe replied, 'I'll definitely be coming to you when I buy my holiday bikinis.'

'Well, I was wondering if you'd like to model them on our website? My other friend Lisa is doing it too and she's never modelled before, so you won't be the only one. You can get some really nice photos and I don't know, maybe you could even forward them on to some agencies or something. I'm sure you have what it takes if you do enjoy it.'

'What me?' Chloe was abashed. 'You're sure you want me to model on your website? Really?' She looked flabbergasted.

'Of course,' Jade replied, amazed that she was so shocked, 'you're completely stunning! When we went shopping that time you had literally everyone staring at you. Even girls just want to gaze at you all day.'

Chloe's face suffused with colour. 'I don't know what to say,' she managed at last. 'Thank you so much. I'd love to do it if you want me. I'm not sure if I'll be any good though . . .'

'Excellent!' Jade was delighted. Chloe was such a sweet, modest girl; just as beautiful on the inside as the outside. She was perfect for the job.

The doorbell sounded and in walked Kelly.

'She's agreed,' Jade informed her merrily.

'Fab, hun. Now come try on this bikini I've just made. It's going to look so beauts with your skin tone and hair colour!'

When Chloe walked in the office wearing their latest new bikini, Jade and Kelly watched her avidly and gasped. It looked nicer than they ever could have imagined.

'Oh my God! Babe, you look like a Victoria's Secret model,' Kelly complimented her. 'Your legs are *so* long. I would kill for them!'

'Thanks,' Chloe said, blushing from head to toe.

'Do you like the bikini?' Jade asked Chloe.

'I love it!' Chloe said with an honest smile. 'You two are so clever.'

Kelly shook her head. 'Babe, she's the intellectual one that comes up with all the ideas. I'm just good at sewing and making the swimwear.'

'Don't put yourself down, Kelly,' Jade told her crossly. 'We'd be nowhere without you. And Chloe, as a thank you for modelling for us, seeing as we can't pay you at this point, we're going to let you and Lisa have a free bikini.'

'Oh thank you so much!' Chloe looked like she genuinely appreciated it. 'I think I'm going to choose this one. It's so nice.'

'You haven't even seen the others yet,' Jade giggled, knowing that Chloe was going to end up loving them all. 'Anyway, I'll pick you up tomorrow night if that's okay? Then take you to the studio and Kelly will do your hair and make-up.'

'Okay, thanks. Thank you so much for asking me,' Chloe smiled, revealing her perfectly straight white teeth.

'Thank you so much for agreeing!' Kelly said. She eyed her over, deep in thought. 'Babe, you may want to come to me tonight for a spray tan. I mean, I know you've got quite naturally tanned skin, but . . . well Lisa is coming and I just think you should both look proper tanned. Obviously you don't have to pay.'

'Thank you,' Chloe said.

'Kelly, she's tanned enough!' Jade protested.

Kelly shook her head. 'You can *never* be tanned enough; you know my motto.'

*

Chloe left Jade's house, feeling on cloud nine. She couldn't believe they actually wanted her to model! Her friends would all be so jealous. Maybe she wouldn't tell them? She hated it when they envied her; they acted all weird and quiet, and she knew they constantly spoke about her behind her back. She recalled the one time when she started going out with the hottest boy from college, Adam Lockwood. Everyone had fancied him and she'd only said yes because all her friends had boyfriends at the time and she wanted to be able to join in conversations about dating and snogging. Her friends had been so bitchy, arranging days and nights out without telling her and not including her in any conversations. It was only when she broke up with him that they went back to normal, as though it had never happened. At first she thought she'd done something wrong,

82

but when she confessed to her mum what was happening, she told her they were simply jealous, and that jealousy brought out a very vicious and nasty side to people. She didn't want everyone to hate her but nothing could stop her feeling excited about tomorrow. She was going to have her own professional photos done as well as a free bikini and Kelly, who always looked gorgeous in her opinion, was going to be doing her spray tan, hair and make-up! Then to top it all off, she was going to be featured on their website! Chloe couldn't wait to tell her mum. Sam and her dad might not like the idea of images of her wearing nothing but a bikini online so maybe she wouldn't tell them for now. Her dad was so over-protective and old fashioned and she just knew he would ramble on about weirdos and perverts looking at her photos online. Sam looked out for her, but he wasn't over the top like her dad, so maybe he would be okay with it.

Her mobile started ringing and Chloe was surprised when she saw Adele's number flashing on the screen.

'Hi Adele. You okay?'

'Hello, babe,' came the husky reply. 'Yeah I'm good thanks. You?'

'Yeah I'm really well,' Chloe said. 'Thanks again for the other night.'

'That's fine, honey. I only ended up going back to Sam's didn't I? God we were so wasted,' Adele gave a little laugh.

Chloe was stunned and didn't know what to say. Sam was with Jade; what on earth was he playing at? 'Oh. What happened?' She closed her eyes, trying to block out the thought of it.

There was a long pause. 'Well it's a bit awkward saying seeing as you're his little sister, but I slept with him.'

Chloe felt sick. She'd always respected Sam so much and Jade was lovely. She never thought he would cheat on her. How could he? 'Oh,' was all Chloe managed to finally reply.

Adele exhaled what Chloe guessed was a cloud of smoke. 'Yeah I know. I'm not exactly proud, but it takes two to tango doesn't it?' she replied robustly.

'Yes, I suppose so,' Chloe mumbled.

'Anyway, babe. The reason I was calling is because I know I can trust you with something. It's a long story, but basically Kelly and Jade have stolen my business idea and I know they're going to be asking you to model the bikinis for their website.'

Chloe didn't like the sound of this. She was sure Jade and Kelly would never steal Adele's ideas, but Adele scared her too much for her to say that. She swallowed hard. 'Yes, they did mention something about it,' she answered wanly.

'Oh good. I knew they would. Anyway hun, like I said, me and you go way back and I know I can trust you. I'll need you to get in with them and report back to me what they're doing and any new designs they come up with. I can count on you, can't I, Chloe? You won't let me down after I helped you the other night, will you?' Adele's voice was hectoring.

Chloe felt a feeling of dread wash over her and gulped. 'Errr . . . yeah, sure,' she replied feebly.

'Great! Thanks, babe. Anything you find out let me know. You mustn't leave a thing out.'

Chloe felt despondent and like the biggest traitor on earth. 'Got it, I won't miss out a thing.'

'You'd better not,' Adele answered tersely. Then her voice changed to friendly again. 'Anyway, hun. I'd better go. You'll have to come out with me soon for a drink or something. I'll be in touch! Have fun at the shoot!'

'Thanks. Bye Adele.'

Chloe couldn't believe how quickly her mood had changed. How could Adele ask her to do that? Spy on Jade and Kelly's plans and bikini designs and report them back to her? It was wrong, so wrong. Not only that, but now she knew that Adele and Sam had cheated behind poor Jade's back! Chloe had a fearful feeling in the pit of her stomach. She'd always liked Adele; she'd never been anything but kind to her. But there had been an underlying threat in that conversation and it terrified her to the core. She hated trouble or confrontation of any kind. Why was this happening? Adele was definitely not the kind of person you wanted to mess with; she was good to have on your side. Would Jade really steal Adele's idea? Her dad always said to never trust anyone where money was concerned, so maybe she had? Besides, Adele *had* helped her in Sugar Hut that night; she supposed this was her way of returning the favour? But she liked Jade and Kelly and she was going to feel so appallingly two-faced doing this, especially seeing as Jade was Sam's girlfriend. As she wondered what to do, a text pinged on her phone.

> *Obviously don't mention anything to anyone, especially Jade and Kelly! Knew I could count on you. Will be in touch. Adele x*

Great, Chloe thought nervously, I have literally no choice but to be her spy. What alternative did she have? She knew she was betraying her brother as well as Jade and Kelly, but going against Adele and facing her wrath? No chance.

*

Kelly kissed Billy on the lips and put her arms around his neck. 'Will you miss me tonight?'

'I always miss you when I'm not with you,' he gushed, kissing her forehead softly.

He hadn't been in from work long and was still wearing his suit, which Kelly thought made him look even sexier.

'Ahhh . . . you're so sweet when you want to be,' she

85

exhaled, kissing his lips again. 'I'm going to quickly get ready and then I'll leave.'

'Where are you going again?' he asked, gently brushing the hair away from her face.

'We've got this photo shoot in Hertfordshire. I only came round quickly to say hello.' Kelly added some lip gloss, because it had been kissed off.

'Okay, babe. Have a good time and make sure you get some good images for your business. Close-up shots and everything.'

'We will,' Kelly smiled lovingly, finding it adorable that he always tried to help.

'Oh before you go, I wanted to ask you if you're free next Wednesday? Gary has asked us to go to dinner with him and his girlfriend.'

'Course I can,' Kelly agreed, despite the fact she hated Gary. He was always undermining her and trying to make her look like a fool. Like the time when he laughed at her and brusquely informed her that Europe was a continent and not a country. How many people must make that mistake – yet he spoke to her like she was stupid! Or the time when they were discussing clay pigeon shooting and she said she thought it was horrific that people harmed poor innocent little birds. Gary had laughed and in a scathing voice told her it was clay shells they shot and not the actual pigeons. Like it was obvious or something! He was such a Mr know-it-all and Kelly always had a bad feeling when he was around. He made her scared to speak because he just constantly criticised her every word. But Billy thought he was wonderful unfortunately, and there was nothing she could do to convince him otherwise.

'Gary hasn't got it in for you,' he'd told her one night when they'd all gone out for drinks to celebrate after they'd done a big deal. 'He just thinks you're funny. You have to admit you say some funny things at times.'

'Yes I know that, but he looks down on me,' she'd replied, raising her eyes lugubriously. 'He hates me.'

'He doesn't hate you! Don't be so silly,' Billy laughed. 'You have to remember that he let me go to Marbella. I pretty much left him in the lurch because I was down at the time and wanted to get away and he let me. I've known him and his family for years and he's done a lot for me. He's a great friend and I promise he doesn't hate you.'

Kelly still didn't believe him. Of course Gary disliked her. Why would he constantly try to put her down otherwise? His girlfriend, Charlotte, was quite nice. God only knew how she put up with him, she thought, as she kissed Billy goodbye one last time and made her way outside to her white Mini.

Lisa, Chloe and Jade were already there when Kelly arrived at the studio. The photographer, Martin Lee, was in his late forties with an immaculate head of thick dark hair, which he kept brushing over to one side.

'Hi,' he said politely, 'you must be Kelly.'

'Hi, babe,' she said, shaking his hand.

'Nice to meet you. Jade has already said you need to do the girls' hair and make-up. We're going to be using the plain white and black backgrounds for now, but as I was telling Jade, when the weather improves you could always do a weekend shoot and we can go outside. I have a swimming pool and we can get some fantastic shots in the sunshine – if it ever comes out!' he said jokingly.

'Oh my God, that would be amazing,' Kelly said, imagining how professional their website would look. 'We one hundred per cent have to use the swimming pool when it's hot.'

Lisa walked over. 'Come on, sort me out. I need making over. I'm so tired today and have huge bags under my eyes,' she said, pointing them out.

'You'll look as good as new in no time,' Kelly smiled, getting out her make-up bag. Forty minutes later, Lisa and

Chloe looked phenomenal. Kelly had used her MAC black kohl eyeliner and grey, silver and black eye shadow on Lisa for a sexy, smoky look, with her long dark hair dead straight in a centre parting. Chloe was going to be modelling the lighter, pastel-coloured bikinis, so she'd made her hair big, wavy and bouncy and used more natural make-up with a touch of mascara and pink Dior lipstick and blusher, which gave her a girly, innocent face.

'Okay,' Martin said to Lisa, who was going first. 'If you want to stand there so I can do a light test.' He snapped away on his camera.

'Should I be posing now?' Lisa asked dubiously.

'No, it's fine. I'm just testing,' Martin explained.

It didn't take Lisa long to relax and before they knew it she was posing and getting the hang of it, with Martin's help. Kelly had a sneaky look at the images on Martin's camera. They looked fantastic, especially the ones with the black background, which really made the colours in the bikini stand out. Next, it was Chloe's turn. She walked on set nervously, looking like a rabbit caught in the headlights, but after about ten minutes she was moving in positions without Martin even needing to tell her.

'That's beautiful!' Martin exclaimed as she twisted and pouted, 'you're a natural.'

Kelly agreed. Chloe was definitely a natural, and the camera, not surprisingly, loved her. She looked like a gorgeous angel, or a pretty doll, and Kelly knew anyone that saw these images would want to buy the bikinis.

'Chloe babe, you look unreal,' Kelly admired. 'How do you know what to do?'

Chloe gave a nervous laugh. 'I don't! I'm just making it up.'

'Well, keep doing what you're doing,' Martin conceded.

'Thanks so much for helping, girls,' Kelly said when they were finished. 'I can't wait to see the images when they're all done. We'll email them to you. You'll both model them on the catwalk at Essex Fashion Week, won't you? We've signed up to have our bikinis on stage!'

'What? You never mentioned that!' Lisa panicked.

'Oh come on, it's no different to a photo shoot,' Jade told her. 'How can you be worried, with your figure?'

'I could do with bigger boobs!' Lisa said, looking down at her chest.

'Join the club!' Jade agreed.

'I'm seriously considering getting mine done,' Lisa explained as they made their way to their cars.

'I know a great surgeon one of my clients has been to. I'll give you his details if you like?' Kelly offered.

Kelly noticed how quiet Chloe was tonight and wondered if something was wrong with her. She was normally softly spoken and never exactly loud, but she could sense she was worrying about something. She'd been texting on her phone all evening too, and Kelly was certain she'd seen Adele's name on the screen.

'Are you okay, Chloe?'

She nodded weakly. 'Yes, I'm fine. Just tired.'

Kelly nodded, unconvinced.

'Chloe!' Martin called, appearing from nowhere.

She turned with an apprehensive expression. 'Yes?'

'Look, I don't know if you're interested in modelling, but with your height and natural ability I just wanted to give you the contact details of a reputable agency in London. There's no up-front payment or anything like that, and if you send those images in, I really believe you're just the sort of girl that they'd like to take on. Have a think about it.' He handed her a card. 'I can see you getting lots of work.'

Chloe looked like she wanted the ground to swallow her up. 'Thanks.' She took the card, her cheeks turning pink.

'Go Chloe!' Lisa grinned. 'Little model in the making!'

'I doubt it,' Chloe said modestly.

'Good for you, babe,' Kelly grabbed her hand and squeezed it. 'We'll send you your photos and you send them to that agency.'

Chloe smiled sweetly. 'Thanks so much for everything girls.'

'We should be thanking you!' Jade replied graciously. 'What's your favourite bikini?'

Chloe thought for a moment. 'I think the pink one in the "No Carbs before Marbs" collection.'

'Then come over one night this week and we'll have made you one,' Kelly said, reaching for her phone in her bag as it started ringing. She answered it, not knowing the number.

'Hello?'

'Oh hi there,' the unfamiliar voice started. 'Is this Kelly, the beautician?'

'Yes, that's me,' Kelly replied in her most professional-sounding voice.

'Great. I've been recommended to come to you and my friend and I would like to get a manicure and pedicure done if possible?'

'Okay, fantastic. When were you thinking?'

'Tomorrow evening? Six-thirty?'

Kelly was relieved that she was free. 'That should be fine. What are your names please?'

'Hilary Salmon and Susan Jacobs.'

'Hilary Salmon and Susan Jacobs. Perfect,' Kelly replied. 'I'll text you the address to this number. See you then!'

She put the phone down and searched for a pen. 'Has anyone got a pen? And a bit of paper?' she asked, when she couldn't find one in her bag.

'I have a pen, but no paper,' Jade responded, while Lisa and Chloe shook their heads. 'See, I told you, you need a diary! And you've also just reminded me that I don't have

90

mine still. I'm going to have to get another one until Tony gets back and I can look at his house to see if it's there.'

'Oh sod it; I'll just put it in my phone for now. What did I say their names were? Hilary Haddock or something?'

Lisa laughed loudly. 'I'm sure you said Salmon!'

Kelly typed their names into her phone. She loved getting new clients; the more money the better.

Chloe kissed her goodbye as she got in Jade's car and thanked her for doing her hair and make-up again. What a lovely girl, Kelly acknowledged. Still, there was definitely something bothering her tonight though, she would lay money on it.

CHAPTER 6

A few days later, Adele was on her way to see Chloe. She knew she'd most probably have the images by now and she wanted to see what they looked like. Her photo shoot with Skye was booked for tomorrow and she needed her photos to look better. She needed people to want to buy her bikinis instead of Kelly and Jade's, and surely a professional model and photographer would be the answer? Adele marched up the path and rang the doorbell and had to contain her laughter as she saw Chloe's shocked expression as she opened the door.

'Oh! Adele . . .'

'Hi, hun,' Adele said with a forced smile as she barged her way in. She'd always liked Chloe, but her lack of confidence and shy ways were beginning to annoy her. She knew she felt bad about Jade and Kelly, but that was just tough luck. Adele needed to know everything they were up to and Chloe was just the person to tell her, whether she liked it or not.

'You may as well come up to my room,' Chloe said walking up the stairs, 'my dad is in the lounge watching football and my mum is cooking our dinner in the kitchen.'

'Okay babe,' Adele replied, wondering whether they could

perhaps squeeze another plate for her round the table. She'd been sewing bikinis all day and she realised she'd only eaten some toast and two bags of Hula Hoops. A nice home-cooked meal was exactly what she wanted. She needed to go food shopping desperately, but didn't have the time with her new business. Every minute of the day counted and all she'd done for the past several days was work, work, work. She honestly didn't know how people did it all the time. Waking up to an alarm in the morning was torture, but she had to get her website up quickly; there was no way she was losing out to Jade and Kelly. This was a battle she was going to win. She had now designed twelve bikinis, which were all copies from Jade and Kelly's book but slightly different. Better, in her opinion. She couldn't wait to see Skye strut her stuff the next day and put Lisa and Chloe to shame. It was going to be hilarious to see their photos and compare them to hers!

'So,' Adele exhaled, when they reached Chloe's room. 'Tell me everything about the shoot. How was it?' she asked as she descended into a chair and put her feet up on the bed.

'Yeah, I think we did okay,' Chloe said earnestly.

'Show me the images then,' Adele replied casually, drumming her fingers. She spun the swivel chair round to face the computer. 'Are they on here?'

Chloe jumped, as though she'd been electrocuted. 'Errr . . . wait, I'll see if I can find them . . .'

'Don't be shy, Chloe. I know they'll have sent them to you by now and I thought we had a deal. Don't pretend you don't have them because I know you do. They're the ones in the wrong remember? Not me. They've completely stolen my whole business idea,' Adele said indignantly.

'How can you be so sure?' Chloe replied mutinously.

'Chloe, I came up with the idea in Marbella last year! I stupidly told them my plans and now look what they've done! I'm livid,' Adele said, waving her hands as she spoke.

Chloe quailed at Adele's incandescent expression. 'Okay, I believe you.'

'Finally,' Adele replied curtly, rolling her eyes. 'Now show me the images,' she commanded.

Chloe shook the mouse on the computer, making it come to life, and then clicked on her photos so Adele could view them.

Adele was fuming as she clicked through the photos of Chloe looking amazing in their swimwear. How did she look so bloody good when she hadn't even modelled before? she wondered irritably. This photographer was cheap too! She'd seen his prices written in that notebook of theirs! So why did everything look so good? *Oh well*, Adele reassured herself, *my images will be even better than this.*

'Did they discuss any other ideas?'

Chloe faltered. 'Errr . . . I don't think so . . .'

'Chloe?' Adele's voice was harsh and demanding.

'Something about Essex Fashion Week,' Chloe responded hastily, caving in.

'Mmm . . . I read about them doing that already. I've already booked to go myself.'

'Read where?'

'Never mind. Was there anything else? Did they share any other designs they were going to be creating apart from the ones they've already done?'

Chloe shook her head. 'No, I swear they didn't mention anything else.'

Adele believed her. She was a quivering wreck around her and made it so blatantly obvious when she was lying. She almost felt sorry for her. 'Look Chloe, it's okay. I'm your friend, remember? I'm only doing what needs to be done. *I'm* the innocent victim in all this, not them, so don't feel bad for telling me what they're up to. Jade doesn't really like you, silly. She's just nice to you because you're Sam's little sister. I heard her saying it when I bumped into her in Buckhurst Hill the other day. She feels she has to include you so she looks good to Sam. You know that don't you? You understand?'

Chloe nodded, her eyes glistening.

'Don't worry about it. I've known you since you were little and we've always got on so well, haven't we? We used to sit up talking about boys for hours. Do you remember?'

Chloe's mouth curved into a smile. 'Yes, I remember. Do you remember that time when we pranked that girl on the phone who was being horrible to me at school? You called her up and put on that scary voice.'

Adele laughed, 'Yes, I remember that.'

'I'm sorry I doubted you,' Chloe said, her eyes downcast.

Adele was about to say it was all okay when she noticed the model agency card by the computer. 'What's this? Elite Model Management,' she read the silver words printed on the card.

'Oh,' Chloe replied, discomfited. 'Just something the photographer gave me. He told me I should contact them or something stupid,' she waved her hand, dismissing the idea.

A familiar feeling of jealousy crept throughout Adele's veins. 'If he told you that you should contact them, then why don't you?' she demanded.

Chloe gulped. 'I doubt they'll want me. The girls on their website look so tall and slim.'

Adele looked at Chloe. Yes, she *was* stunning, with penetrating green eyes like Sam's, and she supposed she was tall enough too, but a real model? No way. She didn't have a high-fashion, edgy look at all in her opinion. Adele wanted Chloe to send her images across so she got rejected, which she was certain she would. She was aware everyone must always tell Chloe how pretty she was; she deserved to be knocked down a peg or two. Pretty by no means equalled model. Adele watched *Britain's Next Top Model*. She *knew* the type of girls that won that show! They often looked like skeletons or aliens, with lank hair and pale white skin. Yes, Chloe needed to realise that she wasn't perfect and was *never* going to be a top model. 'I tell you what. I'll send them across for you. Right now. This could be an amazing opportunity. Of course they'll want you!'

'Do you really think?' Chloe said shyly.

'I *know*,' Adele lied.

She searched through the images for the worst ones. It was hard because they were all really nice, but there were a few not so great that she managed to find. Chloe logged into her emails and typed in the agency address.

'Do you really think those ones?' Chloe questioned, unconvinced. 'There are loads of others I like better. I look like I'm about to blink in that one,' she pointed out.

'Trust me,' Adele said pointedly, 'you can't see which ones look best! You have to get someone else to decide. You are your own worst critic. Have you ever heard that expression?'

Chloe looked into space thoughtfully. 'I think so.'

'Well then.' Adele clicked the send button. 'Done.'

'Thanks Adele. I never believe in myself and maybe I should.'

'Exactly,' Adele replied, her chin rather tight. Then she noticed something else that caught her eye. 'Is *that* one of their bikinis?' she said, rushing over to a pink and silver embellished number.

'Yes. They gave it to me to say thanks.'

Adele laughed derisively. 'Oh, that's hilarious! As if you're going to wear this bit of tat!'

'It looks better on,' Chloe said mulishly, defending the bikini, which she clearly loved.

'Babe, *please*. It looks like it's from Primark or something,'

Adele sniggered. 'I'll give you one of mine and only charge you half price. Mates rates and everything,' she chirped, trying not to feel disheartened about how well the bikini was made. How did they sew it so it all stayed together? she wondered furiously. She'd used the same designs and same bikinis, but hers looked nothing like this one!

'Mmm . . .'

Adele could tell Chloe wasn't impressed, so she changed tack, and sucked up to her. 'That's because you're stunning and everything looks great on you. You're right, I'm sure it looks better on.'

Before Chloe could answer, her mum called her for dinner.

'You don't suppose I could stay too, do you?' Adele asked cheekily.

Chloe nodded. 'I'm sure it's fine.'

*

The following day Adele's alarm clock sounded at eight a.m. and she pressed the snooze button and hugged her pillow even tighter. Waking up this early was such a chore! She couldn't be late today though. She willed herself not to fall back into a nice, relaxing sleep, which she was finding exceptionally difficult.

She had to go all the way to Chelsea today for the photo shoot. She was going to get a taxi, but decided with the morning traffic it was probably quicker to get the tube. The awful, smelly, dismal tube, usually packed with civilians getting on with their dreary lives and their tedious little nine-to-five jobs.

She had given herself time to put some make-up on and get ready. After all, she was meeting a *model* today. She didn't want to look like some tramp next to her. Skye always looked incredible. Adele had Googled images of her professional modelling shots and was fascinated how someone

97

could always look so good. She must have her pick of any men, she assumed resentfully.

Adele plastered on her make-up, always preferring to wear more than less. It made her feel more confident. She would never leave the house bare faced. Even if there was a fire she'd save her make-up bag and apply it as soon as she found safety. She added her Chanel lip gloss and smiled, recoiling as she noticed yellowish stains on her teeth, which she knew were from smoking. She'd tried to quit countless times, but it was impossible. Plus, she enjoyed it and deep down she didn't even want to give it up. She was definitely going to be brave and go back to the dentists in Harley Street to get veneers. She'd been for a consultation before Marbella last year, but bottled it because she was too afraid. This time though she was going to bite the bullet and get them done; she loved the perfect smiles they gave people and she decided she would look amazing with them.

Adele arrived at the studio an hour and a half later, extremely impressed. There were white gloss floorboards, skylights, a separate hair and make-up room and even a small kitchen.

'Hi, I'm Hilary,' the photographer introduced herself, rather snootily.

'Adele.'

She guessed Hilary was in her late fifties. Her hair was short, blonde streaked with grey and she was wearing an electric-blue baggy blazer over a turquoise blouse, with draped pearls round her neck. Had this lady really photographed Madonna? She looked like an uptight grandma. Hilary appeared very serious and glanced over in a supercilious way, her face immobile.

'Help yourself to tea or coffee. What exactly is it we're shooting today? Swimwear garments did you say?'

'Yes.' Adele got the bikinis out and placed them on the white table to show her.

Hilary flicked a condescending glance over them. 'Oh. Right.'

'They look lovely on,' Adele explained, wondering why on earth she gave a shit what this miserable old woman thought. She was paying her to take photos, not to turn her nose up!

'Where is it that you said you were from again?'

'Chigwell in Essex.'

'Yes, I can see that now,' Hilary replied disdainfully, staring into her eyes as though she was weighing her up. 'I take it *you* won't be modelling these bikinis?' She looked horrified at the thought, making Adele want to slap her.

'No,' Adele gave a brittle laugh. 'The model is stunning. She models for huge companies such as Ann Summers, thank you very much.'

'I'm not too sure I know much about Ann Summers,' Hilary replied, as though it was beneath her.

Of course you wouldn't know much about Ann Summers, Adele mused callously, *you probably haven't had sex in decades!* Who would want to do it with an old bat like her? She probably owned nothing but huge grey granny pants.

'Where is this model you speak so highly of anyway?' Hilary enquired, as Adele made herself a cup of coffee.

Good question, Adele thought, looking at the clock on the wall and noticing she was thirty minutes late.

'I'm sure she'll be here soon. There are problems with the tube,' Adele fibbed. 'I'll just go outside and try her mobile.'

'You're more than welcome to try calling her in here. No need to go outside,' the photographer answered suspiciously.

'No signal,' Adele replied with the fakest smile she could muster. What was this woman's problem? She was paying her almost a thousand pounds for the shoot and still being

99

spoken to like crap! If only she had time to use the same photographer as Jade and Kelly. It was too late now. This shoot had to be done today and she had to remember that this lady had shot Madonna. You literally *couldn't* get any better than that.

As she dialled Skye's number she felt a rush of adrenaline. *Answer the phone you skinny cow!*

'Hello?' Skye's croaky voice crackled down the line. She'd clearly just woken up.

Adele bit back the urge to scream at her. 'Skye, it's Adele. Where the hell are you? I'm in Chelsea, waiting for you at the studio!'

She paused. 'Oh fuck! I completely forgot. I only got in from my night out about an hour ago.'

'I really don't care, babe. You need to get here *now*. You agreed to do it and this is bloody unprofessional.' Adele scowled.

'Give me thirty minutes,' Skye groaned.

Adele put the phone down, fuming. She was a professional model! How could she just forget a shoot she was booked for! If she didn't turn up, she would seriously go mad at her. Even if she had to hunt her down, Adele wouldn't be letting this go anytime soon. No one walked all over her and got away with it.

She walked back in the studio, not willing to take any more snooty remarks from grandma, and picked up a large folder on the table and flicked through it as she sipped her coffee. There were pages upon pages of landscape photography. Stunning sea views, country meadows, breath-taking mountains, lakes and forests. Then there were close-up still shots of an eagle, dandelion and an apple on a pine table.

'I shot the sea views at Brighton would you believe,' Hilary piped up from nowhere.

'Oh really, that's good,' Adele replied, deadpan. She couldn't even be bothered to pretend to be interested.

'Stunningly beautiful day it was. Mid-eighties too.'

'Mmm . . .'

She pulled another black folder out of her bag. 'I have other landscape images if you'd like to look?'

Adele looked up at her, puzzled. 'I'd rather see your shots of celebrities to be honest. Do you have the photo of Madonna here?'

Hilary looked incredulous. 'Madonna? My dear, I don't have a photo of Madonna.'

'Oh,' Adele said disappointed, 'would she not let you keep it or something? I suppose celebs have to be careful in case you sell them on or whatever.'

Hilary's face creased into a frown. 'I'm afraid you're mistaken. I've never shot Madonna in my life!'

Adele was confused. 'But it says so on your website. Along with loads of other famous people.'

Hilary shook her head, raising her eyebrows. 'I'm afraid you've got me muddled up. I'm Hilary Burton. I believe the photographer you're referring to is Hilary *Barton*. We're different people, with completely different styles. Unfortunately there isn't much we can do about the fact that our names are so similar. Both our websites appear on Google when you search for either one of us.'

Adele wanted to scream. She'd looked up the first website, obviously the other Hilary's, and then eaten her dinner having a think about it. When she searched again she went straight to the contact page, thinking it was the same website, and not checking. She was so stupid! Why hadn't she checked? Just her luck the photographer she wanted had almost the exact stupid name as someone else! Someone completely annoying, who took photos of poxy apples!

Hilary hesitated. 'I mean I can give the swimwear a go, but . . .'

'Have you ever actually shot people before?' Adele interrupted abruptly.

101

Hilary looked as though she didn't want to answer, her face blank. At last she replied. 'Well not exactly, no. Unless you include snapshots on my camera at Christmas?' She laughed awkwardly, not realising that she was a giggle away from Adele running over and pushing her to the floor.

'I cannot believe this is happening!' Adele kneaded her eyes with her fists.

'I did try to tell you on the phone that I only shot land-scape, but you cut me off and hung up because you were late for your manicure. It's too late to cancel I'm afraid. I'll still need to be paid,' Hilary said firmly, shooting her a threatening glare.

Adele was livid. 'Oh don't give yourself a heart failure; you're still going to be paid, okay? I *can't* cancel. I have to have these images done today. You'll just have to do the best you can!'

Adele's phone started ringing and she prayed it was Skye saying she was close by and needing directions. She frowned when she saw it was Chloe. What on earth did she want?

'Chloe, I'm really busy. What's up?' she answered tersely.

'Adele!' Chloe squealed. 'Guess what?'

'Chloe, I seriously don't have time for guessing games right now. Do you want to just spit it out please?'

'The agency called. The model agency! They want to see me for an interview!'

Great, Adele thought, just as she believed her day couldn't possibly get any worse.

*

'God, I'm tired,' Jade complained as she uploaded another bikini image to their website, which was hopefully going live within the next few days.

'Not sleeping well or something?' Kelly asked, concerned,

sifting through the bags of crystals and picking some for the next bikini.

'No, it's just Lisa. She brings Cupcake round every day at seven in the morning. I then try to get back to sleep and just put the dog in bed with me, but she won't keep still. Then she starts crying and I have no choice but to get up. I really thought one of the positive things about working from home would be not having to wake up too early.'

'Mmm, I suppose that is annoying,' Kelly agreed. 'She's the most adorable dog in the world, but she can be quite a handful I suppose.'

Right on cue Cupcake picked up some finished bikini bottoms in her little mouth and started chewing.

'No!' Jade said, exasperated. 'Put those down now! You're such a naughty dog!'

Cupcake growled and backed away, dropping the bottoms reluctantly. To Jade and Kelly's disgust she then ran into the corner of the office, ignored the puppy pad and went to the toilet on the cream carpet.

Kelly looked at Jade with a stunned expression.

'That's it!' Jade screamed hastily. 'I've had enough! She hasn't even been here a week and she's driving me insane! It's not fair on us and it's not fair on her! Lisa is going to have to make other arrangements for this . . . this . . . monster dog!'

Kelly's mouth was wide open. 'Jade,' she said in horror, rushing over and putting her hands over the tiny dog's ears, 'she'll hear you! Dogs have feelings too, you know.'

'I don't care if she hears me! I *want* her to hear me. She thinks she's so cute with her big puppy eyes and little wagging tail. She's the most disobedient dog in the world. It's like she purposely has it in for me! It's not practical to have this dog while we're working and that's that.'

'She's just a puppy!' Kelly defended. 'She'll learn about

103

going to the toilet outside in the end. She's bored. She just needs more toys.'

'More toys? More toys? She has *plenty* of toys! Look at them! Scattered all round the office and making it look like a complete mess. But does she want to chew her bones? Oh no, they're not good enough for Cupcake. No, Cupcake likes to chew the skirting, or the corners of the furniture or any bikini she can get her tiny paws on!'

'Look, babe,' Kelly said calmly, 'I'll clear up this mess and take Cupcake for a walk. I'll look after her and I'll tell Lisa to drop her to me in the mornings. From now on, I'll be in charge of her. But, we can't say we won't look after her. Lisa would have to get rid of her and it would break her heart.'

Jade felt guilty. She didn't hate the dog, not really. But she didn't ask for her to come and disrupt their lives at work. She knew Kelly loved Cupcake to bits and obviously she didn't want Lisa to have to get rid of her. But this wasn't their problem. Lisa should never have got a dog when she worked full time. She didn't want to be tidying up and worrying about a dog all day. It wasn't fair on Cupcake either and Jade was adamant; Cupcake was going.

Jade took a deep breath and closed her eyes temporarily. 'I'm sorry, Kelly, but she's going to have to go. We're busy all day and she's making unnecessary work for us. You have to admit it. We can't possibly keep her here.'

'Well, I can't tell Lisa. You'll have to. Come on Cupcake,' Kelly said, taking the dog outside.

Jade was stressed out. Pretty soon the website would be going live and they needed to send out a press release to hopefully get some publicity and media interest. All the media contacts they'd been given were in her red notebook, which was nowhere to be seen. She'd even texted Tony while he was holiday and asked him if she'd left it there. He didn't think she had either. Then there was Sam. They'd been getting on amazingly lately, but he seemed paranoid and jumpy all the time. God only knew what was wrong with him, Jade sighed glumly. Jade just hoped it wasn't anything serious.

*

Adele felt a huge weight lift from her shoulders as she heard a knock on the studio door.

'At last she's arrived,' Hilary said raising her eyebrows. 'Unfortunately due to my other commitments we only have a few hours left now.'

'I'm *aware* of that, Hilary. You have told me about thirty times you know,' Adele huffed, making her way over to the door.

'Hi,' Skye slurred when she opened the door, 'sorry I'm late.'

Adele grimaced as the alcohol fumes hit her straight in the face. You've got to be joking, she thought, almost exploding in frustration. Adele glared at her venomously as she opened the door. 'You're drunk!'

Skye looked up at the ceiling. 'I'm not drunk exactly, just had hardly any sleep. Chill out.'

Adele was so furious she couldn't even respond to the 'chill out' comment. 'Look, just hurry up and get ready, okay?' She couldn't believe the state of her. She looked nothing at all like her photos! Her skin was flaky, pale and dry. Skye's hair was greasy and lank and Adele couldn't take her eyes off the two great big spots on her forehead.

'Where's hair and make-up?' Skye asked looking completely uninterested as she threw her cardigan on the floor.

Adele felt her blood beginning to boil. 'What do you mean? I thought you'd be doing your own hair and make-up?'

Skye laughed derisively. 'I can't do hair and make-up for shit.'

Adele wanted to scream. This simply had to be the worst photo shoot of all time and to make matters worse Skye had already been paid up front. Now what was she going to do? 'Oh for God's sake. Come here. I'll have to do it! But, I want a discount.'

'No can do,' Skye said, ready to leave. 'I'm a little bit late I know, but I'm not working for any less. Take it or leave it.'

Adele considered her options for a moment. She would have happily modelled herself if she'd had a recent bikini wax. The thought of spider legs creeping out of the bikini bottoms made her quiver in shame. That was certainly not a good look! Besides, Skye *knew* what she was doing. She did it for a living, after all.

'No, stay,' Adele replied finally. 'We don't have long though, so please take a seat and I'll do your make-up quickly. Do you have any make-up with you by any chance?'

'No. Can we smoke in here?' Skye looked around, catching Hilary's livid glare.

'Under no circumstances,' she replied, appalled at the suggestion.

'Trust me, I'd have smoked a whole pack by now if we could,' Adele muttered under her breath.

Luckily Adele had brought a few bits of make-up with her. She didn't have foundation, but found an old cover-up stick at the bottom of her bag and she dashed it under Skye's eyes to hide the dark shadows underneath them. She tried not to vomit as she rubbed the concealer into her spots. How could make-up artists touch other people's zits without gagging? It was the most revolting thing she'd ever done so far in her life! She had some dark brown eye shadow, an old mascara and Vaseline. That was it. She still looked a complete state and there was nothing else Adele could do. Maybe the hair would make her look more like a glamorous model? She brushed it, parting it on the side, but with no straighteners or curlers it just hung there dismally, the thick grease impossible to disguise.

'Look. This is a very important shoot, okay? You're going to have to get some good images with how you look. *Please*,' Adele pleaded.

'Don't worry,' Skye grinned. 'They'll come out good.'

Adele felt a fraction more confident when Skye started to pose for Hilary. Her body was to die for, and the bikinis would have looked great if they could have blurred her face out. Oh well, Adele thought, maybe she could cut the head off some of the photos? Hilary was an expensive photographer and even though she only shot landscape, it couldn't be that much different to actual people could it?

An hour and a half later, the day was over and Adele finally felt herself relax. She needed a large glass of wine after the day she'd had. Maybe she'd stop over at Lisa and Nicola's? They'd moved in now, but she hadn't had a chance to go over and see them yet. What was she going to do about Chloe too? She couldn't believe the agency actually wanted to meet her! Jammy bitch! Trust Chloe to get spotted by someone. When was someone going to spot *her*? She had to put a stop to it. There must be a way. She couldn't think of anything worse than Chloe rubbing it in her face she was going for this commercial or that photo shoot, expecting her to be *pleased* about it. The only thing she'd be pleased about was when this whole modelling thing was knocked on the head. Chloe wasn't good enough! Surely the agency would see that? She was shy and pathetic; she didn't have any qualities of a model. She would visit her on her way home and see how she could ruin her chances in some way.

*

'Hi Adele,' Chloe answered the door with a cheesy smile. It made her feel sick.

'Hi, babe,' she said, kissing her cheek. 'So, when is the interview?'

'I'm going to see them tomorrow! I'm so nervous!'

'So soon? Wow, they must have been impressed,' Adele replied sarcastically. Looking back, Chloe *had* looked good in the photos they'd sent, but mainly because of all the make-up she'd had on. When they saw her bare faced they'd be in for a shock.

'Do you want a drink?' Chloe asked kindly.

'No, I'm not staying long. I just came to wish you luck and say well done. I knew they'd want you. Look, I got some tips from a top model today I used at my shoot,' she lied. 'I asked just for you. She's given me some advice to pass on to you.'

'Oh my God! That's amazing. Thanks Adele. What did she say?'

Adele thought for a moment conjuring up a plan. 'She said don't wear any make-up. Not even a tiny dot of it.'

Chloe turned up her little nose, looking unsure. 'Really? I hate myself with *no* make-up on. Surely I need some? What about mascara at least?'

Adele shook her head, trying to stop herself from bursting into laughter at Chloe's stupidity. What girl looked better with no make-up on? They'd never want her looking how she did first thing in the morning. 'No make-up. It's *really* important, she said.'

'Okay,' Chloe nodded seriously, hanging on her every word. 'What else?'

'Act really quiet and shy. They *love* that.'

Lines appeared on Chloe's smooth forehead. 'Mmm . . . surely they want someone who is outgoing and confident though?'

Adele shook her head violently. 'Absolutely not!

108

Confidence is seen as arrogance in their industry. They'll think you're a diva and that's the last sort of person they would welcome into their agency.'

Chloe gave a little nod after thinking about it. 'I suppose that makes sense.'

'Anyway hun. I must go,' Adele said with a flick of her hair as walked out the front door.

'Thanks so much, Adele,' Chloe said smiling thankfully.

'That's what friends are for! Good luck!'

*

Sam pulled up at his parents' home, certain he'd just seen Adele's white Range Rover pull away. What on earth was she doing here? he thought with dread. Why was she so set on ruining his life?

Sam had done nothing but replay that night in Sugar Hut again and again in his mind. If he'd have just left without speaking to Adele or if he hadn't drunk all those shots he would never be in this mess. He hadn't been acting himself around Jade lately and felt like there was a time bomb about to go off at any second. She *knew* something was up, but every time she asked him he acted like she was imagining things. Sam had never believed he would cheat on Jade, he certainly didn't want to, but seeing Adele's thong in his bed he realised a lot more had obviously gone on than just polite chit-chat. How he hated her! It was as though she knew when he was happy and purposely went out of her way to ruin it for him. He couldn't have felt guiltier if he tried. He was such an arsehole! He had the best girlfriend ever and he may have slept with his ex-girlfriend, who he knew Jade despised, behind her back when they had their first tiny row. When she found out, which he was certain she would because Adele would make sure of it, she was going to kill him

– and he didn't blame her. He hadn't been sleeping properly since it happened, wondering whether he should confess everything to her, but he just couldn't bring himself to say the words and break her heart. If he did, he would lose her and the thought of that made him panic and feel nauseous. Poor Jade had already been through this once. Her last boyfriend at university, Tom, sounded like a complete scumbag. She'd found his phone and seen he'd been sleeping with someone else behind her back. Sam had always promised Jade she'd never have anything to worry about with him and now look at what had bloody happened. He was never drinking that much again. It wasn't often he got that drunk, but when he did, he blacked out and literally had no recollection of what had happened. Adele must have taken advantage, he thought angrily; she was the most manipulative bitch he knew. He must have been insane to have ever dated her all those years ago! He took out his phone and punched in a message before sending it to Adele.

What are you playing at? Stay away from Chloe.

He slipped his phone in his pocket and rang the doorbell.

Chloe answered the door. 'Hi Sam,' she smiled, sweetly.

'Hey.' He wiped his feet on the doormat, his face creased in a frown. 'Why have I just seen Adele leave here? Please tell me I'm going mad and it wasn't her.'

Chloe shrugged. 'She just came over quickly to wish me luck.'

'Why? Since when are you two friends? Wish you luck for what?' He was thunderous. Why couldn't she just get out of his and his family's lives? She wasn't welcome and never would be! How dare she go to his parents' home!

'She just comes and sees me now and again, that's all.

110

She was saying good luck because I have a meeting with a modelling agency. Anyway,' Chloe retorted indignantly, 'don't moan about me being friends with her. If I were you I would worry about *your* relationship with her. She told me what happened and I'm just shocked to be honest.'

Sam was exasperated. 'What? She had no right to blurt out rubbish and spread rumours! It's not true,' he lied. 'Stay away from Adele, Chloe. Trust me, she's bad news. She lies.'

'I can't,' Chloe murmured.

'What do you mean, you can't? Just tell her to piss off next time she calls!'

Chloe sighed, as though she had the weight of the world on her shoulders. 'You wouldn't understand. We're friends.'

'Why would you want to be friends with her? You tell her from me to keep her big fat gob shut,' he replied curtly, looking furious. She was a nightmare that girl! She was already trying to cause trouble by telling his little sister he'd cheated on Jade.

He called hello to his parents who were busy in the kitchen and sat on the sofa next to Chloe in the lounge, trying to relax. 'So, what's this modelling agency you're talking about anyway?'

'Oh, it's probably nothing,' she replied, with an insouciant shrug of her shoulders.

'Have you told Mum?'

'Yes, she's coming with me.'

'Good,' Sam replied, feeling more at ease. 'So long as you don't take all your clothes off or do anything stupid . . .'

'I would *never* do that!' Chloe replied, looking affronted. 'I've been modelling the bikinis for Jade's website and the photographer told me to contact an agency.'

'What?' Sam was horrified. 'You've been modelling Jade's bikinis?'

Chloe frowned. 'Yes, didn't she tell you?'

'No, she didn't! When you said modelling I assumed you'd have your clothes on, Chloe. I didn't think you'd be that stupid,' he fumed, shaking his head furiously. How could Jade not have told him this? Didn't his opinion matter?

Chloe's chin wobbled, making Sam feel guilty. 'Sorry to snap,' he said after a pause. 'Just be safe, okay? I'm not happy about my little sister modelling bikinis, I'm not going to pretend to be okay with it, but I doubt I can stop you. Just make sure Mum goes everywhere with you.'

'I will,' Chloe replied. 'It's not just bikinis, I promise. You can get all kinds of work in the agency, I've seen on their website. You get paid loads for television commercials,' she explained.

'I'm sure you'll do well,' Sam nodded. 'Just remember what I said; be careful. Make sure it's legit before you sign anything.'

'They probably won't even want me,' Chloe said modestly.

'I'm sure they will,' Sam replied honestly, feeling pleased with himself when he saw her mouth curve into a smile.

'So, how are things with Jade anyway?' Chloe asked him.

'Well, apart from the fact I'm not too happy she didn't tell me about you modelling, they're good,' Sam replied, feeling uncomfortable now because Adele had shouted her mouth off. 'Look Chloe, *please* don't mention a thing to Jade about whatever Adele has told you. You saw how drunk I was that night and if I'm honest, I really don't know what happened. I feel bad enough as it is without you going on at me so please, let's just never mention this again.'

Chloe nodded. 'My lips are sealed.'

'Thanks.'

Sam tried to enjoy himself for the rest of the evening. He didn't see his parents as much as he should and there was nothing better than his mum's roast chicken, which he wolfed down in no time. It was to die for. Try as he might though he couldn't help but wonder the whole night: who else had Adele told? He knew Adele and knew she would be saving this bit of information for a rainy day. She liked playing with people's feelings and emotions and being in control. He'd walked straight into another one of her games, but this time, he seriously didn't feel like playing.

CHAPTER 7

Chloe sat in the reception of the modelling agency nervously. She'd gone straight from college to Oxford Circus
with her mum and luckily it hadn't taken them too long
to find. She couldn't believe she was here. She eyed up
another girl sitting there confidently on her own with a
huge black folder, which must have been her portfolio. She
didn't even have a portfolio; all she had were the images
that Jade and Kelly had sent her online. She hoped that
wouldn't go against her? The building was simplistic and
modern and the reception was so quiet you could have
heard a pin drop. It was like waiting for your driving test
and Chloe felt intimidated even when the receptionist asked
her name and who she was there to see.

She'd done exactly what Adele had said, and hadn't put
on any make-up at all. She didn't feel one bit confident,
but her mum thought she looked nice. She would though,
wouldn't she, Chloe worried. As she looked round at the
framed images of models already represented by the agency
she wondered what she was doing there. They'd never want
her, would they? Would she really be able to get work? She
took a *Tatler* magazine from the huge glass coffee table
and browsed through it, trying to keep her mind

preoccupied. A few minutes later the receptionist called her name and beckoned her to go to the furthest room down the hall on the right. Chloe looked at her mum warily.

'Do you want me to come?' her mum asked, noticing her concerned expression.

'No, I'll be fine,' Chloe replied. She was eighteen years old. As much as she wanted to, she couldn't take her mum with her. How ridiculous would they think she was, needing to hold her mum's hand everywhere? If she was ever going to do this, she had to be brave for once and do it alone.

Chloe reached the door and knocked, her heart thumping in her chest.

'Come in,' the voice called from inside the office.

Chloe walked in, relieved when she saw a friendly-looking woman sitting behind a desk with a wide smile. There were more images of models on the cream walls and all of a sudden she felt excited. Maybe one day her image would be up there?

'Hi.' She felt herself relax a little.

'Take a seat, Chloe.' she signalled to the seat opposite her. 'I'm Francesca, a head booker here at Elite, pleased to meet you.'

'Pleased to meet you too,' Chloe grinned politely.

She was writing something on a clipboard and then looked up at her. 'I hope you found it okay today? You didn't have to come too far?'

'No, it was fine. I just jumped on the Central line and managed to find it easily,' Chloe said as she sat down.

'Good. So tell me a bit about yourself? What makes you want to model?' Francesca stared at Chloe, resting her chin on her palm.

'Errr . . . I'm eighteen and I'm at college . . .' Chloe was stuck already. What sort of thing did she say? That she liked to go clubbing? She doubted that would go down too well. That she liked nothing more than to sit in her jogging bottoms all day and eat chocolate? Hardly the life of a potential model! 'To be honest, I've never really thought about modelling. I did a shoot for my brother's girlfriend's new bikini company at the beginning of this week and the photographer suggested I contact you.'

'Okay.' Francesca was clicking away at her computer and Chloe guessed she was looking through her images again. Finally she spoke. 'So that was your first ever shoot, am I right? You've never modelled before?'

Chloe nodded timidly.

Francesca turned to face her again, her eyes bright. 'Well I must say your images are rather impressive. You have a great figure and you'd be great for our commercial side of the agency rather than high fashion. I can't guarantee anything, as I need to discuss you with our other head booker, who unfortunately isn't here at present. When will you be leaving college?'

'June,' Chloe replied, her heartbeat increasing in pace with excitement.

She noted it down and then looked up with a thoughtful expression. 'I'm very pleased you came in with a fresh face. The amount of girls we have coming through the door plastered in make-up! Of course models wear make-up when they're photographed, I think that's why so many girls come in here getting it wrong. If we put you forward for castings this is exactly what you need to look like. They'll need to be able to see *you*.'

'Okay,' Chloe replied, thanking Adele in her head. She'd been right! Make-up was definitely a no-no.

'The camera loves you,' Francesca said happily. 'Obviously we would need to get you a portfolio done, which we would pay for, then take from your earnings if we take you on.'

Chloe nodded, twirling her hair round her finger; something she always did when she was nervous.

'Is it okay to take your measurements?'

Chloe nodded. 'Yes, that's fine.'

She stood up and Francesca took out a tape measure, wrapping it round various parts of her body.

'Height, five foot nine and a half. Bust, thirty-four inches,' she moved the tape measure down. 'Waist, twenty-five inches and hips, thirty-three. Perfect.'

Chloe didn't have a clue if her measurements were right or not. Was her waist small enough to be a model? Her hips too big?

'You're a great healthy size,' Francesca answered the thoughts in her mind. 'Is it okay to take a few Polaroids?'

Chloe nodded. 'Yes, that's fine.'

She had a full-length photo taken and a head shot and then sat back down and Francesca explained a bit more about the agency. Chloe was glad to hear they didn't take any fees up front, just a percentage of her earnings if they managed to find her work.

After jotting some more on her clipboard Francesca looked up again with a smile. 'So Chloe, any questions?'

Chloe couldn't think of any. Besides, she didn't want to be too chatty. Adele had told her to be quiet and shy hadn't she? She was right about the make-up, so she must be right about that too, she decided, simply shaking her head at the question.

'Okay, well thank you for coming in to see us,' Francesca said, standing up and shaking her hand, leading her to the door. 'I'll have a chat with my colleague and we'll be in touch if we're interested. We may or may not need to see you again so she can meet you. It was good to see you in the flesh!'

'Thanks,' Chloe said, waving as she walked out. 'Bye.'

She had no idea how it went. Did that mean that she wasn't going to be taken on? She'd honestly never thought about being a model before. People had often told her she should be, not any of her friends though of course.

She remembered once when someone stopped her and gave her their card when she was shopping and told her to contact their agency. She had only been fifteen at the time and her friends who had been with her didn't stop going on and on about how they were most probably trying to con her and how they would hate to be models because models had no brain cells. She felt so bad for accepting the card that she threw it in the bin, right then and there, agreeing that she would also hate to be a model. It was only the following year when she told her mum the story that she said her friends had only said that because they were jealous that they weren't given cards. Chloe had never thought of it like that and she hadn't thought about it since, until Martin gave her the card for Elite. Now her mind had started to wonder if she really *could* be a successful model and she was almost there. Now she wanted it more than ever.

*

It had been almost a week since Jade had told Lisa they couldn't dog-sit Cupcake anymore. As much as she felt terrible she knew that she was doing the right thing.

'Why not?' Lisa had asked incredulously, when she came back from work to collect her. 'Has she not been behaving herself? Oh Jade, I'm so sorry if she's been a nuisance,' Lisa told her as her hands flew to her cheeks in mortification.

'It's not her, it's me,' Jade had explained gently. 'I can't watch Cupcake the whole time and neither can Kelly because we're so busy working. She deserves better and I know she'll be fine with someone else. Is there anyone else you can think of to watch her? If you can't find anyone, then of course we will but . . .'

'No,' Lisa had shaken her head sternly, putting her hand up in protest. 'You're busy and I know Cupcake can be a bit naughty sometimes. I'm just sorry I put you in this situation. I'll find someone, no problem.'

Jade felt terrible. 'Lisa, I'm so sorry! Drop her to me until you find someone else, I promise, it's fine.'

'Honestly, don't worry,' Lisa replied, scooping Cupcake up and putting her in the pink bag. 'We'll find somewhere else for you, won't we Cupcake?' she said in a high-pitched voice, looking at the dog.

'Thanks anyway, Jade. See you soon.'

Jade had felt dreadful as she watched Lisa walk off that day. Kelly had said that Lisa was now paying an old lady that lived in one of the flats in her building twelve pounds a day. It seemed like such a lot of money to waste and Jade had contemplated saying they'd look after Cupcake again, until she realised how spotless the office was without her.

The website was finally ready to go live and Jade couldn't wait for Tony to get back from his holiday so he could launch it. She'd composed a press release earlier that day, which they were going to send out to all their media contacts. She was relying on her notebook being at his house so they could send it across. Otherwise, they'd have to spend ages finding all the contacts again. It was so frustrating! When she got the notebook back, she was never going to put it down again.

Her doorbell rang and Jade couldn't help but smile, knowing it was Sam coming over for the evening.

'Hello,' she said, kissing him as he walked through the door.

'Hi,' he said. 'Good day?'

'Not bad. Let's go upstairs.' She led the way to her room and lay on the bed, pulling him towards her and kissing him.

'So, how are things?' he asked.

'Better now I'm seeing you,' Jade said, her face beatific. 'Though I do have a bone to pick with you.'

119

Jade frowned when she saw his horrified expression. Was she imagining it or could he not look her in the eye?

'What?' Sam asked, disconcerted.

'Calm down, it was only a joke. I was just going to say that you didn't text me back last night.'

He visibly appeared relieved, and exhaled sharply. 'Oh, that. Sorry. I fell asleep.'

'Are you okay?' Jade asked, narrowing her eyes. Why had he been acting so odd lately?

'Yeah I'm fine,' he replied tetchily.

'Okay, sorry for asking,' Jade said caustically, as she tucked her hair behind her ear.

'I actually have a bit of a bone to pick with *you*,' Sam said, his mouth a straight line. 'Why didn't you tell me about Chloe modelling your bikinis?'

'I forgot, sorry,' Jade said, wondering if he was upset about it. 'She's great honestly, such a natural, you should see her.'

'I'd rather not see my little sister, who's only eighteen, modelling swimwear, thanks,' Sam responded moodily. 'I think you should have told me about it to be honest. I don't really like the idea.'

Jade sighed. 'I'm really sorry I didn't tell you, I honestly just forgot. Don't be so dramatic. It's not glamour modelling or anything and the poses aren't sexy; it's more like catalogue modelling.'

'Whatever,' Sam said, shaking his head, clearly not up for discussing it further. 'Let's just forget about it.'

Jade rolled her eyes after a minute of silence. So far the night wasn't going as planned. 'Are you okay with me?' she asked.

He kissed her on the nose. 'I promise I'm fine.'

'Oh I forgot to tell you!' Jade exploded, unable to believe she hadn't already told him. 'You'll never guess who lives opposite Lisa and Nicola?'

'Who?' he asked, raising his eyebrows.

'Adele! Lisa is gutted! Of all the people to live in the same building. Apparently she said she'll go over to them so they can have girly nights. Can you believe it? I feel so sorry for Lisa.' She watched Sam as his face froze. He was acting weird again and it was making her feel unsettled.

'Oh well,' he managed, looking the other way and searching for the remote control to turn the TV on with.

'Is that *all* you're going to say?' Jade had expected more of a reaction from him. His mental ex-girlfriend lived opposite her best friend and the best he could come out with was 'oh well'?

'Well, what do you want me to say?' he snapped.

'Sam, seriously. What has gotten into you?'

Sam fiddled with the remote control. 'I'm tired. I had a hard day at work and you're just talking to me about girly rubbish, which I don't really care about. I don't care about Adele and where she lives or what she's doing. She's a complete lying idiot and I don't want to talk about her.'

'You're acting really strange,' Jade retorted, baffled, her forehead wrinkling.

He gave a theatrical sigh. 'Jade, *please* stop saying that. Nothing is wrong, okay?'

'Fine.'

'Now come here and give me a cuddle and let's just relax. I would rather talk about you.'

Jade heaved a sigh. Things had just started to go well again, but she just knew that something was wrong with Sam and it was scaring her more than ever.

*

Adele was the most excited she'd been for ages. She was with Donna in Funky Mojoe nightclub in South Woodford, and she'd just heard a group of girls squawking about there being a Premiership footballer in there. Obviously, he'd have his own table in the VIP section somewhere, she acknowledged; she hoped their table was close by! The club wasn't that big and Adele promised herself she would find him. She wasn't leaving here until she had his number. Being with a footballer had always been a dream of hers. Who didn't want to get treated like a princess and whisked off to the Caribbean and Dubai to stay in five-star hotels at every opportunity? She *deserved* this. She didn't care what he looked like so long as he wasn't *too* bad looking. She could handle a wonky nose or a bit of a monobrow for the right person. Slightly below average looks were acceptable when they were footballers, every girl knew that. It was fate that they had come to this club tonight! Adele was glad she was wearing her brand new Sass and Bide dress, which had been seen on several celebrities in the press recently; it made her feel special and important. She looked at Donna, who actually looked okay for once. She was wearing a slimming black lace one-shoulder dress with ginormous black open-toe Miu Miu heels, and her dark hair had been highlighted with gold and styled in a side bun, with sexy, wavy strands coming loose. Thank God she's made an effort, Adele thought callously. For once it wasn't *that* embarrassing going out with her.

She'd been disappointed that Lisa and Nicola couldn't make tonight. She'd gone over to their flat before she'd left and finally caught them when they were home. She'd tried every night that week, but they always seemed to be out. Lisa had answered, dressed up in an amazing gold dress; she simply *had* to borrow it one day. Nicola had been sitting there in the lounge with a bottle of wine. She hoped that they were going out just to a club or something and she could have convinced them to join her and Donna in Funky Mojoe, but apparently they were going to a friend's private birthday party and couldn't have invited her or they would have. That would have been nice, Adele considered, but she was glad she was here now seeing as a footballer was in the building. She'd gone to their flat anyway and joined them for a glass of wine as she waited for Donna to arrive. It was nice sitting there together and chatting; she'd have to go round there more often in future.

Adele walked over to a member of staff in the club and asked where their table was. As she followed the lady directing them, she overheard a group of girls chatting.

'So which one is it that plays for Fulham?' one blonde girl asked her friend.

'I'm not too sure. I think it's the one in the blue shirt,' came the dreamy reply. 'He's gorgeous.'

Adele was over the moon! They were sitting dead opposite the man they were talking about with the blue shirt! They couldn't have picked a more perfect spot!

'So,' Donna smirked as they sat down. 'Any sign of the guy you know that likes me?'

Adele's face creased into a bewildered expression. 'What? What guy?' Then she remembered that she'd lied in order to get Donna to miss her aunt's birthday. She waved her hand dismissively. 'Oh, *him*. He texted me a while ago saying he was ill. Sorry, you'll meet him another time.'

Donna couldn't hide her disappointment. She looked down at the floor. 'That's a shame. I was really looking forward to it. You made him sound . . . perfect.'

Adele rolled her eyes. 'Get over it. No man is perfect, don't be so ridiculous. It's really not a big deal; you'll meet him some other time.' She picked up the drinks menu, trying to change the subject quickly. 'Now what champagne shall we buy? It's on me.' She flashed a credit card, hoping that would make up for it.

'I really don't mind,' Donna said unenthusiastically.

Adele ignored the sullen look on her face and called the waiter over. Donna was not ruining her night tonight because some made-up person wasn't coming to Funky Mojoe! How desperate did she want to be for God's sake?

'Actually, I'm more up for vodka tonight,' Adele decided, when the waiter appeared. She could see the guy in the blue shirt opposite had champagne, and when they got chatting she'd just get some from him.

'So what was this person's name that likes me anyway?' Donna asked, eyeing Adele suspiciously.

'Donna, there are tons of guys in here tonight. Some really fit ones! Why not worry about them instead? The man I know that likes you is called John,' Adele lied scathingly. 'But he's not here, so just forget about it.'

'John who?' Donna pouted, clearly not believing her anymore.

'John Smith. Okay? His name is John Smith.' Adele changed the subject. 'There are some hot guys opposite us actually. I like the one in the blue shirt.'

Donna looked at them avidly. 'I think they're all nice!' She grinned.

Adele smirked. Donna clearly hadn't heard the girls saying which one was the footballer, so she was none the wiser. She'd be able to chat to him easily now, while Donna chatted to the others without realising what she was up to. Donna was bound to want the footballer too if she knew which one he was. Luckily, she only knew he was in the club and not where he was sitting. Adele looked over, caught blue shirt guy's eye and smiled seductively. He smiled back, making her heart flip. She was one step closer to becoming a WAG already!

'Oh my God, he fancies you!' Donna gasped, almost spluttering her drink in excitement.

'Play it *cool*,' Adele warned, running her fingers through her hair flirtatiously. 'We can't come across as bothered. We have to wait for them to ask us over.'

Twenty minutes later, after lots of eye contact and smiling, to Adele's delight, they were finally asked over to their table. After introducing themselves, Adele made a beeline for the man in the blue shirt, whose name was Neil, sitting down beside him. She wasn't going to mention that she knew he was a footballer, he'd see straight through her. She would act all innocent and naïve when he told her. It was so much more attractive that way.

'So, tell me about yourself,' he said, gazing into her eyes.

She swooshed her hair back over her shoulder sexily. 'I live in Chigwell and run my own bikini business. I design them too.'

'Bikinis,' he said raising his eyebrows cheekily. 'So how long have you been doing that?'

She decided to lie. 'Three years almost. It's an extremely successful business, which I run alone. I've won awards and everything for businesswoman of the year.'

'Impressive,' he grinned as he filled up her champagne glass and then his own. He was a bit of a rebel, she realised; footballers weren't supposed to drink alcohol, were they? Maybe he had some time off.

He was average looking and certainly no oil painting. Never mind, Adele told herself, just think of his bank balance. She looked over at Donna who was deep in conversation with one of Neil's friends who she thought had said he was called Aaron. Not bad at all for Donna, she realised, eyeing him up. At least she looked happy and wouldn't whine about being left alone. She could chat to Neil in peace now.

A few hours later, Adele was feeling drunk. She had cheekily snogged Neil already and made sure she had his number. This was turning out to be such a great night. She'd even seen Donna kissing Aaron a few times, which was the first time she'd ever seen her pull!

'Come for a dance,' Neil slid his hand into hers and pulled her up.

Adele pouted sexily, following him to the dance floor. Everyone was watching them, she just knew it. Every girl was staring at her enviously because she was the one who had bagged the footballer. She'd have to get used to this, she thought and she wrapped her arms around his neck on the dance floor. She would be centre of attention if he became her boyfriend when they went out. Did Fulham footballers ever get papped? she wondered, hopefully. She'd search Google images tomorrow and find out. Besides, she imagined he would end up playing for a better team eventually; Chelsea or Manchester United or somewhere like that. She didn't know much about football, but he looked fit enough and she imagined most players moved up the ranks in the end. Hopefully Neil would soon, she thought, kissing him passionately. She'd have to stop herself from asking him back to her flat tonight; that definitely wouldn't be a good idea. She couldn't be just *another* of his conquests. She had to be special and someone to stick around for. Sex was totally out of the question on the first night on this particular occasion.

She made her way back to the others with Neil. Adele was so happy she felt as though she was floating. Donna also looked utterly euphoric sitting with Aaron, Adele noticed as she made her way over to her.

'You okay?' Adele asked.

'Yes, couldn't be better,' Donna turned her back on Aaron to make sure he couldn't hear and whispered, 'they want us to go back to their place.'

'Well we can't, can we? We don't want to look like slags, Donna. Don't you know anything?' Adele hissed.

'Yes,' Donna replied shamefacedly. 'I suppose you're right.'

Adele shook her head. 'When he asks you again, say no thank you, we need to be up early in the morning. Tell him we'll go out with them one night in the week instead on a double date.'

Donna perked up again. 'Excellent idea! That will be so much fun.'

An hour later they were waiting outside in the cab queue with the boys.

'Are you sure you won't come back? We've got so much booze at ours and we can all just chill out,' Aaron suggested, putting his arm around Donna's shoulder.

'We're sure. But we'll go out in the week,' Donna replied. She gave Adele a knowing glance and Adele smiled and nodded, indicating she'd said the right answer.

'Okay,' Aaron kissed Donna again on the lips. 'I'll call you. We're going to stay at our mate's and he only lives round the corner so we're going to love you and leave you. We can walk from here.'

Adele kissed Neil passionately. 'We'll go out soon, yeah?'

'Definitely,' he said, rubbing her cheek with his hand and staring at her happily.

The boys walked off and Donna almost jumped around on the spot, excitedly. 'Oh my God. I like him so much. I can't believe tonight, I've had the best time!'

'See, I told you not to go to that stupid birthday party! What a load of rubbish that would have been.'

'Thanks for inviting me, Adele. Aaron is totally gorgeous.'

Adele controlled herself from sniggering. He was attractive, yes, but he wasn't a footballer like Neil! Donna looked elated. 'Yes he's actually quite good looking,' Adele said.

'So was Neil!'

'Yes, about Neil. I know something about him. Something that's going to shock you . . .'

Before Donna could answer a rowdy group of men were walking past, talking loudly. 'Yeah, it was definitely him. Just walked past us. That footballer that plays for Fulham. What's his name again?'

Adele smirked, excited to see the look on Donna's face when she realised who Neil was.

'Oh yeah, I know,' another man answered. 'It was that midfielder. Blinding little player. Aaron Bond!'

Adele's jaw almost hit the floor.

'*Oh. My. God!* Did you hear that? It's Aaron! He's the one that plays for Fulham! Remember those girls were saying in the queue on the way in that their friend had texted them saying there was a footballer in Funky Mojoe. I can't believe it's him! It's Aaron!' Donna was thrilled.

'This can't be right!' Adele's heart was galloping in anger. *Please* don't say she'd wasted a whole evening snogging the face off a nobody when there was a Premiership footballer beside her getting it on with Donna! Adele was so furious she could feel the blood rushing to her face. She grabbed her phone, which finally had a signal, and Googled Aaron Bond. News stories about football matches filled the page as well as images of him. She wanted to scream! Maybe, just maybe, Neil was a footballer too? She typed in his full name in the search bar and when nothing came up she felt physically sick.

'Oh my God! He's texted me already as well,' Donna said happily.

Resisting the urge to either throttle her or throw her phone under the next taxi, Adele took deep breaths and tried to remain calm. So fatty had bagged a footballer had she? The sly little cow. 'How did you know he was the footballer?' Adele demanded, her eyes flashing in fury.

Donna's face was blank. 'I didn't.'

'Oh come on,' Adele said hastily, giving her a sinister look. 'Do you really expect me to believe that? Tell the truth!'

'Adele, I had no idea! What are you talking about?'

Adele was livid. She'd gone for the wrong man. The *wrong* one. If she ever saw those thick airhead girls that said Neil was the footballer she would kill them. This wasn't right! *She* was meant to get with the footballer. *She* was meant to be the WAG getting papped in the Seychelles, not Donna! 'Oh whatever,' she replied at last. 'He was ugly anyway.'

'But you just said you thought he was good looking?'

'I lied,' Adele answered, folding her arms imperiously.

'Well it doesn't matter to me anyway. I like him,' Donna beamed. 'I don't even care if he's a footballer either. None of that matters to me.'

'Oh please!' Adele retorted, getting in the taxi.

'I'm being serious!' Donna said, affronted.

Adele looked out the window moodily. 'Whatever. Can we talk about something else please? I'm bored of this now.'

'You know what, Adele?' Donna said, narrowing her eyes.

'What?' she replied haughtily, folding her arms over her chest.

'You can be really nasty sometimes.'

Adele ignored the comment and looked out of the window. She couldn't help being cross, could she? Donna didn't realise the effort she'd put in with Neil! It wasn't fair! So what if Donna thought she was nasty? She needed to get a life, being so bloody sensitive all the time. She didn't *need* her. She thought for a moment about how often she invited her out. What would Donna do at the weekend if it wasn't for her? Yes, Donna often went to the cinema with her boring friend Gill from work or a meal with her annoying cousin Jane, but she had a better time when Adele convinced her to go clubbing. Didn't she? Adele realised at that moment that if it wasn't for Donna, *she'd* probably be stuck most weekends with nothing to do. It was a scary thought. She couldn't lose her as a friend. She'd have to accept that she'd managed to get the footballer this time and that maybe one day . . . that's it, she thought excitedly! 'Oh my God, babe. I've got the best idea!'

'What?' Donna replied, unenthusiastically, clearly still upset by her previous comments.

'You can get Aaron to set me up with one of his friends!'

'You already have been. You were with Neil?'

'No, no, no,' Adele shook her head frantically. 'Not one of his *normal* friends, one of his *footballer* friends!'

'Okay,' Donna replied tiredly. 'Why do you care so much if they play football?'

Adele gave a loud tut. 'Oh Donna, get a life. What girl doesn't want a footballer?'

Donna nodded. 'We'll see.'

Adele felt better already. If Donna could pull a footballer then she sure as hell could.

CHAPTER 8

'What are you going to order, babe?' Billy asked Kelly as he browsed through the menu.

They were in The Blue Boar in Abridge with Gary and his girlfriend Charlotte.

'Mmm . . . the mushroom wellington I think. I'm trying to cut down and be healthy. Mushrooms are vegetables, right?'

Gary snorted with laughter. 'Are you for real? Great choice if you're trying to cut back, Kelly. There's hardly any calories in the chateaux potatoes, blue cheese and herb cream it comes with!' he said sarcastically. 'Honestly! The things you come out with!'

Kelly stared at him straight faced as he sniggered at her comment. Billy gave a little giggle, trying to be polite, which she really didn't appreciate, and Charlotte pretended she hadn't heard anything. So he was starting on her already, was he? They'd barely just sat down and Gary was already making fun of her. If anyone else had said it to her she would have seen the funny side, but not with him. Not when he did it constantly and was laughing *at* her rather than with her. She was annoyed that Billy never stood up for her either. He always thought she was overreacting because he could never see how his precious Gary could do anything wrong. She loved Billy more than anything, but this was one of the small flaws about him that drove her crazy. Gary always seemed to be trying to prove he was more superior and intelligent than everyone else and she didn't like the way he spoke to Billy sometimes either. They were supposed to be partners, but Kelly got the impression that Gary thought *he* was in charge. Billy had put a lot of his own money into their company and he deserved to be treated with respect in Kelly's eyes. Billy was blind to it though and it was extremely frustrating.

'I was reading the paper this morning,' Gary said, turning to Billy as he chomped on a piece of bread, 'how apparently Osama lived in the room he was captured in for five years, according to his wife. Never left it can you believe?'

Billy nodded. 'Yeah, think I read something about that too.'

Kelly was bemused. She had no idea what they were talking about and decided to keep out of the conversation rather than even attempt to join in. This was way out of bounds.

'It stated that Pakistan continues to defend its failure to uncover him. I mean, it's not like they didn't have enough time, is it? He had been living in the Abbottabad region next to a military base for at least the past half a decade!' Gary continued pompously, buttering another piece of bread and enjoying the fact everyone was listening to him. 'Apparently officials have rubbished claims that the country's secret services have links to Al-Qaeda, which I wonder about. What do you think, Billy?'

'Dunno mate,' Billy replied with a nod. 'I just think good riddance and it's a pity it took so long to take Osama out.'

Kelly was amazed. Billy *knew* what he was talking about? The only word she even remembered was Osama. The rest was a complete blur! Half the words she didn't even know, let alone actually understand them.

'What do you think, Kelly?' Gary's eyes bored into her. 'What?' Kelly was aghast. He wanted *her* opinion. He knew she had no idea what he was talking about. Yet again, he was just trying to make her look stupid. If only she could think of something good to say back to shut him up! Why did he always have to talk about the bloody news? She never had time to read newspapers. She read the odd *Heat* magazine she supposed, but come on; was she really going to give that up for a boring old newspaper that would make her fall asleep? Why couldn't he ask her about celebrity gossip? She knew that Kerry Katona had undergone her second lot of lipo recently or that Reese Witherspoon had fallen pregnant, but Osama? What the hell? *Think of something to say! Think!* Kelly cleared her throat, playing for extra time. She was not going to say she didn't know what he was talking about. She was going to answer *something*. 'Errr . . . I think . . . I mean . . . I don't understand why they wanted to take him out anyway? I mean, when you say that, do you mean kill? Because I think he seems like a lovely man. I saw him on the TV the other day and I can't see why anyone wouldn't like Osama.'

'What?' Billy almost spat his drink out. 'Kelly, he's an evil, wicked man who's responsible for killing thousands of innocent people!'

Kelly was stunned. 'Is he? Really? But he's so friendly, polite and well-spoken and has a lovely stylish wife.'

Billy's face creased in bewilderment. 'Wife? Where would you have seen his wife?'

'I don't know, I just remember she was wearing the most amazing Diane Von Furstenberg dress the other day on TV. I even looked it up online to see if I could buy it,' Kelly replied complacently. 'But answer me one thing. If he's so bad then why is he the American Prime Minister or President or whatever it's bloody called?'

Gary shook his head with the biggest grin Kelly had ever seen plastered across his face. 'Oh surely not. This is too good to be true!'

Billy rubbed her arm, comforting her as he let her down gently. 'Babe, we're talking about Osama Bin Laden. Not Barack Obama. He's the President. Osama was the terrorist, remember? They killed him last year.'

'Oh.' Kelly felt her face burn with shame. 'Easy mistake,' she said, with a forced laugh.

Gary was sniggering and Kelly caught Charlotte tugging his arm harshly as if to tell him to shut up. Great, so even *she* felt sorry for her. Kelly was humiliated and embarrassed and wished she'd never even attempted to answer now. She felt like a complete thicko and that was exactly what they all thought of her.

'Oh Kelly, you really are hilarious,' Gary spluttered. 'Imagine getting Osama Bin Laden and Barack Obama muddled up! They couldn't be further apart if they tried. What school did you go to out of interest? Did you pass your GCSEs?'

Charlotte elbowed him in the ribs.

'Ouch, that hurt!' Gary said with a pained expression.

'Just leave her alone,' Charlotte retorted under her breath.

'It's okay,' Kelly replied weakly. Her confidence had completely disappeared and she felt her eyes sting, threatening tears.

'He's alright,' Billy said jovially. 'He's only messing around, aren't you Gal?'

Kelly was disappointed that Billy was completely unaware of how small Gary had made her feel, yet again. Why could he never see things from her point of view?

'Of course I'm messing around,' Gary laughed. 'You're not offended, are you Kelly? It's only a bit of banter.'

'No,' she lied, wanting to kick herself. Why couldn't she just stand up to him and tell him the truth? She was such a coward at times. She looked at Gary who still couldn't contain his laughter; he loved every second of it.

Kelly excused herself after a few minutes and went to the toilets to calm down. She was so angry with Gary! She hated him even more than before, if that was possible. How dare he think he could make her feel so low? And why had she let him? She knew why deep down though; the moment she stood up for herself she would be opening a can of worms and everything would come pouring out. She'd call him out about every time he'd belittled her or Billy, and Kelly guessed it would cause a big problem between Billy and Gary, something she couldn't risk happening. Her eyes were shining as she blinked the tears away. In future, she just wasn't going to talk or say a word around him. Then he couldn't pick on her anymore and make her feel like an idiot. If he did ask her any more questions she would just shrug or change the subject. If only Billy didn't always feel like he had to say yes whenever Gary asked him to go out. But she knew how important his friendship was to him; he felt like they had to be good friends to be good business partners and she supposed she could see his point.

Later on that evening when she was alone with Billy, she decided to tell him her true feelings once again.

'Lovely food in there weren't it, babe?' Billy said, sitting on the edge of his bed and taking his shoes off.

'Yeah,' Kelly murmured.

'You don't sound very enthusiastic,' Billy replied. 'What's wrong?'

'Nothing.'

'Come on, Kelly. I know you better than that to know when something is up.'

Kelly sat next to him. 'It's Gary,' she said finally.

'Oh not this again,' Billy said looking bored.

'He tries to make me look stupid all the time! He talks about all this stuff in the news and God knows what else so everyone thinks he's really intellectual and clever. You can't see it, can you? He puts me down all the time. I don't like the way he talks to you either sometimes. He thinks he's better than everyone; especially us. Why does he always try to talk so posh as well? He's from Essex, not Chelsea!'

Billy shook his head. 'Kelly, it's not his fault if he's well-spoken, interested in the news and knows about what's going on in the world. I doubt he thinks he's better than anyone. It's all in your head. He can't help if he's an intelligent man, can he? He doesn't put you down, he just thinks the things you say are funny!'

'He asked if I'd passed my GCSEs!' Kelly reminded him with a stare, mortified.

'He was joking. You're just being over-sensitive. Look if you hate it that much, I'll have a word with him. No big deal.'

'Yes, please do,' Kelly snapped, annoyed that he wasn't on her side. She gave up. Billy would never see Gary for the nasty piece of work he really was and the sooner she accepted that the better.

*

Adele loaded the CD into her laptop and waited for her photos to appear. She hoped they looked good after the amount she'd paid in the end. As she clicked on the first one she didn't know how to feel. Yes, they looked professional and better than she thought, but Skye didn't look great at all. It was the make-up and hair! Why hadn't she thought to hire people for the day? Oh well, she thought, trying to see the bright side, lots of people probably wouldn't even be looking at the model. They would want to see the bikinis and they looked fine. Some even looked quite nice and she was sure they would sell. Her dad's computer developer had done the whole thing for her, including her Facebook and Twitter pages and all she had to do was add these images and she was good to go! It was a great feeling. She'd have her website up and running before Jade and Kelly. There was no way they could say she copied them now! She'd send them proof of when the website launched if she had to. Then she was going to send out a press release to all their contacts. She'd already paid someone to do it for her that worked in the PR department at her dad's company. She was going to send it first thing in the morning.

She'd called Chloe earlier that day and she still hadn't heard back from the modelling agency, which was good news. They obviously didn't want her; she'd have been snapped up there and then if they did! The thought pleased her immensely. Now Chloe knew she wasn't as perfect as she probably thought. She'd fed her all the usual lines of course. 'Of course they'll call,' she'd told her, practically laughing her head off inside. Chloe could kiss her modelling career goodbye as far as she was concerned. Dream on!

She was about to make herself a cup of tea when she changed her mind. This was a perfect time to go round and see Lisa and Nicola and get to know them better. They could all have a girly night together and watch a film or something. She picked up some DVDs and called her dog.

'Buddy! Come on Buddy, we're going out.' The dog followed her as she shut her front door behind her, walked across the hall and knocked on their door.

Nicola answered with a surprised expression at seeing her there. She looked different, Adele noticed; she was wearing smart black trousers, a pretty yet conservative blouse and less make-up. It made her look more grown up and mature.

'Hi, hun,' Adele grinned at her. 'Thought I'd bring some DVDs round and we can watch them together; have a girly night in.'

'Oh, hi honey.' Nicola opened the door and let her through. 'We're actually just eating our dinner.'

'Oh that's okay.' Adele walked through and her stomach rumbled as she recognised the delicious smell of home-cooked lasagne.

'Hi Lisa,' Adele called to her, glancing through to the kitchen to see if they had any leftovers. She was delighted when she spotted the oven dish still half full with food left inside. 'Girls, you don't mind if I have some, do you? I never had time to cook dinner and this looks gorgeous. You're not having any more are you?' Adele asked, helping herself to a plate in the cupboard and dishing some on her plate along with the salad beside it.

'No, help yourself,' Nicola replied.

'Thanks, babe.'

Adele poured herself some wine, put her dinner on a tray and then walked in to join them.

'Good day at work, girls?' Adele asked brightly as she sat on the sofa next to Lisa.

'Yeah, it was good thanks,' Lisa replied unenthusiastically, her eyes not leaving the television.

'Ah bless. I don't know how you girls wake up so early every day.'

'Some of us have to,' Lisa replied curtly.

Adele ignored her remark and decided to play it safe and stay on her good side. She was just jealous, she decided, and who could blame her? She had the perfect life; rich parents, a stunning flat bought for her, good looks and now her own business. Not that Lisa knew about her company just yet though. She would be sure to run off and tell Jade and Kelly and she didn't want them to know just yet.

'Are you watching this?' Adele asked, picking up the remote control. *EastEnders* was on the TV and it really wasn't Adele's cup of tea. 'Why don't we put a DVD on?'

'Sounds good to me,' Nicola agreed.

'I want to find out what happens to Billy,' Lisa said in an irritable tone.

'Okay, sorry,' Nicola responded. 'Didn't know you were watching it.'

Adele rolled her eyes at Nicola, but she turned the other way, looking awkward.

The minute the show ended, Adele jumped up and put *The Hangover* on.

'I've seen this loads of times,' Lisa complained. She was beginning to get on Adele's nerves complaining about everything all the time.

'Choose another one then,' Adele replied, pointing to the rest she'd brought round as Lisa reluctantly searched through the collection. Really, why was she so miserable? Adele wondered. Nicola was so easygoing and nice, but Lisa was hard work. Hopefully they'll fall out and Nicola can come live with me, Adele hoped wistfully.

Lisa opted for *Pretty Woman*.

'Good choice,' Adele smiled at her. 'I just love the old classic films. They remind me of being young.'

'Me too,' Lisa agreed.

'You've got such lovely hair, babe,' Adele complimented Lisa as she brushed it, sitting back on the sofa.

'Thanks,' Lisa said, giving a half-smile

At last, Adele thought relaxing, Lisa was finally perking up. She still had the feeling she wasn't overly keen on her, though she knew that would change soon, when she really got to know her. She was a nice person and never understood why Jade and Kelly wouldn't give her the chance? Well, she didn't need them now she had Lisa and Nicola. Buddy jumped up at the sofa, too tiny to get himself up and Adele pulled him up and put him on her lap.

'Where's Cupcake?' Adele asked, realising the dog was missing.

Lisa's eyes flashed with sadness. 'Oh, a lady upstairs is looking after her in the daytime now. She went out for the day and isn't home yet. She'd going to drop her off when she's back. Jade and Kelly were meant to look after her, but, well . . . it didn't work out.'

'Oh.' Adele didn't know what to say. It was obviously a touchy subject. 'So, you pay this lady?'

'Yes, it's £12 a day, which is £240 a month. If I'm honest, I don't think I can afford to keep her. Not now I'm paying to live here as well.'

Adele could tell she was devastated. As she watched Lisa's eyes start to glisten the perfect idea came to her. It was a way in. A way to be friends. 'Babe, why don't you just bring her to me every day?'

Lisa's face lit up, but then she looked doubtful. 'Oh, I couldn't. It wouldn't be fair.'

'Hun, don't be ridiculous! I love dogs. I work from home and this way, you'll get to keep her, right? You won't have to give Cupcake up?'

'I'd have to pay you . . .'

Adele held her hands up in protest. 'No way! I want to do it. I already have one little dog. I may as well have another. It's no problem. I'd never take money from a friend.' Adele gave a shrug of her shoulders.

Lisa had a dubious expression, but then her face lit up. 'Really? You promise you wouldn't mind?'

'I promise,' Adele smiled sweetly. 'That's what friends are for!'

'Oh my God! Thanks Adele. That's really kind of you. I can even leave you a key so I won't wake you or anything. You can just let yourself in and pick up Cupcake in the day if that's okay? Then I'll come straight to you in the evening and get her.'

'No problem,' Adele said, feeling really good about herself. She was even getting a key now! This plan was going fantastically. She was a hero in Lisa's eyes and she really loved the feeling.

'Ah, babe, that's well nice of you,' Nicola said, looking pleased for Lisa.

Lisa looked emotional. 'I literally can't thank you enough.'

'It's no bother really. I want to do it,' Adele assured her.

The atmosphere completely changed after they'd had that conversation, Adele realised happily. It was like the tension had been swept under the carpet and they were starting afresh. She watched *Pretty Woman,* feeling very pleased with her bright idea.

*

Lisa felt the happiest she had all day as she gazed down at her little dog that had just been dropped off. Cupcake was tired for once, thank God and had fallen fast asleep on her lap. She'd sat down at lunch earlier that day and worked out how much money she'd have left each month if she had to pay for a dog-sitter every day as well as vet bills, rent, house bills – the list went on. It wasn't very much. She'd literally have to eat cereal for dinner and stay in every night and no matter how hard she tried to come up with a solution, she just couldn't think of any. It was then she had realised she was going to have to give Cupcake up and sell her to someone that could look after her. The thought had broken her heart and she'd felt irritable and sad all day. She wasn't annoyed with Jade or Kelly; she completely understood where they were coming from and thought back to how she'd never really asked them if they could do it; she just assumed they would. It was a big responsibility and a lot to ask them and she realised that she hadn't thought it all through. She was astounded that it was Adele who had answered her prayers. Who would have thought it? She clearly wasn't all bad if she was willing to do that for Lisa for nothing. She felt slightly ashamed with herself for being so cold and abrupt with her every time she'd come over to see them. Yes, she got in their faces a bit too much and helped herself to their dinner and drink, but the fact that she was happy to put herself out and take Cupcake every day went a long way in Lisa's book. Lisa knew Adele had done some strange things in the past to Jade and Kelly, but she believed deep down she just wanted to be their friend. There were things that she didn't like about her of course, but who was perfect? Everyone had flaws and she believed Adele deserved a second chance. She had redeemed herself.

Lisa looked over at Nicola who was busy texting on her phone. She'd been on a couple of dates recently with a guy called Charlie and she could tell she was falling for him. She was on the phone constantly, her face lighting up when she read her messages every five minutes, and as much as Lisa would miss her to go out with if he did become her boyfriend, it was nice seeing her so happy. 'What's he been texting?' she asked, as Nicola grinned again after reading his message.

Her smile didn't falter. 'Oh, he just wants to take me out one night after work. Nothing really.'

'Who's this, babe?' Adele questioned.

'Just someone I've been on a few dates with, honey. He's called Charlie.'

'Nicola's in *looove*,' Lisa teased.

'Leave off!' Nicola giggled. 'But yes, I do like him.'

'Where's he from?' Adele looked over at her, interested.

'Loughton. I love Essex boys, honey,' Nicola said, her eyes gleaming.

'Me too.' Adele nodded in agreement with a yawn. 'Right, I'd better go.' She stood up and kissed them both on the cheek. 'Thanks girls. See you tomorrow babes,' she said to

Lisa. 'Can't wait to look after Cupcake. Shall I take the spare key now?'

'Yes, one minute,' Lisa replied as she went to find it in the kitchen. This was such a perfect idea. Now she could just leave Cupcake when she went to work, knowing that Adele would be round soon afterwards to pick her up. She had felt awful when she woke Jade up every morning at just gone seven. Jade must have wanted to throttle her every day having to wake up so early, but she hadn't shown it. Lisa was lucky to have such good friends. She handed the key to Adele and thanked her once again, then went to get ready for bed. As she drifted off to sleep she wondered what Charlie was like. He must be nice for Nicola to be so keen, she mused. Hopefully it would all work out for her.

*

'So you're sure it's not there?' Jade asked Tony on the phone, trying to control her panic.

He sounded sympathetic. 'No. I'm sorry, Jade, but I've searched everywhere I can I think of. There is no red notebook here at all.'

Jade sighed heavily. It was lost then. It had simply disappeared because she'd been so careless. She swallowed hard. 'Okay, I'll have to buy a new one,' she said resentfully.

'On the plus side, your website has just gone live. Have you done the press release?'

'Yes, it's all done. I had to make note of all the media contacts again, which took ages to do, but I sent it out yesterday.'

Tony was pleased. 'Excellent. Now all you need to do is follow it up with some phone calls. Journalists can be a nightmare and unless you go out of your way to chase them, they may never get back to you.'

'Okay, I'll do that now. Thanks Tony.'

'No worries. Call me if you need anything.'

She hung up the phone and Kelly looked up at her with a hopeful expression.

'Anything?'

'Nope, it's gone,' she replied miserably.

'Oh that's shit, babe,' Kelly said as she carried on sewing at the little desk they'd bought. 'Did he say the website is live now?'

Jade nodded, feeling her hopes rise. 'Yes, Vajazzle My Bikini is officially open for orders!'

Kelly beamed. 'I'm not being funny, but how exciting is this?'

'I know. I'm going to call a few magazines now and chase them up about the press release. Let's hope they'll be interested in writing about us. We need to advertise and could really do without paying for now.'

'Exactly, hun. We have the most reem bikinis ever. I bet they'll love it.'

'Fingers crossed,' Jade replied, crossing her middle and index fingers on both hands.

Jade looked through the list and decided to try *Allure* magazine first.

'Hello, *Allure*,' a posh woman answered.

After Jade explained why she was calling, the woman stopped her halfway through abruptly. 'We already have something too similar we're writing about. Thank you.'

Jade sat there agog as the phone went dead. How rude, she thought, stunned, as she looked through the list for another magazine to call. What a lie the woman had told about there being something similar. They'd done their research thank you very much, and they *knew* that no one was doing anything like them at all.

Jade dialled the fashion desk number for *IT Girl* magazine next. Her heart was racing as she waited for the answer.

'Hello, *IT Girl*,' the cheery voice answered.

Jade calmed down a fraction as she read out the passage she'd written earlier on. She put on the most professional accent she could muster. 'Oh hi. I'm calling from a company called Vajazzle My Bikini. We sent a press release to yourselves . . .'

'All press releases are handled by Chelsea. One moment and I'll connect you,' the girl replied hastily as the phone beeped.

'Hello, Chelsea speaking. How can I help?' came the no-nonsense voice down the line.

Jade composed herself again and started speaking in a poised manner. 'Hi Chelsea. I'm calling from a company called Vajazzle My Bikini and we've just launched. We sent a press release to yourselves and were wondering if you've had time to look at it. We can send it again if not?'

'Oh yes, I remember. Vajazzle My Bikini . . . here it is, I've just found the email.'

Jade felt positive. Chelsea sounded excited, she was sure of it. Maybe she was about to tell her some good news. 'Great. Is this something *IT Girl* would be interested in covering?'

'It's a fab idea. I loved the bikini images you sent over, they look lovely. The only issue for us is we've just had a really similar company come up and we're doing an article about them. Maybe we'll be able to squeeze a mention of your website too? I can't promise anything, but . . .'

'Another website?' Jade cut her short, incredulous at what she'd just heard. Isn't that what the other woman said? 'What website? What's it called?'

Chelsea hesitated. 'Oh . . . one moment, I'll see if I can find it . . .' Jade could tell Chelsea knew she'd said the wrong thing. She was unaware that they had no idea there was another similar website. 'It's called Reem Bikinis?'

'Reem Bikinis?' Jade echoed, completely bewildered. That

was one of the options they'd written down when they were deciding what to name *their* website. She wondered if it was possible she'd sent the wrong name on the release? She double checked her sent items quickly and when she noticed she hadn't just felt even more confused.

'Yes, that's right. They do similar bikinis to what you do for pool parties. Did you not know about them?'

Jade felt the blood pulsating round her head. Know about them? There had to be some sort of mistake. 'Sorry, I'm a bit confused,' Jade said with a nervous laugh, noticing Kelly was now looking at her with a worried expression. 'You're telling me that there is another website, called Reem Bikinis, doing the exact same glamorous swimwear that we're doing?'

'Yes,' Chelsea replied abruptly, sounding bored. 'To be honest, I thought you were the same company at first, but then I noticed your images were slightly different. Anyway, thanks for your call. Maybe we'll do you a little mention if we can.'

Jade gulped despondently. 'Thanks.'

'Okay, bye!' Chelsea hung up.

Jade was galvanised by what she'd just heard. She turned to Kelly, who was waiting for the news and watching her closely.

'Oh my God, Kelly,' Jade shook her head morosely.

'What, babe? Did I hear you say there's another company?' Her eyes were wide open with fear.

'Yes, that's what she just said. There can't be though, can there?' Jade looked at Kelly disbelievingly. 'We checked any kind of competitors about a week ago, didn't we? There was no one doing anything like us.'

'Maybe she's over-exaggerating?' Kelly said hopefully, biting her lip. 'Maybe the website is nothing like ours but she just didn't want to write about it?'

'Well there's one way to find out.' Jade typed 'Reem

Bikinis' into Google and held her breath. It couldn't be the same, it just wasn't possible. It was too much of a coincidence that someone else had come up with the same idea and given their website a name that they had even considered! Kelly stood behind her as they waited for the page to load. When it did, they both gasped in unison.

'*Oh. My. Good. God!*' Kelly exhaled, closing her eyes and shaking her head, wanting to block out what she was seeing.

Jade couldn't believe her eyes. She was finding it hard to believe that after all their hard work, someone, somehow had the same idea! These people were creating and customising pool party swimwear. And not just any swimwear, but almost the exact same designs as their own! 'How is this possible?' Jade's face crumpled with anger and frustration. 'I don't understand.'

'Someone has got there before us, I can't believe it,' Kelly said, her voice cracking. She was obviously gutted.

Jade looked at the website and clicked on their categories. 'Wait. Look at this, Kelly!' She pointed to the screen in indignation. 'They've copied. I don't know how, but these people, these *thieves,* have copied us!'

Kelly read through their swimwear categories. 'Viva Las Vegas, Marbella Belles, No Carbs before Barbs . . .' She looked at Jade with a puzzled expression. 'No Carbs before Barbs? What the hell is Barbs?'

Jade opened her mouth to respond, then shut it quickly and looked back at the screen, not exactly knowing the answer. 'Ah-ha! It says here. Barbs is short for Barbados. It's a Caribbean section.'

Kelly inhaled sharply. 'They've copied us! They've just changed the words slightly! They were our categories! It's meant to be No Carbs before Marbs, not Barbs!'

Jade was just as appalled. 'I don't believe it. I just can't understand who would do this? And how the hell do they know about us?'

Kelly shook her head and narrowed her eyes angrily. 'I don't know, but they're pathetic, whoever they are. They're so jell of us and our ideas that they've copied them all. Losers!'

Jade chewed her nails disconsolately. 'We need to find out who it is. They're completely out of order.' She was devastated. Whoever it was had managed to get their website up and running before them, and now they were going to be advertised in magazines as though they were the first company to think of the idea! It was so wrong and unfair. She'd never felt so furious in all her life.

'Do they have a contact number?'

Jade searched the website and clicked on the 'contact us' page, disappointed when only an email address appeared. 'No, just an email. We can't very well send them a message saying "who are you, you bastards, you copied us", can we?'

'No, babe. We'll look well silly. We have to look as though we're not bothered. We have to make sure our website is better than theirs. To be honest, I think ours is already anyway.'

'Me too,' Jade agreed, trying to muster some positive thoughts. Her mobile vibrated, making her jump. It was a text message from Sam asking if she'd found her notebook yet. She texted back.

No, it's officially gone. Tony didn't have it. X

As she clicked the send button her heart began to gallop when she realised what had happened. The notebook. The missing notebook with all the information in was the reason for this other website. Someone had found it and copied them! 'Kelly, I've just thought. I lost my notebook and now someone else is doing the same thing. That's it! The person who has my notebook is the one that's copied! We even had other names we were going to consider calling our website and Reem Bikinis was in there!'

'Yes!' Kelly slapped her forehead, as though she should have known that all along. Then she winced because she'd done it harder than she meant to. 'But who? Who could possibly have found it? You must have dropped it in the street?'

Jade shook her head and then answered slowly. 'I have no idea. There is one thing I do know though,' she said seriously.

'What?'

'This means war.'

CHAPTER 9

Adele couldn't believe how well the press release had gone. So far she'd heard back from six magazines and two newspapers wanting to write a piece about her new website. It was even going to be featured in *The Sun* the next day; she couldn't believe it! She'd already had two orders and was on her way to the post office, which fortunately was down her road. They were slightly delayed being sent because the two customers had been bigger sizes than she had, so she'd had to quickly decorate them first. One wouldn't stop emailing about when it was going to arrive and she was driving her nuts. She hoped not every customer was like this annoying one. She wondered if Jade and Kelly knew about her website yet. She hoped so. They would be wondering what genius came up with the same idea. They wouldn't have to wait long to find out either; Essex Fashion Week was two days away and she couldn't wait. She had booked five models from top agencies and had even gone to meet them to check they weren't minging in real life, like Skye. They were perfect. Tall, slim and naturally beautiful.

She could see why Jade and Kelly didn't want to look after Cupcake. The dog had so much energy and was constantly chewing anything she could get her tiny paws on. Buddy didn't like her either, but she left them both in the kitchen together so they didn't disturb her. They were worse than children!

She was pleased when she heard her mobile ring and saw Donna's name flashing on the screen.

'Alright, hun?'

'Hi Adele. You alright? Just returning your call.'

'Yeah. It was about Saturday night actually. I've booked a table at Movida in the West End. It's going to be an amazing night, babe . . .'

Donna paused. 'Oh, I can't do Saturday, sorry. What about Friday or something?'

'What do you mean you can't do Saturday?' Adele asked, disappointed. If she had another ancient relative's birthday again, she could forget it.

'Aaron is taking me out for a meal. I've been out with him twice already! He's lovely. We get on so well. I can't describe it; it's like we were made for each other. It's official too; he's asked me to be his girlfriend. I know it's happened fast, but it just seems so right!'

Adele had forgotten she'd been on a few dates with him. Donna had told her Neil had wanted her to go too, but she couldn't think of anything worse! Sitting there with a complete goon while Donna played footsie with the footballer all night was not in any way, shape or form her idea of fun. Now Donna was turning down her offers because she'd met a bloke. It was ludicrous! Saying they were made for each other? The only person Donna was made for was someone like James Corden! The thought made her smirk. How could Aaron seriously want Donna for his girlfriend when he could have anyone? 'Tell him you can't go. See him another night or something. Don't you think you're rushing into this?'

'I can't. He's taking me somewhere nice and it's all

planned. You never mentioned Saturday before and I've said yes, already. What about Friday night? Or lunch Sunday?'

Adele was livid. Talk about use her when she was single and ditch her when she had a boyfriend! Why on earth would she want to go to lunch on Sunday with Donna? Who was she supposed to go out with now on Saturday night? Was this some sort of sick joke?

'Oh do as you please, Donna. But when it all goes wrong and he cheats on you, don't come crying to me,' Adele scolded bitterly. She knew she was going over the top but she couldn't believe the cheek of her. If it hadn't been for her booking the table and flirting with Neil, she never would have got chatting to Aaron in the first place. What did he see in Donna anyway? Adele was so envious she could almost taste it. He would be taking her to some amazing restaurant in London, most likely. Donna wouldn't have to pay for a thing. Life was so unfair! A thought came to her. Donna may be going out with Aaron for a meal, but that didn't mean she couldn't meet them both afterwards. She would have had her veneers done by then and she was going to make sure she dressed up to the nines to show Aaron what a mistake he'd made.

'Please don't be like that, Adele,' Donna begged unhappily.

'I just think you're being selfish. We *always* go out together on Saturday nights and now you're ditching me for a man.'

'I'm not, I swear. I can do any other night, I . . .'

'Just listen for a minute,' Adele interjected rudely. 'I'll meet you after your meal with that Neil thing and we can all go to a club together. How does that sound?'

'I can't,' Donna replied ruefully. 'He's taking me to The Fat Duck in Berkshire. We're staying over in a hotel and I won't be back until Sunday afternoon.'

Adele was so fuming her hands were shaking. She was being taken to The Fat Duck! That restaurant had three

Michelin stars and Adele was always begging her dad to take her there! This was just so typical! Adele had been so close to the perfect life and she had picked the wrong man. Now Donna was living the life *she* was supposed to have. This romance between them simply had to be stopped. She wasn't sure how just yet, but she was going to make sure Aaron realised what he was missing by being with Donna. When he knew Adele was interested in him, surely Donna would be dropped like a hot potato?

*

Two days later, Jade was backstage at Essex Fashion Week with Kelly, Lisa, Chloe and Chloe's friend, Chanel, who was also going to model. They'd decided they needed three in the end and Chanel was tall, slim with light brown hair, so they had the perfect mix. Kelly had already given them a spray tan the night before and they were seated, ready for her to do their make-up.

'I think big, bold, smoky eyes and nude lips. Maybe put a bit of glitter on too,' Jade suggested.

'Obviously I'm going to use glitter, silly,' Kelly said, as though it was absurd that Jade had asked. 'Don't worry, babe, these girls are going to look beauts. I'm using two sets of fake lashes on each. Their eyes are going to look unreal.'

Jade smiled, trusting Kelly implicitly. She also did a great job where beauty was concerned. Over the top, but today it would be perfect.

'I'm so nervous,' Chloe admitted timidly.

'Me too.' Lisa held her hand out. 'I'm nearly shaking.'

'Girls, you'll look so gorge you'll want to get out there and show off. Keep calm and be reem,' Kelly grinned, holding Lisa's hand and wiping over her nail varnish. She looked baffled as she rubbed Lisa's nails over and over with a cotton pad, the pink nail varnish not budging. 'Babe, what nail varnish have you got on? It's not coming off?'

'It's just normal Barry M nail varnish,' Lisa shrugged, equally as puzzled.

Jade giggled as she noticed what Kelly was trying to remove it with. 'Maybe it's not coming off because you're using make-up remover?'

Kelly laughed gaily. 'So I am, maybe the nerves are getting to me too!'

A lady came over to them dressed in black with a clipboard and walkie-talkie.

'Hi girls. Just checking you know when you're going on stage?'

'No,' Jade replied. 'We've haven't spoken to anyone yet.'

'Okay, no worries.' She looked at the bikinis set out, ready for the catwalk. 'Oh! You must be Reem Bikinis. I read about you in the newspaper the other day and couldn't wait to see them in real life. Wow, they're lovely!'

'*What*?' Kelly dropped her lip gloss in astonishment. 'Reem Bikinis, did you say? They're here too? At Essex Fashion Week?'

Jade felt just as angry and turned to the woman. 'We're actually called Vajazzle My Bikini,' she told her sternly.

The lady looked abashed. 'Oh sorry, my mistake. I must have got you muddled up with someone else, never mind. Here you are,' she ticked them off her list. 'You're going on eighth.'

'Is that before or after Reem Bikinis?' Jade enquired.

The lady eyed her clipboard. 'After.'

'Well is there no way we can go on before?' Kelly whined.

'Afraid not. All the programmes for the catwalk show have gone out. They're being sold now and we can't change it. They requested they were first on. To be honest, I think they even paid extra.'

Jade was exasperated. If Reem Bikinis went on first,

everyone would find their bikinis boring because they were almost identical! They'd paid a lot of money to be there and put a lot of hard work into their business. She knew there was always going to be competition, that was business, but for someone else to be stealing their ideas and ruining things for them just wasn't on. 'Who owns Reem Bikinis? I want to speak to them now.'

The lady looked concerned, seeing how infuriated Jade appeared. 'I'm not too sure of her name I'm afraid.' She looked around. 'I can't see her at present, but she's around here somewhere. Anyway, you're on eighth. Someone will come round nearer the time to get you prepared. Good luck.'

'I can't believe this,' Jade exhaled. 'It's not enough that they need to copy our website and launch theirs first, but now they've even followed us here and have made sure that they're going on before us! I can't wait to see who it is and give them a piece of my mind.'

'I know, babe. It's seriously starting to piss me off now,' Kelly said as she applied blusher to Lisa's cheeks. 'Let's just concentrate on our bikinis and models and forget about them. Let's forget they even exist!'

Jade knew Kelly was saying the right thing, but it didn't help the horrible, sick feeling she had inside. How could she not let this affect her? She'd been in such high spirits a few minutes ago, but now she felt as though the rug had been pulled from under her feet. She inhaled slowly, trying to calm herself down. *Just focus on what matters*, she told herself. An hour later, Lisa, Chloe and Chanel were good to go. Their eyelashes were fluttering, hair big, bouncy and perfect and heels gigantic, making them all four inches taller. Every company had two changes and the final bikini was their favourite one; the Essex Showgirl, which Chloe was going to wear. She knew that one was going to be a big hit and couldn't wait to watch the audience's reaction. She hadn't managed to find the owner of Reem Bikinis yet, as they hadn't been around when their models were going out. She had seen a couple of sequins and beads fall off when the models had walked out and had laughed with Kelly childishly. Up close, they definitely weren't as nice as their bikinis. The patterns weren't even and the beads had been sewn on all wrong, often patchy where the creator was clearly lazy and couldn't be bothered to spend too much time and attention on them. They were pretty shabby really, though the models looked great in them; they would look amazing in anything though, she noticed.

'Vajazzle My Bikini?' The lady in black was back.

Jade nodded, feeling nervous suddenly.

'Models ready please. You're up next.'

Lisa walked to the entrance. 'There are so many people out there. I'm scared! Look how high the stage is! I'm scared of heights as well!'

Kelly wrinkled her nose as she looked. 'It's not *that* high.'

'It is!' Lisa protested. 'Aren't you scared of heights?'

Kelly shrugged. 'Babe, have you seen the size of my heels? Of course not.'

'You'll be fine,' Jade said, rubbing Lisa's shoulder affectionately. 'Just walk straight, go to the end and pose for a few seconds. Good luck.' She watched through a gap as Lisa strutted down the catwalk like a pro. She looked like a Mediterranean goddess with her shiny, long dark hair swishing and her olive skin shining. Next was Chloe, and she too looked fantastic, Jade thought happily.

'God, I'm jell of her figure,' Kelly said as she gazed at Chloe walking back towards them.

Chanel came off the catwalk and sighed. 'Oh my God, I loved it! Can't wait to wear the next one!'

Jade was pleased. She'd watched the cameras flashing when the girls had walked down the catwalk and she'd been able to lip-read several people in the crowd saying they liked them. Maybe it didn't matter about Reem Bikinis after all?

*

Adele was overjoyed. Her models were the tallest and slimmest around. She kept well out of Jade and Kelly's way today, sneaking off to the audience throughout the show, so they still had no idea she owned Reem Bikinis yet. She was so happy she'd had the wise idea to make sure her bikinis had gone on first. She'd paid extra, but it was worth every penny. Everyone loved them. She made sure she was listening to people in the audience and all she could hear were gasps about how one girl had to have the purple one for Vegas, or that another needed to buy some for her swimwear photo shoots. She felt proud that she'd actually created something people were talking about. She'd never felt this way before in all her life. It didn't matter how good she felt though, she still had an annoying niggling reminder that none of this was actually *her* idea. Still, she was the one that had made the swimwear. She was the one that had sat up all day and night sewing sequins.

She sorted through the next lot of bikinis quickly, to give to the models for their second change. As they were heading back towards her, to her horror she pulled a thread of beads by accident on one of the bikinis and the whole row came tumbling off, hitting the floor and making tiny tinkling sounds.

'Shit!' she murmured under her breath, not wanting anyone to see. The panic was rising inside her; she had ruined her final one! It was the best bikini that she was saving until last. The one she envisaged being her best seller. Now what was she going to do?

'What are we wearing next?' one model asked her, removing her top in a split second to reveal perfect, pert breasts with no shame whatsoever.

157

Adele handed each of them a bikini and told her favourite model to wait one moment. She had an idea.

'But we need to go on soon!' the model protested.

'Just wait a moment,' Adele retorted tersely. 'It's my company and you'll go on when I say, got it? I won't be long.'

The model stood there agog as Adele darted in and out of the sea of people backstage. Then Adele saw exactly what she wanted; the Essex Showgirl bikini. The best part was that it was unattended. Jade, Kelly and the others were discussing something by the stage and not even looking, the fools! This was the only one Adele hadn't copied. The pattern was too difficult and she didn't have the patience. Not only that, but they'd also run out of the embellishments the girls had used. No doubt they'd bought them all, she thought, grabbing the bikini and running back. It was gorgeous and now it was hers. She looked at the label sewn inside with VMB printed in silver letters and took a pair of scissors from her bag. Two snips later and the label was gone.

'Here you are,' she sang to the anxious model. 'You're on last please.'

'Thanks. Wow, this one's my favourite! Talk about save the best until last!' She looked pleased as she slipped it on.

'Thanks,' Adele replied tightly. She then hurried back to the front of the stage where her seat was to watch.

*

Jade walked back to the bikinis to get the next three ready.

'Right Lisa, you're wearing this one from the Ibiza category.' She handed her a leopard print monokini with lace trim. 'Chanel, this one is for you,' she said passing over a turquoise and gold two-piece, 'and Chloe, you're wearing the Essex Showgirl one . . .' Jade frowned when she realised it wasn't where she left it. 'Kelly, have you seen the Essex Showgirl?'

Kelly was concentrating as she reapplied Lisa's lip gloss. 'No, babe. It was on the table, wasn't it?'

'It's not here!' Jade began to panic. 'It's gone.'

Kelly stopped what she was doing. 'It can't be gone; it was there just a minute ago. I saw it. There was no mistaking the electronic blue colour.'

'Electronic blue?' Lisa tried not to giggle, knowing this was a serious matter. 'You mean electric blue, hun,' she said kindly to Kelly who nodded. 'You're right though, I saw it too; it was right there,' Lisa agreed, pointing to the table.

'What colour is electric blue?' Chanel asked in wonderment looking at the ceiling.

'It's bright blue,' Jade replied quickly. 'Can everyone help look for it please?' Jade looked under the table and in places she just knew it wasn't going to be. It was worth a shot though. They needed that bikini!

'Is it like that colour?' Chanel pointed to a tall brunette model about to walk onto the catwalk.

They all stood with rapt attention, watching the girl about to go on stage.

'Oh my God!' Jade shouted. 'That's it! Stop that girl!'

'Oh my God!' Kelly echoed as they ran over to the entrance of the catwalk.

Jade was so close to grabbing the girl back, that she even felt the silkiness of the material. It was too late though; the girl had gone. It was a nightmare. Their favourite bikini they had spent hours designing had been snatched, and all the credit would go to Reem Bikinis.

'How could it have been taken?' Lisa asked, stumped. Jade saw the concerned look in her eyes and could tell she felt sorry for them.

'I didn't see anyone,' Chanel said shaking her head.

Jade glanced at Chloe, who looked uncomfortable. She

obviously felt bad for them too; she couldn't even look her in the eye. 'Chloe?'

Chloe was so disconcerted she jumped.

'Are you okay?' Jade continued, staring at Chloe.

'Yes, I'm fine,' Chloe said hastily. 'Just wondered what on earth happened, that's all.'

'It's so obvious,' Kelly said, her voice getting louder the more she got worked up. 'Reem Bikinis stole it, just like they stole our website. If only we knew who owned it we could give them a piece of our mind! Right now, I'd have so much to say! If only we knew whose it was.'

'It's mine.' The voice was powerful and striking, like the sudden sound of thunder.

Everyone turned and Jade knew who it was instantly; perhaps she'd known all along? It was Adele.

'I should have guessed it was you,' Jade responded with a poisonous glare. Lisa ushered Chloe and Chanel away so they could chat in private.

Kelly couldn't hide her exasperation. 'It's you! Why did you steal our website, Adele? Then not only that, but our bikini as well? What's wrong with you?'

'Girls, girls,' Adele said superciliously waving a hand as if to shut them up. 'Let's not run away with the fairies. I didn't steal anyone's ideas. I have absolutely no idea what you're talking about. Come on, this is all just silly nonsense.'

'Where did you get my notebook? That's what I want to know,' Jade accused.

'What notebook?' Adele looked as though she had no idea what she was talking about. Jade began to doubt Adele had it, but then remembered she had practically copied all their designs. They were all on her website. The only way to know their designs was to look through the notebook. There was no other explanation. 'Look girls, let's be mature about this,' Adele retorted robustly, folding her arms. 'We're mature enough to have a civil conversation, aren't we?

160

We're businesswomen after all. I'm sorry if you've got the wrong impression, but I haven't copied you. Yes, I knew you decorated the odd little bikini in Marbs, but I didn't have any idea that you were starting your own business up. How would I? I'll admit, I thought the idea of customising swimwear and designing it properly was a good one, which is why I've started Reem Bikinis. But copy you two? I wouldn't dream of it.' Adele creased her forehead disparagingly.

'You stole our bikini for the show. How do you explain that?' Kelly eyed her disdainfully.

'Oh that! Oh you're not annoyed about that, are you? Girls, come on, there are like a million garments flying around backstage. It's hard to keep up! Our bikinis are similar and I apologise, I wasn't backstage to supervise my models. One of them picked up your one by mistake. It's an easy error to make. You can have it back of course.'

'Thanks,' Jade replied sarcastically. She couldn't believe the cheek of her! She was acting like she was doing *them* a favour by giving them their own bikini back.

'Listen. It just so happens that we've all come up with the same idea. I launched my website a few weeks ago. What about you two?'

Jade and Kelly looked at each other, both thinking the same thing. She had launched her website before they had. How could she have possibly had her website built so fast? If she did somehow have the notebook, she couldn't have had it for very long. It didn't make any sense. 'We've just launched,' Jade finally said.

'Oh, so that means mine was running before yours? So I could say, if you think about it, that *you* copied me?' She gave an irritating, pathetic little laugh.

'Look Adele. We can't stop you from starting your own business. But, we just think it makes no sense to copy our designs when you can think of your own.'

'I don't copy . . .'

Jade cut her short. 'In fact, it makes no difference to us what you do, not really. Copy all you like. It's quite flattering actually.'

Adele smiled tightly, her voice like steel. 'I don't need to copy. I have my own ideas. Thank you all the same though, Jade.'

'Well, if you don't mind giving our bikini back, we'll be going,' Kelly asserted stonily. It was strange to see Kelly in this mood. She never hated anyone and was always so warm and kind. That's the effect Adele has on people, Jade reminded herself.

'Of course.' Adele gave a fake smile as she turned. A minute later she was passing the bikini back to them. 'How are you two anyway?' Adele's tone was friendlier all of a sudden.

Jade rolled her eyes at Kelly. Did she really think they wanted to chat with her? Was she insane? 'Yes Adele, we're good. Very busy though, so we must dash . . .'

'Sam's looking well recently, isn't he?' Adele gave her a look that made Jade shudder.

Jade folded her arms across her chest defensively. 'How would you know? You haven't seen him since Marbella.'

Adele's eyes sparkled mischievously. 'Did he not tell you about when we bumped into each other? Oh dear. And there was me thinking you two were close. I thought you were all loved up and told each other everything?'

Jade felt sick. What was she getting at? Why hadn't Sam mentioned anything to her? She decided to lie so she didn't lose face. 'Oh, come to think of it. I do remember him mentioning something about it.'

'Oh really?' Adele questioned. 'That's surprising actually, because I'm pretty certain that night he told me how you had no time for him. Kept blowing him out and letting him down I think he said? I got the impression you two may have been going through a bit of a bad patch.'

Jade felt her blood run cold. He said *what*? She felt nauseous as she realised it must be true; how would Adele know otherwise? Why would Sam tell Adele something so personal about them? He hated her! She'd tried to keep them apart! She hesitated, not finding the right words to say. 'Well . . . yes . . . I mean, no. It was a little issue, but it's resolved now. We're fine. We're perfect in fact.'

Adele smiled imperiously. 'Well, that's just great news then.'

There was something about that smile, which Jade couldn't look at. Something that told her Adele was hiding something; that she had a secret. 'Anyway, we need to get going,' Jade said. 'Bye Adele.' Kelly followed her as they walked.

'Bye girls.'

'I just can't believe that girl copying our website and stealing from us yet again! What is wrong with her?' Kelly fumed as they marched towards the others.

'I honestly don't know,' Jade shrugged, her mind elsewhere.

'She's just so irritating! I wonder how she got all our ideas? It's like she's obsessed with us and what we're doing! She was exactly the same in Marbella.' Kelly glanced at Jade and noticed the disturbed expression etched on her face. She paused. 'Did Sam really tell you he'd bumped into Adele?' Kelly knew Jade better than anyone. She had clearly known Jade had made it up.

'No.'

Jade didn't know what else to say. The question was on both their lips: Why?

CHAPTER 10

The following day, Jade pulled up outside Sam's flat anxiously. He was making chicken fajitas, her favourite dinner – and the only thing he knew how to cook. She didn't mind though, she much preferred to do the cooking herself normally. Jade wasn't exactly Delia Smith, but she did like to experiment and work from cook books. She found cooking a great way to escape sometimes when she was stressed and she had to admit, she made the best seafood risotto in the world.

Jade exhaled loudly as she thought about what she needed to say. She was going to ask him why he hadn't mentioned he'd run into Adele that night in Sugar Hut and why on earth he'd told her their issues. It was so unlike him to talk about problems, especially to Adele, of all people. Something was definitely not right and she was determined to get to the bottom of it. The thought of Sam confiding in his psycho ex-girlfriend hurt like hell.

'Hi,' he said, kissing her lips softly as he opened the door.

'Hi.' She walked into his flat, which was spotless as usual. If they ever moved in together she definitely wouldn't be moaning at him to keep the place tidy; it would be the other way round by the looks of things. Sam had changed

164

out of his work clothes into casual jogging bottoms and a white t-shirt. Even dressed down, he was still painfully handsome. His tanned skin was emphasised by the white top, his fair hair was messy and sexy, without any gel and his piercing green eyes were the most striking eyes she'd ever seen. He was so masculine and tall and just by holding her, he made her feel protected and safe. Jade still couldn't believe he was her boyfriend.

'Dinner is nearly ready.' He seemed proud that he'd cooked it all on his own as usually she helped him at some point. 'Take a seat and just relax. Drink?'

'Just juice if you have some.'

Sam poured her a glass of orange juice and handed it to her, before going back to stir the chicken, onions and peppers, which smelt divine.

'So how did the fashion show go yesterday?' Sam asked as he spooned the guacamole dip into a small dish.

Jade sat down at his modern glass dining table. 'It went well. We handed out lots of leaflets to people and then it was the fashion show. There was a good response and loads of girls commented that they loved the swimwear. We've had quite a few orders already.'

Sam nodded. 'That's great. My mum was saying how Chloe loved it when she called me today. I still hate the idea of her prancing around in swimwear though.'

'Come on, lighten up; there were loads of girls in swimwear there. Your sister is stunning,' she said honestly, sipping her juice. 'She could easily model as a career. She has the height too.'

'Mmm,' Sam looked uncertain. 'I'm never going to like the idea of it to be honest. Maybe I'm just being over-protective.'

Jade always thought it was so sweet how Sam looked out for Chloe. Her own older brother, Simon, had always been the same with her growing up and she knew it was only because he cared. There was a much bigger ten-year age gap between them though and Simon never had to worry about his friends eyeing her up when he turned his back. The same definitely couldn't be said about Sam's friends, who often joked about Chloe to wind Sam up.

Sam brought her plate over and her stomach rumbled. She waited for him to sit opposite and then wondered when the right time was to bring up Adele. She felt slightly sick. What was he going to say? She was terrified to find out the answer, but knew she had to. There was no way she could leave it as it was. Besides, she trusted Sam. He wouldn't do anything behind her back. The only thing she could think of was that perhaps he didn't bring Adele up because he knew how much Jade hated her. Adele *had* tried to keep them apart in Marbella so perhaps he didn't want to bring her up in conversation, which was understandable. But the thing she couldn't work out was, why, when she'd told him the day after she'd bumped into Adele, did he not mention what a coincidence it was that he had too? That was his perfect chance to say it. It was the fact he had remained silent about it that was making her panic. Sam had had the perfect opportunity, yet he hadn't mentioned anything.

'Our final bikini was stolen at the end of the show,' Jade said trying to appear nonchalant, as she rolled her tortilla wrap. 'Did Chloe tell your mum that?'

'No, she didn't actually.' Sam took a bite of his fajita, his face wrinkling into a frown. 'What was that all about? Why would someone steal it?'

'Well, do you remember me telling you about the other website? The one that has clearly copied us?'

Sam dipped his wrap in some salsa. 'Yes.'

'Well, we now know who it is. She also stole our bikini and used it as one from her own collection for the show.'

'And who is it?' Sam asked bewildered.

Jade studied his expression as she said her name. 'Adele.'

Sam's eyes opened slightly wider in shock. If she hadn't been watching his reaction so closely, she could easily have missed it. Adele's name had made him look uneasy and he shifted in his chair uncomfortably.

'Oh. That's odd. What a bitch.' His face reddened and he stood up and got a glass of water.

He's terrible at trying to hide anything, Jade noted nervously. Sam was, without a doubt, acting very peculiar. She had to continue, even though she hated every second of it.

'We accused her at the end of the show of copying us and she denied it of course. She said she had just happened to come up with the idea.'

Sam sat back down and took another bite of food, fiddling with the sour cream dip on the table. 'Maybe she did?'

Jade stared at him. 'I told you before; all the bikinis are almost identical. There is no way that's possible. Somehow she must have got hold of my red notebook.'

Sam's eyes flickered with alarm. 'You're just being paranoid. There is no way she found your notebook. How could she have?'

'When was the last time you saw her?' Jade questioned casually. She begged him not to lie to her. Her heart was thumping hard against her chest.

Sam's face twitched awkwardly. 'Who? Adele?' Sam looked up at the ceiling as if trying to remember. 'God knows.'

Jade glared at him and put her wrap down. 'That's funny. She told me at the show that she saw you in Sugar Hut the other week? The night we were supposed to go out to dinner, remember?'

Sam couldn't look her in the eye. Jade hadn't intended this to be an argument, but Sam's shifty movements were starting to freak her out and now he was pretending he didn't know the last time he had seen Adele. She could feel herself becoming more irritated and angry with him.

'Oh, yes!' Sam said, as if just remembering. 'That's right. I did see her quickly that night.'

'Did you say much to her?' Jade demanded.

His eyes opened wide. 'Not really. Why are you asking me this?'

Jade could tell he knew something was up. Sam looked nervous.

'I may have said a couple of things, I don't really remember all that clearly. She stuck up for Chloe in the toilets when a group of girls started on her, which was nice,' Sam continued after a pause.

Nice? Jade thought furiously. So now Adele was *nice* in his eyes?

'You told her things weren't going that well between us because I was busy with work. Do you remember that?' Jade retorted tartly, as she pierced a pepper with her fork.

'Who told you that? Adele?' Sam looked slightly worried.

'Yes. I want to know a) why you never mentioned you saw her, especially when I told you I'd bumped into her, and b) why you were telling *her*, of all people, about our relationship? Funnily enough, she's the last person I want to know my business. She's a complete troublemaker. I thought you felt that way too, but clearly not.'

Sam looked shaken. 'I do think that! I'm sorry if I mentioned anything to her; I'd had a few shots and can't really recall every word I said. I was upset; she just happened to be there. I only went to say thanks for helping Chloe out and she started asking me about us.'

Jade was fuming. 'So why didn't you just tell me this a moment ago when I asked you? Why did you never mention you'd seen her?'

Sam kneaded his eyes with his fists. 'Because I knew how much you hated her. I thought you'd be paranoid about it. I'm sorry. I just didn't want to talk about Adele with you. Can we just move on from this please?'

Jade felt sick and pushed her plate away. So, he *had* lied. He was willing to not tell her things if it meant getting him in trouble. All she ever wanted was honesty and she really thought that with Sam, that was exactly what she got. It was a horrible shock knowing that he was capable of keeping things from her. Important things.

'I just don't understand why you haven't told me this before? You've just sat there and lied to my face saying you didn't remember the last time you bumped into her. Do you not realise that by not telling me and then me hearing from Adele how bad that looks? It looks like you're keeping it from me for a reason.'

Sam put his head in his hands as though he couldn't deal with the conversation any longer. 'For God's sake,' he looked up at her. 'I didn't want to tell you something that is so *unimportant*. I've apologised. I'm not hiding anything. Can we *please* talk about something else now? I'm not saying another word about it. You're being ridiculous. Sorry I spoke about us to her. I won't do it again. There is nothing more I can say.'

Jade felt completely let down. He was shutting himself off from her and not allowing her to ask all the things she wanted. She knew that wasn't the end of it; she had a gut instinct because of the way he was acting. She saw the panic in his eyes when she mentioned Adele's name and she wasn't going to be forgetting about that anytime soon. She didn't and would never trust Adele. Wherever she went and whenever she was involved there was trouble. She was a selfish, manipulative individual, who only ever thought about herself. She was the type of girl that hated it when others were happy or successful. Jade fully expected her to stir up trouble, but Sam was involved in this case and there was something he wasn't telling her. She left the rest of her fajita, not being able to eat another mouthful.

'Do you want to watch a film or something?' Sam said

easily, clearly relieved they'd no longer be talking about Adele.

Jade wasn't in the mood to be in his company any longer. She'd really had high hopes for Sam and genuinely thought if they ever had issues they could talk about them and resolve them. She needed to leave, because all she could think about was the fact he was keeping something from her. 'To be honest, Sam, I'm tired. I know I've not been here long, but I want an early night tonight and I'm going to head back I think.'

'You can stay here if you like?' Sam looked crestfallen.

'No, I need to do a bit of work so it's best I go back.' Jade knew her foul mood wasn't going to budge tonight.

Sam took a deep breath and ran his hands through his hair. 'And this isn't because of the conversation we just had?'

Jade lied and shook her head. 'No.'

Sam nodded, believing she was just tired. How can he believe that? Jade questioned tetchily. Of course she was leaving because of the conversation! Why were men so stupid? They would believe anything for an easy life and to prevent confrontation. It was obvious she was upset. How could he not see that? How many other nights had she simply eaten her dinner and then gone home? She picked her plate up and emptied the leftovers in the bin.

'Leave all that, I'll do it,' Sam said, taking the plate out of her hands.

'Okay. Well, thanks for dinner.'

'Come here,' Sam said opening his arms, which she fell into reluctantly. What was the point in getting close to him when she knew he wasn't being completely honest? How could their relationship last? The thought saddened her immensely.

'I'd better go.' Jade headed towards his front door and he followed behind.

'Okay. Drive safely.' Sam pulled her back one last time and kissed her.

'Thanks for dinner. Bye Sam.'

Jade sighed as she sat in her car with a heavy heart.

*

Sam tidied his kitchen and watched Jade's car pull away from the window by the sink. Tonight had shaken him up, that was for sure. He couldn't believe Adele had copied Jade's website and then blabbed that he'd seen her and moaned about his relationship! What a complete cow! He felt sick with nerves. What on earth was he going to do? He'd got himself into a huge mess and if he managed to get out of it with Jade still by his side it would be a miracle. He didn't realise he'd even told Adele that Jade was working and neglecting him. What an idiot he was. If only he could go back to that night and change everything! Their relationship had been pretty much perfect until then. Yes, Jade had other priorities and he'd felt let down, but they'd got over that in no time and now he saw her as much as he wanted to. He loved Jade. *Really* loved her. He didn't even want to imagine how hurt she'd be if she knew what Adele was claiming had happened. It didn't bear thinking about.

When Jade had mentioned the red notebook, he knew instantly what had happened. She *had* left it in his room and Adele had clearly found it and stolen it. If Jade put two and two together he was in deep shit. If only that night wasn't a complete blur and he knew for sure he was innocent! Then he wouldn't keep acting so guilty. He knew he was a terrible liar. He blushed and couldn't look the person in the eye and made it so blatantly obvious that he might as well just own up. He didn't have the guts to tell Jade the truth though. How could he? He was so happy with her; he didn't want to lose her. It would break his heart as much as hers. He couldn't carry on lying though when she asked him questions. He was certain that wasn't going to be the end of it. He probably wouldn't sleep well tonight as he was terrified that Adele was going to open her big trap yet again and tell Jade she'd slept with him. He needed to warn her not to, he decided, getting his mobile and starting a new message.

Adele, stop stirring to Jade and causing trouble. I'd appreciate it if you kept quiet about that night in Sugar Hut. I know you took her notebook as well. That's low. I hope you're proud of yourself.

He didn't expect her to reply, seeing as she'd ignored his last message telling her to leave Chloe alone, and deep down he knew Adele was probably enjoying seeing him sweat. He switched the TV on in his room, but couldn't concentrate. He was serious about Jade. He wanted to be with her forever. Maybe the best thing would be to just come clean? If she didn't want to know him it was his own fault, but at least it meant she'd hear it from him instead of Adele. He would just beg her to forgive him forever until she took him back. He never thought he'd be in this situation. He hated lying and cheating and never agreed with any of his friends when they lied about where they were to their girlfriends and made him cover for them.

The worst thing about the whole sorry situation was that he didn't even know what had gone on that night. Say Adele was just making the whole thing up? He wouldn't put it past her. The image of her pink thong flashed through his head and he cringed. If nothing had gone on, why did he have her underwear in his bed?

*

Adele was in a great mood. She'd had a deep mahogany spray tan, her hair extensions redone and blow dried to perfection, fake eyelashes reapplied, but best of all, a stunning set of pearly white veneers, which she'd had done in Harley Street. She couldn't stop looking at herself in the mirror. She hadn't looked so amazing in ages! Getting veneers was one of the best ideas she'd ever had. The fact she smoked meant her normal teeth were never as white as she wanted, despite the fact she had them whitened on a regular basis. Her veneers were perfect and she couldn't believe she hadn't got them sooner. Her smile could have been on a toothpaste advert she thought ecstatically, as she grinned at herself in the mirror yet again. Of course, it had cost her dad fifteen grand, but seeing the smile on her face had been worth it, she told herself. She was his daughter after all and obviously he wanted to see her happy. It wasn't as if he couldn't afford it anyway; it was a tiny amount to him.

She thought back to the text message she'd received from Sam a few days ago telling her to keep her mouth shut. He was clearly worried and so he should be. She'd ignored it completely, hoping that would make him panic even more. It was his own fault he'd been drunk and careless that night and if she wanted to tell people about it, then that was up to her. Calling her low because she stole the notebook! They had no proof it was her, so they could all go to hell as far as she was concerned. It had been difficult to conceal her delight when she told Jade she'd seen him in Sugar Hut that night. Jade always spoke to her like dirt and treated her like a nuisance or bad smell lingering around. She'd soon shut her up, informing her that her precious boyfriend had moaned about their perfect relationship. The look on Jade and Kelly's face had been priceless. Jade clearly didn't know Sam as well as she thought, did she?

Her phone started ringing and she answered, seeing Donna's name flashing.

'Hi Donna. You okay, babe?'

'Yeah, I'm good. Just wondered what you were up to tonight?'

Adele wondered if it was because Aaron had dumped her already and she needed a shoulder to cry on. 'Why, what's Aaron up to? How was The Fat Duck?'

'Oh Adele, I can't explain just how happy I am. I've completely fallen for him. The Fat Duck was fantastic and he took me to this lovely hotel called The Coworth Park afterwards and bought me a necklace. He certainly knows how to treat a girl.'

'That's probably because he's had so many,' Adele retorted bitterly. She could feel the anger rise inside her. A necklace? She couldn't even bring herself to comment or ask her where the necklace was from. She didn't want to know the answer.

'Don't say that.' Donna sounded wounded. 'He's only had one girlfriend before me.'

Adele didn't want to upset her; not when she needed her to go out with. 'It was only a joke, Donna, lighten up. So what's up? Did you want to meet up?'

'Yeah. I just felt bad about last Saturday and thought if you were free we could meet tonight instead? The King William?'

'Yes, sounds great,' Adele replied, happy she had somewhere to go out seeing as she looked so good. 'Bring Aaron and one of his friends or something.'

'Really? I thought you would have wanted it to be just the two of us?'

Adele gave a little laugh. 'No, it's fine. I'm sure you want to see him, don't you? Besides, it's good for him to get to know your friends. Tell him to bring one too.'

'Who shall I get him to bring? Neil?'

'Whoever,' Adele replied casually. 'It's fine. I'm really pleased for you and Aaron. Let's meet at The King Will at eight.'

'See you there,' Donna sang happily.

Adele changed into the Victoria's Secret lingerie and admired herself in the full-length mirror. Her cosmetically enhanced cleavage was now her second favourite body part, after her teeth. She had a nice curvy size ten figure that any man would be happy to have wrapped around them. There was only one man she had her eye on at the moment though, and that was Aaron. Now there was a man that knew where to take his girlfriend! She'd never forget the moment Donna declared he was taking her to Cipriani restaurant in the West End for their first date. That was one of her favourite restaurants, where tons of celebrities were spotted! Then he'd splashed out on The Fat Duck and Coworth Park Hotel and who knew where else. Donna was so lucky and she didn't deserve it. Yes, she had a pretty face, but she was *huge* compared to Adele. Why did Aaron like her? She slipped on the new Balmain jeans she'd recently purchased online, with a cream Phillip Lim top which showed her tan off. Tonight, Aaron was going to notice *her*. He was going to see her sitting next to frumpy Donna and wonder what on earth he was doing. Adele was certain of it.

She sighed as she saw four bikinis sitting there that needed to be sewn and finished. She'd had lots of orders to keep her busy since Essex Fashion Week and hadn't got round to some of them because if she was honest, she couldn't be bothered to make them all. It was tiring and she'd had other things on her mind, such as getting her teeth done. Two of the customers had been emailing constantly asking when they would be receiving them, but she'd just fobbed them off, explaining they were on their way. Then there were the irritating customers that just constantly called up and wanted her opinion on every single bikini and whether it would suit them or not. Did they really think she had nothing better to do than sit talking about whether lavender would suit their skin tone or sequins would be too over the top for a family holiday? They needed to get a life and sometimes she just ignored her flashing mobile, not having the energy to be helpful and nice to boring women droning on. At first she had just wanted the website to be email only, but there was no way she was losing customers to Jade and Kelly, just because they had a phone number to call and she didn't. Not letting them get her down tonight, Adele brushed the thought of the unfinished bikinis to the back of her mind, promising herself she'd do them tomorrow. Nothing was going to put her in a bad mood. Even the sun was still shining, making her excited for summer and holidays ahead. If her plan worked, maybe Aaron could whisk her off to the Maldives or Hawaii? Just imagine the type of room he'd be able to afford! Donna wouldn't appreciate it as much as she would; she didn't care as much about money and wealth. Adele was accustomed to the finer things in life and she wanted that fact to remain. She couldn't live off her dad forever and she needed a man who could keep up with her demands. A lovely big Essex home was a must-have, as were designer clothes, bags and shoes. Men who made lots of money were so much more attractive to her and always had been. In her eyes it wasn't acceptable to date someone just barely scraping by; it would be far too embarrassing and she'd hate to not be able to afford her weekly blow dry and spray tan. Cutting back wasn't an option. Her mum, Janice, had always told her to marry a rich man; no one knew better than she did just how important it was. Her mum had come from nothing, brought up in a tiny council house in Dagenham with six brothers and sisters. Apparently, at one point, her mum and two sisters had shared a single bed in one room and her three brothers a single bed in the other. They were box rooms too, she was often told, and there wasn't enough room to swing a cat in either of them. Then her mum had met her dad at school and luckily he'd been successful, earning decent money from the age of eighteen when he started his own property development business. Now her mum had a six-bedroom house in Chigwell, three holiday homes abroad, a private yacht and top of the range sports cars. That wasn't including the fact she was often draped in huge diamonds, had her own personal trainer and cosmetic surgery as and when she wanted it. It was often she wanted it as well, Adele thought wryly, remembering the state of her beloved mum after her latest facelift. It had been horrifying and like something out of a horror movie. She hadn't stayed with her mum for long because the sight of her with bright red, bloodshot eyes and bruised cheeks had made her want to vomit; she'd simply made her excuses and left, waiting a few weeks before she'd gone back to visit.

Her phone rang and without looking at the caller ID, Adele answered it.

'Hello?'

'Oh hi there,' the high-pitched woman's voice came down the phone. 'Is this Reem Bikinis?'

Adele huffed in annoyance and rolled her eyes. 'Yes. How can I help?'

'I was just wondering when you're getting new stock in . . .'

Fifteen minutes later, Adele finally hung up, relieved the boring phone call was over. That was the third time that week she'd been asked about new bikinis coming out. It must be because there weren't that many to choose from at present, she realised, thinking of her selection. She needed new ideas and fast, but she'd racked her brains, and being creative wasn't exactly one of her strong points. She wondered what other designs Jade and Kelly had come up with. There was one way she could find out she decided, and dialled Chloe's number.

'Hi Adele,' Chloe answered in her usual jolly voice.

'Hi, hun. How are you?'

'I'm really good thanks. I've been meaning to tell you that I . . .'

'Listen,' Adele interjected, not wanting to listen to what she assumed was frivolous rubbish Chloe was going to tell her. 'I need to know what new designs Jade and Kelly are coming up with. You need to find out for me soon. I don't know how you're going to do it. Maybe just go over there and ask them. They'll tell you and then you can tell me.'

'Well, they may not tell me,' Chloe replied feebly.

'Of course they'll tell you! They have no reason not to! Just grow up and do it, okay? You owe me, remember?'

'I'll try,' Chloe said dubiously.

'Thank you. Of course they'll tell you,' Adele softened now that Chloe was cooperating. 'You're their model and they trust you. I can't believe they don't even pay you to do it, to be honest. Then again, I suppose seeing as you're not going to be a *real* model, it's a bit of fun for you.' Adele couldn't resist the little dig.

'But Adele, that's what I was trying to tell you! The modelling agency want me! They've taken me on as a model. I have a casting for an advert at the weekend and I'm so nervous. I don't know how to thank you for your advice . . .'

'What?' Adele interrupted, furious. She couldn't believe her plan had backfired and Chloe had been taken on! 'That's great news,' she forced herself to say, seething with jealousy.

'I'm in their new faces section. Hopefully I'll get lots of work. They're paying for me to have some head shots too. It's so exciting!'

'Just brilliant,' Adele said unenthusiastically. 'I need to go now anyway. Find out for me about the bikinis and I'll speak to you soon.'

'Okay. Speak soon, Adele. Bye.'

Great, Adele thought glumly, trust that little cow Chloe to ruin her good mood. Hopefully tonight Aaron would be able to change all that.

CHAPTER 11

'Seriously, babe, I know we were told we would sweat doing that yoga, but I didn't realise it would be that bad!' Kelly was exasperated. After being told by a client about Bikram yoga, which was basically just yoga, but in a room that was one hundred degrees Fahrenheit, she had managed to persuade Jade to join her in a class. After all, her client had informed her you could burn off up to eight hundred calories an hour, and that wasn't information she could ignore. They were at Epping tube station waiting for a train. There wasn't anywhere to park at the yoga class so they thought it would be easier than driving and searching for ages for a parking space somewhere. Kelly turned to Jade. 'I'm not being funny, but I'm half tempted to go and get a blow dry or something. I look like a drowned rat and I'm meeting Billy now!'

Jade giggled. 'I'm sure he won't mind. Just have a shower quickly before he comes over. You don't even look bad as you are.'

Kelly looked down at her outfit. She always made an effort with her appearance, even when going to the gym, and she'd opted for a baby pink Adidas crop top with a hot pink Ralph Lauren hoody unzipped over the top, bright pink matching Adidas leggings, with her hair tied back in a matching pink hairband. In her opinion you could never wear too much pink; it was her favourite colour. She'd even put rollers in her hair that morning to give it a bit of bounce, but now it was just flat and stuck to her scalp. She had no choice but to wash and dry it quickly. There was no way Billy was seeing her like this.

They could see the train making its way to the platform in the distance and Kelly watched it coming. 'Babe, I was thinking. Do you reckon you can get a tan on the tube because it's so hot and obviously you've got the bright lights as well? I swear everyone that works in the City looks like they have sun-kissed skin and I was thinking it must be to do with the tube or something.'

Jade looked at her like she had two heads and then her mouth twitched and she burst into laughter. 'Kelly, are you kidding? I mean I know you come out with silly things sometimes, but seriously. Of course you can't get a tan on the tube!'

Kelly stared at the train thoughtfully in disbelief. 'I still reckon there's a chance you know.'

Jade rolled her eyes and gave an amused laugh. 'Okay, Kelly, if you say so. I should have brought my factor fifteen in that case.'

Suddenly, Kelly screamed at the top of her lungs. 'Oh my God! Get it off me! Help! Quick!' She threw her hoody to the floor, running away and throwing her arms wildly in the air.

Jade had never been so puzzled in her life. 'What are you doing? What's wrong?'

Kelly was gasping for breath and swallowed hard. 'There's a bug on my jumper, babe. You know I don't do bugs; I can't handle anything that crawls.'

Jade sighed, breathing out sharply. 'For God's sakes, I thought it was something serious for a minute. Quick, the train is coming. Give it here, I'll get it off.' She walked over

181

to her pink hoody cautiously, picking it up carefully with her fingertips.

'Be careful!' Kelly cried, covering her eyes with her hands because she couldn't bear to watch.

Jade gently shook the jumper, gave it the once over and then realised that nothing was there. 'Kelly, there is no bug. What are you talking about?'

Kelly lifted her chin defiantly. 'There is! It was on the right side on my chest and it was green.'

The train pulled in and Jade looked once more and then felt the laughter rising in her throat. 'Do you mean this?' She pointed to the trademark Ralph Lauren horse logo, which was green. Kelly had clearly thought was a bug.

Kelly's eyes widened when she saw it. She shook her head uncertainly. 'No.' She hesitated and then turned to get on the train, taking it back. 'It had wings, it can't have been that.'

Jade laughed and she could see the smirk on Kelly's face as she turned her head momentarily before taking a seat on the train.

Kelly took a seat and then got her make-up bag out of her gym bag.

Jade gaped at her. 'You're not doing your make-up on here are you? The train will be shaky, how will you keep a steady hand?'

Kelly said proudly, 'Hun, when you can do your make-up on public transport perfectly, you can do anything. Trust me, I'm a professional.'

Jade shook her head. 'But you're having a shower when you get back. How will you not get your face wet?'

Kelly looked at her as she curled a set of eyelashes. 'Experience, babe. I don't have time to do my make-up after showering because Billy will arrive and there is no possible way that boy is seeing my bare face!'

Jade laughed, obviously unsurprised. Kelly had been with

Billy for over nine months and he'd *still* never seen her without make-up. Kelly made sure she set an alarm to wake up early before Billy could see her make-up free.

Shortly after, they arrived at the station and went their separate ways.

Kelly selected a white pair of 7 for all Mankind jeans and a tight All Saints denim shirt for Billy's arrival, which she buttoned just under her cleavage. She blow dried her hair quickly and retouched her make-up, just on time. Her mum was away for the weekend with her partner, Peter, at a spa, so luckily she had a free house. Her nan was looking after Lord McButterpants too, so Billy had agreed to stay over and keep her company for a few days and she was looking forward to it.

'Hey babe,' she said, opening the door and kissing him. He was dressed in a black work suit with a blue tie, his hair sleek to the side as normal and Kelly thought about how lucky she was to have such a handsome boyfriend. Something was up though, she noticed, as she spotted the frown lines on his forehead. He looked worried.

'Hi,' he said, following her in the house. His shoulders were slumped and his voice was low. She could tell something was wrong before he even told her. Normally he was chirpy, upbeat and would practically scoop her up in his arms and hold her tightly because he was so excited to see her.

'Are you okay?' Kelly asked, her big blue eyes open wide.

He took a deep breath and sighed dramatically as he loosened his tie. 'It's just work problems, babe.' He sat on the sofa in the lounge and took his shoes off.

She exhaled sharply; glad it wasn't anything to do with his mum. He had her worried for a moment there and she'd first thought that she may have got worse again. She sat next to him and rubbed his knee gently. 'Do you want to talk about it?'

He thought for a moment, staring at the coffee table in front of him. 'I tell you what, why don't we just eat dinner first and I'll tell you after. I'm bored of thinking about it.'

Kelly nodded and then realised she didn't have any dinner. Was she supposed to make him some? Normally when he came over her mum cooked dinner and they would all sit together. She couldn't cook to save her life and wasn't even sure what food they had in the house. 'Errr . . . Billy . . . I haven't actually made dinner as such.'

'Babe, it's fine,' he said, putting his legs up on the sofa. 'We can get a takeaway if you like or I'll help you make something?'

Kelly thought for a moment. Maybe she should treat him and cook him a meal, seeing as he'd had a bad day? After all, she was his girlfriend and she'd never done it before. She wanted to do something nice for him and cooking couldn't be that hard could it? 'Look, you sit here and relax and I'll go and make you a nice home-cooked meal. How does that sound?'

Billy looked doubtful for a second, but then smiled. 'That's really lovely of you, babe. You sure you know how to cook though, yeah?'

She rolled her eyes and put her hands on her hips, slightly annoyed that he didn't have faith in her. Then she fibbed. 'Yes, I do know how to cook, thank you very much. Mum and I take it in turns and her and Peter love my cooking, so there.'

Billy laughed as he flicked through the channels. 'Okay, keep your hair on. So what we having then?'

Kelly turned on her heel. 'It's a surprise,' she said as she made her way to the kitchen. *What on earth am I going to do?* She panicked as she frantically searched through the freezer, fridge and cupboards. She picked up a questionable cucumber and a bag of pasta. Could she make cucumber pasta? she questioned in desperation, before putting it back and cursing herself for being so stupid. How could she hand Billy that for dinner? He didn't think she could do it, she had seen it there in his eyes. Well, she would soon show him, she promised, hunting through the kitchen drawers to see if she could find a cook book. She was relieved and overjoyed when she stumbled across a book called *Thirty-Minute Home Cooked Meals*. She searched through the pages and found a chicken in white wine sauce recipe that didn't look too difficult. She knew she didn't have all the ingredients, but she could improvise and make a few adjustments here and there; Billy would never know the difference. She pulled out a bottle of white wine from the wine rack. At least she had one of the main ingredients, Kelly thought happily, as she opened the bottle and poured herself a generous glass before hunting through the freezer for some chicken. Luckily, there were four frozen breasts. Frozen chicken was okay to cook, wasn't it? The recipe didn't say anything about whether it should be frozen or not, so Kelly assumed it must be fine. Next she was lucky enough to find an onion, celery and a couple of carrots in the bottom drawer of the fridge, which she didn't even know existed until that moment in time. They were all in the recipe so she chopped the carrots and celery as best she could and then got started on the onion.

'You okay in there, babe?' Billy called from the lounge.

Kelly wiped her forehead with a tea towel, already feeling flustered from the stress of cooking. 'I'm fine, hun!' she replied hastily, not wanting him to come in and disrupt her. She gulped down some more wine and then tried to slice the onion in half with difficulty. 'Keep still you little bugger,' she said, as if the onion could hear her. She yelped as half the onion shot away onto the kitchen floor as she sliced it. She washed it under the tap and then continued chopping in no particular order. As her eyes started to water, she panicked about her make-up running and rushed over to

185

the mirror, thankful she'd worn waterproof mascara. How do people do this for a living? Kelly wondered as she placed the chicken in a dish and added the vegetables on top. She glanced again at the menu as she took another slug of wine. She needed a bay leaf and some peppercorns, which she didn't have, to add on top of the chicken. Instead she simply sprinkled on some pepper, hoping that would be okay. Now for the sauce, she thought to herself with dread as she filled her glass with some more wine.

*

Adele batted her long lashes at Aaron as he spoke and flicked her hair over her shoulder, letting out a soft, sexy laugh.

'Oh Aaron, you're hilare!' she said, brushing his arm with her hand.

Donna cleared her throat, shooting Adele an icy look. She tapped his shoulder. 'Aaron, do you want another drink?'

Aaron turned to Donna and gently rested his hand on hers. 'Babe, don't be silly. I'll get them in. What does everyone want? Same again?'

'Yes please,' Adele said, pouting her lips at him and waving her empty wine glass.

Donna looked at Neil who had decided to join them on their night out. He looked well and truly fed up. 'So Neil, Aaron tells me you went scuba diving recently on holiday. Adele, you love scuba diving don't you?'

Adele narrowed her eyes at Donna, knowing exactly what she was trying to do. She wanted her and Neil together and there was just no way that was going to happen! Neil was ordinary and boring. He worked at an accountant's for God's sake! He couldn't be further away from being a footballer if he tried!

Neil perked up a bit and his eyes brightened. 'Yeah, I

love it. I was in Thailand last year and the water was crystal clear. Absolutely beautiful. So, you like diving as well, Adele? Whereabouts have you been?'

Adele rolled her eyes, annoyed that he was even trying to speak to her. She'd made it pretty clear tonight she wasn't interested in him. She'd only spoken to Aaron the whole night, so why wouldn't Neil just get the picture? 'Yeah, it's okay. Been loads of places. The sea looks the same most of the time,' she replied flatly.

'Do you have your diving licence?' Neil asked enthusiastically.

'Mmm,' Adele murmured with a little nod as she sipped the last of her drink. She jumped up quickly. 'I'm going to go help Aaron with the drinks. See you in a bit.' She turned before she could see Donna's face, which she assumed would look like thunder. Oh well, Adele thought to herself as she made her way over to Aaron at the bar, she was going after what she wanted in life. If Donna had a problem with that then she was clearly worried about Aaron being easily persuaded. She'd be doing her a favour if he cheated and left Donna for her! Donna would forgive her eventually and if she didn't, then so what? Adele would just make friends with all the other WAGs and they could go away to spa weekends or shopping trips to Milan and Paris. It was obvious Aaron would prefer Adele to Donna anyway. Who wouldn't? If she hadn't made a beeline for Neil in Funky Mojoe that night, Adele was certain that Aaron would have tried it on with her instead. He hadn't had a choice that night and he got left with Donna. She looked over at Donna who had made an effort tonight. Her hair looked nice, it had been dyed a bit lighter and was down and wavy, she had to give her that. She supposed her make-up looked pretty too, especially her eyelash extensions. It still didn't mean she was skinny though! She was a size sixteen for goodness' sake! Though as she looked over at

Donna, she noticed that she actually looked a bit slimmer. Had she been dieting?

'Hey,' Aaron said to her as she stood by him.

She smiled and eyed him up and down seductively. 'Thought someone should help you with the drinks.'

He nodded and handed her two glasses of wine, which the barman passed him. 'Thanks. That's nice of you.'

'Anytime,' she grinned, sticking her chest out so he could see her cleavage. She swung her hips from side to side sensuously, swishing her hair as she walked back, hoping he was watching.

A few minutes later, they were all sitting back at the table.

'So when are we going to Venice?' Donna beamed at Aaron, before turning to Adele and Neil with a smile. 'Aaron said he's going to take me to Venice because I was saying the other day how I've always wanted to go to Italy. I can't wait to visit the Grand Canal, Bridge of Sighs and Doge's palace.'

Adele had to fight the urge to throw her drink in Donna's annoyingly joyful face. It sounded so boring too. Who would want to go all the way to Italy to look at a bridge?

'As soon as I get some time off footy,' Aaron promised her. He grinned. 'I already know the hotel I'm going to book, but don't ask which one as I want it to be a surprise.'

'Lovely,' Adele said, blankly. 'Though I doubt Aaron is going to want to look at the boring stuff you just mentioned, Donna.' She let out a hollow laugh.

'I'm actually looking forward to seeing those places,' Aaron said, gazing into Donna's eyes lovingly. 'I can't wait to go to St Mark's Square and St Mark's Basilica and take you on a gondola as well.'

Donna turned to Adele. 'We have all the same interests,' she giggled, blissfully happy. She waved her hand. 'I know you may think they're boring, Adele, but that's why Aaron and I get on so well.'

Adele couldn't believe this. Now Donna was making Aaron think that he wouldn't be compatible with her! 'Well of course that St Mark's place sounds interesting,' she huffed, annoyed with Donna. 'It was just the bridge place and the canal that you mentioned, Donna, that sounds a bit dull. I've been all over Italy and I've seen them before,' she fibbed. Her idea of a perfect holiday was simply lying in the sun all day, followed by shopping and a meal in an expensive restaurant. 'The bridge is nothing to write home about, trust me. Though you'll love the food in Venice, Donna.' She smirked at her and was glad when Donna's smile faltered. Then with a little laugh, she added spitefully, 'I know how much you *adore* your food.'

'Nothing wrong with that,' Aaron stuck up for her quickly and kissed her over the table, much to Adele's irritation. 'I like a girl with some meat on her bones. Nothing worse than dating a stick insect that lives on lettuce leaves.'

Adele watched in surprise as they continued to stare at each other with love in their eyes, holding hands across the table. What on earth was wrong with him? All foot-ballers dated skinny WAGs, didn't they? *She* was supposed to be dating a footballer, why couldn't he see that? This was harder work than she first thought and she needed a plan to get him alone. As Neil sat and chatted to her, she barely concentrated on what he was saying, only thinking about how to get Aaron by himself. Neil and Aaron had both driven there separately and Donna had picked Adele up on the way. Somehow she needed to get Aaron to take her home. She pretended to send some messages on her phone.

'Donna, I'm actually going to stay at my nan's tonight now if you don't mind dropping me there? I've just got a message from my dad asking to go round and help her with a few things.' She watched Donna's reaction. Donna knew Adele's nan lived completely in the opposite direction and at least thirty minutes away. It made sense for Aaron to take her who was going the same way home.

'Okay, I don't mind taking you,' Donna said, raising her eyebrows.

Adele was furious. That wasn't the answer she was hoping for! She brushed the hair away from her face and added quickly, 'Unless it's easier if Aaron takes me? I was just thinking that my nan lives completely out of your way and I feel bad because you have to get up early for work.' She tried to sound casual, as though she had just realised that this made more sense.

Aaron nodded and shrugged his shoulders. 'No probs. I'll take you if it's easier.'

'I really don't mind,' Donna repeated.

Aaron shook his head. 'Donna, you were saying how tired you were this morning and you have to wake up at six tomorrow. Let me do it. It makes more sense.'

Donna exhaled slowly. 'Okay fine, you take her.'

Adele beamed broadly; at last things were going her way. She downed the last of her drink and then stood up. 'Just nipping to the ladies.'

'Me too,' Donna said hastily, jumping to her feet and following.

When they reached the toilets, Donna turned Adele to face her, tugging her arm back towards her.

Adele threw her eyes to heaven and sighed sharply. 'What?'

'Are you flirting with Aaron?' Donna accused, exasperated.

'Oh for heaven's sake!' Adele spat. 'Get a grip! I'm just being friendly and trying to know him better. You're my friend and I felt like I should take an interest in him.' Adele stared at her, wondering if she'd believe her lies.

Donna looked unconvinced, her eyes becoming thinner as she watched Adele suspiciously. 'Adele, you've been talking to him all night, laughing at his jokes, ignoring me and poor Neil who's trying to make conversation with you. What's going on? Do you fancy Aaron or something?' Donna's voice broke and she looked hurt by the thought that Adele was trying to steal her boyfriend.

'No Donna, I do not fancy Aaron,' Adele puffed, folding her arms across her chest imperiously. 'I thought you'd be pleased I was making an effort. I'm making an effort for *you*. Trying to get to know *your* boyfriend better. I'm so sorry if I've laughed at his jokes and tried to be friendly. I don't know why I even bother! Don't take your insecurities out on me.'

Donna bit her bottom lip and considered what Adele was saying. 'Sorry,' she mumbled looking at the floor. 'I guess you're right. I'm just so happy, I'm worried something or someone is going to ruin it. I know you wouldn't try to steal him from me; we're good friends after all.'

'That's okay,' Adele said, turning away from her. She actually felt a bit guilty for once and couldn't look her in the eye. Donna really trusted her as a friend. Still, Donna was the one with the footballer, not her, and Adele couldn't accept that fact. Adele wanted Aaron more than ever before and some stupid sob story wasn't going to stop her.

They were in the car park ten minutes later saying goodbye. Adele looked at Aaron's silver Aston Martin convertible admiringly, noticing it was a new model; glad she wasn't getting in Neil's Renault Megane. Now this was the kind of car her boyfriend should have, she thought, as she sat on the expensive-looking leather seat.

She waved at Donna through the window, who waved back and drove away.

Adele smiled at Aaron as he sat beside her. 'You smell delish,' she complimented him in the sexiest voice she could muster.

'Thanks. It's D & G,' Aaron replied as he started the

ignition. 'So, how do you feel about Neil? He said he really liked you after that night in Funky Mojoe.'

Adele paused and fiddled with the strap of her cream Chloe bag. 'Babe, he's not really a bit of me to be honest. Nice guy, but I like more athletic men to be truthful.' She looked at Aaron, hoping he would realise she was talking about him, but he was concentrating on the road ahead.

'That's a shame,' he replied politely. 'Donna was saying she hopes you meet someone nice soon, as you deserve it.'

Adele felt a stab of guilt and swallowed hard. 'Bless her,' she managed. 'She's never actually had a serious boyfriend,' Adele told him, hoping it would put him off.

Aaron shook his head. 'I really don't see how. I haven't had many serious relationships either though I suppose.'

'Same,' Adele chimed in. 'I can never find men that like me,' she sulked with a pout.

'Nonsense,' Aaron waved a hand dismissively. 'Plenty of men would want to be with you. You must have them queuing up outside your front door.'

Adele let out a loud, throaty laugh. 'I wish,' she replied huskily, noticing his CD collection and having a look through. She frowned as she read the titles of the CDs. He had albums by The Shins, Andrew Bird, Tanlines and Miike Snow. Who the hell were these people? Adele had never heard of them.

Aaron noticed her looking. 'That's my favourite album there by The Shins at the moment. It's amazing. Donna bought it for me a few weeks ago and I haven't stopped playing it.'

Adele's face crinkled even more into a frown. Donna knew this music? She actually bought this for him? She went along with it, pretending she was into the same kind of thing. 'I adore The Shins. So cool,' she lied.

'Aren't they just,' Aaron agreed with a nod. 'So you're into indie music as well then?'

Adele tried to sound enthusiastic. 'Oh yeah. Big time. I love The Shins the most. This album in particular.' She noticed Aaron's eyes light up. God, he must really be into this rubbish, she realised, disappointed. Give her chart music any day.

'What's your favourite song on the album?' Aaron asked, quickly glancing at her.

Obviously not knowing any of the songs, Adele quickly put the CD in the player and clicked to number four. 'This one. I could just listen to it all day.'

He nodded, satisfied. '"Bait and Switch". Great choice,' he said, singing along.

What a load of crap, Adele thought despondently, looking out of the window and wondering whether he really was her perfect man after all. Adele remembered Donna listening to the same sort of music in her car before she would force her to switch the radio on. She winced as he turned the volume up. It just sounded like noise in her opinion and the loud bits were making her head hurt. Why couldn't he be into Rihanna or something she actually liked to listen to?

Aaron interrupted her thoughts. 'I'm going to try to take Donna to Reading or Glastonbury this year. She'll love it, won't she? You should come too.'

Adele scrunched up her nose. She wouldn't be seen dead wearing wellington boots and sleeping in a tent! How vile! Those people didn't wash and just acted like slobs all day, drinking beer in mud, without a brush, hair dryer or straighteners in sight. What was wrong with him? Donna had been a few times and when her photos were uploaded on Facebook, the dishevelled-looking people in them made Adele want to gag. 'Sounds totes amaze,' she said coolly, keeping up the facade.

As he pulled into her nan's road, Adele realised it was now or never she was going to have to make a move. She forced herself to think of his money and his car. She pictured changing him into the person she wanted him to be. They could scrap Venice and go to New York or the Caribbean. And he could forget about Glastonbury and take her to see Beyoncé in concert instead, in a VIP box of course.

He stopped the car and turned to face her. Adele could feel her heart beating faster as she imagined herself leaning into him and kissing his lips. He had lovely dark eyes and hair and although he wasn't exactly drop-dead gorgeous, he was definitely attractive. He was looking serious all of a sudden and she felt certain he must fancy her. He appeared tense and slightly awkward.

'I need to ask you something,' Aaron said finally, his eyes gazing into her own. 'You have to promise you won't tell Donna. I just can't keep it in any longer. I *have* to tell you.'

This is it! Adele screamed with happiness inside. She always knew she would go out with a footballer one day. 'I think I know what it is,' she replied huskily, rubbing his shoulder with her hand.

He frowned slightly and Adele lunged towards him, plastering her lips on his mouth and holding the back of his head with her hands and drawing him closer.

He jumped back, looking as though he'd been scalded. His eyes were wide open in horror. 'Adele! What the . . . what are you doing?'

Adele cringed, realising she'd made a mistake and that he wasn't just playing hard to get. Whatever he was going to tell her, she could tell judging by the look on his face it wasn't that he fancied her. 'I thought . . . I . . . I'm sorry,' she said breathlessly, wanting the ground to swallow her whole. She was so mortified she didn't know where to look.

Aaron wiped his mouth as though she was contagious and looked at her, disgusted. 'Why the hell did you just do that?' he demanded, his eyes darkening.

'I'm sorry!' Adele exploded, wishing she could go back

in time. She rubbed her eyes. If he told Donna, she would never want to talk to her again. She needed him to keep this quiet. She had *never* been knocked back by anyone before. This was beyond humiliating! She knew she wasn't right for Aaron anyway; the thought of listening to those CDs of his made her shudder. She'd gone too far this time and now she felt bad. Donna had always been nothing but good to her, she realised. From going anywhere she asked her to, to helping out in a shoe crisis and lending her Louboutins, she was there for her. When she thought about it, despite only becoming really close to her since she'd been back from Marbella, Donna was her best and only true friend. She breathed hard. 'Please Aaron. Just forget that happened. Don't tell Donna. It was a huge mistake and I'm really sorry.' Her eyes were hot and Adele blinked her tears away.

The shocked expression was still engraved on Aaron's face. His voice was calm and serious. 'I don't see why I shouldn't. You're supposed to be her friend.'

Adele nodded, closing her eyes and trying to block out the horrified look on his face. 'I know, I know, and I am her friend. I promise I am. It was just a silly mistake. Donna never needs to know about it.' She looked at him, her eyes pleading.

He thought for a moment and then exhaled. 'Okay, I won't say. But please don't think it's because of you that I'm keeping this a secret. I'm only thinking of Donna and her feelings. She'd be so hurt if she knew what you just tried to do. Just don't do anything like that again. I'm with Donna and I love her. That's what I was going to tell you. I'm even going to propose; I want her to be my wife.'

Adele's jaw popped open. He was going to propose to Donna? Talk about a bad time to try to snog him! She felt a wave of envy wash over her, but brushed it away, trying to feel happy for her friend like she knew she should. 'That's great news!' she spluttered, leaning forward and going to give him a hug. Aaron leaned back, a terrified look on his face. Adele gave a nervous laugh. 'Okay, maybe a bit too soon for a hug after what just happened. I'm really happy for you though; I mean it. Donna is going to be over the moon.'

Despite the situation, Adele watched as Aaron smiled happily. 'I may not have been with her for long, but I've never felt this way about anyone. It feels right.'

Adele nodded and grinned. 'You're perfect for each other.' As she said the words, she realised that she meant them, too. Donna and Aaron were a perfect match. 'Thanks for the lift,' she said as she opened the car door to get out.

'That's okay,' Aaron managed a lopsided grin. 'Remember; not a word to Donna about the proposal and I won't say about what just happened.'

Adele signalled her lips were sealed by moving her hand across her mouth. 'I promise I won't say.'

He nodded and started the engine. 'Bye Adele.'

She waved him off and then walked through the gates of her nan's huge house. What a waste of time, she thought miserably, now she needed to get a taxi home. She couldn't believe it; Donna was going to be getting married. Would this mean that everything was going to change? There was no way she was ever going to want to go to Faces or Nu Bar anymore now she was going to be someone's wife! Adele wanted to be happy for her, but no matter how hard she tried she couldn't help but wonder; where did that leave her?

CHAPTER 12

Kelly looked at the state of the kitchen and sighed. There were vegetable peelings everywhere, mess on the floor and empty packaging, pots, pans and cutlery spread out all over the kitchen surfaces. It didn't matter though; she'd done it. Kelly had finally prepared her first ever meal and she couldn't wait to impress Billy with her new-found cooking skills. The chicken in white wine sauce was going to be delicious and thank God, it was now in the oven, ready to be cooked. She quickly checked her appearance in the mirror, grimacing as she wiped her slightly sweaty forehead on a tea towel. Cooking was hard work! She didn't even sweat this much when there was a sale on in Selfridges! She filled her empty glass with some more wine, which she poured from the second bottle she'd opened. By the time Kelly had to make the sauce, she realised she'd almost drunk a whole bottle to herself. Well, it was stressful and she needed it, she consoled herself as she filled another glass for Billy. As she made her way into the lounge, Kelly realised she actually felt quite tipsy.

'Alright, babe?' Billy asked, looking up from the programme he was watching as Kelly walked into the room.

Kelly walked over to him and sat on his lap, wrapping

her arms around his neck and kissing him on the lips. 'I'm fine,' she hiccupped. 'You're going to be so proud of my cooking.'

Billy rubbed his lips together and tasted them. 'Have you been drinking?'

Kelly giggled. 'I just had a couple of glasses of wine while I was cooking. I've got you a glass as well,' she said as she nodded to the coffee table.

'Thanks.' Billy leaned forward and picked up his wine. 'I need a drink after the day I've had.'

Kelly climbed off him and sat up straight. 'You can tell me all about it over dinner.'

Billy flicked through the channels on the television and patted his stomach. 'Can't wait, I'm starving. How long until it's done?'

Kelly smiled, looking forward to serving it to him. 'Thirty minutes.'

Twenty-five minutes later, Kelly went in the kitchen to check on the dinner. She inhaled deeply by the entrance, trying to catch a whiff of the delicious cooked chicken and was baffled when she couldn't smell anything.

'How is it looking, babe?' Billy called in to her.

'Errr . . . I'm just checking it,' Kelly shouted back, as she made her way over to the oven with dread. Her heart sank as she opened the oven door to reveal cold darkness – meaning she'd forgotten to actually turn the oven on! *How could I be so stupid?* Kelly cursed herself, blaming the wine. She jumped as she heard Billy behind her.

'Let's have a look at this lovely dinner then,' he said, placing his hands on her waist.

She turned to face him with a sheepish grin. 'Billy . . . I . . .'

He looked behind her at the uncooked meat lying in the dish and his mouth started to twitch as it dawned on him what had happened. 'You didn't turn the oven on, did you?'

198

Kelly bit her bottom lip and looked at the floor like a naughty schoolgirl. 'No.'

Billy burst into laughter and Kelly slapped him playfully.

'Shut up, Billy! I *can* cook, you know. I just forgot that one simple thing! Anyone could forget! People do it all the time!'

Billy held his stomach as he continued to laugh. 'Oh, you make me laugh so much. How could you forget to switch it on?' He looked closer at the dish and made a face. 'Kelly, is that chicken frozen?'

Kelly frowned. 'Yes, why?'

Billy shook his head, incredulous. 'Kelly, you can't cook chicken from frozen like that! You need to defrost it. We could have got salmonella poisoning!'

Kelly's mouth opened wide. 'Oh my God, shut up!' She thought for a moment, her forehead creasing into a frown. She wasn't going to admit that she only thought you could get salmonella poisoning from salmon, he was laughing at her enough as it was. But really, salmonella from chicken? How bizarre. She was annoyed with herself for messing it up, just like he guessed she would. Why couldn't it have just gone right? She wanted Billy to be proud of her and to think that she was at least capable of making a decent meal. She sat down at the kitchen table, depressed. 'I really wanted to make you a nice dinner,' she sulked, sticking out her bottom lip.

Billy looked at her lovingly and walked over to her, putting his hand on her shoulder gently. 'Oh babe, don't get upset. It's lovely that you tried, I really appreciate it. It doesn't matter. Come on, why don't we go out and have an Indian? My treat. You can cook me dinner another time.'

Kelly looked up at him and managed a weak smile. 'Okay, Indian it is then,' she mumbled, feeling defeated.

Thirty minutes later they were sitting in Jaipur Indian

restaurant in Chigwell, munching their poppadums. Billy broke a piece off and dipped it in some mango chutney. 'I'll explain what happened today,' he said as he chewed a mouthful.

'You know you can tell me anything.' Kelly stopped eating and squeezed his hand across the table.

Billy paused and took a deep breath before clearing his throat. 'There's a bit of a problem with this guy called Alfie, who's been supplying us with various tickets for our clients. Basically, we've bought tickets from him for the last few months and he's been great. He's the cheapest around and we've never had any problems with him. But, we recently bought a lot of tickets for Wimbledon, the Olympics and a rugby match at Twickenham and we can't get through to him. Our clients have paid us and we've paid him. The rugby match is a week and a half away and we should have received everyone's tickets to send out to them, but we haven't. Now he won't even answer the phone; Gary is fuming.'

Kelly's big blue eyes opened widely. 'Oh no! What are you going to do? Does he work for a company? Can't you just call the company up?'

Billy shook his head and exhaled sharply. 'No. He just works for himself, from home. He's been given all our clients' money for tickets, which he hasn't sent to us yet. The last we heard from him he said they were on their way. But now he's just ignoring our calls. He's never normally like this; we've bought from him quite a bit in the past and the tickets are always on time. I don't know, maybe we're panicking over nothing. Maybe the tickets will turn up tomorrow. I'm just really worried.'

Kelly didn't know what to say. She knew how important Billy's business was to him and he rarely told her anything that went on. If she was honest, she never really understood half of what he usually told her and just nodded along and pretended she was keeping up with him. The fact that he was telling her he was worried made her feel uneasy; things must be bad. 'How much money has this Alfie been given?' Kelly asked, curious.

Billy took a deep breath and paused. His voice was shaky. 'Just over a hundred grand.'

Kelly's heart sank. She was hoping it wasn't going to be much, but a hundred grand? That was a huge amount of money! She panicked for him.

'So what happens if he doesn't send the tickets?'

Billy shook his head and took another bite of poppadum. 'It doesn't even bear thinking about. We're not insured so it means we will lose all our clients' money, every penny we've invested in the company and I reckon we'll have to close it down.'

Kelly was horrified. 'How come you're not insured?'

Billy shook his head and swallowed hard. 'I don't know, babe. I've always been worried about it, but Gary always insisted it's a waste of money and we don't really need it. I wish I'd kept on at him now.'

Kelly gasped and put her hand on her lips. Why would Gary convince him that they'd be fine without insurance? It seemed odd. Billy would be heartbroken if he had to close his company down. His company was everything to him. No wonder he seemed like he had the weight of the world on his shoulders, the poor thing! She tried to remain positive for him and hope for the best. 'Don't worry, hun, I'm sure the tickets will turn up. Maybe Alfie is ill or something? Maybe he's lost his phone?'

'We've emailed him too,' Billy said blankly.

'Maybe he's lost his computer?' Kelly realised how stupid that sounded. 'Or . . . or . . . or not lost his computer, maybe it's broken? That's it; maybe he's lost his phone and his computer is broken? Stranger things have happened.'

Billy looked doubtful as he ran his hands through his

hair and sat back in his chair. 'Thanks for trying to cheer me up, babe. Let's just hope the world has gone crazy and you're right.'

Kelly nodded as she placed her napkin on her lap. 'It will all be okay, you'll see,' she said with as much conviction as she could muster. For some reason she couldn't explain though, she had a very bad feeling about this indeed.

*

Jade brushed through her long hair, which had recently been highlighted a bit blonder for summer, and stepped into her beige Giuseppe Zanotti heels. She'd had a spray tan and was wearing a pretty nude-coloured Reiss dress to show off her bronzed legs, teamed with a white blazer. It was a Saturday and she was waiting for Kelly to pick her up and take her to Lisa's, as the three of them were going to go for lunch. Jade decided to take her cream Jimmy Choo bag, which had lasted her for years. She smiled as she remembered buying it. It was just before she'd gone to university and she didn't want to spend a fortune, so she was just going to buy a cheap copy from a Chinese website she'd found online. No one would know the difference anyway, she'd told herself. Kelly had come over and spotted the website up on her computer. Jade recalled how Kelly had gasped and made a face as she clicked through the fake designer bag website.

'A real friend would *never* let a friend wear fake designer!' Kelly had declared, outraged that Jade was even considering it. 'Just save for a real one if you can't afford it just yet. That's what I do. My bank account always wants me to stop shopping, but my heart doesn't.'

Jade had laughed and promised Kelly she'd save for a real one. Jade's dad had wanted to get her a 'going away' present in the end, so he'd helped put some money towards it, and Kelly, Jade and Lisa had gone to Harrods for the day. She had so many happy memories with her friends and didn't know what she'd do without them.

Twenty minutes later, Kelly and Jade were outside Lisa's flat. She opened the door looking stunning as always in tight jeans, a black vest and cropped leather jacket. Her long, dark hair was as shiny as ever and Jade always felt a pang of envy whenever she saw it; Lisa certainly didn't need hair extensions.

'Come on in, girls,' Lisa said with a smile as they made their way into her flat.

Princess Cupcake came running over excitedly and Kelly bent down to stroke her. 'Hello my little beaut,' she said as she lifted her up. 'I should have brought Lord McButterpants today, shouldn't I? Then you would have had a little friend.'

Jade walked over to Princess Cupcake and stroked her soft fur. She seemed to have got bigger and a bit calmer. It was amazing how quickly she was growing up. She did look adorable in her little red frilly dress, she thought to herself. She hated to admit it, but she'd actually missed the little dog. Yes, she had been hard work at times, but her little cheeky character was actually quite endearing and Jade realised now, she had only been disobedient because she was a puppy and needed to learn. As she stroked her, Princess Cupcake licked her hand and Jade felt that it was her way of telling her she was forgiven for telling Lisa they could no longer dog-sit. All of a sudden she heard a little bark, which wasn't coming from Cupcake. Jade was stunned as she saw a miniature Yorkshire Terrier come bundling towards her, which was the dog Adele had told them she was getting. The dog jumped up at her and Jade bent down to stroke him.

'Babe, is that Buddy?' Kelly asked Lisa the exact question on Jade's lips.

'Errr . . . yeah,' Lisa answered, hesitantly.

Jade frowned, confused, and stood up. 'Why is Buddy here in your flat?'

Lisa brushed her hair back from her face and hesitated. 'I'm just looking after him for a bit until Adele gets back from the gym. It's not exactly hard seeing as she lives dead opposite. She'll be back soon and then we can go.' Lisa turned, unable to look either of them in the eye.

Kelly's brows knitted and her jaw dropped. 'What? Since when do you talk to Adele and do her favours?'

Lisa turned to face them, her face a little pink. 'I don't. It was just a one off. I don't know why we're even talking about this.' She batted her hand in their direction, dismissing their baffled expressions.

Jade was incredulous. Why was Lisa even in contact with Adele, let alone looking after her dog? She guessed Adele must be taking advantage of Lisa's kind nature. 'Lisa, if she's been coming round here and just dumping her dog on you to look after, you have to stand up to her. You know what she's like! She'll walk all over you, now you've agreed this one time. Say something, before it's too late.'

Kelly was nodding furiously beside her. 'I bet she keeps coming round here trying to be friends, doesn't she? Just wait until she knocks to pick up Buddy; I'm going to give her a piece of my mind.'

'Please just stop it you two,' Lisa said with a theatrical sigh as she sat on the sofa. 'It's not a big deal. I don't mind looking after Buddy for one morning. Adele really isn't that bad when you get to know her. It's the least I can do for her.'

Jade's eyes narrowed. 'Why? What does she ever do for you?'

Lisa exhaled sharply and said heavily, 'If you must know, she's been dog-sitting Cupcake for me every day.'

Kelly was exasperated, her eyes getting rounder by the

second. 'Oh my God, shut up! *Adele* is Princess Cupcake's dog-sitter?'

Lisa held her hands up. 'Yes. There. Now I've said it. Adele is Cupcake's dog-sitter.'

Kelly inhaled sharply and put her hand on her heart. 'I don't believe it!'

Jade was just as shocked and stood with her hands on her hips. 'You do realise that Adele is a psychopath?'

Lisa let out a loud tut. 'Oh, don't be so ridiculous, you two. I really don't have much choice, do I? You two can't dog-sit for me, my mum wouldn't dream of it, I can't afford the lady I had previously and besides, Adele does it for free. I know you both hate her and she can be a bit weird, but honestly, I don't think she's all that bad deep down. How are you both even sure she stole your notebook?'

Kelly shook her head. 'She did Lisa, trust us. You just can't use Adele, no way. Oh my poor little Princess Cupcake!' She ran over to the dog and stroked her before Cupcake ran off in the other direction. 'How could you give that precious little animal to such a two-faced beast?'

Jade sat down, still unable to believe that Lisa was actually associating with Adele. She felt betrayed. 'After everything she's done to us, you're really speaking and seeing her every day?'

Lisa shut her eyes briefly and lowered her voice, looking regretful. 'I don't want to give Cupcake up. What choice do I have?'

Just as she said the words they heard barking in the distance.

Lisa jumped up to her feet frantically. 'Did you close the front door behind you?'

Jade and Kelly looked at each other and raised their eyebrows.

'I thought you did,' Jade said to Kelly, shrugging her shoulders.

Lisa ran to the entrance of the flat and then whispered and gesticulated as she called the girls over. 'Quick! Come and look at this.'

Jade and Kelly walked over to her quickly and put their hands over their mouths as they looked across the hall at Adele's flat, which had the door open and the dogs running around in it. There was Adele sprawled out on the sofa, fast asleep.

'I thought she was meant to be going to the gym?' Kelly hissed, not impressed that Lisa was still dog-sitting when Adele was fast asleep.

Jade pointed to Adele's gym bag by the sofa. 'I think the intention was there.'

Lisa giggled. 'We need to get the dogs back in here before they wake her up. Adele always leaves her door on the latch because she's always coming in and out and somehow the dogs have pushed their way in.'

Jade sighed. 'Good, I hope they do wake her up. We've been waiting to give Buddy back to her so we can go out. Why don't you just leave Buddy in there, get Princess Cupcake and then we can go?'

Lisa nodded before she whispered back, 'I suppose we could do that. Come help me.'

The girls walked to the entrance of Adele's flat and stifled giggles as Adele's loud snores became clear.

Kelly beamed broadly. 'No wonder she's single! She snores as loud as a warthog!'

Jade clamped her hand tightly over her mouth to stop her laugh escaping. She managed to compose herself. 'How do you know warthogs snore?'

Kelly looked up to the ceiling, thoughtfully. 'They just sound like they do, don't they?'

Jade laughed and Lisa elbowed her playfully. 'No time to talk about that girls, help me get Cupcake back. Remember to be quiet so we don't wake Adele.'

'Cupcake!' They hissed at the dog as quietly as possible but she ran out of sight in the opposite direction.

'Cupcake!' Lisa whispered as loudly as she could.

They all froze when Adele stirred and then breathed a sigh of relief as her snoring started again.

All of a sudden Cupcake came bounding round the corner with something in her mouth, running straight towards Jade, Lisa and Kelly.

Lisa bent down and took the torn piece of paper out of her mouth. She lowered her voice. 'You naughty dog, Cupcake! I've told you not to chew!'

Cupcake sat with her tail still wagging, looking very pleased with herself, despite being told off.

'What is it?' Kelly asked.

Lisa had a quick glance down at the paper as she stood up. 'Oh, I don't know. Just a bit of rubbish.'

Something caught Jade's eye on the paper that made her freeze. '*Oh. My. God.*'

Kelly stared at Jade. 'What? What is it?'

Jade took the paper from Lisa and showed Kelly. 'Look! It's a page from my red notebook! That's your writing, Kel. Look, there are hearts instead of dots!'

Kelly's mouth opened wide and her eyes were bulging as she noticed the familiar writing. She was so angry that she forgot to whisper and shouted loudly. 'I can't believe it! Now we have proof Adele stole it!'

Adele jumped hearing Kelly's loud voice, and her head jerked up to see where the noise was coming from. 'What are you lot doing here? How did you get in? What time is it?' she croaked, disorientated as she sat up, and rubbed her eyes.

Lisa stepped forward. 'Sorry, Adele, but your door must have been on the latch again and the dogs just ran in. We heard them barking so we followed them and were trying to get them out. It's one-thirty.'

'That's alright, hun. Can't believe it; I must have fallen asleep. I planned to go to the gym as soon as *Gossip Girl* finished, but obviously dozed off.' Adele sat up and ran her fingers through her tangled hair. She lifted her arms up, stretching before she noticed Kelly and Jade standing behind Lisa. 'Alright girls?' she asked, with a sarcastic smirk.

Kelly stepped forward, her chin lifted proudly. 'Not really Adele, no,' she started boldly. 'We're going to ask you one more time. Did you steal our red notebook?'

Adele rolled her eyes and yawned loudly. 'Oh not all that again. Please girls, give it a break, yeah?' She turned to Lisa. 'Thanks for looking after Buddy, hun. It's nice we can do these things for each other isn't it?' She narrowed her eyes in Jade and Kelly's direction with a smarmy grin. 'That's what real friends do for each other, after all.'

Jade stepped forward, not willing to listen to any more; she was fed up with Adele and how manipulative she was. 'If you didn't steal our notebook, Adele, then please forgive me for asking, but why did Cupcake come running to us with this in her mouth?' Jade demanded, waving the torn piece of paper in the air. 'She found it in here, which is your flat I believe.'

Adele's smile was frozen solid. 'I have no idea what you're talking about,' she said, looking away from them, trying to keep her cool.

'Liar,' Kelly accused. 'The notebook is in here. We know it is! This is a page from it. Those are my love hearts above the I's!'

Jade and Kelly walked through the doorway and Adele jumped up and stood in front of them, folding her arms.

'Don't you dare come in here making accusations!' Adele's voice was bold and abrasive as she ushered Jade and Kelly to the door. 'Get out of here now!'

'We know you stole it!' Kelly cried as she stumbled

backwards, being forced by Adele. Her eyes flashed with anger. 'Why don't you just get your own ideas, you saddo?'

'You're pathetic,' Jade agreed as they stood by the door where Lisa was standing.

Lisa sighed. 'Please, can everyone just stop arguing?'

Jade gasped and turned to face her. 'Don't tell me you're taking Adele's side?'

Lisa shook her head. 'Of course not. Adele, just admit you took it? You were out of order and they deserve an apology.'

Adele glowered at Lisa. 'I would rather die than ever apologise to those two!'

'Fine!' Jade bellowed. 'You want a war, Adele, then you've sure as hell got one.'

Adele looked at her with a smug grin. 'Bring it on.'

Lisa shook her head and stared Adele straight in the eyes. 'If you won't apologise then you're just as much of a nasty cow as Jade and Kelly have said you are.'

Adele looked mad as she put her hands on her hips and replied viciously, 'Find someone else to look after Cupcake then if that's how you feel. Oh, I forgot, you can't, because you haven't got anyone else.' Adele gave a derisive cackle and gaped at Lisa with a spiteful look on her face. 'You'd better kiss Cupcake goodbye; such a shame.'

'That dog isn't going anywhere,' Jade said assertively as she noticed Lisa's chin shake. 'Kelly and I will dog-sit Cupcake from now on. Just admit the truth, Adele, and we'll be on our way.'

Lisa squeezed Jade's arm as if to say 'thank you', and Jade knew she'd made the right decision. How could she not look after Cupcake after she'd brought them the evidence they needed? Cupcake was on their team and if it meant Lisa could keep her by them dog-sitting, then so be it. Jade would never want to see Lisa upset and she felt guilty that Lisa had needed to accept Adele's offer in the first place. At least she could make it up to her now.

Adele gave a little shrug and exhaled sharply. 'I didn't take anything. God, it's getting so boring now I could actually fall asleep again.'

Kelly held the piece of paper in front of her face. 'We have the evidence! How can you deny it?'

Adele flicked her hair over her shoulder and pouted at Kelly. 'I'm surprised you even recognised your own writing, seeing as you're such a blonde bimbo.'

Kelly went pink with rage. 'Well at least I don't look like a horse with those stupid, huge, ridiculously white fake teeth! Who are you trying to be? Simon Cowell's twin? You look like the daughter of Bugs Bunny!'

Adele gave a short, frosty laugh. 'You're just jell.'

Jade laughed and Adele shot her a chilling glare. 'I don't know what you're laughing at, Jade. I didn't *steal* the notebook; I was given it.'

Jade threw her eyes to the ceiling, wondering what other lie she was going to come out with now. 'Oh really?' she said sarcastically. 'Tell us then, Adele. Who was it that gave you *my* notebook?'

Adele's eyes glinted. 'Sam did when I stayed at his flat after Sugar Hut that night.'

Jade felt her head pulsing with blood as she heard the sentence. She felt as though she'd been punched in the face and was lost for words; was Adele lying or telling the truth?

'What an absolute load of rubbish,' Lisa chimed in. 'Sam would never let you stay at his flat. He's obsessed with Jade; everybody knows that. He's a decent person, unlike you.'

'Don't listen to her, Jade,' Kelly said gently as she saw the horrified and confused expression on her friend's face. 'Sam would never do that. Adele is just a born liar. Don't fall for her lies.'

Adele threw her head back and gave a bark of laughter. 'Ask him, Jade. Go and ask your precious little Sam. Not only did he tell me all your problems, but he invited me back to his flat where we slept together; that's when I got the notebook. I stayed there all night and left in the morning. You saw me arriving back that day, Lisa, remember? It was the day you came to the flat.'

Lisa opened her mouth, about to call her a liar, when the memory of Adele that morning came flooding back to her and she closed it. She remembered her wearing her dressing gown at the door, saying she'd had a big night, and Nicola asking her what his name was. 'Like we said, Adele. Sam would never do that to Jade,' Lisa finally replied, not entirely convinced by her own words.

Jade felt her eyes become hot and she turned so Adele couldn't see. 'I really don't have time for this,' she muttered, her voice trembling. She could hear Adele laughing as she walked back to Lisa's and she burst into tears as soon as she walked through the door. She knew Sam had been acting weird lately and she had also been certain he was keeping something from her. But this? Was this true? What would she do if it was? She never, ever, in her wildest dreams thought he would do anything as low as sleeping with his awful ex-girlfriend. Never did she imagine he could hurt her this bad; especially when he knew how distraught she'd been about her ex-boyfriend, Tom, when he'd cheated on her. Jade would never accept any man cheating; she had far too much self-respect for that. Lunch today was cancelled; she had no option but to go meet Sam and confront him. In fact, she couldn't do it quickly enough.

CHAPTER 13

'Why don't we just have lunch in?' Lisa suggested to Kelly.

Jade had just left and they were sitting in the lounge in her flat, both completely shocked by what Adele had said to them. Lisa felt so sorry for Jade. What was it with Adele and Sam? Why did Adele have such a problem with him dating Jade? It was as though she was always trying to ruin things between them. They both agreed that they just couldn't imagine Sam cheating on Jade and they hoped, for Jade's sake, that Adele was lying. Jade had been through all this before; it just felt so cruel if she was to go through it all again. Their friend was the perfect girlfriend in their eyes; gorgeous, caring, thoughtful and loyal. What more could a man want?

'Okay babe. Let's just make some sandwiches then, yeah?' Kelly agreed.

Lisa made her way into the kitchen. 'Ham and pickle okay?'

Kelly followed her, turning her nose up. 'No babe. Just plain ham for me; never been a fan of that Branston pickle stuff.' She paused and thought for a moment. 'That Richard Branston has got his fingers in all the pies, hasn't he? He's got aeroplanes, Virgin trains, TV and even bloody pickle!'

Lisa's mouth curved into a smile. 'What? It's Richard *Branson* you wally and he doesn't have pickles! It's *Branston* pickle,' she burst into laughter as she opened the bread bin.

Kelly frowned. 'Oh right. I thought it was a bit random for him to have pickle,' she said with a giggle.

Lisa laughed as she buttered four slices of bread. 'Kelly, you're hilarious.'

Kelly smiled, but Lisa noticed it didn't quite reach her eyes. 'I know. Who would everyone laugh at if I didn't exist?'

Lisa gazed at her. 'We're laughing *with* you, not at you. Everyone has blonde moments, but you just have a few more than most people and you have to admit, you *are* funny.'

Kelly nodded, but Lisa noticed she didn't look her usual happy self. Was Kelly offended? She always laughed at herself in these situations, but today something seemed to be on her mind.

'Are you okay, Kelly?' Lisa asked. 'You know I was only joking.'

'I know,' Kelly said as she attempted a smile.

Lisa could tell that she clearly wasn't up for discussing it further so left it at that.

The girls sat eating their sandwiches and after a few hours, Kelly left to spend the rest of the day with Billy as she'd planned.

Lisa sat down and turned on the television, wondering whether she should go on a date that evening with a guy she'd met at a bar in London the previous week. The problem was, she already knew she didn't like him in that way and she would just be using him so she had something to do. She hated the thought of being a user, so decided against it; she would just let him down gently. She thought about Jade and hoped she was alright. Lisa had texted her twenty minutes ago asking how things went, but she hadn't had a response yet; she guessed that Jade just wanted a bit of time alone if she was upset.

Lisa heard the key in the door and smiled as Nicola walked in the flat. She had stayed the night at Charlie's and as always looked completely glammed up. Her long platinum blonde hair had been curled and her wedges were so high Lisa guessed they made her almost six feet tall.

'Alright, honey?' Nicola said with a smile, her large chest bouncing as she walked.

'Hey. Good night?' Lisa asked, smiling back.

'Unreal night, babe. Charlie is just getting this gorgeous shabby chic mirror I just bought out of the car, he'll be here soon and you can meet him. It's beauts.' Nicola sat down on the sofa next to Lisa.

'How's things going with you two then?' Lisa lowered her voice in case Charlie was nearby and overheard.

'Honey, this is seriously like, the most reem relationship ever. You know when you just know someone is perfect for you?' Nicola's eyes sparkled as she spoke. 'He's just so completely amaze; I hope you like him.'

'I'm sure I will,' Lisa replied as she shifted on the sofa.

They both looked up as Charlie arrived, holding the mirror. He was wearing light blue jeans and a blue t-shirt and Lisa could instantly see the attraction. He had dark brown hair, naturally tanned skin and intense coal-coloured eyes. He was the complete definition of tall, dark and handsome.

'Hi,' he nodded at Lisa with a wide smile, revealing perfect teeth. 'I'm Charlie. I would shake your hand, but . . .' he laughed and nodded towards the mirror as he carried it to Nicola's bedroom.

'He's gorgeous,' Lisa mouthed to Nicola.

'I know,' Nicola said dreamily. 'I'm practically obsessed with him, honey.'

'That's so sweet,' Lisa replied, feeling happy for her friend.

Charlie walked back in the room and sat down on the armchair opposite them. 'So you're the amazing Lisa Nicola speaks so highly of,' he said as he stared at her intently. There was something about his eyes which made Lisa feel strange inside. She didn't know what it was, but the feeling unnerved her. She told herself she was imagining it.

'Ahhh that's nice, Nicola,' Lisa said, turning to her friend. 'Yes, that's me.'

Nicola stood up. 'I'm going to quickly re-curl my hair before we go out, Charlie. I don't want it to drop out, that would be a complete nightmare! Won't be long. I'll leave you two to get to know one another.'

Lisa paused for a moment, wondering what to say. When she looked up at Charlie, he was already looking at her. His large brown eyes were rimmed with the most perfectly curled lashes Lisa had ever seen. 'So, things are going well with you and Nicola?' she asked, tucking her hair behind her ear.

'Yeah, I suppose. It's early days yet,' Charlie said, still gazing at her. 'What about you? Are you single? Or has some lucky fella snapped you up?'

Lisa felt herself blush and gave a short, light laugh. 'No, I'm still single. Came out of a very long-term relationship and I've been on my own for about nine months now.'

Charlie nodded, his eyes never leaving her face. 'What kind of idiot let you go?'

Lisa was beginning to feel even more uncomfortable. He'd only just met her; why was he talking to her like this? She supposed he was just being friendly for Nicola's sake. 'It wasn't really like that,' she replied finally. 'It's a long story.'

He raised his broad shoulders. 'Fair enough. All I'm saying though, is whoever had you and let you go is crazy.'

Lisa flushed and gave another nervous laugh, desperately trying to think of how to change the subject. 'So where are you and Nicola off to this evening? Anywhere nice?'

He ran his hands through his thick, dark hair. He really was good looking, Lisa thought; she wasn't too sure about his personality though. 'I don't know yet, we haven't decided. Why don't you join us?' he asked, his mouth curving into a smile.

Lisa frowned. 'No, it's fine thank you. I'm sure you want to be alone together and I have plans already,' she lied.

Charlie looked at her seriously. 'That's a shame.'

Lisa smiled awkwardly, wondering if it would be rude to say she had to go out all of a sudden. Why did he keep looking at her in that way? He was acting so odd that she didn't know where to look. 'Another time,' Lisa said airily.

'We'll have to arrange a date,' Charlie said with a twinkle in his eye. 'When are you free?'

'I'll speak to Nicola and we'll arrange something,' Lisa said hastily, swallowing hard and wishing she could magically disappear. 'Maybe I'll bring a date along or something,' she decided to add. She didn't like the way he was now looking at her legs.

Charlie's eyes flicked back to her face. 'Maybe,' he said, eyes narrowing as he nodded, as though he was weighing this up.

What is wrong with him? Lisa questioned. He was saying the most inappropriate things to his girlfriend's housemate, especially one he had just met! Lisa could easily see how Nicola had fallen for him though. As well as his good looks, Charlie had this way of looking at you as though you were the only woman in the world. If it wasn't her friend's boyfriend and they'd just met in a bar or something, she probably wouldn't find it so creepy.

Nicola waltzed back in the room and Charlie stood up. 'Hair looks gorgeous,' he complimented her, running his fingers through her blonde curls.

'Thank you, honey. You ready? Shall we make a move?'

'Cool with me. Lovely to meet you, Lisa.'

Lisa looked up at him and gave a little wave. 'See you.'

'Charlie, you get in the car, I'm just going to grab my bag,' Nicola said, walking off to her room.

'Look forward to seeing you again soon,' Charlie said, looking over his shoulder before he left the flat. His intense eyes blazed into her, and Lisa looked away, glad that he was gone. She exhaled a sigh of relief.

Nicola came bounding round the corner. 'Well honey, what did you think? How gorge is he? Did he say anything about me?'

Lisa smiled tightly. 'Yes, he's really . . . errr . . . really nice. He said you were getting on well,' she fibbed, trying to make her friend happy.

Nicola squealed excitely. 'How lucky am I to have him? He's completely adorable.'

Lisa's smile froze on her lips. She decided to tell her about the invite. 'He's very friendly, isn't he? He asked me to come out with you tonight,' Lisa explained with a frown, worried about Nicola's reaction.

Nicola beamed broadly. 'Ahhh, bless him! How sweet is he? I told him you were single, so he was probably worried you had no one to go out with. He's been asking all about you after I showed him your photo the other day. So cute that he takes such an interest in my friends.'

Lisa felt a wave of unease as she recalled him asking her if she was single. Why did he ask her if he already knew? It was so strange.

'Don't worry, honey,' Nicola said, noticing Lisa's unsettled expression. 'He's over-friendly to everyone. When you get to know him, you'll love him as much as I do! Have a good night, honey. I'd better go as Charlie is waiting.' Nicola bent down and planted a big kiss on Lisa's face, leaving a red lipstick print.

'Bye Nic, have fun,' Lisa called after her as she left.

Maybe Nicola was right then. Maybe Charlie was just over-friendly to everyone?

*

Sam was relaxing in bed, playing his PlayStation. He loved days like this; he had nothing to do until the evening and could completely chill out and do as he pleased all afternoon. No getting up early and putting on an uncomfortable suit or sitting on a packed, stuffy train; it was a great feeling. He was taking Jade to the theatre tonight as a surprise. He had told her it was just dinner in London, but he'd booked tickets to see *Blood Brothers* as well, as he remembered her saying she'd love to see it. He didn't even have to think about getting out of his bed until about five-thirty, he thought happily, as he considered ordering a pizza. He ate healthily most days and was always in the gym, so one treat wouldn't kill him and besides, they would be having a late dinner tonight after the show. He felt his phone vibrating on the bed and when he saw Jade's name flashing, he assumed she was calling about their arrangements for later that evening.

'Hi Jade,' he said, eyes fixed on the screen in front of him as he played his computer game.

'Sam, are you home now?' Jade asked. Her peremptory tones weren't lost on him and immediately he felt disturbed.

'Yes, I'm in my room. Why?' He had a feeling of dread and paused his game.

'I'm outside,' she replied with a steely edge to her voice. 'Let me in; we need to talk.'

'Okay, I'm coming,' Sam said, jumping to his feet and walking to the front door nervously. Something was definitely wrong and he had a very bad feeling. 'What's up?' he asked her with a concerned expression as he let her in.

Jade gave Sam a sinister glare. 'I need to talk to you,'

she said as she marched through to his bedroom and sat on the bed, folding her arms.

Sam followed Jade and sat down beside her. He attempted a joke. 'You've interrupted a brilliant computer game here, so I hope it's good.'

Jade's expression was frozen; she looked upset and angry, but her voice was calm as she spoke. 'I need you to be honest with me for once. Tell me exactly what happened that night in Sugar Hut. I want to know everything.'

Sam exhaled and looked at the floor. She had clearly been told something and he had no choice but to come clean. He only wished he'd been brave enough to tell her before she'd been told by someone else. 'Who have you spoken to?' he asked. 'Adele?'

'Yes, I've just seen Adele. Now tell me everything.' Jade's hands were shaking and she looked nervous. All he wanted to do was cuddle her and tell her everything was going to be okay, but he didn't dare.

Sam breathed harder and harder until he finally spoke. 'Okay. I went to Sugar Hut that night and I admit, I got really drunk. I saw Adele in the queue and she tried to speak to me, but I brushed her off. It was only when Chloe told me she stuck up for her in the toilets against some horrible girls that I went over and thanked her and then obviously spoke about us. After that, it's a complete blur; that's the truth.'

'So, she's telling the truth then? You slept with her?' Jade asked sharply, hurt and anger flashing in her eyes.

Sam's face darkened and his voice was wobbly as he spoke. 'I don't think I did, no. I just don't remember anything, Jade, you have to believe me. Ask Chloe, she'll tell you what a state I was in. I would never cheat on you, ever, but I blacked out.'

Jade's eyes thinned into slits. 'So let me get this straight. You don't *think* you slept with her, but you can't be certain?'

Sam winced and he stared into space. 'I can't remember anything. I would never do anything to hurt you though. I just wish I could think back, but I can't. I hate Adele, you know I do. There is no way I would have invited her back here so she must have just followed me, you know what she's like. I can't bear the girl.'

Jade shook her head and a tear slid down her perfectly bronzed cheeks, creating a white streak. She sniffed, choking on her tears as she spoke. 'That's not good enough, Sam. After everything I went through with Tom, and after every-thing Adele tried to do to keep us apart, I just can't believe you would be so stupid. You've let me down badly. I hated it when she told me she'd spoken to you, let alone stayed the night at your flat!'

Sam felt sick. He didn't have the words to make every-thing alright and it killed him. He didn't want to lie any-more, but the truth sounded terrible and he was petrified she was going to leave him. 'Please don't cry, Jade. Come here.' He put his arms out, but she bit her bottom lip and shook her head, sobbing.

'Just leave me,' she sniffed before she exhaled sharply and composed herself.

'I don't know what to say,' Sam said honestly, feeling like he wanted to cry himself, but trying to be strong. 'Adele could be making the whole thing up, which she probably is, but I want to be honest with you about what happened and the truth is, I just don't know.'

Jade was suddenly calm. 'She said she slept with you and she stayed here all night. Was she here in the morning when you woke up?'

Sam shook his head. 'No, she wasn't.' He paused. 'Jade, I'm so sorry. I'd do anything for you. I love you more than ever and I don't want this to be the end. It would kill me.'

Jade took a tissue from her pocket and blew her nose. She turned to him and looked him in the eye, sadly. 'Sam,

I can't accept the fact that you may or may not have slept with Adele behind my back, I'm sorry. We've all been drunk before and not remembered what happened, but someone is claiming to have had sex with you on this occasion and I'm never going to know the truth.'

Sam shook his head and his voice cracked. 'Please, Jade. I can't lose you. I honestly don't think anything happened. I was too drunk to raise a smile, let alone anything else!'

'But we'll never know though, will we?' Jade was adamant as she stood up. 'I can't do this, Sam. It's over.'

Even though he knew she was going to say it, Sam couldn't believe his ears. This couldn't be it! He may have got drunk and blacked out, but there was no evidence he actually did anything wrong! The image of the pink thong he found in his bed popped into his mind and he pushed it away. It didn't matter though; he knew how drunk he was that night and doubted very much he'd even been able to kiss someone, let alone have sex with them. Adele was making it up, he was almost certain. Sam jumped up and ran after Jade, grabbing her hand and trying to pull her back.

'Please Jade! I didn't do anything! I can't have done. Don't go!' He knew he sounded desperate, but that was exactly what he was.

'Leave me,' Jade said breathlessly. 'I just can't do this, Sam. I feel humiliated and let down more than ever by you.'

He nodded. 'I know. I love you, Jade. I'm so sorry,' he managed, as he watched the girl of his dreams walk out of his life. What on earth was he going to do without her?

*

The following day Chloe danced about on the spot, ecstatic at the news she'd received from her agency. She had landed a speaking role in a commercial! She had been terrified at the casting; the waiting room had been filled with the most beautiful girls she had ever seen and she had honestly thought she didn't stand a chance.

'Mum!' she called, as she ran downstairs to tell her the good news. She sighed as she realised her mum must have already gone out for the day. Chloe decided she would wait until she got home later rather than call her up. The money for the commercial was fantastic; her mum was going to be so pleased for her! Maybe she'd offer to take her on a shopping trip to New York with her earnings?

Chloe couldn't stop smiling as she made herself some toast. This was the best day of her life for sure! Out of all those girls, *she* was selected; it was the best feeling in the world. When the doorbell rang, Chloe hoped it was a dress she'd ordered online turning up. Her friends had asked her to go out at the weekend and she'd bought it especially. There was no way she'd be telling them about the commercial, she decided, as she made her way to the front door. They wouldn't be happy for her in the slightest. No, she wouldn't mention this to them unless she had to.

As Chloe opened the door, her jaw dropped. It was Adele with the fakest smile plastered on her face, revealing her new veneers. 'Hi Adele.'

'Morning, babe. Ohhh is that toast in your hand? Make me some, will you?' Adele pushed past Chloe and made her way down the hall into the kitchen, where she descended into a chair at the table.

'Two slices?' Chloe replied feebly as she put some bread into the toaster.

'Please. Make me a cuppa as well please, hun. One sugar.' Adele took out a cigarette and lit it.

Chloe grimaced as Adele exhaled a cloud of smoke. 'Adele, my mum will go mad if you smoke in here! Put it out.' She waved her hands in the air, trying to magically make the smoke disappear.

Adele flicked her hand in Chloe's direction, dismissing her comment. 'Oh chillax, will you? Your mum isn't even here and I'm sure by the time she gets back the smoke will be gone.'

Chloe huffed angrily, wishing she was brave enough to tell Adele to get lost. Instead she slumped to the kettle with a heavy heart to make tea. As much as she'd love to, she simply couldn't defy Adele; the consequences were too frightening. Besides, Adele looked out for her; they were friends.

'Cheers, babe,' Adele said when Chloe placed her mug of steaming tea in front of her. 'How's the modelling going?' she asked.

'Good,' Chloe nodded meekly, as she sipped her tea.

'Landed any jobs yet?' Adele smiled in a patronising way. When Chloe didn't answer straight away Adele added, 'Don't worry if you haven't, babe. No offence, but you're just *another* young girl wanting to be a model. There are tons of girls out there who are going to be better looking than you and better at modelling; it's a tough industry and you'll just have to get used to knockbacks.'

'Actually,' Chloe finally replied with a twinkle in her eye, desperate to tell someone her news, 'I just landed my first commercial! My agency called me up a moment ago and told me the good news!'

Adele smiled tightly and swallowed hard. 'Well done.' She flicked her hair over her shoulder. 'Anyway, let's talk about something more important than all that trivial model-ling nonsense. Do you like my new teeth? They're totes amaze aren't they?' She smiled, showing off her pearly whites.

Chloe nodded and sat at the table in front of her. 'They look really good, you're right.' Deep down she thought they looked a bit too over the top, but obviously they made Adele happy so she didn't want to ruin it for her.

Adele munched her toast, deep in thought, before turning to Chloe with a serious expression. 'Okay, let's get down to business.'

This was what Chloe was dreading. She hadn't been able to sleep the previous night because she felt so guilty about what she was about to do. She knew Adele was her friend, but no matter how hard she tried, she simply couldn't imagine Jade and Kelly stealing her business. Chloe was certain Adele must have got it wrong and now here she was, helping Adele copy everything they did.

Adele continued. 'I take it you got what I asked for? At the end of the day, you know you have no other option but to show me.'

Chloe sighed, feeling like the world's biggest traitor, gave a little nod of her head and walked out of the kitchen to get Adele what she wanted. Everything in her life was going well apart from this. When was Adele going to stop asking her to sneak around? She felt completely trapped by her at times. Chloe walked back in the kitchen and handed the several pieces of paper to Adele.

Adele scanned the sheets, her eyes like saucers and Chloe felt like her heart was in her mouth as she waited for her reaction. Adele put the papers down on the table and smiled so widely that she reminded Chloe of the Grinch. 'Great work,' she declared, approvingly.

Chloe turned away and began to tidy up, unable to say anything because the guilt was eating away at her. She couldn't believe she'd stolen and photocopied the papers with Jade and Kelly's new bikini designs. She'd gone to see Jade one evening and when she'd used the bathroom upstairs had crept off to her office, like Adele had told her to. She'd found the bikini sketches in no time, quickly photocopied them using Jade's photocopier and stuffed them in her bag. Now she'd handed them over to their biggest rival; Adele.

'Loving these new designs they've come up with, especially the bikinis with the flowers,' Adele said, drumming her long, rock-hard acrylic nails on the table. 'Have they made any of them yet?'

Chloe shook her head, wishing Adele would just leave and stop asking questions. 'Not that I know of, no.'

Adele gave a bark of laughter. 'I'll just have to beat them to it then and make them faster.'

Chloe winced at the sound of Adele's rough, gravelly laugh. She stared at Adele. 'Why don't you just come up with your own ideas?'

Adele's mood changed suddenly and the smile was wiped off her face instantly. She stood up and walked over to Chloe, looking her square in the eye. Chloe was terrified.

Adele's voice grew louder as she spoke. 'Do you really think I have time to come up with stupid designs, you silly little girl? I have orders to attend to, bikinis to make; it's not easy this job you know! Those two idiots, Tweedle Dee and Tweedle bloody Dum have each other, whereas I work alone! Don't ask me stupid questions like that again, Chloe.'

Despite Chloe being taller, she visibly shrunk in front of Adele. 'Sorry.'

Adele's demeanour changed again and she smiled sweetly. 'That's okay. Listen, we're friends, aren't we?' she asked with a casual laugh, as if to say this was all silliness.

Chloe nodded hesitantly. Yes, they were friends, but sometimes it felt like Adele was just using her.

'Good. Now, just do as I say in future, don't ask pathetic questions and we'll get along just fine.'

Chloe attempted a smile, but a lopsided one was all she could manage.

Adele grabbed the papers on the table and turned. 'Must dash, I'm so busy it's a joke. Oh, I must ask you before I go though; how are Jade and Sam getting on?' Adele's eyes sparkled in anticipation.

Chloe was puzzled. 'Jade and Sam? Why? They're happy as far as I'm aware.'

'So Sam didn't come back here last night upset or anything?' Adele looked disappointed. 'Did you speak to Jade yesterday?'

Chloe felt even more confused. Had something happened? 'No, I didn't see or speak to either of them yesterday, why?'

Adele nodded. 'Oh no reason,' she said coolly before heading towards the front door. 'I'll be in touch about any new stuff Jade and Kelly are doing in a few weeks. See you!'

Chloe closed the front door behind her and stood there in wonderment. Maybe she should go and see Sam and see if anything was wrong? It was Sunday and the only thing he might be doing was playing football, but it was still early and she doubted he'd gone anywhere just yet. That night in Sugar Hut replayed in Chloe's mind. She would bet her life on it that Adele had caused some kind of trouble between them; she was learning that that was what Adele was best at, after all.

*

It was a beautiful day, Sam thought as he looked out his window, before closing the blinds again. After weeks of nothing but cloud the sun had finally decided to make an appearance, indicating that summer was on its way at last. Inside, Sam felt exactly the opposite of the weather; depressed, gloomy and miserable. So this was heartbreak? It was awful. He'd barely slept a wink the previous night and the thought of eating made his stomach turn. After Jade had left, he'd waited about thirty minutes and then texted her asking her to meet again as he wanted to make it work. He would do *anything* to make it work. She'd replied that it wouldn't and could he stop calling and texting

226

because he was only making it harder for her. That didn't stop him though. He guessed he'd tried calling her around fifteen times, but she never answered; it had driven him crazy! He had never felt this way before in all his life. He had flashbacks to when girls in the past used to call him and he'd ignored them. They would ring and ring despite him never answering or calling back, and he used to wonder why they had no pride or self-respect. Now Sam knew the answer; when you wanted to talk to someone that badly, pride simply went out of the window. It was the most awful feeling when you urgently wanted to speak to someone but got nowhere. Each unanswered call only made him feel more desperate and determined. After about fifteen calls though, he knew he had to stop. Jade didn't want to speak to him and he had no choice but to accept it. He was supposed to be playing football today, but he couldn't do it. He normally loved the game, but he didn't want to see or talk to anyone. Besides, there was no way he would play well when he hadn't eaten or slept and had so much on his mind.

There was a knock at the door and his heart thudded violently in his chest. Was it Jade? *Please say it's her*, he thought as he got up and went to open the door. He was surprised to see Chloe standing there.

Chloe took one look at his dishevelled hair, tracksuit bottoms and stained t-shirt and her face fell. 'So, it's true then? You and Jade are going through problems? I can't believe it,' she said shaking her head as he made way for her to go through.

'What? How do you know? Have you spoken to Jade? What did she say?' Sam asked all at once as he followed Chloe into the kitchen.

'Wow, calm down a bit,' Chloe said with an anxious expression. 'I haven't seen Jade. Adele just came over and asked about you both,' she explained.

Sam looked enraged. 'What? Adele has been round to you today? I'm going to kill her,' he said, marching round the kitchen deep in thought, his hands on his hips. He put his hands through his fair hair. 'What did Adele say?'

'What is all this about?' Chloe asked, biting her nails with worry. 'She just came round and asked how you and Jade were, as though something had happened.'

Sam screwed up his hand into a fist, looking furious. 'Oh, I bet she did. I bet she was fishing to find out that Jade broke up with me! Just like that bitch wanted.'

'Oh my God,' Chloe said sadly as she stared at him, stunned, her huge green eyes open wide. 'I can't believe it. What happened? Tell me everything.'

Sam sat down and put his head in his hands. In a way he was glad Chloe had come over. He wanted to talk to someone about it and it wasn't like he could cry down the phone to his mates, was it? Men didn't do that. He would call his mates when he wanted to get drunk and forget about Jade, not to talk about what happened. Girls sat there for hours with their friends, discussing their feelings and thoughts about their most recent break-ups, but with men it was the opposite. No talking, just drinking. He explained to Chloe what had happened. He told her everything – from the pink thong to the text messages he sent to Adele. He knew he could trust Chloe and that everything he said would stay strictly between the two of them.

'So you really don't know what happened that night then?' Chloe asked curiously. She'd never been that drunk in her life and couldn't imagine not being able to remember what happened.

Sam shook his head with a tormented expression. 'I honestly don't. I don't believe I was capable of doing anything though.' He flushed a little, embarrassed to be talking about sex in front of his little sister.

'If only I'd have stayed at yours that night to make sure

you were okay,' Chloe said, staring into space. 'Then Adele couldn't have done anything because I would have been here.'

'If only I hadn't got so drunk,' Sam said with a sigh.

'Adele is so out of order,' Chloe announced.

Sam was baffled. 'Then why do you stay friends with her? Why does she go round Mum's house all the time? I tried telling you to stay away from her.'

Chloe shifted in her chair and cleared her throat, not knowing how to answer. 'It's a long story,' she said finally, too ashamed to admit the truth. 'We're friends.'

'Chloe, Adele doesn't have *friends*. I'm sorry to break it to you, but she's a user. The only person Adele will ever care about is herself. Try to stay away from her,' Sam said, wagging a finger in Chloe's direction. 'She's a nasty piece of work and I don't want her anywhere near you. I bet she's made this whole thing up.'

Chloe nodded as she thought about what Sam had just said. 'Me too.' The more Chloe thought about Adele, the more she suspected he was right. Was she *really* Adele's friend? Adele only ever called her and came over to see her when she wanted news about Jade and Kelly. 'Poor Jade,' she whispered.

Sam winced as she said Jade's name. 'I know. What can I do to get her back?' He looked up at Chloe, his face alight with hope. 'You talk to her sometimes, don't you? Can't you go round and tell her you think Adele has made it up? You saw me that night, you know how drunk I was. Please.'

Chloe looked doubtful. 'I don't think it will change anything, but I'll try if you want.'

Sam sighed with relief and closed his eyes momentarily. 'Thank you.' He stood up and put the kettle on, hoping that a miracle would happen and somehow Chloe would be able to bring Jade back to him.

*

Lisa walked out of her office wondering where she should go for lunch. She had a new book in her bag she couldn't wait to get started on.

'Lisa!' she heard a man shout.

She squinted in the sunshine as she tried to make out who was calling her and was surprised when she saw Charlie making his way towards her.

'Hi Charlie,' Lisa said with a friendly smile. 'You meeting Nicola for lunch or something?'

'I came here on the off chance that Nicola could meet me, but she's too busy,' he shrugged. He looked her up and down, making Lisa feel self-conscious. 'You look like a sexy secretary in that black skirt and white blouse.'

Lisa tried to laugh it off as she felt her face redden. 'I don't know about that.'

'Where you off to?' Charlie asked, his smouldering eyes making her want to look away.

'Not sure yet, just about to get some lunch,' Lisa told him, hoping this was her chance to leave. 'I haven't got long, so better get going.'

'I may as well join you then,' Charlie grinned as he put his hand on her shoulder. 'Will be nice to get to know Nicola's roommate a bit better.'

Lisa didn't know what to say. How could she be rude to her friend's boyfriend and tell him no? Having lunch with Charlie was not only the last thing she felt like doing, but also it was weird. This was Nicola's boyfriend and she'd only met him once! Lisa felt nothing but awkward around him. Seeing no way out, Lisa tried to smile back as they began to walk in the direction of a row of restaurants and cafés.

They decided on a little Italian café and Lisa kept looking at her watch, wondering when she could make her excuses and leave. Charlie hadn't taken his eyes off her the whole time and Lisa was worried what Nicola would make of them going to lunch together; it felt wrong. He didn't eat much, Lisa noticed, as she sipped her small bowl of soup.

'Today was nice,' Charlie said as they left. 'We should definitely meet for lunch again sometime.'

Lisa looked away from him uncomfortably. 'Yeah. We'll have to make sure Nicola can come next time.'

'Maybe,' Charlie said as he kissed Lisa's cheek to say goodbye.

Lisa waved goodbye, relieved her lunch was over. She would rather have been sat in work, she thought resentfully.

'Hi, honey.' Nicola's voice made Lisa jump as she walked to her desk.

'Hi Nic,' Lisa said merrily, as she sat down. She was about to say she'd just seen Charlie, but Nicola spoke first.

'I had an amazing lunch with Charlie today,' she gushed. 'He had a day off work and took me to a lovely Turkish restaurant,' she explained, fluttering her eyelashes.

Lisa couldn't believe her ears. So Charlie had already been to lunch with Nicola? That's why he was near their offices, not because he'd come on the off chance! Why did he lie? *Because he wanted to spend time with you*, a voice inside her head sounded, which Lisa tried to ignore. No wonder he could only manage a soup, she thought, annoyed that he was so deceitful. He was so weird! Lisa wanted to tell Nicola, but she didn't want her to get the wrong idea and be upset, not when she looked so blissfully happy. Lisa knew then and there Charlie was definitely someone she needed to avoid at all costs.

*

A week later, Donna felt herself drifting off as the masseuse worked her magic on her shoulders, rubbing in some beautiful scented lavender oil. This is the life, she thought, as she felt herself go into a world of complete relaxation. Thirty minutes later she was gently tapped by the masseuse, who informed her that her massage was over.

'Just relax and take your time getting ready. We'll see you outside,' the lady said in her silky, soothing tones.

Donna nodded sleepily, and then glanced over at Aaron who was lying on the bed adjacent to hers.

He was already looking at her with a smile. 'Enjoy that?'

Donna yawned. 'Oh my God, it was amazing.'

Donna had had the most enjoyable weekend of her life. Aaron had surprised her and whisked her off to Claridge's in Mayfair. It wasn't your typical London hotel; it was the most luxurious, exclusive, iconic hotel she'd ever stayed in and Aaron had even booked them a suite. It was huge! Donna wouldn't have minded living in it; she would have swapped it for her poky flat any day. Donna felt so blessed to have met Aaron; he was, quite simply, the best thing that had ever happened to her. She never had good luck, but that night at Funky Mojoe someone had been looking down on her, because her life had changed for the better in every way. Donna knew Adele would be pea green with envy if she could see her now, living life like an A-list celebrity, but Donna genuinely just wanted Aaron. Of course, being treated like a princess was wonderful, but if Aaron had nothing to his name Donna would still love him. Things didn't need to be dressed up in bells and bows for her to be happy. She hadn't told him she loved him yet, but she did. She was certain he felt the same too; they were made for each other. When she was with him she felt as though she'd known him for years. He accepted her for who she was and she loved him for that. She'd always felt conscious in the past when she went out in Essex. Most men hardly glanced her way and she guessed it was because of her size; most girls desired to be a size twelve and under in Nu Bar and Faces. Aaron was constantly complimenting her figure though, telling her how much he adored it and loathed waiflike skinny girls. Aaron always went to the gym after football practice and Donna had started to join him so they could spend some time together. She had slimmed down a fair amount already without even trying and actually had started to enjoy feeling healthier. She didn't want to be a slender size eight or anything; she agreed with Aaron, there was nothing better than a curvy figure, but she did enjoy exercising surprisingly, especially if it meant more time with Aaron. She smiled at him and his eyes sparkled.

'Let's go back to the room,' he grinned lustily, with a suggestive glint in his eye that made Donna's heart flip.

That was another thing. They had so much chemistry in the bedroom department and Donna could have sworn she'd never truly enjoyed sex until she'd met him. She was so comfortable with him and felt completely uninhibited; she literally couldn't get enough. Probably another reason why I'm losing so much weight, Donna almost laughed to herself out loud.

'Come on then,' she said, getting up and throwing her clothes back on as quickly as possible. She giggled as Aaron tugged at her underwear as she was trying to get her jeans on.

'I'm not sure I can wait,' Aaron whispered breathlessly as he pushed himself against her.

Donna gave in; she couldn't wait either. 'Quick then and don't make too much noise,' she laughed before kissing him hungrily.

It wasn't long before it was over. They were far too excited and the prospect of someone walking in had hurried them along.

'Look at the colour of my face!' Donna exclaimed, as she rubbed her blotchy red skin. 'They'll know what we've been up to!'

Aaron shrugged as he zipped up his trousers. 'The amount

they charge to stay here, we should be allowed to do that anywhere in the building.'

Donna followed behind him, guiltily holding his hand as they exited the room, and thanked her lucky stars the staff were so busy talking to other customers they barely noticed how long they'd been.

'Thanks,' Aaron said, slipping two ten-pound notes on the table to pay for both their masseurs' tips.

The lady looked up with a smile. 'Thank you. Enjoy your stay.'

'I can't believe we just did that and got away with it!' Donna giggled excitedly as they made their way back to their room.

Aaron smiled, squeezed her hand and kissed her gently on the forehead.

Donna got ready for the evening, slipping into a gorgeous little black dress which Aaron had bought her that day from Dolce and Gabbana in Bond Street. It was plain and simple, but she felt a million dollars in it and she actually loved the way it showed off her curves in all the right places. She was down a dress size to a size fourteen now and felt better than she had in ages. She made her hair wavy with her curling tongs, added a layer of fake tan and then decided on the smoky-eyed look to compliment her dress. Her eyelash extensions looked great and she honestly couldn't remember a time she felt so happy with her appearance. Or maybe she just couldn't remember being so happy? She had a beautiful black Mulberry clutch that she'd bought at work and it matched her outfit perfectly. Then she slipped into some sleek Gucci heels and caught Aaron staring at her in awe.

'Babe, you look absolutely . . .' He was lost for words and she couldn't believe that she was having this effect on her gorgeous Aaron. Donna didn't think it was possible to feel this content. She kissed him tenderly.

'Thank you,' she said, not even needing to hear his last word.

'We're going to Gordon Ramsay's restaurant downstairs,' he told her.

Donna gasped. 'Oh my God, really? I've always wanted to go there!' She beamed, remembering seeing it was there when they'd arrived at the hotel and hoping they would get to go.

Ten minutes later she was being seated by the waiter and poured champagne. Donna clinked glasses with Aaron and beamed broadly. 'Thank you so much for this. You're the best boyfriend ever,' she told him, her eyes glistening with happiness.

'You're worth everything and more,' Aaron said earnestly. 'I told you before; I've never met anyone like you. You make me happy.'

'That makes two of us,' Donna said, leaning over for a kiss.

They sat through the most fantastic meal and Donna had to pinch herself that this was actually happening to her. Here she was, sitting in a top restaurant in a renowned hotel with her famous footballer boyfriend!

After dessert, Aaron took her hand and stared at her seriously. 'Donna. I've been meaning to speak to you. There is a reason I brought you here this weekend.'

Donna's grin vanished in a split second. Why was he shaking? Was he about to tell her something bad? 'Is something wrong?' she blurted out, worried he was about to let her down.

Aaron gave a nervous laugh. 'No, no. Nothing is wrong; quite the opposite actually.' He began to breathe harder and slower, as if he was trying to build up the courage to say something. 'The thing is,' he managed before wiping his forehead with a napkin, 'the thing is, I've fallen in love with you.'

Donna's chin wobbled and her eyes filled with tears. 'Oh Aaron! I love you too!' She grabbed his hand and rubbed it gently, thinking how sweet he was to tell her his feelings. She was so glad he felt the same way she did.

'That's not all,' he laughed again, his hands still trembling.

Donna's mouth flew open wide as she watched Aaron drop to one knee in front of her. She looked down at his happy, yet petrified face and felt more emotional than she ever had in her life.

Aaron swallowed hard and cleared his throat. 'Donna, since I've met you I've had a smile on my face every day. I may not have known you for long but I feel like I know I want to be with you forever. Will you do me the great honour of being my wife?'

Donna screamed with happiness and Aaron laughed as people in the restaurant started to look round to see what all the noise was about. She bent down and kissed him. 'Yes! Yes! Yes! I'll be your wife!' She shrieked in delight as he placed the biggest diamond she had ever seen on her finger. The restaurant had become silent and suddenly there was a huge round of applause, making Donna and Aaron flush with happiness. Out of nowhere the waiter appeared, bringing two more glasses of champagne, and the waitress handed a huge bouquet of red roses to an ecstatic Donna.

'I love you,' Aaron said, gazing into the hazel eyes of his wife-to-be.

'Oh my God! I'm going to be your wife!' Donna shrieked excitedly as she kissed him once more, tears of joy rolling down her cheeks. 'I can't believe you've proposed! I had no idea,' she said, smiling and sniffing at the same time.

He dabbed at her eyes lovingly with a napkin. 'I decided a few weeks ago. I know you're the one and I want us to get married and move in together as soon as possible.'

'I can't wait,' Donna said, staring at him in amazement. He was actually going to be her husband!

'We can have the most amazing wedding day ever. I want you to have nothing but the best,' Aaron announced as he sipped his champagne.

Donna grinned. 'I already have the best; I have you.'

Aaron beamed. 'Thanks. Seriously though; if you want a big wedding, then that's what we'll have.'

'I'm so excited,' Donna said, shaking her head as she thought about all the plans they'd have to make. She had always dreamed of getting married and couldn't believe it was finally happening to her. She gazed down at her engagement ring, which glittered and sparkled in the light; it was absolutely gorgeous and must have cost a fortune. It fit perfectly too she noticed, just like they did.

'To us,' Aaron clinked glasses with her and they sipped their champagne.

Donna was on cloud nine. She felt so lucky that she had a warm, glowing feeling sweep over her making her feel like she was floating. Her smile froze on her lips as she thought about breaking the news to Adele; boy was she going to be jell!

CHAPTER 14

Jade gasped in horror as she saw the images flash in front of her eyes. 'Oh my God! Kelly, come look at this!'

Kelly looked up from the sewing machine, where she was finishing the last of the bikinis from their new line. 'What's up, babe?' she asked as she made her way over to the computer.

Jade pointed to the computer screen, devastated. 'It's Adele's website! I was on Facebook a moment ago uploading some of the images of our new bikinis and someone had commented on Adele's bikini page and it flashed up on my screen. I then went to her website and you're not going to believe this! She's got the same bikinis as us again!'

Kelly looked like she'd seen a ghost as she watched Jade flick through the images, mesmerised. The colour drained from her face as she watched their designs displayed across Adele's website. 'I don't believe this! How on earth did she copy us this time?'

Jade felt like crying. All their hard work felt like it had been for nothing. Adele had not only copied them again, but managed to beat them to it and start selling the same designs earlier. 'Look,' Jade said, clicking back on Facebook to Adele's bikini page. 'She uploaded these images last week.

I don't understand. They're practically identical to ours! Even the colours are the same. The only difference is that hers are slightly cheaper!'

Kelly was just as perplexed as she scratched her head. 'How has she copied us? I don't get it.'

'Me either,' Jade said, shaking her head, frustrated beyond belief. Vajazzle My Bikini had been doing really well and the girls had quickly realised they needed to keep updating their stock to keep customers interested. Jade mainly designed the bikinis and Kelly bought the best materials and embellishments, as well as making them. They worked so well as a team and hadn't argued about anything so far. Orders were coming in thick and fast seeing as it was early summer and Jade took care of all enquiries and advertising as well as dealing with the courier company they used to send the bikinis out to their customers. They were both continuously busy, but they wouldn't have it any other way. Customers were of the utmost importance and Jade and Kelly made sure they received their orders as soon as possible. They had decided to wrap them in hot pink tissue paper, tied with a big pink bow and silver sticker which had their company logo on. They prided themselves on being professional and reliable and Jade often wondered how Adele was coping running her business alone. If it was as busy as theirs was, she must have been struggling. They had been so pleased with their new designs, but now somehow Adele had managed to ruin everything by copying them again. Jade racked her brains, wondering how on earth she could have known what they were going to do.

'Check where the design papers are,' Kelly suddenly suggested. 'Do we still have them?'

Jade opened a drawer and pulled them out, flashing them in front of Kelly. 'They're here. So there is no way Adele can have them. It just doesn't make any sense.'

Kelly nodded. 'I know, hun. I just can't work out how

she's taken our ideas. It's definitely no coincidence our designs are identical; this is Adele we're talking about.'

Jade sighed. The past week had been so difficult for her not being with Sam anymore and to take her mind off it, she'd thrown herself into work. It helped having something else to focus on; God only knew how she would have coped otherwise. The doorbell rang and Jade ran to answer it, surprised to see Chloe standing on her doorstep.

'Chloe, hi,' she said, opening the door and letting her in. 'How are you?'

'Hi,' Chloe said softly, as she walked through. 'I've been meaning to come and see you, but I've been quite busy recently. I'm so sorry to hear about you and my brother splitting up.'

Jade didn't know what to say. She had tried to prevent herself from thinking about Sam because it made her too upset and now here Chloe was on her doorstep, with those piercing green eyes, so like her brother's. She reminded her so much of Sam it was uncanny; from her fair hair, to her perfectly golden, smooth skin tone, it was obvious for anyone to see they were siblings. She pointed upstairs. 'Kelly is here working. Shall we go up?'

Chloe nodded and followed Jade to the upstairs office where she took a seat.

'Hi babe,' Kelly said, glancing up from the sewing machine where she was back working.

'Hi,' Chloe smiled and gave a little wave.

'Do you want a drink?' Jade offered. She took a seat when Chloe shook her head.

'So, how have you been?' Chloe asked Jade.

Jade briefly raised her eyebrows, trying not to get upset. She swallowed hard and cleared her throat. 'As well as can be expected, I suppose.' She was glad that she'd made an effort today and had actually put some make-up on. Her long hair was in a side plait and she was wearing jeans instead of the Abercrombie tracksuits she'd been slouching around in for the last few days. Kelly had told her in no certain terms that just because she was feeling upset, it didn't make it okay to have bad fashion sense and that under no circumstances was Jade to wear them again in front of her, as they were an eyesore. Kelly always made Jade laugh when she was down and she was grateful that she worked with her, especially since she'd split up with Sam. Jade was thankful that she looked quite nice; hopefully Chloe would go back to Sam and say she was doing just fine without him, even if that wasn't the case.

'I saw him the day after you split up,' Chloe explained. She shook her head as she remembered the state of her brother. 'Sam's terribly upset. Is there definitely no way you can work things out?' She looked up at Jade, her face full of hope.

'Did he tell you everything that happened?' Jade questioned, secretly glad that Sam was finding it as hard as she was, though she'd guessed because he'd tried to call her so many times. At least it showed he still cared, Jade consoled herself.

Chloe nodded and tucked her silky, long blonde hair behind her ear. 'Yes. I was there that night though and honestly Jade, he was so drunk. I just can't believe that anything happened between them. I truly think that Adele is making it all up!'

Jade shook her head sadly and fiddled with the end of her plait. 'But I'll never know, will I? Besides, Sam lied to me. He didn't tell me anything about that night and I asked him time and time again what was wrong and why he was acting strange. He shouldn't have got himself in that situation in the first place.'

'Yeah, babe,' Kelly supported Jade, looking at Chloe, 'you have to see it from Jade's point of view.'

'I know,' Chloe agreed. 'I just was wondering if there

241

was any way you think you could talk to Sam or meet up . . .' Her eyes flicked to Jade's cynical expression and then down to the floor. Chloe paused. 'But I can see now it's out of the question. I know Sam was wrong, but it's just such a shame. He's still crazy about you and he's really devastated.'

'I was crazy about him too,' Jade said sullenly. 'But it's over. He ruined it.'

Chloe nodded as if she understood where Jade was coming from. 'How have you been?'

Jade was glad to change the subject and turned to her computer. 'Well, it looks as though Adele strikes again. Come and look at this, Chloe,' she said, showing her the copied designs on Adele's website.

Chloe looked uncomfortable and awkward as Jade showed her the images. *She obviously feels sorry for us and doesn't know what to say*, Jade thought to herself.

'Can you believe it?' Kelly asked Chloe, getting angry once again. 'We just can't understand where she's getting our designs from.'

Chloe couldn't look Kelly in the eye and picked her bag up. 'It's really weird, isn't it? I wonder . . . how . . . how she stole your designs?'

'I know. We just can't work it out,' Kelly said, watching Chloe as she put her jacket on.

'I can't stay for long,' Chloe said hastily, 'I have to be home for dinner. I just wanted to check you were alright, Jade.'

'Yes. Thanks for coming round, Chloe. I know it's a shame about Sam and me, but unfortunately it just can't be helped.'

Chloe waved her hand as she walked to the door. 'Bye Kelly, see you soon. Don't worry Jade, I'll let myself out. Speak soon.'

'Bye,' they chorused.

Jade looked at Kelly, surprised to see a suspicious look on her face. 'What are you looking like that for?'

Kelly opened her mouth to speak, but then hesitated. 'It doesn't matter,' she said finally as she pinned red flowers on black bikini bottoms.

'What do you mean it doesn't matter?' Jade replied. 'Just say what you were about to. I hate it when you do that.'

Kelly stopped what she was doing and stared at Jade. 'Okay fine, I'll say.' She took a deep breath. 'It's something about Chloe that I'm unsure of. I know she's a lovely girl who wouldn't harm a fly, but did you see how strange she was acting when you told her about Adele stealing our ideas again? She couldn't get away quick enough.'

Jade frowned, bemused. 'That's just because she felt awkward for us. Why are you saying this?'

Kelly exhaled. 'Look, I get she feels awkward for us, but could it be because she had something to do with it? That day at the photo shoot I remember her acting quiet and a bit offish and she was texting all day on her phone. I remember I caught a glimpse of who she was texting; I've never mentioned it before because it didn't have any significance, but now I'm not so certain.'

Jade was baffled. What was Kelly getting at?

'Who was she texting? I remember seeing her on her phone a lot too, but so what? This whole thing has nothing to do with Chloe.'

'She was texting Adele.'

Jade shook her head, certain Kelly couldn't be right. Chloe was lovely. There was no way on earth she would betray them and give their designs to Adele. Kelly was crazy! She sighed and finally spoke. 'Kelly, you must have got it wrong. Chloe is on our side, not Adele's. Maybe she has another friend called Adele; have you thought of that? How could you even suggest she may be in on it? She's one of the sweetest, nicest people I know.'

Kelly put her hands up. 'I can't help it if that's what I think! I'm telling you, she was texting Adele. It's not exactly the most common name in the world! I'm being serious. I was watching her just now and she was acting guilty. Maybe she just mentioned what some of the designs were like to Adele without thinking?'

Jade thought about it for a moment. Chloe spying for Adele and discussing their designs? There was just no way. 'Kelly, you've got it wrong. Now please stop accusing innocent people. You'll probably be saying it's me next!'

Kelly gave a sulky pout. 'I know what I saw and I have a good read of people's reactions. Don't believe me then.'

'I won't,' Jade said firmly as she typed an email to a customer.

'You never take anything I say seriously,' Kelly huffed, lifting her chin in the air defiantly. 'I bet if it was Lisa saying it, you'd listen.'

Jade tutted loudly. 'Stop being so stupid, Kel.'

'Well it's true,' Kelly muttered as she pinned some more flowers in place.

Jade shook her head, thinking how silly Kelly was being. 'Look I have enough on my plate thinking about Sam all the time without thinking about Chloe now as well. Let's just forget it, yeah?'

Kelly nodded reluctantly. 'Okay, but I'm not going to change my mind and I promise, I'm going to do my best to get to the bottom of all of this.'

Jade sighed, wondering why Kelly couldn't just forget about it all. She felt drained and exhausted. Chloe was such a lovely girl and Jade was certain that Kelly was barking up the wrong tree. She just hoped she didn't make things worse in any way; Kelly saying she promised she was going to get to the bottom of everything was a very worrying thought.

*

Adele rolled her eyes as she listened to the customer at the other end of the line.

'I'm sorry, but I've received my bikini and one of the flowers has already fallen off. I've only just tried it on. Another two of the flowers are loose as well and I must say, I'm really not impressed with the quality at all,' the angry woman explained.

Adele really couldn't be bothered with this. She had another five bikinis to make and send out and the college girls she had hired to help make them were over thirty minutes late. 'So the flowers were on the bikini when you received it, yes?' Adele asked.

The lady sighed. 'Yes. But then I tried the bikini on and one fell off. When I looked closely there were some others loose as well.'

Adele paused and then exhaled sharply. 'Look, I'm sorry but if the flowers were attached until you tried it on then I can only imagine you're too big for the bikini, meaning you've stretched it and made them fall off.'

The woman was exasperated. 'Excuse me? I'm a size eight! All I did was try it on and it practically fell apart! I want a refund!'

Adele yawned, bored of the conversation; there was no way she was giving this woman her money back. She ordered it and she was getting it. 'No can do I'm afraid,' Adele asserted.

The woman gasped in shock. 'But it's a faulty product!'

'Correction,' Adele interjected. 'The product was fine until *you* tried it on. You said so yourself. It's been worn by you and we cannot give you a refund. You ruined it and when you tried it the flowers came off. So if I were you I would get sewing, babe.'

'I tried it on, that's all! It still has the hygienic strip inside the bottoms. I haven't worn it anywhere! This is disgusting!' The woman was clearly irate as she huffed down the phone.

'No refunds, sorry. Is there anything else I can help you with?' Adele asked in a cheery tone, much to the woman's annoyance.

'I can't believe this! How can you sell me a faulty product and not give me a refund? This is so unprofessional! I'm going to report you. In fact I'm going to go to the citizen's advice bureau right now! I have rights! I . . .'

'If there's nothing else, then I must go. Thanks for the call,' Adele said with a smirk as she hung up the phone and then switched it on silent in case she decided to call again. Some customers really were just nothing but a nuisance. They complained about *everything*! So what if a couple of flowers fell off? Big deal. Why didn't she just stitch them back on? Adele glanced at her Cartier watch and sighed. The two college students she had hired, Libby and Megan, were late again. She gave them all the bikinis to make and usually pretended she was doing other work or had meetings to go to while she left them and just went for a spray tan or pedicure. Running a website was actually hard work and hiring the two students meant she wasn't earning as much. She only paid them six pounds an hour, but this still ate away at her profit margins. She didn't think the girls were actually any good, they spent far more time chatting than sewing, but she knew they needed the cash and she was more than happy to give them the work rather than sit there and do it herself. The doorbell rang and Adele jumped up to answer it.

'About bloody time,' Adele said as she flicked her hair behind her shoulder when she opened the door.

Libby looked nervous. 'Sorry Adele. We got held up at college.'

Adele raised her eyebrows. 'Whatever, just get on with it. I need these five bikinis made within the next two hours before the post office closes.' She threw the material and flowers on the floor in front of them, making Megan flinch. 'Now, I must go out,' she said, pausing as she tried to think

246

of an excuse, 'I have an important business lunch.' Adele put on her oversized Dior shades and turned, her head held high as she walked out.

Thirty minutes later Adele was relaxing as her feet were being soaked in soapy water before her pedicure. This bikini business really was quite tiring, she acknowledged as she picked a bright pink colour for her toes.

'I want lots of crystals on the big toe too,' Adele asserted to the beautician. 'And go right to the edges this time. The last girl gave me hardly any.'

After a pedicure and eyebrow tint, Adele felt much better. It was a warm day even though the sun wasn't shining and she decided to have a walk around the shops in Loughton before they closed. Shopping always cheered her up, she thought as she purchased a brand new Forever Unique dress for three hundred pounds; now she just needed somewhere good to go to wear it. As she walked out of the shop she spotted Donna on the other side of the road.

'Donna!' she called, practically jogging to catch up with her.

Donna glanced over and waved, waiting for Adele to cross over.

'Alright babe?' Adele said, giving her a kiss. She looked Donna up and down; she looked great, Adele thought in surprise. She was slimmer, that was for sure and Donna looked like she was glowing with happiness. Had she done something new with her hair? 'Hair looks gorge,' she admired. 'Are you wearing extensions?'

Donna instantly put her hands on her hair as she spoke, stroking her longer locks. 'Thanks. Yeah, I had some extensions put in and I dyed it a bit lighter.'

Adele's eyes suddenly focused on the huge rock on Donna's wedding finger. So Aaron had done it then, she thought dismally. She forced a smile and wagged her fingers. 'Something to tell me?'

Donna blushed a little, as she beamed broadly. 'I'm engaged!' she blurted out with an excited laugh.

'I can't believe it!' Adele replied in mock surprise. 'Such amazing news,' she said as her stomach rumbled. It was a good job she'd bumped into Donna, perhaps she'd go for dinner with her? The last thing she wanted to do was cook tonight and there was a lovely Thai a short walk away that she fancied. 'Let me take you to dinner to celebrate and you can tell me all about it.'

Donna hesitated. 'Sorry Adele, that's really kind of you, but I said I'd go to my parents' house for dinner tonight.'

Adele flapped her hand. 'Then tell them you'll go another night. Tonight I'm taking you out to celebrate. You can go home any time.'

Donna looked uncertain. 'But my mum may have already started on the di—' Donna paused when she saw Adele's mouth press into a hard line. 'Okay, dinner sounds great.'

*

'So, have you started wedding planning yet?' Adele asked, as she dipped her Thai crackers into some sweet chilli sauce.

'Not yet. He only asked me at the weekend,' Donna explained.

Adele stopped munching and stared at her with a serious expression. 'I want you to know I'm here to help as much as possible. You know fashion is one hundred per cent my thing, so I'll help you choose your dress. Obviously you can take your mum as well and all that, but seriously, I know a good dress when I see one.'

Donna nodded, looking a bit shocked. 'Thanks Adele, that's really sweet of you.'

Adele shrugged. 'That's what maids of honour are for, silly.'

Donna frowned, looking awkward. 'What?'

Adele sighed. 'Maid of honour. I take it I'll be yours, won't I?' she demanded, as she tucked her napkin into her top. She needed *some* part in this wedding. The whole event would be swarming with footballers and she wanted to stand out and be noticed; who knew, maybe her turn would be next?

Donna looked uncomfortable, her eyes looking round the room. 'Well, I haven't decided yet and I know my sister may be a bit put out . . .'

Adele's jaw dropped. 'Donna, don't be so ridiculous! I was with you when you met Aaron. I'm your best friend, surely? Sod your sister. You told me before that she only ever talks to you when she wants you to babysit her brats!'

Donna turned red and lowered her voice. 'I didn't call them brats, Adele, please don't say that,' she said, as she looked behind her to check there wasn't anyone she knew listening to them. 'I haven't even decided those kind of details yet. It's only just happened.'

'Well, decide now,' Adele said, glaring at her, tapping her long fingernails impatiently on the table.

Donna held her breath and then finally spoke. 'Okay, you can do it. You can be my maid of honour. My sister can just be bridesmaid.'

Adele squealed. 'Thanks Don! This is going to be amazing. When shall we go shopping? When do you think you'll get married?'

Donna smiled as she spoke. 'Aaron wants to get married right away, so I guess booking a venue will be the first thing. I feel a bit awkward really,' Donna said, tucking her hair behind her ear. 'He's told me I can have whatever I want, you know, go all out. Nothing is too much he said. But, I'd just feel uncomfortable spending all his money. I mean, I have some savings, but not a lot, and my parents aren't in any position to help. Maybe we'll just have a quiet wedding?'

Adele was more envious than she'd ever been in her life. Here was her friend, marrying a footballer who had told her to spend as much as she wanted on the wedding and she was actually feeling awkward about it. Adele smiled tightly and tried to persuade her otherwise. If she was going to be maid of honour then she wanted to wear an expensive designer bridesmaid dress, drink the best champagne and eat exquisite food. What was the point in marrying a footballer otherwise? She took a deep breath and spoke to her as though she was addressing a child. 'Donna, if he's told you to spend as much as you like on the wedding then I really think you should. It's not as though he's strapped for cash, and you wouldn't want to hurt his feelings, would you?'

Donna shook her head with a thoughtful expression.

Adele's lips curled upwards. 'I think he must obviously want a big wedding himself and that's why he's left you in charge, thinking that's what you'll organise. You wouldn't want to take that away from him, would you?'

Donna frowned, deep in thought. 'No, of course not.'

Adele gave a short laugh. 'Well then, organise a huge wedding, silly. It's *our* day . . . I mean *your* day to enjoy yourself. You only get one day, Donna; make it a good one.'

Donna digested Adele's words and then nodded. 'You're right. You're totally right. I'm only ever going to get married once; I may as well go crazy and have the biggest and best wedding ever!'

'Exactly!' Adele smiled, exhaling a long breath and clapping her hands together excitedly. 'We'll go shopping next weekend. Obviously Vera Wang will be our first stop for you, I'll arrange the appointments, then Browns Brides, which have amazing bridesmaids dresses and obviously you can see more wedding dresses too. A family friend got married not too long ago and her bridesmaids' dresses were from there; the most gorgeous Monique Lhuillier gowns ever. Then after that we'll go to Temperley London, Jenny Packham and Valentino.'

Donna sipped her white wine spritzer and nodded. 'Okay, sounds good. I'm excited now.'

'Me too,' Adele announced and she clinked glasses with Donna. 'To your wedding; the most amazing event you'll ever experience.'

*

Kelly pulled up outside Billy's house and felt the usual bubbles of excitement in her stomach. She was surprising him with a visit tonight, something she never normally did. He'd been busy with work and really hard to get through to in the last couple of days; she just hoped everything was okay because Billy wasn't giving much away on the phone. She coated her lips with some MAC lip gloss she found in the glove compartment. Make-up and hair spray were all she had in there and Billy had laughed his head off when he'd opened it one day. What else did a girl need in her car? Kelly wondered, baffled as to why he found it so amusing. Maybe she should add some portable straighteners, she decided. She ran her fingers through her long blonde hair, satisfied with her appearance, and walked to his front door to ring the bell.

After ringing three times to no avail, she wondered whether Billy was actually home and was about to call him until she saw the upstairs curtains moving. A few moments later, the door opened and Kelly's mouth opened wide with shock as she was greeted by Billy. He looked as though he hadn't slept in days, with the worst bags under his eyes Kelly had ever seen. His usually sleek, shiny hair was dishevelled and greasy and his usually smooth skin was dry, stubble covering his jawline. What on earth had happened?

'What's going on, babe?' Kelly asked, her voice full of worry.

He opened the door and Kelly walked in, wondering what he was about to tell her. She was worried for him. The whole house was in darkness and Kelly caught a glimpse of the state of the kitchen; there was a pile of washing up on the kitchen surface – this was so unlike Billy! Kelly followed him through to the lounge and sat down. He sat next to her and put his face in his hands.

Kelly gently touched his hands and moved them from his face. 'Come on, tell me what's wrong. I'm really worried.'

Billy took a deep breath and looked up at the ceiling. He shook his head sadly, his voice a whisper. 'I've lost it all, babe. Everything; it's gone.'

Kelly stomach flipped over with nerves. 'Bill, what are you talking about? Work?'

He nodded, his shoulders hunched, looking defeated. 'Yep. Alfie has wiped us out. He's taken the lot.'

Kelly shifted in her seat and moved closer to him. 'Oh no, babe. Tell me everything that happened,' she said sympathetically, now understanding why Billy hadn't been acting himself recently on the phone. He had kept saying he was busy, but she could now see that was a lie; he'd been sitting in, alone, devastated by what had happened. The thought made her sad; why hadn't he told her?

Billy sighed, his eyes now firmly fixed on the floor as he told the story. 'I told you the other week about that guy Alfie, didn't I? The one we bought over a hundred grand's worth of tickets from?'

Kelly nodded, remembering the story.

'Well we called him, texted him, emailed him, but there was no answer. He was just blanking me and Gary; we even went to his house, but surprise, surprise, no one was there. When we looked through the windows it looked as though no one lived there at all. The whole place was empty. Anyway, obviously we started to worry. Then I spoke to Jonny's uncle, who runs a similar hospitality business, not in the same line as us, but similar, and I asked him what we could do.'

Kelly watched Billy as he told the story; he seemed to have aged overnight. She could see he had the worry of the world on his shoulders and she hated it. 'What did Jonny's uncle say?' Jonny was Billy's best friend and his uncle, who ran a similar business, had actually given Billy lots of advice in the past and been really helpful.

Billy sighed. 'He couldn't believe how naïve we'd been buying tickets from someone who didn't own a proper company. He said most likely we'd been scammed and he doubted there was anything we could do apart from call the police.'

Kelly thought that was the best idea too; surely this man couldn't just get away with it? 'So did you? What did the police say?'

Billy sat back on the sofa, his brows knitted. 'Gary did call them eventually, but he kept trying to hold it off. I think he was hoping by some kind of miracle that Alfie would get back to us and the tickets would be delivered. He didn't want to admit that we'd been scammed and would have to call all our customers and tell them their money was gone. We've reported it and they said they'd look into it, but they don't seem to be doing much.'

It seemed a little bit odd to Kelly that Gary hadn't wanted to call the police; she would have called them straight away. 'What did your clients say?' Kelly asked him, taking his hand and holding it so he knew he had her support.

'That they wanted their money back. Most were furious. You have to remember that they had purchased these tickets through us to take *their* clients out. Not only have we lost their money and cannot afford to pay it all back, but they have to let their clients down, which is both embarrassing and unprofessional.' He shook his head as he recalled some of the conversations. 'Some even threatened to take us to court.'

Kelly exhaled sharply. 'Oh babe, I'm so sorry this has happened. I know how hard you worked to build this company up. I don't know what to say. You definitely don't have insurance?'

Billy shook his head and kneaded his eyes with his fists. 'No. I always knew we should have. Gary used to say it was a waste of money and that he'd sort it eventually, which he never did.' He looked at her, his eyes shining. 'We're going to have to liquidate the company. There is no way we have a spare hundred grand to refund everyone. I've lost it all. All the money I put in the business to start with has just gone. All that hard work we did, for nothing.'

Kelly sat there wondering what liquidate actually meant but not wanting to ask him; it wasn't the right time. She assumed it meant close down and her heart went out to him. 'He won't be able to get away with this,' Kelly said, more confidently than she felt.

'Well, not much seems to be happening,' Billy explained. 'The police have seen us a few times and we've told them everything and they said they'd be in touch. Either way, the company has to close.'

'I'm so sorry, Bill,' Kelly said, kissing him and wishing that would make it all better. Then a thought came to her. She cleared her throat, unsure whether to say what she was about to. 'There's no way that Gary is in on it, is there?'

Billy flinched and looked at her in horror. 'Kelly, Gary has been furious with Alfie like I am! Our family have been friends with the Jacobs for years and there is no way Gary would ever do that. How can you even suggest something like that? For God's sake, I know you don't like Gary, but you're taking it a bit far now.'

'Well I was just saying, you never know,' Kelly replied huffily, irritated that he was getting so angry with her.

'Well don't say, okay? I've known Gary Jacobs since I

was about twelve. I know you come out with some stupid things sometimes, but that one tops the lot,' Billy snapped.

Kelly felt her eyes brim with tears. She was only trying to help him, but now his anger had turned towards her. She needed to leave. 'I'm going to go, Billy, okay?' Kelly's voice cracked as she stood up and headed towards the front door. She heard Billy sigh loudly.

'Now I've upset you, haven't I? Kelly I'm sorry, I didn't mean it to come out like that and I shouldn't take it out on you. Please don't leave,' he pleaded as he jumped to his feet and put his hand on her shoulder.

Kelly turned to face him. 'I know you're gutted and I'm sorry for you, I really am. But you need to get up, washed and dressed and face the world again; be like the Billy we all know and love. That's all I can say to help you. I'm not going to lie, what you just said hurt me. I know I come out with silly things sometimes, but I'm *not* stupid. I know some people think it, but for you to say it to me; that's what hurts the most. Look, I just need to go,' she said firmly, as she opened the door.

'I didn't mean it, Kelly, I'm sorry,' she heard Billy call as she walked along the path.

Kelly climbed in her car, refusing to even glance up at Billy who was standing by his front door. She had been looking forward to spending the evening with him and she couldn't believe the turn of events. She started the ignition, wanting to get away as soon as possible. No sooner had she turned out of Billy's road than the tears started. She understood that Billy was mad right now, but that was no reason to take it out on her, just for asking if it was possible that Gary could be involved. She wiped her eyes and sniffed. He had told her she said stupid things, which she knew she did, but just hearing him say it stung. He usually laughed at the daft things she came out with and she laughed along with him, but she wasn't stupid and sometimes she just wanted people to take her seriously. Lately it had been bothering her that people didn't listen to her opinions; first Jade and now Billy. They had just brushed her ideas under the carpet, telling her she was wrong. She pulled up at the traffic lights and looked in the mirror, glad her mascara hadn't smudged. A black Porsche pulled up alongside her, music blaring. Kelly admired the car; she'd love a convertible one in silver. As the man in the passenger seat sat back, Kelly caught a glimpse of the other man driving the car and to her astonishment noticed it was Gary. She watched as he threw back his head giving a throaty laugh about something. He was beaming from ear to ear. How was it, Kelly wondered, that Gary could look like he didn't have a care in the world, laughing and joking casually when Billy was in pieces sitting at home in the darkness? Once again Kelly's suspicions arose. This didn't look like someone who was about to lose loads of his own money and liquidate his company at all. It looked more like someone who had committed a crime and got away with it. Kelly needed to dig deeper and find out the truth; the question was, how?

CHAPTER 15

Lisa was chilling out on the sofa watching some old episodes of *Sex and the City*, completely relaxed after a long day at work. She'd gone straight home afterwards, but Nicola had met up with Charlie in a bar on the way back. Just as she felt herself dozing off, she heard the key in the front door and Nicola and Charlie entered, laughing.

'Hi. Good night?' Lisa asked, sitting up and fastening her dressing gown tighter around her.

'Yeah, we only went for a few. I'm completely shattered,' Nicola said with a yawn.

Charlie, who worked in London as well, was dressed smartly in a grey suit. He gave her a smile as he sat on the armchair opposite. 'You should have joined us,' he said with a penetrating stare that Lisa found creepy. She'd been willing to start afresh with Charlie and forget about the fact he lied about meeting Nicola for lunch that day, but immediately he was putting her on edge.

'Too tired, and I had some washing I wanted to get done,' she lied.

'Tea, anyone?' Nicola said, making her way into the kitchen.

'Oh no, I'm okay thanks,' Lisa said as she stretched,

feeling a bit uncomfortable being alone with Charlie; there was just something about him that made her feel uneasy.

'Yes please,' Charlie shouted to Nicola. 'No sugar, I'm sweet enough.'

Lisa looked at him and he winked, making her cringe. She stood up and went to get a glass of water.

'Charlie is staying tonight by the way, honey,' Nicola said as Lisa reached for a glass in the cupboard. 'I hope that's okay.'

Lisa nodded. 'Of course, that's fine.'

'It won't be a regular thing, I'll stay at his most of the time because he lives alone, but he was adamant he wanted to stay here tonight.'

Lisa frowned. 'How come?'

Nicola shrugged. 'I'm not sure. He said he felt bad leaving you alone here and taking me off all the time. How cute is that? Totes adorable.'

'Mmm,' Lisa murmured, unsure what to make of that information. 'Anyway, I'll give you two some space. I think I'm going to call it a night and go to bed. It's half ten already,' Lisa said as she glanced at her watch.

'Okay honey. See you in the morning,' Nicola replied, kissing her friend on the cheek and making a 'mwah' sound.

Lisa took her glass of water and walked into the lounge. 'Night Charlie. I'm going to bed now,' she said politely.

'Already?' Charlie asked, looking disappointed. 'It's still early.'

Lisa yawned. 'I'm tired,' she said lightly, with a friendly smile. 'Night, see you in the morning.'

'Sweet dreams,' Charlie replied in a soft voice.

It didn't take long for Lisa to fall asleep; soon after her head hit the pillow she drifted off. It was in the middle of the night when Lisa woke up and she glanced at her clock which lit up in the dark; four-fifteen a.m. As she was dozing back to sleep, a very quiet noise, which sounded like her door opening, made her look up. A dark figure loomed in the doorway. Was she dreaming? Lisa couldn't speak; she felt paralysed with fear, took deep breaths and assured herself it was a dream, closing her eyes. When she woke again, it was morning.

'Morning, honey,' Nicola said when Lisa met her in the kitchen as she put the kettle on. Nicola was wearing a gorgeous pale pink silky nighty and somehow her long platinum blonde hair extensions looked perfect, full of bounce and waves. Nicola had decided to have a boob job a few years ago and Lisa admired her big but natural-looking bust, wondering whether she should go through with it too. It was weird; some days Lisa wished she had bigger boobs, especially when she was wearing a backless dress or something, but other days she felt extremely content with her B cup chest and felt that a larger chest would make her figure look generally bigger and a bit out of proportion. Who knew, maybe in the distant future when she'd had children she'd treat herself, but she felt too indecisive at present.

'Morning,' Lisa said, helping herself to some Special K and walking to the fridge for the milk. 'I had a horrible nightmare last night. I imagined someone was in my room.'

Nicola raised her eyebrows as she put a spoonful of coffee in two mugs. 'Really, honey? I hate nightmares. Do you want a coffee?'

'No, it's fine,' Lisa replied in between mouthfuls of Special K. 'I'm going to make tea for myself.'

Nicola nodded, picking the two mugs up and walking out.

An hour later, Lisa was standing on the very packed Central line with Charlie and Nicola. Once again, Lisa felt a bit uneasy in Charlie's presence; every time she looked up, he was staring at her.

'What are you doing tonight?' Charlie asked Nicola.

Nicola flicked her long blonde hair over her shoulder, which nearly hit some poor man behind her in the eye, making Lisa giggle. 'We have some girl's leaving drinks tonight after work, don't we honey?' Nicola said to Lisa.

Lisa nodded, 'Yeah. Hopefully it won't be as messy as the last time,' she smiled.

Charlie cleared his throat. 'Perhaps I should take Lisa's number,' he suggested. 'Last time you had no signal, Nic, and I couldn't get through to you.'

Nicola nodded breezily. 'Okay.'

Lisa frowned as she told Charlie her number. Why did she not have a good feeling about this? Luckily Charlie got off the train at Liverpool Street, leaving Lisa and Nicola alone for the rest of their journey.

'So, things still going well with you two?' Lisa asked her.

'Yeah, really well,' Nicola smiled.

'That's good then,' Lisa said, finding it slightly frustrating that she was going to have to keep seeing Charlie, but happy for her friend at the same time. Lisa didn't want Nicola to get hurt, but she didn't trust Charlie as far as she could throw him.

They got off the train at Oxford Circus and walked to their offices together. They said goodbye as they walked in opposite directions to their desks and Lisa felt her phone vibrate in her bag.

As she read the text message, she froze to the spot, her heartbeat quickening and blood pulsating round her head. She didn't know what to do about this, but she was most definitely in a very tricky situation. She glanced down and re-read the words, checking she had read them correctly. A chill went through her and she shivered as she read them again.

You look so pretty when you sleep. C xx

*

The following day, Kelly was lost. She had been searching for Sam's road for the past ten minutes. She'd only been there once with Jade, and couldn't for the life of her remember where it was. She drove down a street which looked familiar, though she'd thought that about the last two as well. However, this one definitely looked like it could be right, Kelly thought with satisfaction as she pulled up by a set of modern flats. It was seven p.m. and Kelly hoped he was home from work by now. She buzzed up and Sam answered.

'Hello?'

'Hi Sam. It's Kelly. Can I come and speak to you please?'

She could tell he was surprised by his voice. 'Kelly? Yeah, sure, come up.'

He opened the door in a pale pink shirt and black trousers, his tie loose around his neck, indicating he'd just got back from work. Suddenly Kelly felt a bit awkward. Her plan to visit Sam had seemed like a good one an hour ago, but now she wasn't entirely sure. She liked Sam; as well as good looks he had a lovely, warm personality and they had always got on well, but she'd never been on her own with him in his flat before and she knew he must be wondering why on earth she was there.

'Here, take a seat,' he said walking through the lounge and signalling for her to sit down.

Kelly sat down and Sam sat opposite. She looked around with admiration. She'd never actually been inside before, just waited outside once when she picked Jade up. His flat was beautiful; it was very stylish yet simple, with stunning wooden floors. Kelly was impressed and told him so. 'Love your flat, babe. Reem.'

'Thanks,' he said looking round. His eyes flicked back to her. 'How's Jade?'

He had a hopeful look on his face and Kelly realised he thought she was here because of Jade. She felt sorry for him. 'She's good,' Kelly replied. 'I'm not actually here about her though,' she said uncomfortably, tucking her long blonde hair behind her ears and shifting around in her seat. 'It was Chloe I wanted to ask you about actually.'

Sam squinted and he frowned. 'Chloe? What about her?' he asked, surprised.

'Look, I'm not accusing her of anything, but I just wanted to check it wasn't her. You know our website was copied by Adele when she stayed . . . you know . . . ended up back here that night?' Kelly watched Sam carefully and saw him wince when she mentioned that dreaded night.

Sam heaved a sigh. 'Yeah.'

'Well recently, it's happened again. Somehow Adele has managed to copy all our designs and we just can't see how. I just wondered how close Chloe and Adele were? I know she may not have meant any harm, but I thought maybe Chloe let slip some of the things we were doing?' There, Kelly had said it; had told him that she thought his sister might be behind it.

Sam looked thoughtful for a moment before he finally spoke. 'I don't think Chloe would blab behind your back, she's not like that. But, I must say, she does see Adele quite a bit. Adele goes round to my parents' house sometimes to see Chloe. I wish she would just get lost, I can't stand the girl. I've told Chloe to steer clear. To be honest, I don't even think Chloe likes her much; that's the impression I get anyway.'

Kelly was confused. 'Why would Chloe be friends with her if she didn't like her? Why would Adele go round to see her?'

Sam shrugged, just as baffled. 'I'm not too sure. Maybe because Adele helped Chloe that night in Sugar Hut when those girls started on her? No idea, but I know she goes round to see her.'

Kelly nodded, getting a better understanding of the situation. So Chloe met with Adele regularly? That meant it *was* Adele on the phone to Chloe all those times, just like she thought. Something just wasn't right here. It had to be Chloe passing information on to Adele, Kelly decided. Maybe Adele was threatening her? Chloe was nothing but sweet, soft and gentle; an easy target for Adele to manipulate. She was glad she'd come to see Sam now, she felt like she was getting closer to the truth. She stood up to go. 'Thanks Sam. Sorry to bother you.'

He jumped up. 'That's okay. Hope I helped.' He walked Kelly to the front door and then added quickly, 'Kelly. I'm so sorry for that night in Sugar Hut. I'd do anything to change what happened. I really don't think I did anything with Adele though; I know I'll never be able to prove my innocence, but I just wanted you to know. I've lost Jade and I'm gutted. Tell her I miss her, will you?'

Kelly felt terrible for him and as she looked into his eyes she could see the pain and heartache he was feeling. No matter how hard she tried, she just couldn't picture Sam cheating and she believed him. 'I'll tell her,' she replied to placate him, but she didn't want to bring this meeting up to Jade, as she knew her friend needed to move on. 'Bye, Sam.'

'Bye, Kelly,' he said sadly, closing the door behind him.

As Kelly made her way downstairs she could hear some voices on the ground floor. As she walked down she could hear what they were saying.

'Look, this is the second time my Merc has been keyed parked outside here and I want to watch the CCTV to see who's doing it. I want to report these scumbags to the police,' the angry voice asserted.

'I understand you're upset,' the other male voice replied, 'but please calm down. As I told you over the phone we can watch the CCTV footage and hopefully get this matter sorted.'

Kelly froze to the spot as an idea popped into her head. If the CCTV footage was available to watch, maybe somehow she could watch the night Adele claimed to have slept with Sam and see what time she left his flat? Maybe there would be an answer as to what *really* happened in the video? Kelly marched along to where the noise was coming from, lifting her chin in the air, her skirt a bit higher and pulling her top down to reveal more cleavage. She cleared her throat, interrupting the two men, who turned and gaped at her.

'Excuse me, but I couldn't help overhearing the fact that you have CCTV footage filmed outside these flats. Is this right?'

The security man looked at her curiously, his mouth open as if he was mesmerised. 'Who the hell are you?' he asked, scratching his beard.

'Kelly,' she smiled, batting her long fake lashes.

The security man frowned looking at Kelly with suspicion. 'Sorry, but we can't just let *anyone* watch the CCTV.' He pointed towards the other man in front of him. 'This young man has had his property vandalised. Why do you want to watch it?'

Kelly tried to think of a reason why she'd want to watch it. To check if her hair was bouncy enough from the back on camera? No, they'd just tell her to look in the mirror or something; she needed to come up with a better plan than that. Maybe she'd try being a damsel in distress and hopefully they'd feel sorry for her. She pouted and put on a distraught expression. 'If you must know, I think my boyfriend is cheating,' she exhaled sharply, playing with her hair and trying to put on her most sexy voice. 'I just have to know. There is only one night I need to see.'

The security man nodded and Kelly spotted him staring at her chest. His eyes flicked back to her face. 'Well darling, if he's cheating, he's an idiot.'

'Agreed,' the other man said, his eyes wide open, staring at Kelly's legs.

The security man turned to him. 'I'll come by soon and we'll deal with the vandals, okay?'

The other man nodded, quickly adding before he went back to his flat, 'If he *is* cheating, I live at number two.'

Kelly smiled, and then continued her sob story to the security man. 'Is there any way I could see the footage? It's just one night?' She tried to persuade him by giving him an innocent, doe-eyed look.

'Mmm,' he murmured, thinking about it as he scratched his beard again. 'I suppose it won't hurt. Just the one night though, okay?'

'Thank you so much, babe,' Kelly said, gently touching his arm. 'What a lovely man you are.'

He blushed a little and dismissed the comment. 'Let me know the date and I'll get the footage as soon as I can. Write your mobile number down in my phone,' he told her, handing his mobile over.

'Thanks, hun,' Kelly beamed, believing she was a step closer to finding out the truth. If it turned out Adele did stay all evening then she would just forget about it and not tell Jade; she didn't need to be hurt any more. Maybe it would show Sam and Adele walking back that night together holding hands or something? Maybe, Kelly thought, though for some reason she very much doubted it.

*

'Oh my God, Donna! That's the one. You look almost as slim as me in that dress!' Adele gasped as Donna exited the cubicle, with the sales assistant holding the train waddling behind her. They were in Vera Wang; the best bridal store in history in Adele's opinion.

'Do you like it?' Donna asked, standing on the platform and gazing in the mirror as she twirled and turned.

'It's totes amazing. I'm actually well jell of you right

now,' Adele admitted, swigging another mouthful of champagne and finishing the glass. She tapped the glass and looked at the assistant. 'Any chance of another?'

'Just one moment,' the sales assistant replied sweetly as she walked off with the empty glass.

'It's gorgeous, but it's only the fifth one I've tried on though,' Donna said as she looked down, admiring the lace. 'My mum isn't here either.'

Adele tutted. 'Babe, mums are never any help. They're all old and frumpy and probably want you in something dull and boring. You just *have* to be a Vera bride and you just *have* to get that dress. It's the one.'

'It is nice,' Donna agreed, turning to Adele with a grin. Her mobile started ringing in the cubicle. 'Can you just grab my phone, Adele? I can't even walk in this dress!'

Adele huffed, annoyed she had to get up, and walked to the changing room to quickly get it. 'It's Aaron,' she told Donna as she handed her the phone.

'Hi Aaron,' Donna said, unable to contain her smile.

Adele sat back down and looked at her phone, seeing a blank screen. No messages, no calls, no boyfriend. This would have been her dream, picking out her wedding dress in Vera Wang and having no limit on the budget. Donna seriously didn't realise how lucky she was! Adele was going to make sure they picked the best bridesmaids' dresses ever. The only good thing about Donna getting married was the fact the wedding was going to be swarming with footballers and she was definitely going to get with one, even if it killed her. *She* was dying to be a WAG, why did Donna get to be one when she didn't even care about that sort of thing? Life was just so cruel sometimes. Adele looked at her business phone quickly and saw several emails sitting there waiting to be read. How boring, she thought, as she read a couple; both were people complaining about the quality of the bikinis. She rolled her eyes in annoyance; this website was nothing but stressful. She was no way giving these people refunds and there was nothing they could do about it. Donna interrupted her thoughts.

'Oh my God! Guess what, Adele?' Her hand was covering her mouth as she spoke.

'What?' Adele asked.

'Aaron said there has been a cancellation at Orsett Hall, the venue where we want to get married, and he's booked it for two weeks' time! I'm going to be his wife in two weeks!' Donna looked shocked but thrilled.

'Donna, don't be so ridiculous,' Adele replied curtly. 'You cannot organise a wedding in two weeks! That's not giving anyone enough notice!'

'Two weeks?' the sales assistant echoed as she handed Adele her champagne. She shook her head. 'Oh dear. Our dresses have to be ordered at least eight months in advance. There is no way we'd have one in time. In fact, I think you'll struggle in most places to find a dress that quickly.'

Donna's happy face faded and she lowered her voice. 'Oh well, I'll just have to kiss this dress goodbye then.'

'Just tell him you can't organise it in two weeks for God's sake!' Adele exploded, making the sales assistant jump.

'He wants to marry me soon, before football season starts again. I'll just have to get another dress. Maybe I can get someone to make it?'

Adele put her perfectly lacquered nail to her forehead, taking deep breaths. 'You're going to . . .' she could barely say the word, '*make* your wedding dress?'

'Not me, someone else,' Donna responded, not understanding why that would be so bad.

Another sales assistant walked past and stopped in her tracks, oohing and ahhing over Donna's dress. 'That dress looks stunning on you. Just divine. It's such a shame as a customer of mine recently bought the same one and has now changed her mind about the whole wedding and was wondering whether she could get a refund or not.' The lady gave a little laugh. 'Of course we told her she couldn't, it had been adjusted to fit her. The poor thing is lumbered with a dress for nothing.'

Donna's mouth dropped open. 'What size was she?'

The lady thought for a moment. 'About a fourteen I think. Why?'

Donna explained the situation and Adele couldn't believe how jammy she was. The lady was going to call her customer and get her to contact Donna so she would get her perfect dress. All she'd need to do was get it altered to fit her. Donna seemed to have dropped a dress size recently and was now down to a size fourteen, Adele realised glumly, wishing she was too big to fit into the dream dress she'd just been offered. The lady explained it was £10,500, but she was sure the other lady would give her a discount. Adele had to literally bite her tongue from screaming about the injustice of it all! Donna was going to wear a dress that cost over ten grand and she didn't even bat an eyelid when the price was mentioned! Adele ordered another glass of champagne to cheer herself up and reminded Donna that it was time to go to Browns Brides for the bridesmaids' dresses now; it was her turn.

'My sister said anything apart from strapless, because she hates her chest,' Donna told Adele forty minutes later, as she sat outside the changing room.

'What? You've got to be kidding me?' Adele fumed. She was in the middle of trying a stunning Monique Lhuillier strapless gown. She was already compromising on the colour, which she wasn't thrilled about; Donna had opted for lilac.

'No. Please Adele, it's the only thing my sister has asked.'

Adele was annoyed. The strapless dress she was trying on fitted her perfectly. She hated all the ones with straps in the shop and there was no way she was wearing one of them. This dress was beautiful and it did wonders for her figure. She exited the cubicle with a smile and turned in front of Donna.

'Well, what do you think?'

'Oh Adele, it looks beauts,' Donna replied looking at Adele in awe. She shook her head sadly, 'But it's strapless. What about that one-shoulder one we saw?'

Adele put her hands on her hips and exhaled sharply. 'It's got straps inside the dress, silly. They attach and hook on the dress,' she lied.

Donna perked up. 'Oh, really? Oh, well that dress is perfect then.'

'Agreed,' Adele beamed walking back into the cubicle. 'Now, let's quickly buy them, as I'm sure you have a million and one things to organise.'

'Don't remind me,' Donna said, putting her face in her hands.

Adele smirked as she took the dress off. She'd just have to inform them she was mistaken when they asked her about the straps on the dress. They'd never have time to look for new dresses; there was hardly any time now! As she changed into her own clothes, Adele congratulated herself on somehow always managing to get her own way.

*

'So how is the business going?' Lisa asked Jade at lunch. They were sitting outside in the King William beer garden and it was a beautiful sunny day.

'Really well,' Jade grinned. She was so pleased with how busy they'd been. 'We're going to be mentioned in *Reveal* magazine next week because they love our website, which is great. All the people that buy them seem to love the bikinis too. We even received a thank you card from a happy customer the other day,' Jade explained. 'Kelly's pinned it up on the wall because it was pink and matched the room,' she laughed.

Lisa giggled. 'Sounds like Kelly. That's amazing that it's going so well though. Well done you two.'

'How are things with you?' Jade asked. She finished the last of her pasta and pushed the bowl away, feeling completely stuffed.

Lisa looked a bit unsure and pulled a face. 'Something really weird happened to me.'

Jade frowned as Lisa told her the story about having lunch with Charlie and then about him peering in her room at night and sending her the text message. Jade couldn't believe what she was hearing!

'Oh my God, shut up! I can't believe he actually did that! What a perv!'

Lisa cringed. 'I know. He just stares all the time as well and says really inappropriate things. What do I do? Nicola is in love with the guy and I can't bear to be the one to break it to her that her boyfriend is a complete weirdo.'

Jade sympathised. What an awkward situation to be in; she didn't envy her one bit. 'I would perhaps tell him it's not acceptable and say if he carries on you'll have no choice but to tell Nicola? That way you're at least giving him a chance?'

Lisa nodded. 'Yeah, you're right. That sounds like a good idea. Just the thought of even speaking to him makes me shudder. He's so strange.'

Jade thought Lisa looked stressed out over the situation and tried to change the subject. She told her about Kelly and the fact she thought Chloe was the one going behind their backs and telling Adele all their business plans.

'No way! She can't possibly think it's Chloe. Chloe is adorable. I can't imagine her ever doing anything malicious. She really likes you and Kelly too, I can tell, so why would she go behind your backs? It makes no sense.'

270

'That's exactly what I said, but Kelly is certain it's the only way Adele is finding out,' Jade replied, arching an eyebrow.

'Heard anything from Sam recently?' Lisa asked.

Jade looked down at the table miserably. No matter how hard she tried, she was unable to get Sam out of her head most days. She missed him so much it hurt, but he had let her down in the worst way possible and she was far too proud to allow him to talk her round. 'No, he knows I don't want to talk to him. We're over.'

Jade looked up and Lisa nodded. 'It's just such a shame. You were so happy with Sam and it's so hard to imagine him cheating with Adele. It was clear for everyone to see how much he loved you. I just don't understand. Have you met anyone else you like? I know it's early, but sometimes it helps to go on another date to try to move on.'

Jade looked into the distance thoughtfully. 'Funnily enough, your cousin, Tony, asked me out for a drink the other day when I told him me and Sam had split up,' she confessed.

'Really? Did he?'

Jade nodded. It had been a surprise to her too, but she'd told him she wasn't ready. 'I still can't imagine being with anyone apart from Sam if I'm honest, so I told him it's too soon.'

'What did Tony say?' Lisa asked.

'He understood,' Jade replied. 'He's a lovely bloke, but I still have feelings for Sam. I wish I didn't.' Feeling herself becoming emotional, Jade swallowed hard and changed the subject. 'Been on any more dates recently? Any new men in your life apart from Pervy Pervison?'

Lisa gave a little laugh. 'I'm actually getting a bit sick of dating, you know. I'd actually like to find a boyfriend now, but it's hard. I mean, I know I did the right thing with Jake, but sometimes I can't help thinking about him and how happy he is with his new fiancée. I looked at his Facebook page for the first time the other day and saw photos of their holiday together. It was so strange.'

'I bet it was!' Jade replied, finding it difficult to imagine Jake with a girl other than Lisa. 'I looked at Sam's the other day as well. There weren't many updates, but I forced myself to delete him as a friend as I don't want to torture myself by looking at his page every five minutes.'

Lisa stared at the floor, thoughtfully. 'Maybe I should do the same with Jake. I'm over our relationship, but it's just weird seeing him with someone else.'

Jade smiled at her friend. There was no way she was going to have trouble finding a new boyfriend eventually; even dressed in jeans and a casual white top she looked stunning. 'You'll find someone when you least expect it,' Jade told her confidently.

Lisa exhaled heavily. 'Not you as well. My nan always says that to me!'

Jade sipped her white wine spritzer and looked Lisa in the eye. 'Everyone says it because it's true! When you least expect it, he'll come along.'

CHAPTER 16

Chloe couldn't wait to see the commercial she'd just finished filming on the television; it was going to be amazing. Everyone had been so nice to her at the shoot and she'd had people doing her hair and make-up the whole time, making her feel like a film star. Since she'd joined the modelling agency Chloe had started to feel more confident. Adele had been wrong about one thing and that was that she should act shy. Her agency constantly drummed it into their models to be self-assured, with a positive attitude, and Chloe had learned behaving like this was the only way she would ever book jobs. She had now shot her first commercial and had also been to four other castings, where she had successfully booked one other job so far. She was going to be in *Look* magazine modelling their best fashion picks for the summer and she couldn't wait. She played Cheryl Cole's latest hit, 'Call my Name' on her iPod and lay on her bed, flicking through a magazine. Five minutes later, Chloe saw her mum appear at her bedroom door.

'I've been calling you for ages, but I can see why you couldn't hear me now. Adele is here to see you,' her mum informed her.

Chloe's heart sank and she switched her music off. She

sat up on the bed and whispered to her mum. 'Just tell her I'm not in,' she pleaded.

Her mum sighed. 'Don't be so ridiculous. I've already told her you were in your room. Honestly Chloe, please stop being so rude.'

Chloe threw her eyes upwards, annoyed that her mum couldn't just lie for her. 'Go on then, send her up.' Chloe stood up, ready to face her. She'd had enough of Adele's bullying ways and although she was terrified of her, she decided there and then she wasn't going to dance to her tune anymore. Maybe it was the new burst of confidence she gained, but she realised it was time to tell Adele to get lost. Chloe had accepted Adele bossing her around because she had truly believed they were friends. But how could Adele be a true friend and treat her the way she did? The more Chloe had thought about it, the more she realised Sam was right; Adele was using her. Just who did she think she was, coming to her house, treating her the way she did and threatening her all the time?

'Hi, babe,' Adele grinned like a Cheshire cat as she walked into Chloe's room.

'Hi Adele. What's up? I'm a bit busy,' Chloe replied firmly, wanting her to leave already.

Adele ignored Chloe's irritable tone and sat on her bed, putting her feet up and leaning comfortably on her hands. 'Need you to do me a favour, babe. You see, Jade has just tweeted about Vajazzle My Bikini being in *Reveal* magazine next week and I want to know how they managed to worm their way in there and what the article is about. Reem Bikinis is better than theirs and if anyone should be written about it's my company. I need you to find out who their contacts are.'

Chloe felt her heart hammering in her chest and her hands were clammy. She couldn't take this anymore. She didn't want to spy any longer for Adele and she knew she had to stand up to her. Jade and Kelly didn't deserve it and she felt terribly guilty about what she'd done in the past; this had to stop now. She knew Adele saw her as nothing more than a walkover and someone to do her dirty work. Well not anymore, Chloe decided. Adele's gruff, masculine voice interrupted her thoughts.

'Errr hello? Chloe? Did you hear what I said? I need this info ASAP!'

Chloe cleared her throat. 'No,' she answered meekly.

Adele's mouth flew open and her face scrunched up, making her look ugly. 'What did you just say?'

Chloe heard the doorbell ring downstairs and wondered if her mum would be too distracted to hear her cry for help if Adele decided to thump her one. Chloe stood up tall and folded her arms across her chest. 'I said no,' she repeated, more boldly this time.

Adele's face contorted with shock and rage. 'What do you mean *no*?' she asked in a loud voice, standing up and putting her hands on her hips.

Chloe closed her eyes momentarily, knowing it was now or never. She looked Adele square in the eye and with all the force she could muster, spoke as assertively as physically possible. 'I mean no, Adele. No, I won't find out anything else for you. I've had enough of you bullying me and getting me to sneak about for you. I'm going to come clean to Jade and Kelly and tell them what happened. Now, get out and leave me alone!' Chloe gasped for breath as she finished, shocked that she'd actually managed to finally speak that way to Adele.

Adele took deep breaths, her face turning red and her eyes glinting like a mad person. 'After everything I've done for you, Chloe, this is how you choose to repay me! I should have just let those girls beat you up in the toilets that night, shouldn't I?'

Feeling more confident than ever, especially seeing as

Adele hadn't even touched her yet, Chloe stood up to her. 'I said thank you that night, Adele, and ever since then you've tried to manipulate me and boss me around. You're just as bad as those girls in the toilets that night!'

Adele started to walk away, clearly stunned by Chloe's outburst. 'Whatever, Chloe. You're just a child and when you need me in future, you can dream on if you think I'll be there. You did exactly what I asked you to and went behind Jade and Kelly's backs, so spare me the innocent act. Jade and Kelly will never speak to you again after I tell them who my little spy was. I'm going to go round there right now and tell them everything you did. I'm going to laugh when they never speak to you again. They're going to hate you.'

Chloe's eyes became hot with tears and a lump grew in her throat. Adele was right; they were going to be furious with her. 'I didn't want to do it,' she gulped. 'You made me! You threatened me!'

Adele smirked callously. 'That's just your word against mine.'

Chloe jumped when she heard another familiar voice behind her.

'And we know whose word we're going to believe. Don't worry Chloe, Jade and I won't hate you.'

Chloe turned round to see Kelly standing there, staring at Adele in outrage.

'Oh my God, Kelly!' Chloe cried, squeezing her tightly in a hug. Chloe had never been so pleased to see her before.

'Your mum just let me up, hun, and I heard everything. I actually guessed that this is what had happened anyway; that's why I came here to see you,' Kelly explained, before turning to Adele with a threatening glare. 'So now we know how you copied and came up with all the same ideas, don't we?'

Adele shrugged, as though she couldn't care less. 'Believe

Chloe all you want, but she happily told me everything I wanted to know. I never had to push her into anything. In fact, I think she enjoyed going behind your backs.'

'She's lying!' Chloe protested in self-defence. She turned to Kelly. 'I promise I didn't want to tell her anything or give her your new bikini designs, but she wouldn't leave me alone, she knew how much I was frightened . . .'

'Don't worry, hun,' Kelly interjected, 'I know how much of a twisted cow she is.'

'Who do you think you're calling a cow, you thick bimbo?' Adele sneered.

Kelly flushed with anger and she lunged forward and slapped Adele hard across the cheek. 'Never copy us again and don't you *ever* call me a thick bimbo!'

Adele's mouth was wide open in shock as she stood there holding her cheek, which was getting redder by the second. 'Get out my way,' she spat as she barged past Chloe and Kelly. 'I need to get out of here before I actually do some damage to the pair of you! Don't think I'm letting you get away with slapping me, Kelly. You did it last year in Marbs too and I haven't forgotten.'

'You deserved it then just as much as you did now,' Kelly snapped. 'You're a bully and a coward, Adele. If you have a problem, let's sort it out right now.' Kelly stood with her head held high, waiting for a response.

Adele looked her up and down and shook her head. 'Nah, you're not worth it. I have better things to do with my time, thanks very much. I don't know why I bothered copying your website anyway because quite frankly, it's a load of crap,' Adele hissed, slamming Chloe's bedroom door behind her.

Chloe faced Kelly, exhaling slowly. 'Thank God she's gone.'

'Hopefully for good,' Kelly added. 'I can't believe I hit her like that. I've never slapped anyone in my life apart from Adele – twice!'

Chloe sat down, feeling a little shaken. 'She deserved it. The look on her face was priceless,' she said with a little laugh.

Kelly joined in, giggling, and sat down by Chloe's computer on the chair. 'I saw her constantly calling you that day of the first photo shoot and I thought you seemed stressed. When you stopped by at Jade's the other day I could tell how uncomfortable you were when we spoke about Adele copying the designs and I just knew it had to be you telling her. It wasn't that I thought you would do it on purpose, I had a feeling Adele was forcing you, especially after I spoke to Sam. I was right.'

Chloe still felt guilty. 'I'm so sorry. Can you and Jade forgive me?' she asked, hopefully.

Kelly's pink glossy lips curved into a smile. 'On one condition.'

'Anything,' Chloe said, ecstatic that Kelly didn't hate her.

'Will you model for us on our next shoot? I heard you're doing well now after joining the agency, but remember, we found you first,' Kelly joked.

Chloe sighed with relief. 'Of course. I'll model whenever you need me.' Chloe sat chatting to Kelly about the modelling jobs she'd got and blushed when Kelly told her how impressed she was. 'Do you want a drink?' she offered, ten minutes later.

'No, hun. Thanks for the offer but I'd better go.'

'Off to anywhere nice?' Chloe asked her.

'I wouldn't say nice,' Kelly informed her. 'But trust me; I have people to see and some very important places to go.'

*

A few hours later it was beginning to get dark, the perfect time for Kelly to set off on her next mission. Dressed head to toe in black, including a black baseball cap, Kelly made her way out the door, once again racking her brains to remember where Gary lived. They'd picked him up once before a meal and Kelly knew he lived in Loughton near the station, but that was about it. There was no way she could ask Billy for his address – not only would he think she'd gone crazy, but she was still upset after the way he'd spoken to her.

Luckily it didn't take Kelly long to find Gary's house because she recognised his Porsche outside. She parked her car a few houses along so she wasn't spotted by him. Kelly wasn't even sure what she was doing or what exactly she was trying to achieve by visiting Gary's house. She just had a bad feeling about him, like she always did, though this time it was more serious. Maybe she would overhear an important conversation? Or perhaps she would see him laughing and joking with this Alfie creature about how they'd pulled the wool over her poor Billy's eyes?

Wishing she hadn't worn her five-inch black patent Prada heels, because they made a clip-clop sound when she walked, Kelly slowly made her way to Gary's house, walking as carefully as possible. The blinds were shut in the front window, meaning no one would see her approaching and Kelly quietly opened the side gate and made her way round the side of the house, heart pounding violently in her chest. What if they saw her? she panicked as she silently closed the gate behind her. Kelly ducked down low, bending her legs as she passed a window at the side of his house. She could hear voices and stayed deadly still to see if she could hear what they were saying. It was no good, she couldn't hear a thing. Kelly stood up and peeked through the window as inconspicuously as possible, ducking low. She gasped as she spotted Gary sitting in the lounge with his feet up watching television. There was a woman opposite him, but she could only see the back of her head. They had a bottle of wine open and Kelly felt the anger rise inside her as once again she watched Gary laugh. He looked as though he literally didn't have a care in the world; the complete opposite to poor Billy. Kelly was certain Gary had something to do with the demise of the company; she would bet every pair of her Jimmy Choos on it. She took a photo on her iPhone and congratulated herself when it came out perfectly clear of Gary, mid-laugh. Maybe this will change Billy's mind, Kelly hoped, as she tried to take a few more. The only problem was this didn't prove anything, she realised as she made her way round the back of his house into the garden. She needed to hear what he was saying in case it was something important. It was really dark outside now and Kelly tried to be careful as she crept along with her back against the wall. She shakily knelt down by the back door, where she could hear their voices much more clearly because there was a window open. Kelly realised after a few seconds that she was trying to be so quiet she was forgetting to breathe and let out a huge gasp. Gary was only a few feet away and it amused her that he had no idea she was there.

'I agree that Mexico would be nice or how about Dubai? You've always recommended it, haven't you? I could just book a nice five-star hotel for a few weeks and relax. Sounds heavenly,' Kelly heard Gary say, much to her surprise.

Kelly was disgusted. How could he be booking a holiday if he'd lost all his money? Kelly felt more certain than anything that she was right; Gary had been involved in the scam.

'Yes, your father and I loved Dubai when we went. Expensive, but a beautiful place if you can afford it,' the woman answered, who Kelly now realised was Gary's mum.

As Kelly tried to move even closer to the back door, her heel got caught in one of the paving stones and as she panicked and yanked it out, she fell to the side and knocked over a tin watering can, which she'd been unable to see in the dark. There was an almighty crash and Kelly lay there, frozen to the spot, her heartbeat reminding her of the sound of banging drums.

'Shit,' she muttered under her breath, trying to get up. Her ankle was twisted and sore. 'Shit.'

'What on earth was that?' she heard Gary's mum cry out.

Before Kelly could get to her feet and run, Gary and his mum had opened the back door and were standing there staring at her, their mouths popped open in astonishment.

'Who is that?' Gary demanded in a steely voice. Kelly turned round slightly. 'Kelly? Is that you?' Gary questioned, his eyes wide open in confusion and shock.

Kelly stood up finally, brushing her knees and hands, which were covered in gravel. She was hoping the baseball cap would have disguised her, but clearly there was no such luck. She had never felt so embarrassed in her life and had no idea what to say. She could feel her face burning in shame and was hoping it was too dark outside for them to see.

'Do you know her?' Gary's mum asked, looking at her son in puzzlement.

'Yes, I do. Kelly, will you please answer and tell me what you're doing in my back garden at ten-thirty at night?' Gary asked her in a no-nonsense tone.

Kelly gave a nervous giggle trying to come up with a valid excuse as to why she would be creeping around his back garden. Her voice was light and breezy as she spoke. 'Alright Gal? I didn't realise you lived here. I was just playing ball with my friend and it came into this garden so I came to look for it,' she explained as she noticed a football near the fence. 'Oh there is it!' Kelly beamed, tottering in her Prada heels towards the ball, 'panic over!'

'Kelly, that's *my* football,' Gary asserted firmly, his eyes glinting with suspicion.

Now what do I say? Kelly asked herself, dropping the ball as though it had scalded her. 'Oh really? It looks just like the one we were playing with. Maybe it went over the other garden instead,' Kelly suggested, pointing to the garden to the left, 'I best go and find it.'

'Where is this friend of yours anyway? You came from this garden did you say?' Gary asked pointing to the right, as he frowned.

'Yes that's right. My friend . . . my friend Lucy lives there,' Kelly lied.

'Well, where is Lucy now then? There is no one in that garden. Besides, I've lived here for over a year and I've never even met a girl called Lucy next door,' Gary said with a wary look in his eye, clearly not believing a word Kelly said.

'She must have gone in. I'll call her if you like. Lucy!' Kelly called into the garden, praying no one came out of the house and asked what the hell she was on about. 'Lucy!' she hissed, 'I still haven't got the ball back!'

Gary huffed. 'That's quite enough, Kelly, you'll wake people up. I have my mum round for tea this evening and this is a rather inconvenient time to be honest. You'd better just head back over to your friend's house,' Gary commanded, with a stern look on his face.

'No probs, sorry to bother you, Gary,' Kelly replied, feeling like a reprimanded child. 'Sorry to hear about the company too by the way,' she added.

Gary's face was emotionless. 'Mmm, thanks.'

Kelly looked at him and then realised he was waiting for her to go over the garden. Damn, she thought, he's really going to make me go over there. Say the people next door catch me? This night had gone horribly wrong. 'I'll just be heading back to Lucy's then,' Kelly smiled tightly.

'Hey, don't I know you?' Gary's mum asked as Kelly made her way over to the fence, wondering how she was going to climb over it in her huge heels.

Kelly turned around, her eyes squinting in the dark, trying to look at her face. There was something about her which Kelly recognised. Yes, maybe they had met before?

Gary gave an awkward laugh. 'Don't be so ridiculous, Mum, you've never met Kelly before. Now go inside before your mug of tea gets cold.'

Kelly shrugged and Gary's mum made her way back inside the house.

'Bye,' Kelly called as she fell into next door's garden and landed in a shrub.

'Bye,' Gary said in a flat voice before taking one last glance at her and then walking away.

This was a complete and utter disaster. Kelly held on to the fence as she managed to pick herself up again. The bush had scratched her arm, her ankle was painful and her beautiful new Prada shoes had thick mud on the heels. Not only that, but now she was stuck in someone's garden. Kelly crept along to the house and heaved a loud sigh when she noticed that there wasn't a side gate, meaning she had to climb over into the next garden along. She looked at the fence with dread; this one looked even higher than the last!

Three gardens later Kelly had found a way back to the road but she felt worse than ever. A dog had barked in the last one and Kelly had literally run for her life! The dog definitely sounded bigger than Lord McButterpants and Princess Cupcake, judging by its ferocious bark. At least she had heard Gary talking about jetting off to sunny Dubai; it showed her that he wasn't one bit bothered about his company. Or maybe he wants to book a holiday to get away from it all? a voice inside her head told her. Maybe he's stressed and needs a break? That would be understand-able. Perhaps she just had this whole thing wrong and it wasn't Gary at all? She hoped he didn't tell Billy about finding her in his garden, what on earth would she tell him? Firstly, Billy knew all her friends and she had never mentioned anyone called Lucy, and secondly, he would know she was lying as soon as Gary mentioned the word football. She hated football with a passion unless it meant gazing at Ronaldo's legs for ninety minutes. Billy had tried to explain the offside rule to her about five times and she still had no idea what it was.

Kelly climbed into the driver's seat of her car and thought for a moment. She had successfully solved the case with Chloe and Adele, but there was nothing else she could do about Gary except hope that she had been wrong. Perhaps Alfie would be arrested soon and then Billy could get back to normal and concentrate on starting again, the poor thing. Kelly hoped so more than anything.

CHAPTER 17

A few days later Lisa was walking home from Grange Hill tube station, relieved the shoot she'd been working on had finished early for once. Wrapping up before six was almost unheard of and most shoots went over by hours. Lisa opened the door and frowned, hearing that the television was on. Had Nicola left it on this morning? She hadn't worked on the shoot with her today and had stayed in the office. It was unlikely she'd be home this early, Lisa thought in confusion. She walked through to the lounge and stopped dead in her tracks when she saw Charlie sprawled out on the sofa, beaming from ear to ear when he noticed her baffled expression.

'Oh hi, Lisa. Hope you don't mind me being here, but Nicola gave me the spare key and I was just waiting for her to get back from work,' he said, looking amused by her obvious discomfort.

Lisa tried her best to appear offhand by giving a little shrug and flicking her hair over her shoulders, her voice cool as she replied, 'Oh that's okay. I have work to do so I'll keep out of your way and go to my room so I can concentrate.' She could tell from his expression that he didn't believe her, but she didn't care. Spending time alone with Charlie was the worst thing Lisa could possibly think of. She had avoided him since he sent the creepy text message and feeling too embarrassed to bring it up, she just wanted to forget it ever happened by keeping well out of his way.

'I've made you dinner,' Charlie said finally, touching his bottom lip with his index finger. 'I've made a Thai green curry for all of us. Nicola said it was your favourite.' Charlie looked up at Lisa, his burning gaze on her.

'That's nice of you,' Lisa murmured as she began to walk away. 'I'll eat when Nicola gets home.'

'Do you want a cup of tea?' Charlie asked hopefully just as Lisa reached the kitchen to get a drink, making her jump. He had followed Lisa and was now standing by the kitchen door, gazing at her.

'I'm really quite busy,' Lisa replied hastily, feeling a bit claustrophobic that he was blocking the exit by standing there.

'Just one drink?' Charlie begged, his voice soft and gentle as though he meant no harm. 'I'd like to get to know Nicola's friend better, that's all. I don't bite,' he said with a short laugh, watching Lisa closely with his intense, dark eyes.

Lisa felt flustered as she downed a glass of water. She needed to get away from Charlie, and fast. Why couldn't he just leave her alone? His presence was unnerving. 'Honestly, I really must get on.'

Charlie walked towards Lisa and she felt as though her heart was in her mouth. As he drew nearer, Lisa took a step back. He stood in front of her, smirking, his eyes fixed on her lips, his brow arched. 'Lisa,' he said in a husky voice. 'You know there is something between us. Stop trying to deny it.'

Lisa was frozen to the spot, the panic inside her rising and her cheeks burning red. Inside she was screaming for him to leave her alone but nothing would come out.

Suddenly Charlie stepped forward, his lips pressing hard against hers, his desire bursting out as he kissed her eagerly. Lisa tried to pull away but his hands gripped the back of her head, pulling her face as close to his as physically possible. As Lisa managed to push him off forcefully, she heard a loud cry.

'Oh my God!' Nicola screamed, bursting into tears and running away.

'Nicola!' Lisa shouted breathlessly, shoving Charlie out of the way. Nicola was sitting on the sofa sobbing, her head in her hands and Lisa ran over and touched her gently on the shoulder. 'Nicola, it isn't what it looks like. He just kissed me. I tried to get him off; I tried to push him . . .'

'Just leave me alone, the pair of you!' Nicola shouted, running from the flat in floods of tears.

Charlie stood there watching Nicola leave, appearing totally unfazed by what had just happened.

'Get the hell out of here now and don't come back!' Lisa glowered at him with a menacing expression. If Charlie had ruined her relationship with Nicola, Lisa would be devastated. 'There is something wrong with you! Nicola is my friend who you're dating, might I remind you, and you've just forced yourself upon me!'

Charlie gave a slight shrug, but Lisa could tell he was surprised by her sudden outburst and grabbed his jacket quickly.

'Get out, you lunatic!' Lisa screamed at him again, wanting him gone. She slammed the door behind him, feeling the hot tears forming in her eyes. What if Lisa thought she was kissing him back? How long had she been standing there? She would probably never want to speak to her again, let alone live with her! Lisa was so angry with herself for not confronting Charlie sooner about his behaviour she could scream. Maybe it wouldn't have happened if she had? She thought she'd made it so clear she wasn't interested.

Lisa called Nicola on her mobile but there was no answer – and who could blame her if she thought Lisa was trying to steal her boyfriend?

Lisa stood up with a heavy heart and made her way over to the freezer to get the one thing that comforted her when she was feeling down; strawberry cheesecake Häagen-Dazs ice cream. Damn you Charlie, she thought as the ice cream melted like heaven in her mouth, not only was he causing havoc with her friendship, but now her waistline too.

*

Kelly was half asleep when she heard her phone ringing. She reached across the side of her bed and answered to a phone number she didn't recognise.

'Hello,' she said in a croaky voice. She cleared her throat and sat up.

'Hi there, is that Kelly?' came the gruff reply. 'Sorry if I've just woken you up.'

Kelly frowned, not having a clue who she was speaking to. 'Who is it?'

'It's Derek, the security man. You wanted to watch the CCTV footage outside the flats?'

'Oh yes, that's right,' Kelly replied, feeling the excitement bubble in her stomach. Did he have the video ready?

'I've got the footage from the night in question, so if you want to come to the offices this morning, you can have a look. Do you have a pen handy so I can give you our address?'

Kelly jumped up and hunted through her drawers to write the address down. She could only find a red lipstick, so ended up jotting the address down with that on a copy of *Now* magazine she found. Forty minutes later, she was showered and ready with a full face of make-up, wearing a tight lemon Alice and Olivia summer dress and pretty jewelled sandals from Reiss. She would have to tell Jade she wouldn't be in the office until this afternoon, she decided, as she picked out a pair of shades seeing as it was a nice day. She hadn't yet told her the news about Chloe and couldn't wait to tell her that she had been right. She dialled Jade's number.

'Hi Kel,' Jade answered.

'Hi, babe. I'm really sorry, but I won't be in this morning,' she told her, trying to come up with a good excuse.

'Why not?' Jade sounded a bit put out. 'We have five new orders and we need bikinis made. We need to send them out as quickly as possible so we're providing a good service. Besides, we're written about in *Reveal* magazine this week and I just know it's going to be manic.'

Even though where Kelly was really going was actually for the benefit of her friend, she still felt guilty leaving her for the morning when it was going to be busy. 'Babe, I'll get there as soon as I can, I promise. It's my teeth,' she lied, 'they've been aching all night and I need to go to the dentist because I'm in a lot of pain.'

Jade sighed heavily. 'Very well. But don't even think of eating any of the Haribo sweets in the office like you usually do then; not now your teeth are hurting.'

Damn, Kelly thought, why did I say teeth? She loved Haribos more than anything and Jade always put them in bowls round the office, which Kelly ended up eating all day. Oh well, hopefully she could come clean if she found anything important out. 'Okay, babe, see you as soon as I can.'

'See you soon,' Jade replied before hanging up.

Kelly climbed into her Mini, re-touched her lips with Dior lip gloss for good luck and punched the postcode of the address the man had given her into her sat-nav.

Kelly arrived at the small building fifteen minutes later and pressed the buzzer, before she was let in by Derek.

Derek smiled at her sympathetically as she walked into the room. 'Let's hope your boyfriend hasn't done anything wrong, eh?'

Kelly gave a half-smile, her voice soft and gentle. 'I hope so, I really do,' she said, going along with him.

'Okay, so we'll fast forward until you see him,' the man said as he picked up the remote control. 'What time do you want to start from?'

Kelly thought for a moment. She doubted Sam would have been home before midnight, even if he was drunk. 'Say eleven-thirty, just in case,' she told the man.

'No problem young lady,' Derek replied. 'I'll fast forward very slowly from eleven-thirty, and you just tell me when to stop.'

Kelly sat in anticipation biting her nails, which had just been applied with hot pink shellac vanish. There wasn't much going on at first and Kelly couldn't imagine she was going to see anything important at all. There were the odd couple of people coming back to the flats, but that was it. When the footage got to two a.m. Kelly knew they must be close to seeing Sam and at twenty-four minutes past she jumped up and told Derek to stop the tape. 'That's him! That's Sam. Can we go back please?'

Derek did as Kelly asked and at first Kelly thought Adele had completely lied about going back to Sam's altogether, as she could only see Sam on his own. Sam looked very drunk as he staggered through the entrance to the flats. About thirty seconds later, Kelly inhaled dramatically as she saw Adele jog along to catch up with him.

Derek was shaking his head. 'Sorry, love. If it makes you feel any better, I must say the man is a complete idiot for cheating on a lovely girl like you.' He rubbed his beard again thoughtfully.

Kelly ignored the comment, feeling disappointed. She was so sure that Sam hadn't cheated, but seeing Adele jog after him like that and how drunk he appeared to be didn't give her much hope anymore.

'Is that enough?' Derek asked.

'No,' Kelly told him firmly. 'I want to know how long she was there for.'

Derek shrugged. 'Shall I fast forward quickly?' he asked, obviously thinking it was a waste of time if the girl had stayed the night.

'Maybe a bit quicker, but not too fast,' Kelly told him as she watched the screen, concentrating. She began to feel a bit bored and as though this was a complete waste of time when suddenly someone appeared to be leaving the building thirteen minutes later. 'Stop again! Please rewind that,' Kelly asked Derek, feeling a ray of hope. Had that been Adele? As Derek rewound the footage, Kelly gasped as she watched Adele leaving Sam's flats. She felt like squealing with joy. Adele had lied! She hadn't stayed at Sam's all night at all; she'd only been there for thirteen minutes, which meant she was likely to be lying about sleeping with him too! Kelly knew some men didn't last long in bed, but thirteen minutes was really taking the biscuit. Besides, Adele would have had to get up the stairs, get undressed, do the deed and then get dressed again and leave the flat in thirteen minutes. Judging by the state of Sam walking, he wouldn't have even been capable of kissing someone, let alone anything else.

'Well, there she is again,' Derek said, his forehead creasing. 'I don't really know what to make of that.'

Kelly beamed broadly, 'I do Derek, I do. Thanks so much for your help. Is there any chance I could have this footage somehow?'

'I'm really not supposed to. I don't think we're actually meant to give it out . . .' He stopped as he watched Kelly's bottom lip rise.

Kelly pouted and she played with her hair with her index finger. 'It would be such a big help,' she muttered in a butter-wouldn't-melt tone.

'Okay,' Derek nodded, smitten by Kelly's charms. 'But don't tell anyone, okay?'

'Dezza, you have my word, babe,' Kelly said joyfully, kissing him on the cheek and leaving a lip-shaped glossy print behind. She smiled as Derek flushed beetroot red. He took the DVD out of the player and handed it to her.

'Good luck with everything,' he called as she made her way to the exit.

'Thank you, Dez,' Kelly replied. 'You'll never know how much this means to me.'

Derek blushed again and dismissed her with his hand. 'Bye Kelly.'

*

Jade was rushed off her feet. There were tons of emails to reply to as well as bikinis to be made. Jade wasn't bad at sewing, but she was nowhere near as talented as Kelly and she wished her appointment would hurry up so she could get here to help.

Picking up some crystals to sew on a turquoise strapless bikini, Jade's eyes flicked to the photo of her and Sam in Nu Bar for Billy's birthday the year before, just after Marbella. She loved that photo and knew it was probably time to take it down. Jade often looked at it when she was working and her eyes often wandered over to it ever since they'd split up. But she was certain it wasn't helpful to have it sitting there, staring her in the face every day. Jade picked the photo up and studied it, feeling the familiar wave of sadness that overcame her every time she allowed herself to remember being with Sam. Their faces looked beatific and anyone could tell from this photo how in love they were; a moment of pure happiness had been captured and Jade wished, not for the first time, that things had turned out differently. She didn't normally allow herself to dwell on her failed relationship for long; when she did, there was an ache in her heart which hurt so badly, she wondered if it would ever heal. Despite what had happened, Jade still loved Sam. Why couldn't she just switch off her feelings? she wondered, as she picked up Princess Cupcake and sat her on her lap. She'd grown closer and closer to the little dog as every day went by. Jade would actually miss Cupcake now if Lisa took her away. She smiled down at the gorgeous furry creature and tickled her under her chin. Since being toilet trained, Cupcake was hardly any trouble anymore. She'd finally learnt what her own toys were and what she shouldn't touch, much to Jade's and Kelly's delight. Lord McButterpants was having a birthday party soon and Jade had taken Princess Cupcake out and bought her the most amazing frilly pink dress and sparkly party hat; she would definitely be the best-dressed dog there, Jade thought fondly. Cupcake was great company, especially on days like today when Jade was feeling a bit down. She looked at the photo of herself with Kelly and Lisa and thanked God for having such amazing friends. Kelly had been acting a little odd the past few days – Jade couldn't put her finger on what she was up to, but her mind had constantly seemed elsewhere and she knew Kelly hadn't seen Billy in a few days, which was definitely strange. Jade hoped nothing was up with them, they made a great couple and she hadn't seen Kelly so happy in ages.

Fifteen minutes later the doorbell rang and Jade jumped up to let Kelly in, carrying Cupcake in her arms.

'Hi Kel,' she said as she opened the door.

Kelly was smiling broadly. 'Oh my God. I have got so much to tell you I don't even know where to start,' she said as she walked in.

Jade was intrigued. 'Let's go to the office and you can tell me everything. How was the dentist? I hope it's nothing serious?'

Kelly shook her head. 'Have you got a DVD player, babe?'

Jade frowned, trying to keep the irritation out of her

voice. 'Kelly, we don't have time to watch a DVD. I've only just started on the first bikini, we need to get going!'

Kelly exhaled and raised her eyebrows. 'Trust me, we'll get them done. I need to show you something and it's *really* important.'

Jade gave a little nod and walked through to the lounge. 'There's a DVD player here.'

Kelly faced her with a serious expression, her eyes brightening. 'I have something else to tell you first. It's about Adele and Chloe.'

Jade rolled her eyes as they both descended onto the cream sofa. 'Kelly, I really wish you'd stop blaming poor Chloe. She'd never do anything like that to us.'

Kelly shook her head, her eyes widening as she spoke. 'She's confessed everything. I went round there to see her and overheard a conversation between Chloe and Adele,' Kelly informed her, before explaining exactly what had happened that day to Jade who sat there, open mouthed. 'Oh my God, shut up! It was Chloe all along? I can't believe it!' Jade was astounded. Never would she have expected it of sweet and innocent Chloe, of all people. She couldn't believe Kelly had been right. 'Well done, Kel. That's amazing finding that out. I don't think it's possible to dislike someone as much as I dislike Adele. If I never saw her again, it would be too soon. I can't believe she stooped so low as bullying Chloe, what a cow. I'm just sorry I ever doubted you.'

Kelly took Cupcake into her arms and cuddled her. 'That's okay,' she replied, kissing the dog on her head. 'Sometimes I just get a gut instinct and it's usually right.'

Jade nodded thoughtfully. 'What's the DVD got to do with Chloe and Adele though? I don't understand.'

'Nothing. Now this is even more important,' Kelly announced, looking pleased with herself. She looked up at Jade, biting her lip, and Jade noticed she suddenly looked a bit awkward. 'Okay, now I know this is going to sound a bit weird, but I went to Sam's recently.'

Jade's jaw dropped in surprise. 'What? Why?'

'I just needed to know about Chloe and I wondered if he knew anything,' Kelly replied quickly. 'I didn't go to see him about you or anything, don't worry.'

'What did he say? I can't believe you went there,' Jade replied, swallowing hard, a million questions flashing through her mind. Did Sam mention her? Or was he completely over their relationship now? They hadn't been broken up for long, so she hoped not. Why did she still even care after what had happened?

'I just asked him about Chloe and to see if she spoke to Adele and he told me that Adele often went to see her. He asked about you though,' Kelly said with a mischievous smile. 'There is no way he doesn't still love you; I can tell a mile off. He looked disappointed when I told him I wasn't there about you.'

Jade felt her eyes brimming with tears and she blinked them away, furious with herself. 'It's all his fault,' Jade said breathlessly. She looked at Kelly as a tear plopped on her nose. 'I know I never say it, but I miss him, you know. I miss him every day and I try to not think about what we had, but it's always there in the back of my mind,' Jade said as she hugged her knees morosely.

Kelly nodded. 'I know, babe. Don't get upset.'

Jade sighed. 'I've been trying not to get upset for the past few weeks we've been apart. I hold it in, bottle it up. I've never cried about Sam in front of anyone, but I can't help it,' Jade sniffed, wiping her eyes with the sleeve of her cardigan. 'I just can't believe he slept with Adele.'

Kelly beamed broadly and Jade frowned. 'Why are you smiling? It's not funny.'

'Babe, he didn't do it!' Kelly exploded in a high-pitched excited voice. 'Adele was only in his flat for thirteen minutes, so unless he's that bloke from *American Pie* he couldn't have! I have it all here on camera. That's what the DVD is!'

Jade sat in silence as Kelly told her the whole story about how she'd overheard the security man talking and managed to get her hands on the footage. Kelly then proceeded to show Jade the video.

'OMG! Kelly, I can't believe you did that! I can't believe you got your hands on this!' Jade said, her jaw wide open, touching her bottom lip with her index finger. She felt a mixture of emotions. Happy, because Adele had been lying; by the looks of things Sam didn't even realise she was following him and she'd actually only been there for thirteen minutes and not all night. Angry, because Adele had purposely gone out of her way to cause trouble again in the lowest way possible, causing the demise of their relationship. Lastly, Jade felt confused. What did this now mean for her and Sam? Should she forgive him for keeping this secret from her and accept it was just a one off?

'There is one more surprise,' Kelly said softly, interrupting Jade's thoughts.

'What?' Jade asked in a small voice, wondering what else Kelly could possibly have up her sleeve.

'Go to the front door and look outside,' Kelly said, her mouth twitching.

'But why?' Jade asked, feeling suddenly nervous for some reason.

Kelly nodded towards the front door. 'Just go. I'll be getting on with the bikinis upstairs.'

Jade nodded and walked to the front door, opening it anxiously. At first she didn't see anything, but as she turned to her right her heart skipped a beat and her blood raced round her body. There, sitting in his car and staring at her with his gorgeous green eyes, was Sam.

CHAPTER 18

Lisa hadn't seen Nicola all day at work, which was unusual. She had dialled her extension number five times without getting an answer and was now walking down the corridor to where Nicola sat. She needed to explain the deal with Charlie desperately and was so glad that she hadn't deleted his weird text message; at least she had some proof he was being inappropriate well before he moved in for the kill. *Please believe me, Nicola*, Lisa thought unhappily. Nicola hadn't come back to the flat at all since she'd walked in on the incident and Lisa guessed she must be staying at her parents' house. Lisa had texted her saying she needed to talk and called her several times, but Nicola hadn't responded so far. The lift pinged and Lisa got out and nervously walked along the floor to where Nicola's desk was. As she turned the corner, she was surprised when saw it was empty. Dina, a kind middle-aged woman who sat opposite Nicola, looked up from her computer.

'You okay?' she asked Lisa, with a concerned expression. Dina moved her glasses further up her nose, waiting for Lisa to respond.

Lisa was frowning. 'Errr . . . yes. I was just looking for Nicola. Do you know where she is?'

'Nicola isn't well today, sweetheart. She called in this morning with a stomach ache. Didn't you know that already though? I thought you two lived together?'

Lisa hesitated, not wanting to give too much away. 'She stayed out last night so I wasn't sure if she'd be here. I'm not surprised as she wasn't feeling well yesterday and then she left. I'm not sure where she stayed though,' she lied, knowing that Nicola wasn't in work because she was obviously upset. At least her reason for not coming into work appeared a bit more genuine now.

'Maybe she stayed with that gorgeous boyfriend of hers,' Dina said, with a little cheeky grin.

'Maybe,' Lisa smiled back politely. 'See you.'

Lisa walked back to her own desk and hoped that Nicola was okay. She prayed to God that Charlie hadn't got to her first and made up a load of lies, she would be furious. Nicola had been such a great friend since Lisa had split up with Jake and she didn't know what she would do without her now. Knowing that she had to put things right before she went crazy, Lisa decided at that moment to visit Nicola's parents' home straight after work; this way Nicola would have no choice but to face up to things and finally talk to her.

*

Sam watched Jade walk over to his car and felt as though his heart was in his mouth. She looked stunned to see him sitting there and he couldn't blame her because he'd normally be at work this time of day. As soon as Kelly had called him and told him the news he'd fibbed to his boss and told him he had an important doctor's appointment and needed to take a half day; there was simply no way on earth he could have waited any longer to see Jade, not when the footage Kelly had got hold of might very well change things between them. Jade looked stunning as always; she was only wearing a casual pair of tight white jeans and a peach top, but she still looked like the sexiest girl in the world to him. Her long highlighted hair was loose and tousled, just how he liked it, and she was wearing minimal make-up, which he preferred. Jade didn't need much to look beautiful he thought, as she opened the car door and sat in the passenger seat. He wanted to grab her and kiss her, tell her over and over he loved and missed her, but he sat there and took his time; this conversation couldn't be rushed and he was petrified if he said the wrong thing he'd ruin it.

'Hi,' Jade said awkwardly as she sat down.

'Hey,' Sam replied, glancing at her with a half-smile. 'You look nice.'

Jade gave an insouciant shrug and arched an eyebrow. 'I look awful, but thanks anyway.' She looked him in the eye, quickly making his heart flip over, but then looked down again uncomfortably.

'How have you been?' Sam asked, clearing his throat. He wanted to know everything; what she had been up to, where she had been. It had been nothing but torture being apart from her this whole time and never knowing anything about what was going on in her life.

'I've been okay I guess,' Jade said as she heaved a sigh. 'What about you?'

'Mmm, I've been better,' Sam answered, hoping she understood that he was never going to be 'great' when he wasn't with her. 'So, did Kelly show you the video?' he asked hopefully to break up the silence. This was so weird; they were never silent when they were together.

'Yes,' Jade said, staring out of the window, deep in thought.

Sam sat there, his heart thumping in his chest. Jade certainly wasn't giving much away. 'So? Do you believe me now? Do you believe I didn't sleep with Adele? Can you see that she lied now? She told everyone that she'd stayed the entire night; Kelly told me she could see from the video that she followed me in and left after thirteen minutes.'

Jade nodded. 'Yes Sam, I believe you. I believe you didn't sleep with her.'

Sam exhaled sharply, wanting to scream with happiness. 'I didn't do anything with her, I knew it. I always knew she was lying deep down.'

Jade turned and looked at him with a stern expression. 'This still doesn't excuse your behaviour afterwards though, Sam. You lied about seeing Adele and it's very worrying that you got that drunk and didn't remember anything. I find it so hard to trust men, you know that, and if you'd just been honest from the start and explained the situation, if you hadn't kept this huge secret . . .'

'I know, I know,' Sam agreed, not wanting to hear any more. He should have just told Jade straight away, but he couldn't turn back time now, he could only apologise. 'Jade, I was terrified of losing you,' he said, finally leaning his head back on the car seat and running his hand through his hair. 'When I woke up that morning, I honestly didn't know what to do. I got too drunk and I was ashamed that I couldn't remember anything, so I didn't tell you. I wish I did, but the thought of you leaving me was too much to bear. When I saw a text message from Adele the following day I felt like crying and I didn't know what to think. But I'm so glad now that we know for sure that she was lying. She's a twisted cow who wanted to ruin us again.'

Jade's eyes were watery as she spoke, her voice croaky. 'You shouldn't have even spoken to her that night, you know she's trouble. You shouldn't have ever put yourself in that situation where she can manipulate and ruin things. You hurt me so much.'

Sam closed his eyes, knowing everything Jade was saying

was true. 'I know.' He looked at her seriously. 'Jade, I swear to God, if you find it in your heart to give me another chance I would never, ever do anything stupid like that again. I'll be honest with you about everything; I'll never get myself into a situation like that and let you down again. I have missed you more than I ever thought possible. I have been in pieces without you and I've laid in my bed, night after night, asking myself why I let this happen. I love you, Jade, so very much . . .' Sam stopped when his eyes felt hot and blurry with threatening tears, and wiped them forcefully, shocked that all this emotion was finally coming out. 'Please give me another chance; I haven't stopped thinking about you since you left my life. Nothing is the same without you. If I ever mess up again in any way, you have every right to leave me, but I know I won't. Not this time: not ever,' Sam choked.

He gazed at her intently and his heart leapt as she slowly smiled lovingly. 'Oh Sam, I've missed you so much,' she said, leaning over to hug him. Sam took in the scent of her hair, which smelt like apples, and thought he'd burst with happiness. He pulled back, looking into her beautiful blue eyes. 'Does this mean . . .?'

Jade beamed a broad smile and said in a soft voice, 'Yes. One more chance. Please don't make me regret it.'

'Never, I promise,' he replied breathlessly. He kissed her softly at first, but when he tasted Jade's sweet lips, he pulled her head closer to his, realising how much he'd missed her touch. He'd been forgiven and Sam felt overjoyed; he had meant every word he said to Jade and there was no way he was ever going to mess this up again. He was the luckiest man alive; he'd been given another chance and he couldn't thank Kelly enough. 'Let me take you out for the rest of the day, now I have you back, I don't want to leave you,' he said as he gazed into her twinkling eyes.

'I can't,' Jade said regretfully, as she shook her head. 'We have so much work to do and I need to go and help Kelly with the bikinis, calls and emails. She'll tell me she can manage alone if I ask, but I know it'll be a struggle and it's not really fair. It's a really busy day today.'

'Okay babe. Anything I can do to help?' Sam offered, holding her hand and running his thumb along her smooth skin.

'Well, you could answer the phone to customers?' Jade said with a little giggle. 'Though I doubt you know much about swimwear.'

'I'm a quick learner,' Sam smiled, opening his car door. 'Now come on, let's get this work done and I'll treat you and Kelly to dinner afterwards.'

'Okay, but remember who's in charge here.'

Sam saluted in mock seriousness, 'Yes, boss!'

*

Kelly sat down in the lounge, sipping the cup of tea Jade had just made her. It had been a difficult day with plenty to do, but they had got there in the end with Sam's help. The phone hadn't stopped ringing and Sam had been answering the calls, while she and Jade had been finishing the bikinis to the highest quality to ensure they got to their customers on time. She smiled to herself as she watched Sam kiss Jade when she handed him his mug of steaming tea. He looked elated now that he had Jade back. His eyes were sparkling and he couldn't stop smiling; it was so romantic and Kelly felt proud that it was all down to her doing. Jade too, looked thrilled, constantly laughing and smiling at every opportunity; Kelly was thankful that Adele hadn't managed to break up two people that were clearly so in love.

'Fancy coming for dinner with us, Kelly?' Sam asked, glancing in her direction as Jade went back into the kitchen.

Kelly shook her head, knowing that she had to see Billy

at some point; they had hardly spoken since she'd been to his house that day. Kelly had wanted to find out some more information about Gary before speaking to Billy about it, so she'd been really quick on the phone when he'd called and made up excuses as to why she had to go. If she was honest, she was also still hurt about the way he'd spoken to her as well; calling her stupid had really upset her. 'That's really nice to ask me, Sam,' Kelly replied, blowing the top of her mug to cool her tea down, 'but I need to see Billy tonight. Besides, you two probably have a lot of catching up to do and I wouldn't want to get in the way.'

'You wouldn't be getting in the way, I promise. I owe you big time and wanted to treat you. You sure you won't come?'

'Another time,' Kelly smiled.

Jade walked in and switched the television on and they sat and relaxed together.

Half an hour later, Kelly left the two love birds and called Billy to check if he was home.

'Hi Kelly,' he answered, sounding surprised to hear from her. 'I was just about to call you actually.'

'Oh were you? I just wondered if you wanted to meet up tonight?'

'Kelly, I wanted to ask you something,' Billy said in a serious, firm tone. 'I just called Gary and he told me he found you in his garden late the other night. Apparently you'd lost a football?'

Oh no, Kelly thought pulling a face, *I knew that football story would come back to haunt me*. She could tell by his tone he knew she'd lied to Gary, but she was too embarrassed to tell him she was spying. 'Yes, I was messing around in the garden with Lucy.'

He sounded incredulous. 'Lucy? Who the hell is Lucy? Kelly, I know you'd never play football so you may as well come clean and tell me what you were doing there. Gary didn't sound too impressed that he found you in his back garden at night and to be honest, this whole thing is looking rather weird and creepy.'

I only did it to help you! Kelly wanted to scream. Besides, why was he so certain that she didn't play football in her spare time? She wouldn't, but that wasn't the point. 'For your information Billy, I've actually become rather a fan of football recently and Lucy and I *were* playing in her garden; I didn't even know Gary lived next door! I support a team and everything.'

'Okay,' Billy replied sounding sceptical. 'Which team do you support?'

Damn, Kelly thought, racking her brains for the name of a team. Were Arsenal Villa one? No, she was sure that didn't sound right. If only she wasn't speaking on her mobile she could have quickly looked one up. She didn't know the first thing about football! Who did that hot player, Frank Lampard play for? Her mind went blank. 'I support . . .' *Think, Kelly, think.* 'QVC,' she said in a jovial, triumphant voice. *Ha! Take that, Billy!*

She frowned when she heard him laughing.

'Do you mean QPR?' He sniggered. 'I think you're getting muddled up with the shopping channel, babe.'

Oops. Kelly sighed; she still wasn't going to tell Billy the truth. She had most likely been barking up the wrong tree, but at the time she had truly believed that Gary had something to do with the scam. She didn't want to admit to Billy she was wrong. 'Yes, that's what I said, babe,' she answered.

'Whatever, Kelly,' Billy replied suspiciously. 'I know there's more to it.'

Kelly thought she would check how things were to change the subject. 'Any more news on this Alfie bloke?'

Billys' lowered his voice. 'No. I've been going round to Gary's to try and sort things out, but the CID dealing with it doesn't seem to be getting anywhere.'

'Ah babe, I'm sorry.'

Billy cleared his throat. 'Me and Gal are doing all we can. Gary's completely pissed off and down like I am; he's completely cut up about it and it's horrible, I've never seen him like this.'

Kelly frowned. Both times she'd seen him he'd been laughing. Once again a feeling of doubt crept up on her. 'Did he say anything about going on holiday, hun?'

Billy sounded bemused. 'Holiday? Kelly, don't be so ridiculous. As if now would be a good time for either of us to go on holiday! Why are you asking that?' he said questioningly.

Kelly bit her lip, wondering whether she should tell him. 'Look, I saw Gary the other day after I left yours driving in his Porsche and he was laughing his head off with some man in the car. I just find it hard to see how you can say he's in bits when I've never seen him look happier. When I went to his garden . . . to find the football, I could hear through the wall and I heard him say something about going on holiday.'

'Kelly, please don't say you're going to start on about all this again! You must have heard wrong; I can assure you Gary isn't going anywhere. Look, babe, I appreciate that you want to help, but please don't point the finger at one of my best mates. I've said before, Gary Jacobs is like one of the family. If you want to blame anyone, blame Alfie Salmon!'

Kelly's brows knitted as he said the last words. *Alfie Salmon?* Why did that name ring a bell? She racked her brains for the answer, but it wouldn't come. 'Okay Bill,' she said to placate him, 'I'll forget about it. Now am I seeing you tonight or what?'

'I hope so, babe. I've missed you the last few days. Come round about eight?'

'See you there.'

Ten minutes later, Kelly put rollers in her hair to give it lots of volume and reapplied her make-up, coating her lips in Bobbi Brown pale pink gloss. Why had that name *Salmon* stuck in her mind? She doubted it was significant, but it was bugging her. Then she remembered that she'd had a client with that last name not too long ago. What was her first name? Kelly grabbed her beauty diary and found the name. It was a pedicure and manicure, she was sure of it. She ran her index finger along, searching through all the dates, pleased with herself when she spotted what she was looking for. Oh yes, that was it; Hilary Salmon and Susan Jacobs. Kelly froze on the spot. *Jacobs and Salmon.* Then it clicked. That was where Gary's mum had recognised her from that night in the garden! It was Susan who she'd given a manicure and pedicure to that time! There was a link and Kelly was certain at that point that Gary and this Alfie bloke were in on it together. Their families clearly knew each other! There was no way this was a coincidence. Leaving her rollers in her hair, Kelly grabbed her car keys and ran out of the door.

*

Lisa rang Nicola's doorbell nervously, hoping that Nicola would answer. She'd never been inside her parents' house before and would probably feel rather awkward if they'd heard from Nicola why she was staying there. She waited patiently, reassured that someone was home when she heard some movement from inside the house. Lisa had to prevent herself from gasping when a tall, blond-haired man answered the door, with the most smouldering blue eyes she'd ever seen.

He gave her a half-smile, his voice soft and sexy when he spoke. 'Can I help you?'

Lisa felt herself blush and cursed herself; she was

completely giving away that she found him drop-dead gorgeous, how embarrassing? 'Oh hi. Is Nicola here? I'm her roommate and really need to see her.'

He nodded and opened the door. 'She's actually just popped to the shops for some milk, she won't be five minutes. Come in,' he said walking into the biggest kitchen Lisa had ever seen.

Wow, Lisa thought, so this is where Nicola grew up? The place was huge!

'Take a seat,' the blond man smiled at her. 'Do you want a drink?'

Lisa shook her head. 'I'm fine thanks,' she replied, unable to look him in the eye for long without feeling her face go hot.

'I'm Ben, Nicola's older brother, by the way,' he announced.

'Lisa,' she beamed broadly, feeling butterflies in her stomach. What was wrong with her today? She watched Ben as he started tidying up the kitchen. She could tell he and Nicola were related, even though they didn't look that much alike. They both had intense bright blue eyes, and were tall, as well as sharing the same cute ski-slope noses. Ben had a gorgeous, masculine jawline though, Lisa noticed.

'She shouldn't be long,' he assured her.

'That's okay,' Lisa replied cheerily, playing on her phone for something to do. A few seconds later Lisa heard the front door opening.

'Ahhh,' Ben said walking towards the front of the house. 'That must be her.'

Lisa could hear their muffled voices and she stood up as Nicola walked in the room. She looked completely different; her long hair was scraped back off her head and she had no make-up on whatsoever, which was unheard of.

'Hi Nic, are you okay?' Lisa asked, her voice full of concern. 'I'm sorry to come here, but I didn't know what else to do; I really needed to talk to you.'

Nicola nodded slowly. 'Come up to my room and we can talk,' she told her, walking to the stairs.

Lisa looked round Nicola's bedroom in awe. She had a stunning king size four-poster bed with ivory drapes, and a French shabby chic chaise longue, which Lisa sat on. The whole house was absolutely beautiful and Nicola's room was no exception.

'I was going to come back to the flat tonight,' Nicola sat, sitting on the bed.

'You were?' Lisa was surprised. 'Look, I don't even know where to start about the whole Charlie thing.' Lisa took a deep breath and closed her eyes for a second, trying to think of the best way to word it. 'The truth is, Nicola, I always thought Charlie was a bit of a creep; even from the first time I met him. I can't explain why, but my initial thoughts were only confirmed when he started making odd comments to me. They were just a bit inappropriate, you know? He told me once that you couldn't meet him for lunch and invited himself along with me. Then when I went back to the office, you told me you'd already been with him! Do you remember that day I told you I'd dreamt someone came in my room at night?' Lisa asked her. This was going to be a hard thing to tell Nicola.

Nicola nodded glumly.

'It was Charlie,' Lisa cringed as she said it. 'Look, I'll show you the text,' Lisa said, fishing for her phone in her bag.

'There's no need,' Nicola said with a sigh.

Lisa gazed at her, hoping she hadn't taken Charlie's side somehow. 'Oh?'

Nicola attempted a smile. 'I know he's a complete sleaze, honey. He followed me back here that day I saw him trying to kiss you. He fed me all the lines; that it was you coming on to him, he loved me, etc. So when he went to make me a drink I looked down his phone because I didn't believe

308

him; I just knew you would never betray me like that. I'd never normally feel the need to look down anyone's phone; you know I don't believe in being with someone if you can't trust them.'

Lisa nodded sadly. She dreaded to think what Charlie had on his phone.

'There were tons of messages, honey. Texts to loads of girls I didn't know. I saw the one he sent to you as well; he's sick in the head and I told him straight there and then! I threw his phone at him and told him never to come back.' Nicola shook her head, still in disbelief. 'I suppose I knew he was a flirt, but I didn't think he was up to anything like that.'

'Oh Nic, I'm so sorry,' Lisa said, leaning forward and giving her a hug.

Nicola shrugged. 'I'm not going to lie; I have been a bit upset. But I was thinking about it today and I'm a hundred per cent better off without him.'

'More like a zillion per cent,' Lisa giggled.

'Exactly, honey,' Nicola agreed. 'I heard my brother telling his mate Adam earlier that he was going to meet him for some drinks in Switch Bar in South Woodford. Adam is unreal, honey. I've had a crush on him for ages. Shall we go?'

Lisa tried to act casual about it, even though she felt her heart flutter at the thought of being in the same place as Ben all night. 'Yeah, why not?' She laughed. 'You don't waste time, do you?'

Nicola smiled. 'Best way to be, honey, trust me. When one door closes another one opens,' she beamed. 'What did Ben speak to you about earlier?' Nicola asked as she took her hair down and plugged her curlers in.

Lisa looked down at her nails awkwardly. 'Not much.'

Nicola's mouth hung wide open. 'Oh my God, honey! You're blushing! You don't have a crush on Ben, do you?'

Nicola said, grimacing at the thought of anyone fancying her brother.

Lisa's hands flew up to her cheeks. 'No! Keep your voice down,' she hissed. She'd be mortified if Ben overheard.

Nicola couldn't contain her grin. 'Secret is safe with me, honey,' she winked. 'Adam is the same age as Ben; they're twenty-five. This night could turn out better than I first thought, eh?'

Lisa's mouth curled upwards; she sure as hell hoped so.

*

Adele rolled her eyes for what felt like the twentieth time that day. 'For goodness' sake, Donna! You're the bride. If anyone should go through with it, it's you! Just stay still!'

Donna's eyes were wide open in terror as the doctor stood there, holding the needle just inches away from her face. 'You promise me it doesn't hurt?' she asked in a shaky voice.

'You'll feel a tiny, sharp prick, but no, it won't hurt any more than that,' the doctor assured her in his calm, gentle tones. 'Just stay very still for me now.'

Donna knocked his hand away. 'Just give me a minute; I'm scared of needles!' she gasped, breathlessly.

'Okay, take your time,' the doctor replied patiently.

Adele huffed. 'Oh this is just getting ridiculous!' she scoffed. Her voice was clipped. 'Just bloody lie still, close your eyes and relax. It doesn't hurt; I've told you a hundred times! Do you want smooth skin on your wedding day or what? Everyone has Botox nowadays, it's completely normal!'

Donna took deep breaths, her hands trembling as she lay back down. 'Okay, okay.'

Adele sighed. Donna better do it this time, she thought to herself irritably; she was holding a Botox party and the more people that went through with the procedure, the cheaper hers would be. Donna's constant hesitation was seriously pushing her to the limit. She sighed with relief as the doctor slid the needle expertly into Donna's forehead.

'It's actually not that painful!' Donna giggled.

'I told you that,' Adele replied curtly.

'I can hear the skin pierce, but that's the worst bit,' Donna said, as she laid there with a grin on her face.

'It's honestly nothing to be worried about,' Adele smiled at her other guests who then relaxed and carried on their conversation. They were three of her mum's friends who she didn't know that well. Adele's mum had fillers and wasn't able to make it.

When the Botox party was over, Adele glanced at her reflection in the mirror and pouted. She loved cosmetic surgery; it was the best thing ever invented. 'I'm going to get my eyebrows tattooed,' she informed Donna, who was sipping a glass of rosé wine. 'There is this brilliant semi-permanent make-up artist in Essex that all the celebs go to. Maybe you should get it done with me before your wedding?'

Donna nearly spat her drink out. 'More needles? I'd have a heart attack! I'm just fine for now,' she informed her, looking horrified at the thought of it. 'It's so nice to just relax for one evening and not have to think and worry about the wedding. I can't believe it's only a week away!'

Adele couldn't wait. She had a week to make herself look even more beautiful so she was ready to bag her footballer. 'Does Aaron have lots of friends going?' she asked hopefully.

Donna nodded. 'Yeah, quite a lot I think. There are around a hundred guests in total. I'm so excited,' she said, her voice raising an octave higher.

'How are you having your hair?' Adele wondered. She had to admit Donna's extensions looked lovely; so much so that she was going to the same woman in two days' time to get the same ones, though she hadn't admitted that to Donna. She couldn't believe how slim she was looking either. There was a radiant glow about her and it wasn't the Botox, as Adele knew from experience that it wouldn't show until a few days' time.

'I'm getting Kelly to do my hair and make-up,' she told her, without noticing Adele's face suddenly becoming contorted in shock and anger. Donna continued as she ran her hands through her long hair, 'She's going to curl it and do half up and then I just want lovely natural make-up,' Donna grinned, imagining her big day.

'Why would you ask *that* airhead?' Adele glowered. 'Surely you can afford someone better than her? She's rubbish and if you ask me I think you're making a *huge* mistake,' she said, folding her arms across her chest sulkily.

Donna tutted. 'Adele, don't be like that. Kelly is lovely and I love the way she does my hair and make-up. I was going to pay for her to do yours too.'

Adele's mouth dropped open. 'I wouldn't let her touch me with a bargepole!' She scowled with a grimace. 'I'll get my own hairdresser and make-up artist thank you very much.'

Donna shrugged and took another sip of wine. 'Suit yourself. Though I'll never understand why you have such a problem with Kelly, she's so nice. I've invited her to the wedding.'

'*What*?' Adele was horrified. 'You've invited her to the wedding as well?'

'Yes,' Donna frowned. 'I honestly don't get what the big deal is? I've known Kelly for about two years; she always does my beauty treatments.'

Adele huffed. 'Oh whatever,' she said, rolling her eyes. Then the thought of her getting with a hot footballer and rubbing it in Kelly's face ran through her mind; maybe it wouldn't be such a bad thing after all? Adele smirked at the thought of making Kelly jealous. Adele was looking forward to the wedding now; she may not be the bride on this occasion, but she was going to make damn well sure that *she* was the centre of attention.

CHAPTER 19

'Slow down,' Billy told Kelly firmly. 'I can't understand what you're saying. What are those things on your head by the way?' he asked, lifting his eyebrows as he glanced at the bright pink rollers in Kelly's hair.

'They're rollers, babe; make your hair well amaze. Anyway, that's not important right now. Just listen to what I'm saying. I recognised Gary's mum in the garden that night and didn't know where from, then when you told me Alfie's last name was Salmon I knew it from somewhere and checked my diary. That's when I remembered having two customers that were friends, with the last name Salmon and Jacobs! It was Gary's mum! I'm certain of it now. Gary's in on it, Bill, I swear he is.' Kelly showed Billy her beauty treatment book and opened it on the page to show him. She pointed with her perfectly manicured nail.

Billy's brows knitted in puzzlement as he saw the name Susan Jacobs; it was dawning on him for the first time that Kelly might actually be right. 'That's weird,' he said, sitting down.

'Gary's mum's name is Susan, yeah?' Kelly asked breathlessly. She felt a weight had been lifted off her shoulders and was so glad she'd told Billy her discovery.

Billy nodded as he frowned. 'Yeah. So his mum has a good friend with the last name Salmon,' he muttered to himself, scratching his head. 'It could be a coincidence that Susan's friend has the same last name. I still can't imagine Gary doing this to me,' Billy said, but Kelly noticed he spoke without the usual conviction in his voice.

'Look at this pic, babe.' Kelly showed the image she'd captured of Gary laughing.

Billy looked even more astonished as he saw his friend who was supposedly completely distraught, laughing his head off. 'Something isn't right here,' he whispered. 'I need to see him,' he quickly added, calling him straight away on his mobile. 'Voicemail,' he said, disappointed.

'Go round and see him?' Kelly suggested.

'You know what babe, I think I will,' he said standing up. 'Coming?'

'Sure am,' Kelly said, glad that she'd finally convinced Billy that Gary wasn't whiter than white. She stood up with her head held high, ready to take on the world.

'Errr Kelly, can you just do me one little favour?' Billy asked, narrowing his eyes.

'Anything,' Kelly said, wondering what it could be.

'Take those bloody things out of your hair!' he laughed, making his way to the front door.

*

When they pulled up outside Gary's house, Billy looked perplexed as he watched a man knocking on Gary's front door. 'That's the CID,' Billy told Kelly, as he watched Gary open the door, smile at him and let him in. Luckily he didn't spot them sitting in Kelly's car. 'Why has Gary not told me about a meeting with him?' he wondered, shaking his head in confusion.

'Try calling Gary on his home phone and ask him what

he's up to,' Kelly suggested. 'It'll be interesting to see what he says, babe.'

'Good idea,' Billy agreed, picking up his mobile once more and dialling the number, putting it on loudspeaker so Kelly could hear. Kelly watched the phone in anticipation and sat on the edge of her seat as they waited.

'Hello,' Gary answered.

'Alright, Gal? It's Bill.'

He sounded a bit startled. 'Alright, mate?'

Billy cleared this throat. 'Yeah, all good. Just wondered what you were up to tonight and if you fancied going for a drink? Maybe we can discuss our next step with the business?'

'Mate, it's a bit late for that now. I'm having a quiet night as I'm not feeling great. Going to go to bed soon if I'm honest. We'll discuss it tomorrow, yeah?'

Kelly's mouth popped open; she couldn't believe he'd just told them a big fat lie! He was having a meeting with the CID and he hadn't even told Billy about it. She watched the shocked look appear on Billy's face and knew he was just as surprised. He thought of Gary as one of his best mates, the poor thing.

'Okay, no worries pal. We'll speak tomorrow,' Billy finally answered with a frown.

'Bye,' Gary said before hanging up the phone.

'Oh my God!' Kelly gasped. 'Now do you believe me?'

Billy bit his bottom lip. 'Something definitely isn't right and I'm going to find out what,' he said, opening the car door.

'Billy, what are you going to do?' Kelly worried. 'Wait! I have an idea,' she told him as she pulled out the black baseball cap and hoody from the boot. 'He has a side gate and we can disguise ourselves with these and check on what he's doing in there.'

Billy eyed her suspiciously. 'Are you still going to tell me you were playing football next door that night he found you in the garden?'

Kelly's mouth twitched and Billy laughed.

'Good work, Kelly,' he said, impressed, knowing for certain she'd been spying. He put on the baseball cap and followed Kelly round the side of the house through the gate.

'Follow me,' Kelly whispered, stopping again at the window at the side of the house, which once again was open seeing as it was a warm evening. She froze when she looked through and realised Gary was standing right by it. She pointed to Billy and he stooped low alongside her and peered in. They could hear Gary's voice, loud and clear.

'So that money should be in your account by the end of this week,' he said to the CID man. 'I'm going to Dubai for a while next week, so if you need to speak to someone, call Alfie.'

Kelly inhaled sharply and noticed Billy's eyes widen.

'Someone say my name?' another man asked jovially, walking over with three glasses of champagne.

'That's Alfie!' Billy hissed, looking livid.

'Shut up! That's the man from Gary's car the other day, babe. I remember seeing his awfully long sideburns and thinking they could do with a trim!' Kelly whispered as they continued to watch the men inside.

'Here's to a great little business deal,' Gary grinned, clinking glasses with the two men.

'That's it!' Billy fumed, not able to watch anymore. He walked back through the gate and banged on the front door furiously, with Kelly following behind him.

Kelly couldn't believe what they'd just seen. The CID wasn't the police at all! He was in on the act! She stood behind Billy as he continued hammering on the door.

Gary answered with a bemused expression, wondering

317

who was so desperate at this time of night to be let in. As his eyes focused on Billy and Kelly his face dropped and he went to shut the door again, but Billy managed to get his foot in first.

'Not so fast, Gal,' Billy sneered. 'I think me and you need a little word,' he smirked as he barged through the door.

'Billy! What do you want?' Gary asked, trying to act normal suddenly as Billy faced him with a face like thunder. 'I told you I was going to bed.'

Billy's face scrunched up in anger. 'What do I want? What do I bloody well want?' Billy said, shoving past him and walking through the hallway, searching for Alfie and the CID who were clearly hiding. 'I want to know why you have *Alfie Salmon* here as well as the CID? Or should I say fake CID as let's face it, at the moment he's looking about as legitimate as a Burberry bag from Romford Market.'

Kelly bit her lip, trying not to giggle at the comment. She always laughed when she felt nervous. She'd never seen Billy this mad since she'd known him and it was scary to watch.

Gary flushed and he looked afraid. 'What are you talking about?'

Billy turned to him and pointed a finger in his face, his eyes like slits. 'You know damn well what I'm talking about, so let's cut the crap. You almost pulled the wool over my eyes, pretending to be gutted about the business, but when I think about it now, you must have been laughing at me the whole time. It was *you* that always dealt with Alfie, you made sure of that didn't you? And it was *you* that called the CID. I offered to call the police, but you were adamant that *you* dealt with it and I can see why now. You tried to act like you were doing me a favour! But the whole time you were plotting against me. After all the years I've known you, Gary! How could you do that to me? You were going to run off with all that *stolen* money and leave me to pick up the pieces.' Billy looked enraged, but Kelly could see there was hurt in his eyes as well.

Gary looked at Billy with venom. 'You don't know what you're talking about,' he said, shaking his head.

Billy's face darkened as the fury rushed through his veins. 'Don't you dare deny it, Gary! At least give me some respect. Be a man and admit it!' he spat.

'I'm not admitting a thing,' Gary shrugged, trying to remain calm. Kelly could tell he was most certainly rattled though; he was like a shaking rabbit caught in the headlights.

Kelly could hear movement under the cupboard by the stairs and opened it, revealing Alfie and the fake CID standing there in shock. 'Here they are, Billy. Here are the two we were looking for,' she announced. The two men came out sheepishly and made a run for it towards the front door.

'You won't get away with it!' Billy shouted after them. 'I'm calling the police and telling them everything!'

'Look, you don't realise the stress I've been under,' Gary said, wiping the sweat from his brow. 'I needed the money, Billy. I wasn't going to leave you, I swear. I would have come back and sorted it out eventually. Please, don't get the police involved. I'm one of your oldest mates.'

Billy gave a short laugh. 'A mate? You think this is how *mates* behave, do you? The sad thing is, Gary, I never even thought for a minute that you may be involved in this. I'm just lucky that Kelly realised in time. You're not getting away with this, I can promise you that.'

'I can explain everything. *Please*. You don't need to involve the police,' Gary said, shifting on his feet uncomfortably and panicking.

'He does and he will,' Kelly informed him. She'd heard enough of Gary's begging for one day; he was a complete lowlife in her eyes.

'Who asked you?' Gary scorned. 'This isn't about make-up and hair, Kelly, keep your nose out and go and read *Heat* magazine, you dumb cow; it's between me and Billy.'

Billy's whole body tensed and he lunged towards Gary and punched him full pelt in the nose. Kelly watched in horror as Gary's nose exploded and blood gushed out like a fountain. 'That's for speaking to Kelly like dirt!' Billy shouted. He punched Gary again in the stomach, winding him and making him bend over in pain. 'And that's for the business,' Billy muttered under his breath. 'Come on Kelly, we're off.'

'Are you okay?' Kelly asked Billy timidly when they were outside.

'I'm fine,' Billy said attempting a smile. 'Well my hand hurts a bit, but apart from that.'

Kelly giggled. 'I can't believe you punched him. He deserved it though, babe,' she said as she opened the car door.

Billy sat down in the passenger seat and stared at Kelly intently. 'Kelly, I can't even begin to tell you how sorry I am for not listening to you. I'm embarrassed that I didn't take your opinions seriously and I said you come out with stupid things. You're not stupid at all, not even close. If it wasn't for you, who knows what would have happened. Thank you,' he said, taking her hand and kissing it.

Kelly kissed him gently on the lips. 'That's okay, babe,' she told him. This was the second time this week someone was apologising to her and Kelly was overjoyed that she'd helped out two of the closest people in her life.

'I'm going to go to the police station first thing tomorrow

and tell them everything,' Billy said gingerly. 'Do you think that's the right thing to do?' he asked Kelly.

Kelly felt glad that he wanted her opinion. 'I think it's your only choice,' she told him softly. 'Gary isn't your friend, babe. I'm so sorry, I can imagine how betrayed you must feel.'

Billy nodded and Kelly knew he was a bit too choked to talk. 'Let's go home,' he told her and Kelly started the car.

*

Lisa woke up with a smile on her face as she remembered the night before. Even her throbbing temples couldn't put her in bad spirits. She'd kissed Ben in Switch Bar and it had felt magical! Just the thought of it made her stomach go over with excitement. She'd been pretty certain Nicola had snogged Ben's mate, Adam, when they left together, because Adam had to get up for work early and offered to drop Nicola back first. Lisa had seen the cheeky glint in her friend's eye when she'd waved goodbye and it had been pretty obvious that Adam liked Nicola too. Nicola had told Lisa that Ben usually hated the thought of his friends with his little sister and normally tried to prevent it from happening, but with Lisa being there he had hardly noticed! *Glad I could be of help,* Lisa thought to herself wryly. It was great to see Nicola enjoying herself and Lisa doubted she'd even thought about Charlie once with Adam around. Adam looked like he lived in the gym; he had the biggest muscles Lisa had seen and she knew that he was exactly Nicola's type. Though Charlie had been good looking, Nicola preferred muscly men to tall and slim, like Charlie's build.

Lisa stretched in bed, wishing she could lie there for longer. Reluctantly, she sat up and reached across for her iPhone, feeling a warm glow when she saw that Ben had texted her.

Morning sleepy head. Great meeting you last night.
You even look lovely when you're scoffing a burger
down at one o' clock in the morning ;) Do you
fancy doing something this weekend? Ben xx

Lisa gasped in horror. *Oh no, the burger!* Memories of her begging the cab driver to stop on the way back so she could get something to eat came back to haunt her. She texted back, unable to wipe the smile from her face. She'd been on so many dates recently, but no one had made her feel like this so far; it was a good sign.

Good morning Ben. I can imagine you have a
stunning image of me in my drunken state last
night with ketchup round my face. Just to let you
know though, I blame you. I told you I didn't want
those last two shots and you made me, meaning
the burger monster comes out, ha. I promise next
time we meet there won't be a burger in sight :)
I'm free this weekend and would love to meet up,
Lisa xx

Lisa was still grinning when Nicola walked into the kitchen.

'Morning, honey,' she smiled back, taking the cup of coffee Lisa had made her. 'Oh my God, what happened with you and my brother last night when we left? Did you pull him?' Nicola's eyes were sparkling with excitement.

Lisa felt herself blush a little and nodded, still beaming from ear to ear.

'Shut up! That's so sweet,' Nicola said in a high voice, taking a seat at the kitchen table. 'Ben hasn't had a girlfriend for a few years and I knew the minute we got in Switch he fancied you,' Nicola informed her knowledgeably.

Lisa sat opposite her. 'So, what happened with you and Adam?' she probed.

Nicola fluttered her eyelashes. 'He is *so* gorge,' she swooned. 'I've fancied him for years. He used to come round when I was younger after school some nights because he's always been friends with Ben, and every time he spoke to me I went bright red. I told him I've always liked him in the taxi last night when I'd had a few drinks, and he kissed me goodbye,' she said, smiling at the memory. 'Such an amazing kisser and I really like him. Last night was hilare, I had such a good time!'

Lisa agreed. Their night out had been planned last minute and Lisa didn't even feel like she was looking her best; sometimes those nights seemed to turn out the best though. 'Your brother has asked me out at the weekend,' Lisa told her, wondering if Nicola was okay with the two of them dating.

'Oh my God! Already? He's keen. Just think, if you two get together properly and get married one day, we'd be sisters-in-law! Just think how cool that would be, honey.'

Lisa laughed, relieved Nicola was fine with them seeing each other. 'We haven't even been on a date yet!'

Nicola shrugged, 'I'm just saying.'

'I'd better get ready for work,' Lisa said when she noticed the time. She jumped up and smiled as she saw the sun shining through the windows. This was the first day for a long while she was going to work with a spring in her step.

*

It was the day of the wedding and Adele was round at Donna's house getting ready. Her eyebrows had recently been tattooed and she loved them; she was going to get semi-permanent eyeliner next, it was such a great way to save time! She was in the middle of curling her hair when

Donna's mum, Jackie, walked in the room looking for the hairdryer.

'I can't believe my baby girl is getting married,' Jackie gushed. 'Her dress had to be taken in again can you believe? I think she's almost down to a size twelve now,' she repeated for the umpteenth time, making Adele want to slap her one. Yes, they all knew Donna had lost weight and was looking much better nowadays, big deal. For the past two weeks she'd been going to a personal trainer with Aaron and cutting down on her food like she should have done years ago. *She'll still never be as slim as me*, Adele smirked. *Cake will find her again eventually*.

Donna's sister, Emma, walked in the room, looking disconsolate.

'Ooh Emma, that dress looks gorgeous on you!' Jackie admired. 'Such a stunning colour, it really is.'

Emma rolled her eyes in exasperation. 'I asked Donna one thing, and that was to make sure the dress had some kind of straps,' she complained, 'but she couldn't do it, could she? Look how humungous my boobs look in this dress! I feel completely uncomfortable and unsupported.'

Donna, who was on her way to the room where they were getting ready, overheard what she said and her face completely crumpled. 'Emma, I'm so sorry! I honestly didn't forget about that. Adele assured me that the dress should have straps that come with it, can't you find them?'

Adele froze when she heard her name. Why couldn't Emma just shut up? she wondered. Her eyes flicked to Emma's bust and she was right, it was huge and the dress gave her no support whatsoever. Goodness, what size were those bad boys? Adele wondered, completely mesmerised; as a guess, they looked about a size 38G!

'Look,' Emma turned to Donna, who was only half ready, 'obviously it's your day and I don't want to make you stressed out or anything, but I seriously look ridiculous in strapless dresses, as you can see; it's the only thing I requested. There aren't any straps that you can attach. The dresses are meant to be strapless.'

Adele turned back round, unable to look Donna in the eye.

'I'm so sorry, the dresses only arrived two days ago and I haven't had time to check them or I would have changed them if I'd known. Adele, you said the dresses had straps you could attach? I told you it was important,' Donna said sharply.

Adele looked at Donna and made a face as she gave a casual shrug. 'Sorry, hun. I thought they did have straps. Oops.'

Donna exhaled, momentarily closing her eyes. 'Emma, I swear I thought they had straps. I never would have picked them otherwise.'

'It's fine,' Emma replied tightly, as she tried to hoist the material upwards to cover her heaving bosom. 'I'll just have to make do.'

Adele smiled to herself. Thank God that was over and done with. She stood in the mirror and twirled around, secretly comparing how good she looked in comparison to Emma standing behind her. *What footballer will be able to resist this tonight?* she thought, arrogantly.

Donna felt terrible for poor Emma as she walked into the other room sulkily to continue getting ready. She knew full well that Adele had known those dresses didn't have straps when she tried it on that day, and cursed herself for not checking before she purchased them or when they arrived two days ago. Why did she believe anything Adele ever said? Adele could sure as hell be selfish at times, though Donna couldn't complain about the amount of help she'd received from her the past few weeks. Yes, Adele was opinionated and manipulative at times, but she'd been willing to help with getting a great photographer, organising the caterers and even the deluxe transport that was taking them to Orsett Hall. Adele had insisted on a top class Bentley and Donna didn't have the time to even question it or consider an alternative, she was just grateful that it was another tick off her everlasting list. Adele must care to help out, Donna assured herself, even if at times she had a very funny way of showing it.

The doorbell rang and Donna knew it would be Kelly turning up to do her hair and make-up. In the end she'd decided on a pretty, sophisticated chignon instead of the half up-half down style and very natural make-up, though she guessed Kelly would suggest applying some individual eyelashes, as she had seemed horrified when Donna had told her at the practice run she was planning to just wear a light layer of mascara.

'Hi, babe,' Kelly said cheerily when Donna let her in.

Donna kissed her cheek. 'Hi Kel, come in. Want a glass of champagne? My mum will get you one.'

'Wouldn't turn down a glass of champers,' Kelly giggled cheekily. 'Thank you.'

After introducing Kelly to her mum and sister, Donna noticed Adele look up from the mirror she was getting ready in and stare at Kelly icily. Why did she have such a problem with her? Donna wondered, as she took Kelly into the other room, away from Adele.

'So are you nervous, hun?' Kelly asked as she got out her hairdryer, brushes and kirby grips.

Donna thought about it. She was a little nervous about walking in front of everyone and saying her vows, but no, she actually couldn't wait to marry Aaron. She couldn't believe that after tomorrow, she would have a husband! It sounded so grown up and surreal. 'Not really, no,' she said taking a sip of champagne.

'It's going to be an amazing day, babe; I'm going to make you look more sensational than ever,' Kelly grinned. 'Where's the dress?' Kelly looked round and spotted the stunning gown Donna had chosen hanging up. 'Oh my God, shut up! Is that your dress? Babe, that is unreal! Where's it from?'

'Vera Wang,' Donna gushed.

Kelly couldn't believe her eyes and her hand flew up to her open mouth. 'Oh my God,' she whispered walking over to the dress in awe. 'It's a *Vera*,' she said, eyes wide open as she touched the material softly, as if it might break. 'It's unbelievable, babe. I bet you look amazing in it.'

Donna flushed. 'I don't know about that, but it is pretty.'

'You'll look gorgeous, Don,' Kelly complimented her. 'The tan I put on yesterday has come out lovely too,' she told her, looking pleased with her work.

Donna nodded. 'Yeah, it's perfect. Thanks. So are you coming to the wedding with Billy?'

Kelly swallowed. 'Unfortunately he can't make it, hun. I'm so sorry I haven't told you sooner, but something really important has come up. Business,' she said, raising her eyebrows.

'That's a shame,' Donna replied earnestly, knowing Kelly didn't know that many other people going to the wedding. 'Why don't you bring a friend to keep you company instead as your plus one? The dinner has been paid for after all. What about your friend I met last time when I came to yours for an eyebrow wax?'

'Jade?' Kelly asked brightly.

'Yes, Jade, that was it. Bring Jade,' Donna answered, remembering her to be nice and friendly.

'You're sure you don't mind?' Kelly asked timidly.

'Course not!' Donna replied as Kelly started brushing her hair.

'Okay, thanks hun. That'll be great,' she smiled.

Donna chatted to Kelly and felt herself starting to relax even more. Why did she have a niggling feeling that something bad was going to happen today? She had been telling

CHAPTER 20

Jade was sitting with Lisa in Belgique in Loughton, eating breakfast.

'I'm so glad you and Sam are back together and happy again. I can't believe Kelly's scheming worked and uncovered the truth. She should be a spy!' Lisa chuckled as she stirred her cappuccino.

'I know! We should call her Inspector Kelly. I'll never doubt her instincts again,' Jade smiled with a little laugh. 'Things with Sam are going great. I hope we never split up. He's actually asked me to move in with him and I said yes.'

'Oh my God, Jade, that's fantastic news!' Lisa reassured her. 'You two are made for each other.'

Jade smiled warmly as she swallowed a mouthful of blueberry muffin. She looked up and stared at Lisa seriously. 'So, tell me everything about Nicola's brother. I told you you'd find someone when you least expected it!'

Lisa glowed with happiness. 'It's early days yet, but we've been on three dates so far and all I can say is I really like him. He's even invited me to a wedding today! I'd normally think that was a bit full on, but with him it feels right. He had a plus one, and was going to go alone until he met me. I'm really nervous as I won't know anyone.

I'm going to get a new dress after here and my hair blow dried.'

Jade grinned. 'That's so exciting! I look forward to meeting him. I'm sure Kelly is going to a wedding today as well. It's a girl called Donna's. Maybe it's the same one?'

Lisa stared into space thoughtfully. 'You know what, the name Donna actually rings a bell. What a small world, if it's the same one? That will be amazing if Kelly is there too.'

Jade rummaged around for her mobile, which had started ringing in the new Marc Jacobs bag she'd recently treated herself to.

'Hi Kelly,' she answered cheerily.

'Hi, babe.'

'What's up? We're still in Loughton if you're finished and want to meet up?'

'Ah thanks, hun, but I'm just about to start Donna's make-up. Listen, I'm just calling you to invite you to the wedding. Billy can't make it and Donna has kindly suggested I invite you instead as my plus one for company. Are you free?'

Jade was stunned. She'd only met Donna once and even though they'd got on really well she'd never expected to be attending her wedding! 'Oh wow, really? Okay, I'd love to come. What time is it?'

As Kelly reeled off the details, Jade decided she was going to go shopping with Lisa afterwards to buy a new dress. Kelly explained she would pick her up in a taxi later on that day and Jade said goodbye and put the phone down. As she looked up at Lisa, she was texting with a smile on her face.

'Ben?'

Lisa nodded. 'I just asked him whose wedding it was and it's Donna and Aaron's.'

'See you there then!' Jade beamed as she filled Lisa in

on the conversation she'd just had with Kelly. 'I only have a few hours and Kelly is picking me up in a taxi.'

Lisa downed the rest of her drink. 'Let's go then. It sounds like it's going to be a good wedding and I desperately need something nice to wear!'

'Me too!' Jade said as she finished her latte. 'It's a lovely day for a wedding,' she added, as they made their way out into the sunshine. It wasn't too hot either, there was a breeze, which made it just perfect. Jade had woken up thinking she had a boring day doing nothing as Kelly and Lisa were busy all day, and Sam was away for the weekend with his friends. She was amazed how her plans had changed in a matter of minutes. She linked arms with Lisa as they made their way to their favourite boutique on Loughton high street. There was a beautiful turquoise dress in the window, which Jade thought would be perfect.

*

Adele was happy when she heard the front door close, meaning Kelly had finally left Donna's house. She marched into Donna's room and eyed her up and down in a super-cilious way. She wrinkled her nose disparagingly. 'Is *that* how Kelly did your make-up? You're actually going to have it like that for your *wedding*?' she sneered. If Adele was honest, she thought Donna looked beautiful, but she hated Kelly and wasn't for a minute going to admit to her friend that she'd done a great job.

Donna's face fell and she looked wounded as she replied. 'Thanks a lot, Adele,' she huffed sarcastically. 'You really know how to make me feel good about myself.'

Adele felt an unexpected wave of guilt wash over her. 'Sorry, you look amazing. I just thought, you know, I just don't rate Kelly's make-up skills.' She drew nearer to Donna. 'It looks really nice up close though and I do like the hair.'

331

Donna didn't look impressed and she walked out of the room to her mum who was calling her.

Adele sighed. She'd had a couple of glasses of champagne and perhaps she'd gone too far saying Donna's make-up wasn't nice. It *was* her wedding day, after all. Oh well, she thought, I'm sure she'll soon get over it. Adele couldn't wait for the Bentley to turn up. She'd made sure Donna had booked the most luxurious transport she could find; there was no way Adele wasn't travelling to the wedding in style. Adele had also suggested the caterers and persuaded Donna to choose the menu that *she* liked; it was the most expensive by a mile, but so what? Aaron could afford it. Donna had been so thankful when Adele had found the photographer too. Little did Donna know that Adele had only been concerned about how *she* was going to look in the images.

Adele had heard that Neil, Aaron's friend who she'd snogged that night in Funky Mojoe, was going to be best man. She had absolutely no interest in talking to him throughout the day and hoped he wasn't going to bother trying.

Donna came back in the room. 'Adele, I hope you don't mind, but my brother is going to take you to the wedding in his car. There isn't enough room in the Bentley for everyone.'

Adele couldn't hide her vexation. '*What?*'

Donna took a deep breath and temporarily closed her eyes as though she was building the courage to speak. 'There isn't enough room. I have my sister and her children, Aaron's sister and my dad. My brother, James, has offered to take you. Please don't cause a fuss, I have enough on my plate.'

'Fine!' Adele snapped, absolutely seething. 'Don't worry about me, the person who booked it for you, I'll just get there in your brother's tin can!'

Donna exhaled sharply. 'Don't be so dramatic, he has a

BMW. Now I need to get in my dress, we don't have long until we have to leave.'

Adele was fuming. After everything she'd done for Donna she had excluded her from the beautiful Bentley. Why didn't she tell her boring sister and her spoilt snotty nosed kids to go with James! She just couldn't believe the audacity of Donna and wanted to scream with frustration. This was an absolute joke! James was in his mid-thirties and about as exciting as a physics lecture in her opinion; what was she going to talk to him about on the journey for Christ's sake? It was a forty-minute drive to Orsett Hall and Adele was dreading it. She made her way to the kitchen, ignoring Donna's family as she stomped through the hallway. Downing another glass of champagne, she promised herself yet again that she would accomplish her mission of finding a rich footballer; it was the only thought cheering her up at this moment in time.

*

Neil had been overjoyed when Aaron had asked him to be best man and couldn't believe the wedding day was already here. He had spent the previous night perfecting his best man speech and felt satisfied it had the perfect mixture of humour and sincerity. He was in a pub near to where the ceremony was taking place with Aaron and the ushers and realised suddenly he was beginning to feel a bit tipsy. He'd been filming Aaron getting ready all morning and downing shots in the pub to play during his speech via a projector. He also had edited clips from his stag party and they were hysterical. Neil had been to a wedding recently and the best man speech had gone down like a lead balloon; it had been seriously dull and depressing. He'd promised himself then and there that if he ever got asked to be best man he would make sure the guests would be laughing. He had his video clips to play as well as hilarious photos of Aaron growing up; it was certainly going to keep everyone entertained. It had just so happened that he got asked to be best man a lot quicker than he'd ever anticipated, but he thought Aaron was making the right decision as Donna seemed like a lovely girl and he hadn't seen his friend smile so much until recently. She was nothing like her awful, shallow friend Adele, Neil thought, as he took another swig of his pint. When he'd first met Adele that night in Funky Mojoe, he couldn't believe his luck. She'd been all over him like a rash and her tongue had been down his throat the majority of the night. But then, when he'd tried to contact her she'd been completely off with him and had even ignored his calls. He hadn't admitted it, but he'd been a bit gutted.

Adele had seemed like such a sweet girl at first and he wasn't sure if it was just the alcohol or what, but it was like she'd had a personality transplant after that evening. The night they'd met up again at The King William, she'd shown her true colours. He realised then what she was all about. Despite her friend, Donna, being loved up with Aaron, Adele had been flirting with him all night like mad and it was clear that the fact Aaron played football appealed to her. Adele had practically ignored Neil all night long and it had made him furious. What a shallow, gold-digging cow, he had decided as he left that evening. Adele was sure as hell ruthless; it seemed she would happily ruin her friendship to get what she wanted. When Aaron had confessed that Adele had made a pass at him that evening, Neil had hated Adele even more. What a bitch! Aaron had needed to tell someone to get it off his chest. He didn't want it getting back to poor Donna as she would have been devastated. How could Adele consider doing that to one of her friends? Neil had been told by Aaron that Adele was even maid of honour today! There was nothing honourable about Adele; she was one nasty piece of work and not only had she tried to destroy her friend's relationship, but she had made Neil look a complete fool. To think he'd really liked her and had rambled on talking about her to his friends, even sending her several texts asking to take her out! It was cringe worthy.

Aaron turned to Neil, bringing him out of his daydream. 'We'd better get going, mate. The taxi is outside ready to take us,' he told him, putting his pint down.

Neil downed the rest of his beer. 'Come on then. Here it goes. You nervous?' he asked Aaron, watching his expression carefully.

Aaron shrugged and shook his head. 'I'm honestly not, no. I love her and can't wait to see her.'

Neil clapped him on the back. 'Alright mate, save all the mushy stuff for your speech.'

Aaron laughed and made his way out of the pub, with Neil following behind.

Neil switched his camcorder to record. 'And here he is,' he said, pointing the camera in Aaron's face, who was grinning. 'He's about to get married and is on his way to the service. Any last words as a single man, Aaron?' he asked with a smile.

Aaron laughed. 'No last words, Neil. Thanks for shoving that thing in my face though.'

Neil laughed and switched the camera off.

Ten minutes later they arrived at Orsett Hall, which was surrounded by beautiful countryside. Neil recorded Aaron again.

'He's arrived. Look at this beautiful place he's taken us to,' he said, filming round the grounds of Orsett Hall. 'Not long now Aaron, and Donna will be your wife.' Neil laughed as he filmed him once more. 'Ahhh bless, look at this man's grin!'

Neil put the lens cap back on the camera as he watched a black BMW pull up. Aaron was making his way to the chapel with the ushers, but something made Neil stay where he was. He heard the car door open and stood there, his breathing getting harder and harder as he watched Adele get out of the car alongside a man he didn't recognise. He noticed her eyes flick towards him and then she turned her head as though she hadn't seen him. *Just who the hell does she think she is, the snobby cow? She's ignoring me as though I don't exist!* Neil couldn't believe how rude she was being as she waltzed past him with her chin in the air, and it only fuelled his anger.

'Adele!' Neil called, unable to help himself.

She turned around, adopting a tone of surprise. 'Oh hi, didn't see you there,' she said, about to turn straight back round.

Neil shook his head and narrowed his eyes. 'Liar,' he replied curtly.

Adele opened her mouth wide, indignantly. 'What are you talking about, Neil? What's your problem? I didn't see you.'

Neil gave a short laugh. 'Whatever.' He gave her an icy glare. 'I can't believe you actually had the cheek to even show up to this wedding, let alone accept the role of maid of honour.'

Adele shot Neil an odd look. 'Why are you saying that?' She frowned in dismay.

'I know what you did after The King William that night, that's why,' he snapped.

Neil watched as the light slowly dawned on Adele's face. 'And what's that then?' she challenged.

Neil sneered at her. 'You tried it on with Aaron, your so-called friend's boyfriend, that's what. Don't even try to deny it because Aaron told me he had to knock you back and how embarrassed he was.'

Adele's eyes were slits as she gave Neil a baleful stare. 'What's wrong, Neil? Are you jealous that I didn't try it on with you, is that it?' she shrugged, nonchalantly. 'Okay, I admit, I did try it on with Aaron, but he chose Donna, which is the wrong choice in my opinion, but it's his loss. They both like the same crappy music, so they're welcome to each other.'

Neil shook his head in disbelief. How could she be so callous about her friend? 'Why did you choose to speak to me that night in Funky Mojoe?' he asked, baffled.

Adele rolled her eyes, huffing noisily as if he was boring her. 'Because *Neil*, I thought *you* were the footballer.' She looked at him as though he was stupid for not realising that sooner. 'But you weren't, were you? You're just a boring little accountant, a *nobody*, so I simply wasted my time and now my friend has ended up with a life of luxury, which should have been *mine*. Now if you don't mind, I'm rather bored of this conversation and Donna has just arrived so I'd appreciate it if you shut the hell up and left me alone.'

Neil's mouth was a perfect 'O' as she stormed off towards the Bentley and helped Donna out of the vehicle.

*

Kelly and Jade were sitting in the chapel together when they spotted Lisa with Ben in front of them. They waved hello and Jade sneakily had a peek at Ben.

'He looks nice,' Jade whispered to Kelly.

'Yeah I know, bit of a sort,' Kelly agreed, her big blue eyes open wide as she stared at him.

'So I hear Donna's husband-to-be is a footballer?' Jade said, as she looked at Aaron who was anxiously waiting for Donna to arrive.

'Yeah babe, he plays for Fulham,' Kelly said knowledgeably.

Suddenly everyone hushed in the room as the song 'She's The One' by Robbie Williams begin to play. Jade looked round along with everyone else to see the bridesmaids enter. There was Adele with a smirk on her face, lapping up the attention of everyone looking at her.

'Wow, someone has overdone the fake tan,' Kelly hissed, stifling a giggle.

Jade bit the inside of her lip, trying not to laugh. Kelly was right; Adele really did look as though she'd been tangoed, not that that was anything unusual. Jade watched as Adele pouted and stuck out her chest, and wondered how on earth Donna liked her enough to ask her to be maid of honour.

The room was completely silent apart from the soft, gentle tones of Robbie Williams and then Donna entered, looking absolutely stunning.

'Oh my God!' Jade whispered to Kelly. 'Her dress is absolutely beauts!'

'I know, babe,' Kelly nodded, staring at Donna as she nervously walked down the aisle. 'It's a Vera.'

Jade gasped. 'A *Vera Wang*?' She had to stop herself from touching it as Donna walked past. The dress was exquisite. It was a beautiful ivory colour, made from the most intricate layers of pretty lace and it fit Donna perfectly. Kelly had always vowed that when she got married her dress was going to be from Vera Wang and she even emailed Jade her favourites every year when the new collection came out 'just in case'. Jade on the other hand had fallen in love with the pretty Alice Temperley gowns as well as the unique Marchesca dresses. She knew she wouldn't get married anytime soon, but looking didn't hurt anyone, did it?

'She looks gorgeous, doesn't she?' Kelly said, her eyes welling up with tears.

'Absolutely amazing,' Jade whispered. 'Her hair and make-up look totes perfect. Great job, Kel.'

Kelly flapped her hand in front of her eyes. 'Weddings make me so emotional for some reason,' she sniffed. 'I was in bits watching Kate and Prince Will get married.'

'Didn't Kate just look so beautiful,' Jade swooned as she remembered.

'She most certainly did,' Kelly agreed quietly. 'I think it's great we get a bank holiday for their anniversary too.'

Jade was confused. Anniversary? 'We don't get a bank holiday for their anniversary. What are you talking about?'

'You know, the Jubilee bank holiday. That's to celebrate them being married for a year,' Kelly whispered wisely.

Jade tried to hold in her laugh by putting her hand across her mouth and blushed as she received unimpressed glances from some of the guests in front. 'It's the Queen's Jubilee, Kel,' Jade laughed as quietly as possible, 'she's reigned for sixty years. It's nothing to do with Kate and Wills.'

Kelly looked disappointed. 'Oh that's a shame. I thought we were going to have one every year to mark their wedding.'

A short while later Jade felt the familiar tingling of her nose as Donna and Aaron started to say their vows, meaning her tears weren't far away. There was definitely something about weddings that got to her.

The ceremony was beautiful and after making their way to an outside garden and sipping champagne and eating delicious canapés the time seemed to fly by, and soon they were ushered into the main room for dinner and drinks. Jade was having a great time and they'd managed to avoid Adele all day luckily. She'd caught Adele's eye once or twice and Adele had just given her a dirty look, which she'd ignored. Adele appeared to be very preoccupied by flirting with every man in sight, Jade noticed, not that it surprised her. As she watched Adele flick her hair as she spoke to a handsome man wearing a grey suit, she just prayed he wasn't going to be another poor soul to fall into Adele's clutches.

*

Adele rolled her eyes as the fairly attractive man in front of her told her a funny story about Aaron's stag night. *Like I care*, Adele thought, *are you a footballer or not?* There was no way she was going to waste time like that night with Neil, so she decided to just come out with it and ask him.

'So are you on Aaron's team? Do you play football?' she asked hopefully, batting her long false eyelashes.

The man laughed. 'Me? Play football professionally? In my dreams!' he replied ebulliently. 'No, I work for my family's dry-cleaning business. You?'

'Run my own bikini business,' Adele gave a wintry smile and sighed inwardly, wondering how she could make a sharp exit. She downed her champagne before he could start asking questions. 'I'm going to get another drink, nice speaking to you,' she lied.

'You too,' he called after her, the disappointment etched on his face.

A few moments later everyone was told to go to their tables and Adele made her way to the top table proudly. It felt good as she smugly walked past Jade, Kelly and Lisa and just completely blanked them. *She* was someone important in this wedding, unlike them. So far she was having a good day. The only problem was, she hadn't managed to meet any single footballers yet; she guessed most of them would be going to the evening instead.

'Ladies and gentlemen,' a man's voice interrupted her thoughts. 'Will you please stand up for the entrance of the new Mr and Mrs Bond!'

The whole room applauded and Adele forced herself to smile. Donna looked happier than ever, beaming broadly from ear to ear and Aaron looked at her adoringly, his eyes gleaming with contentment. Donna was so lucky, Adele acknowledged, she was married to a footballer. She got all the luck! When was it *her* turn to get lucky? Donna walked over to her seat

340

in the centre of the long top table. Adele was looking forward to getting the speeches out of the way so they could enjoy the evening and the other people would arrive. As she browsed the room, she realised there weren't any eligible men and the thought depressed her. She smiled at the waitress as she handed her the starter she had picked for Donna's wedding; at least she knew she liked the food. She'd made sure that Donna had selected all her favourites.

After a lovely meal it was time for Donna's dad to give his speech. The room was silent as he thanked everyone and said what a wonderful day it had been.

He wiped his brow with a handkerchief as he continued. 'When Donna told me she was getting married so soon, I must say, I was slightly concerned and worried that they may be rushing into things. However, after meeting Aaron several times it's clear to see how in love they are. Aaron is a respectable young man and I welcome him to our family and to be my son-in-law. Though maybe I will leave judgement on just how pleased I am until after the best man has had his say and revealed some of the bits I don't know about him!'

Everyone laughed and Adele's eyebrows sank into a disbelieving gaze. *Just hurry up and get it over with.*

Next it was Aaron, who, quite frankly, made Adele want to vomit. His eyes filled with tears as he expressed his love for Donna.

'I can't believe how lucky I am to have met my soul mate and the girl of my dreams. Donna, you have made me happier than you'll ever know and I will love you forever. You're my best friend as well as my wife.'

Adele rolled her eyes once more and searched for her mobile in her bag to distract her from the boring speech. She noticed Donna's mum give her a disapproving stare, which she ignored. If she wanted to look online at Net-a-Porter's new Lanvin dresses then she damn well would!

Everyone applauded Aaron, and Neil stood up. The best man's speech was usually the best, so Adele thought she'd give him a chance and pay attention. Slipping her phone back in her bag, she looked up to Neil as he chatted about growing up with Aaron and how much mischief they got into. Images flashed on a large white screen and Adele giggled. One was of Aaron at around ten years old dressed as a woman, and another was of him asleep outside a villa, obviously where he'd drunk too much. The next one flashed up of him being sick outside a bar on holiday; it looked like he was somewhere ghastly like Kavos or Magaluf. How chavvy, Adele thought, turning up her pert little nose. She looked in wonderment as everyone else seemed to think it was hilarious.

Neil continued his speech and then began fiddling about with his camcorder. A few moments later Aaron and a few of the ushers appeared on a large flat screen, which Adele hadn't even noticed until that point. Neil paused the video.

He cleared his throat. 'Ladies and gentlemen. I could stand here and talk all evening about the funny things Aaron and I have got up to in the past, but I thought a video would be far more fun and would really show you what Aaron's like.'

Everyone cheered as Aaron put his glowing red face into his hands with embarrassment and Neil clicked play.

Adele felt herself laughing and smiling; some of it was actually quite funny and Neil had done a good job. There were lots of clips from his stag do, including a bit of Aaron in nothing but his boxers, tied to a lamppost. *They look like they had much more fun than we did at Donna's hen*, Adele thought enviously; an Ann Summers night wasn't exactly original or thrilling. Then came footage that had been filmed earlier that morning of Aaron getting ready, drinking a pint in the pub and then in the taxi. Everyone was making an 'ahhh' sound as he stated on the video how excited he was for Donna to be his wife, and Adele glanced over at Donna, who was drying her eyes with a napkin. The screen went black and Neil continued his speech.

'I think that just about sums Aaron up,' he smiled. 'The good and the bad.'

Everyone laughed.

'No, seriously mate. I can't express how happy I am for you that you've found your perfect wife. I can't think of anyone better . . .'

A loud voice interrupted him. 'Adele!'

Adele frowned as much as her Botox would let her as people turned to stare at her. Where was that voice coming from and why did she recognise it? Then she heard her own voice and felt her head start pulsing with blood.

'Oh hi, didn't see you there,' her voice echoed through the room.

'Liar,' came Neil's brusque reply.

'Stop the tape!' Adele hissed to Neil, frantically running over to where he was standing. He'd obviously recorded their conversation by accident and it was still playing!

'I'm trying!' Neil said panicking as he pressed all the buttons on his camcorder, which was linked up to the screen.

As their conversation continued through the video, Adele glanced up, her face going puce with humiliation. 'Do something, Neil!' she asked desperately.

'The button on the camera is stuck. I can't switch it off,' he said, helplessly.

'Well, try!' Adele replied wildly.

Neil's voice on the video was loud and the room was silent. 'You tried it on with Aaron, your so-called friend's boyfriend, that's what. Don't even try to deny it because Aaron told me he had to knock you back and how embarrassed he was.'

Adele wanted the ground to swallow her up as she

grabbed the camcorder and pressed every single button there was, urgently hoping she could stop the tape.

'What on earth is going on?' she heard Donna's dad ask furiously.

Neil and Adele's voices continued to echo round the room and Adele winced as she heard her voice again. 'Okay, I admit, I did try it on with Aaron, but he chose Donna, which is the wrong choice in my opinion, but it's his loss. They both like the same crappy music, so they're welcome to each other.'

Everyone in the room was glaring at Adele with hatred, and she literally felt as though she was going to die of shame. As her eyes flicked to Donna, she wished they hadn't. Donna was sitting there, her mouth wide open, giving Adele the most venomous glare she had ever seen.

The tape didn't stop. 'Why did you choose to speak to me that night in Funky Mojoe?' Neil voice resounded.

Adele cringed, closing her eyes and trying to block out the words she knew were about to come. 'Because *Neil*, I thought *you* were the footballer. But you weren't, were you? You're just a boring little accountant, a *nobody*, so I simply wasted my time and now my friend has ended up with a life of luxury, which should have been *mine*.'

Finally, Neil managed to switch off the tape. But it was too late; the damage was done. There were stunned faces everywhere. One lady even had her mouth hanging wide open.

Adele swallowed hard, her face burning. Her voice was light and she gave a little laugh, trying to pretend this was all a big joke. 'Donna, I . . .'

'*Get. Out*,' Donna demanded through clenched teeth. 'I don't want to speak to you. In fact, I don't even want to look at you ever again. Goodbye, Adele.'

Adele gave another little laugh. 'It's a joke, I swear! Don't be like that.' She turned to Neil who was standing there, looking extremely awkward. 'Neil, *tell* Donna it was a joke.'

Neil flushed, bit his lip and looked at the floor.

Aaron stood up. 'It wasn't a joke, Adele,' he said tetchily, 'you *did* try to kiss me.' He glared at Adele.

Everyone in the room gasped in horror, making Adele hang her head in embarrassment.

Aaron looked down at Donna. 'Darling, I'm so sorry I didn't tell you sooner. I didn't want to hurt your feelings.'

Donna nodded as though she understood and held his hand.

Adele threw her hands up. 'I really think that you're all overreacting. Donna, please,' she begged, looking at her. She wanted Donna to say it was okay like normal. Why wouldn't she even look at her? Or at least give her a chance to explain?

'Leave,' Donna said stonily, not even looking up.

'Oh, whatever!' Adele said, rolling her eyes, trying to appear unfazed, when deep down she wanted to cry. As she walked back to her seat to fetch her bag, her face was so hot it felt like her head was about to explode. Adele was shaking with shock and mortification as she walked through the room, past all the tables filled with disgusted faces staring right at her. As she made her way to the exit, the last horrified faces she saw were Jade, Kelly and Lisa's.

Adele called a taxi and the minute she hung up the phone, burst into tears. Well, she'd really gone and ruined her friendship this time, hadn't she? As she sobbed and searched for a tissue in her bag, she realised she'd actually just lost the only true friend she'd ever had.

CHAPTER 21

The wedding had been amazing and Jade had really enjoyed herself. She was still astonished about the performance with Adele right in the middle of the best man's speech though, and she, Kelly and Lisa had spoken about nothing else all day.

'I just can't believe she had the nerve, babes,' Kelly had said earlier that day. 'I mean to try it on with your mate's boyfriend is just unbelievable.'

'She gets worse and worse,' Lisa said, raising her eyebrows.

'That was *so* embarrassing when the recording wouldn't stop. I was cringing for her! Poor Donna,' Jade said.

'I think Donna is a hundred per cent over it,' Kelly giggled and nodded in her direction.

Jade and Lisa joined in the laughter as they spotted Donna on the dance floor, laughing her head off as she danced to 'YMCA' with Aaron.

'That's a good thing then,' Jade said, with an amused smile, 'I wanted to cry for her earlier.'

'God, me too,' Kelly said, flicking her hair behind her shoulder. 'Food was gorge too, weren't it? The only thing I didn't like was that cartier stuff.'

Lisa almost spat out her champagne. 'Do you mean caviar, Kelly?'

'Yeah, that stuff. What is it again? Fish poo did you say, Jade?' Kelly questioned.

Jade burst into laughter. 'Fish eggs, you dope!'

The three of them stood there laughing and Ben came over and asked if they wanted another drink.

'He's hot, Lisa,' Kelly said as Ben walked to the bar to get them three more glasses of champagne.

'I know,' she replied, blushing.

'He must really like you to invite you to a wedding as well,' Jade grinned. 'Glad you finally met someone you like. We'll have to all go for dinner as a trio with our boyfriends soon.'

'Oh my God, shut up!' Kelly gasped, opening her eyes wide. 'That's like, the best idea ever, hun! I love that we're all in love,' she enthused with a friendly smile.

'Whoah, don't know about love for me just yet, I've only just met Ben!' Lisa laughed.

Kelly's mobile started ringing and she walked off to a quieter spot to answer it.

'I bet it's Billy,' Jade said to Lisa, just as Ben approached them with new drinks.

'Thanks Ben,' Jade and Lisa chorused.

A few moments later, Kelly came running over to them, waving her phone in her hand. 'Oh my God, oh my God, oh my God!' she said breathlessly. 'You'll never guess who that was!'

Jade was puzzled and judging by Lisa's and Ben's bemused expressions, they were in the same boat. 'Who?' she asked, anxiously.

'We've won an award! Remember we entered that magazine competition for best new start-up businesses a few weeks ago? That was a lady calling to give us the good news that we'd won! Vajazzle My Bikini has won and they want to write an article about us and our collection! A two-page spread!' Kelly replied, in a high-pitched, excited voice as she jumped up and down.

'OMG, you're joking?' Jade said in disbelief, hugging Kelly.

'Girls, that's amazing news!' Lisa chimed, joining in the hug. 'I'm so proud of you both!'

'Well done girls, that's great,' Ben agreed, clinking glasses.

'Listen girls,' Lisa hesitated and Jade and Kelly stared at her. 'I wasn't going to tell you this until tomorrow when we go for lunch as I wanted it to be a surprise, but I've changed my mind and I want to tell you now.'

Kelly's eyes opened wide. 'What is it?'

Lisa beamed showing her beautiful white teeth. 'I've been in touch at work with a lady that works for *Morning Britain* and they want you girls on the show to talk about your business! They're going to show some of your bikinis on their models and they want you on there for an interview too!'

Kelly's eyes almost popped out of her head. '*Oh. My. God!*'

Jade's voice was an excited squeak. 'Are you being serious?'

Lisa nodded. 'I've been talking to her for the last week and she thinks she wants you on either next week or the week after. Just imagine how many orders you're going to get after being on telly!'

Kelly was flabbergasted. 'What on earth am I going to wear?'

Jade laughed. 'Kelly, trust you to worry about that! Lisa, thank you so much! I can't believe this.' She wrapped her arms around Lisa and squeezed her.

'That's okay. You know I'll do anything to help you two out.'

Kelly stared at Lisa thoughtfully. 'Maybe you could model the bikinis on the show?'

Lisa made a face. 'Me in a bikini, on national telly? No way!' She giggled. 'I'll be working anyway. I tell you who you could suggest though. What about Chloe? She's modelling quite a bit now I've heard.'

Kelly. 'Deffo, babe. That's a great shout.'

Jade agreed; Chloe always looked stunning in their bikinis, with her enviable long legs, toned abs and perfect bust. Though Jade knew she'd have to run it past Sam first.

Kelly turned to Jade with a serious expression. 'I just want to say how happy I am that we're working together on this business which is doing so well. I'm really pleased that I'm doing something other than just beauty. I feel like people are taking me more seriously now, you know?'

Jade hugged her. 'Kelly, you should be pleased with yourself. You're fantastic at so many things that you don't give yourself credit for. I'm so happy that we work together too and I wouldn't swap it for the world. I'll always take you seriously, you can count on that. I'm so proud of you.'

Kelly grinned. 'I do still come out with silly things though, don't I?'

Jade gave a throaty laugh. 'Yes, all the time!'

'We Are Family' by Sister Sledge started playing and Kelly tapped Lisa, who had begun talking to Ben. 'Come on hun, it's our song! Sorry Ben, I need to borrow her,' she said, grabbing Lisa's arm and pulling her to the dance floor. 'Come on, Jade!'

Ben smiled and started talking to a friend and Jade followed them to the dance floor.

Kelly put her arms round each of them as she sang the lyrics, completely out of tune. 'I love you girls!'

'We love you too, Kel,' Jade replied happily.

Kelly sang the words of the song, her eyes closed as she

danced. She looked at them both suddenly and Jade wondered if she was about to say something really important. 'Seriously though, babes. What am I going to wear on TV?'

EPILOGUE

'What do you mean, she won't take no for an answer? Just tell her it's tough luck! No refunds,' Adele told Libby and Megan firmly, losing her patience. Adele had decided to make more use of them, and now the girls, who had previously only helped with the sewing, also answered calls and emails from customers too. The problem was, they were constantly asking her questions so Adele might as well do it herself, she realised angrily.

Adele closed her bedroom door to get some peace and quiet and lay on her bed. It had been about three weeks since Donna's wedding and she hadn't heard a word from her. Adele had texted her once, but she'd got no reply so she decided to leave it at that, not wanting to make a fool of herself and beg for forgiveness. If Adele was honest, she was gutted about her friendship with Donna ending; she always struggled to find girls to go out with now and had even resorted to inviting out Libby and Megan, who were only eighteen. They always jumped at the chance, knowing that Adele usually reserved tables and bought bottles of champagne and vodka. The week after Donna's wedding, Adele had been feeling down, so to cheer her up, her dad had taken her shopping to the West End and splashed out.

Adele had been dying to go out in her new designer wardrobe and truly believed that whoever said money didn't buy you happiness, simply didn't know where to shop. As she gazed at the gorgeous new silver Herve Leger dress hanging up, she couldn't wait to wear it to the Essex Polo that day with Libby and Megan.

'Adele!' Libby called through the door.

'What?' Adele snapped, annoyed that she was being bothered again. Couldn't she be left alone for five minutes?

Libby opened the bedroom door cautiously, her hand over the phone so the person at the other end of the line couldn't hear. 'This woman wants to talk to the manager. She's really irate.'

Adele huffed and held her hand out, snatching the phone and making Libby flinch. She took a deep breath, preparing herself for the earful she was certain she was about to receive.

*

'It's such a shame about the weather, isn't it?' Jade said glumly to Kelly as she looked out the window at the pouring rain.

'I know, babe. I'm so worried about my hair. I've just had it blow dried and it's going to get messed up now! I mean, hair and rain just don't mix,' Kelly said irritably as she sprayed her hair with hair spray. She'd just given them an update about Billy and his business issues, and Jade had felt so sorry for Billy when Kelly explained the whole story. Billy hadn't gone to the police, despite Gary betraying him in such a terrible way. Instead, Gary had just paid all the money back, as well as given up his share in the business. Apparently Gary was now in Dubai for the foreseeable future and Billy was running the business alone after promising he'd never have anything to do with Gary again. Jade couldn't imagine ever being treated by her friends like that and was glad that Gary hadn't managed to get away with it.

'I love your dress, Kelly,' Jade told her, admiring the sparkly, strapless number.

'Thanks, hun. I saw it down Queens Road in a shop window in white and I just said if it comes in sequins or pink, I *have* to buy it. Turned out it actually had a pink sparkly version. Totes me,' Kelly said, looking at herself in the full-length mirror.

'It's definitely you,' Lisa grinned. 'Don't worry, just take an umbrella and your hair will be fine.'

'I hope so,' Kelly said nervously. 'We're going to the Essex Polo after all, and I want to look nice. I had to make the hardest decision ever today about whether to wear my hair curly or straight, the last thing I want is for it to go like a frizz ball.'

Jade gave a light-hearted giggle. The girls were looking forward to going to the Essex Polo, like they did every year. The only problem was the rain, and where there was rain, there was mud. Girls dressed up to the nines at the Essex Polo and it was usually a nightmare when the weather was this bad. The huge marquees were in the middle of a field and about a fifteen-minute walk to get to.

'I've got my wellies to wear until we get in the marquee,' Lisa said, getting them out of her bag. 'Then my Louboutins will be making an appearance when we're inside. There is no way I'm getting them muddy.'

'That's such a good idea!' Kelly said, excitedly. 'I'm going to wear my Hunter wellies. Pink ones to match my dress, *obviously*. Jade, if you didn't bring any, you can borrow my black ones.'

'Thanks, I could definitely do with some. These,' Jade said, holding up her new black Gina heels, 'are not going anywhere near the mud.'

'Don't blame you, babe,' Kelly said, shaking her head.

She looked through her wardrobe for her wellingtons and huffed, throwing shoes around. 'Sometimes, I just wish I had the girl from *Clueless*' digital wardrobe. I can never find anything!'

'You have *so* many clothes, Kelly. You just need to throw some out and make room,' Jade told her, amazed how many items of clothing Kelly had crammed into her wardrobe.

'Don't be so ridiculous! There is no way I'm throwing any of this away,' Kelly looked horrified at the thought. 'Just say I need this top or these trousers one day?' she questioned, pulling out two of the first garments she came across.

Jade wagged her finger at Kelly playfully. 'Kelly, is that a tag I see on that top? So, it's brand new, never been worn, yet you made me go out with you to buy a new outfit for our *Morning Britain* slot!'

Kelly looked away stubbornly, pouting. 'I didn't want to wear any of this. I *needed* something new,' she said firmly.

Jade and Lisa smiled at each other, both knowing how much of a shopaholic Kelly was and how she'd never change.

After the girls had appeared on *Morning Britain* their website had been busier than ever and they were now considering hiring extra staff. The girls had also decided to expand and were now creating customised shorts, vests and kaftans as well as swimwear. It was so much fun and they'd even had some celebrities purchasing from them! Jade and Kelly had also surprised Lisa by telling her they were going to take her away for a long weekend to Ibiza, as a way of saying thank you for getting them on the show; they couldn't wait.

Thirty minutes later they were in a taxi on their way to the Essex Polo.

Walking across the field was even more of a nightmare than the girls had imagined. There was thick, sloppy mud everywhere and no way to avoid it.

'Urgh!' Kelly screamed looking horrified. 'A bit of mud went on my leg!'

'Don't worry,' Lisa laughed gaily. 'At least we're wearing wellies,' she reminded her.

Jade focused on walking, trying to keep as dry as possible, thanking her lucky stars it wasn't raining as they made their way to the marquee. Finally, it was in sight. As Jade looked up with a smile, she came face to face with Adele and her heart sank. *Not you again.*

'Girls,' Adele addressed them smugly, her head held high. She was wearing so much fake tan she didn't look that much different to the colour of the mud and her veneers in comparison looked even more ridiculously white. One hand was on her hip as if trying to block their path, while the other was holding a cigarette.

'Oh what do you want, Adele?' Kelly asked, flicking her eyes upwards with annoyance.

'Can't a girl say hi?' Adele asked, adopting an offended tone. 'I saw you on *Morning Britain* the other day,' she announced. 'It's definitely true that the TV adds ten pounds,' she sniggered, exhaling a cloud of smoke.

'Just leave it will you?' Jade sighed. She really wasn't in the mood for this and would have been quite happy to just ignore Adele today.

Adele opened her mouth to reply, but a young-looking girl tapped her shoulder. 'Adele,' the girl said wanly, her voice barely a whisper. 'There's another customer that keeps calling. I don't know what to say to her,' she explained, passing her a mobile.

'Reem Bikinis,' Adele answered the phone tersely.

Jade, Kelly and Lisa went to walk past, but couldn't help listen and laugh at how rude Adele was being to one of her customers.

'There is nothing wrong with the quality of our bikinis, thank you very much.' Adele paused, closing her eyes

355

furiously as the customer clearly ranted down the phone. 'How dare you speak to me like that!' Adele spat. 'I don't need to put up with this from you!' Adele hung up the phone, shaking with anger. 'Libby! Megan!' Her loud voice shrilled, making Jade shudder. The two girls were at her side in an instant. 'Switch this phone off and don't answer it again!'

'Business going well?' Kelly asked with an amused grin as they walked past.

'I quit!' Adele exploded, her eyes bulging so much they looked like they were going to pop out of her head. 'The business is finished! It's over!' she practically screeched. As Adele went to march away, Jade couldn't believe her eyes as Adele slipped straight over in the mud, falling on her back; it was like something from a comedy show. Jade, Lisa and Kelly bit their lips, trying not to laugh as they heard Adele screaming about the mud ruining her eight-hundred-pound dress.

'Let's go get a drink,' Jade said, raising her eyebrows. All this drama, and the night hadn't even started. Jade couldn't deny that she felt her spirits lift; Adele had finally admitted defeat and quit her website.

As she said cheers to Kelly and Lisa, Jade felt relief wash over her; the war was finally over.

Read Laura's addictive and hilarious novel
ESSEX GIRLS for more adventures from
Jade, Kelly and the gang . . .